Moving toward Reid, stretching on tiptoe, she slid her arms around his neck. Her gaze wide and appealing, her lips tremulous, she whispered, "Kiss me."

He was fast on the uptake. His instant of stiff amazement was barely perceptible before he bent his head and closed his arms around her. She pressed her lips to the smooth and firm contours of his mouth and settled against him until the nipples of her breasts nudged into his chest and her lower body molded to his pelvis.

Reid drew a ragged breath. His hold tightened, and abruptly he took the initiative from her.

Her lips parted under the onslaught of his kiss. Pleasure spiraled up from deep inside her, tingling along every inch of contact between them. Her pulse leaped to a frantic tempo. Heat invaded her body in waves. She accepted the bold and warm sweep of his tongue between her parted lips, and returned it with fervent grace.

Lost, she was lost in half-remembered sweetness, in the revival of sensations she had thought were only imagined. . . .

By Jennifer Blake
Published by Fawcett Books:

Books published by The Ballantine Publishing Group
are available at quantity discounts on bulk purchases
for premium, educational, fund-raising, and special
sales use. For details, please call 1-800-733-3000.

SHAMELESS

Jennifer Blake

FAWCETT GOLD MEDAL • NEW YORK

A Fawcett Gold Medal Book
Published by Ballantine Books
Copyright © 1994 by Patricia Maxwell

http://www.randomhouse.com

Library of Congress Catalog Card Number: 96-97076

ISBN 0-449-15002-X

Manufactured in the United States of America

First Hardcover Edition: June 1994
First Mass Market Edition: August 1997

10 9 8 7 6 5 4 3 2 1

Chapter One

▨ ▨ ▨ *Camilla Greenley Hutton stood in the* middle of the muddy road deep in the game reserve with a .357 magnum pistol gripped in her outstretched hands. The cool rain of a Louisiana spring fell in silver streaks around her. Drops the size of quarters dimpled the surface of puddles caught in the wheel ruts. They clattered in the branches of trees that overhung the road, beaded the wax finish of Cammie's Cadillac Seville on the road's shoulder, and made the green sand-washed silk of the blouse she wore with her jeans cling like a second skin. Wind whipped long, damp strands of golden-brown hair from the green silk tie that held the curling mane at her nape. She narrowed her hazel eyes against the blown rain and flying hair and the fading light of late evening. She waited.

Cammie heard the roar of the Land Rover long before it came into view. Keith was hurtling toward her at reckless speed. He was so intent on staying on her tail in the treacherous maze of game-reserve back roads that he didn't care who or what he ran over in the process. It was typical. Cammie had been depending on it.

Her husband wasn't chasing her because he loved her madly, or even because he wanted her. It was a matter of pride. He couldn't stand the thought that she might be able to outrun him, and hated the idea that she would even try. The thing that drove him most of all, however, was the knowledge that she had managed to survive

1

without any problem since the filing of their petition for divorce. He took it as a personal insult.

The oddest part about the situation was that dissolving their marriage had been Keith's idea. For the first few months after the legalities were in place, he seemed to revel in his freedom, living openly with the girlfriend, nineteen and pregnant, that he'd been keeping in a trailer just outside town. Cammie had expected any day to hear of plans for his wedding. Then, three weeks ago, Keith knocked on her door, his suitcase in his hand, a cocksure grin on his face. He'd changed his mind about the divorce, he said. He wanted to be her husband again.

Cammie had laughed; she couldn't help it. Beneath the amusement, however, there was the painful irony that the man who had shared her life for six long years could fail so completely to understand her. She needed to love and trust the man in her life. Keith had killed those things for her. Without them, there was nothing.

That was when his harassment began.

Cammie had had enough of it. She was tired of hearing her phone ring at all hours of the night, tired of demands that she explain her every movement and appointment. She was sick to death of refusing the delivery of unwanted flowers, and could not bear another visit from her former mother-in-law, pleading her son's case. Most of all, she was disgusted with being spied upon and followed everywhere she went.

She had tried again and again to make Keith realize she wanted no part of being his wife, now or ever, that she was looking forward to the legal end of their marriage in just five weeks. She had told him plainly she didn't like the tactics he was using to try to win her back, but he didn't seem to believe she meant it. There was only one way she could think of to make him see.

Cammie's father had given her the high-powered pistol when she went off to college, and had taught her how to handle it. She was finally going to put that training to use.

The Land Rover rounded the curve in front of her. She waited until she was sure Keith saw her, until there could be no doubt in his mind who she was and what she was doing. Taking a steadying breath, aiming carefully, she squeezed the trigger of the magnum.

It bucked in recoil, jarring her arms and shoulders, flinging up her hands. The concussion blasted her ears.

Glass flew from the Land Rover's right headlight. She saw Keith's wide eyes and the pale blur of his face, his mouth working as he cursed. She steadied her aim again. Firing quickly, she took out the left headlight.

Brakes screamed. The Land Rover fishtailed wildly on the muddy road, spraying mud and gravel as it plowed sideways. The right front tire caught in a rut, spinning the vehicle in a half circle. Motor whining, it plunged into the ditch. There was the hollow thud of metal crunching as it struck a tree, then stillness.

Cammie brought the pistol down, backing toward her car on the side of the road. She stopped abruptly as she saw Keith inside the Land Rover, slumped over the wheel.

He was faking, she knew it. He had to be. Yet it looked as if there was a splatter of red on his shirt.

She couldn't just leave him there. It was impossible, in spite of all the callous things he had said and done, in spite of everything she knew about his weak, manipulating ways.

"Idiot," she said under her breath. She meant herself. Still, she clenched her teeth and walked toward the Land Rover.

She opened the door on the driver's side with care. Keith was breathing; she could see the rise and fall of his chest. There was a trickle of blood running from his nose. Still holding the magnum, she reached out left-handed to touch his shoulder, giving him a slight nudge.

Keith came upright with a jerk. Twisting in the seat, he grabbed her wrist. His slickly handsome features were set in a malicious grin, and satisfaction shone in his yellow-brown eyes. "Fooled you again," he said on a short laugh as he climbed out of the vehicle. "You always were a sucker for anything hurt."

The name she called him was not a compliment.

"Oh, yeah?" Fishing a handkerchief from his back pocket, he wiped at the blood under his nose. "Well, I'm also your husband, and I think it's time you had a reminder. This looks like a good, quiet place for it to me. That should put paid to this dumb divorce petition, plus help make up for the damage to the Rover."

There was a sick feeling inside Cammie, and her heart hammered against her ribs. The falling rain suddenly felt like ice water pouring over her. She made no attempt to release herself, however, but left her wrist flaccid in his grasp. Moistening her lips with her tongue, tasting the rain on them, she said, "If your Rover's damaged it's your own fault."

"Is that so?" A sneer crossed his face, though there was the glitter of a perverse excitement in the depths of his eyes. "I could say the same thing, you know. If you weren't so stubborn, we could have had our reconciliation in a nice, soft bed. As it is—"

He spread his legs and shoved his hips forward, as if inviting her to notice the bulge in front of his pants. At the same time, he exerted pressure on her arm, pulling her toward him.

"Let me go," she said. Raising the handgun in her fist, she pressed the muzzle against his chest.

He snorted. "You think that thing scares me? You're too softhearted to shoot a rattlesnake, much less a man."

"Don't be too sure," she said quietly.

A faint uneasiness flitted across his face before he laughed and reached for the magnum.

In that instant, Cammie brought her knee up toward the juncture of his spread legs. He saw it coming and tried to turn. Still, she caught him a glancing blow. Keith grunted, releasing her as he bent double and clutched at himself.

Cammie danced backward out of his reach. Whirling, she ran toward the Cadillac.

Keith shouted after her. She heard footsteps, hobbling at first, then growing stronger. They splashed and thudded behind her. She redoubled her efforts. Her breath rasped in her throat. He was coming nearer. He would be on her before she could snatch open the car door. There was only one thing left to do.

Cammie swerved and leaped the roadside ditch. At the edge of the trees she spun back and raised the handgun. It spat bullets like a live thing, the reports jolting her until her teeth hurt. Mud and water spouted around Keith's feet.

He yelled, throwing himself backward, landing full-length in the muddy roadway. She didn't look to see if he was hurt. Swinging around again, she put her head down and ran.

The woods of the game reserve closed around her, wet, shadowed, and protective. The dripping branches that she pushed past snapped back into place behind her like gates. She heard Keith shouting at her to come back, but she didn't stop. He was never going to touch her again, not in warped passion, not in revenge, especially not in anger. Never.

She heard the crash and thud of his footsteps. Or maybe it was her own gasping breaths and the pounding of her heart in her ears. She ran harder.

Her marriage was over. The gladness inside her was like a rising shout. Maybe this time Keith had heard it, too.

Trees. They pressed around her. Towering pines with a skirt of slippery needles around their ankles. Whispering cedars so green they were nearly black. Massive sweet gums leafed out in aromatic green. Shivering maples with red veins under their leaves and gray lichen like a tracery of silver on their bark. Gnarled old black oaks. Great, spreading white and red oaks. Hickory trees with leaves like spear points, and decorated with the tiny green blooms.

The connecting branches overhead blocked the last of the watery twilight, turning everything to green-tinted dimness. Seedlings, sprouting thickly around the trees, green along with wildflowers, weeds, saw vines, and briers, the underbrush making it impossible to see more than a few feet in any direction. Also impossible to be seen.

Cammie loved trees; had since she was a child. That love ran in the distaff side of her family. Plants of all sorts, but especially trees, had always been an interest of the Greenley women.

It was her grandmother who had first taken Cammie into the woods, into the game reserve that came to the edge of their property. The elderly woman had introduced her young granddaughter to each variety of tree as if presenting an old and valued friend.

As Cammie grew, she passed through a tomboy stage where she rode limber sassafras saplings like wild ponies, and climbed into the cool upper regions of tall pines to find the privacy and quiet to read. Sometimes, when no one was looking, she would press her palm to the bark of some bay or ash, oak or pine, and think she could feel the life flowing through it.

She had never been lost in the woods before.

When she finally stopped to catch her breath, she realized she could no longer hear Keith behind her, and hadn't for some time. The woods around her stretched quiet and still, and endlessly the same.

A chill wind soughed through the treetops. Cammie shivered, rubbing the wet silk on her shoulders and arms as she gazed around. Apprehension touched her as she realized she had no idea how to find her way back to the road, no inkling of which direction to take to reach her car again.

It seemed a betrayal, as if the woods she loved had turned as false as the man she had married.

That was ridiculous, of course. The dense woods of the game reserve covered more than thirty thousand acres, and she had never ventured far beyond the few acres that came up to the back door of her house. There was no reason she should know every inch of it.

The reserve spread over a large portion of the parish. It circled behind the paper mill, and crowded the town of Greenley. This section she was in might be several miles from her home by road, but could be no more than two or three, maybe even less, straight through the woods. If she just knew how to go, she could find her way to her own back door. There were several roads crisscrossing, winding through the reserve, and even a few houses. If she walked southeast she was bound to hit one of the roads. Someone was sure to come along, someone who could drive her home.

But the gray shadows under the trees were turning black, and there was no way to tell which direction she was pointed. It would be so easy to walk in circles until she dropped. It might be better to stay where she was, wait for morning in the hope that she could see some landmark. However, spending the night in the woods held no appeal.

She moved on again. Her shirt slapped around her, snagging on bushes and briers. Her jeans grew clammy and so soaked that water dripped into her shoes. Rain trickled in a steady stream from her tied hair, dribbling down her back.

Cold and tired, she slipped in the wet, tripping over tree roots and the vines that clutched at her ankles. Once, she sprawled full-length. The .357 magnum went flying. She searched the thick growth of saplings and briers that were matted together with dried grass and pine straw, but couldn't find it in the dim light. She left it.

She could hardly see any longer, but still would not quit. The temperature was dropping as darkness fell. She could feel the wet chill creeping through her, cooling the warmth of her exertion. She had to go on, had to get home. No one knew where she was, no one knew which way to start looking for her.

One minute she was plodding doggedly along, the next she stopped as if she'd reached an invisible barrier. There was something, or someone, in the woods with her; she knew it with an instinct more certain than anything she had ever felt in her life.

Cammie turned slowly, searching the darkness with her eyes. There was nothing there, no movement, no slightest whisper of sound. And yet, she knew she was not wrong.

She felt the brush of dread, as if there was a wild animal or some devil in human form out there, following her, creeping closer. She wasn't fanciful under ordinary circumstances, but there was nothing ordinary about this.

A tree branch shook with a rustle of leaves.

Suddenly she broke into headlong flight, twisting through the underbrush, ducking under limbs, leaping over fallen logs and massed briers. She sprinted between the dark, towering sentinels of tree while her lungs burned and her gasping breaths scraped through her throat. Thorns tore at her blouse and raked her skin, but she hardly felt them. She scraped past tree trunks in a shower of bark, ricocheting off them to blunder onward.

He came from nowhere. One instant she was alone, the next, the dark shape of a man moved from behind a tree directly in her path.

She crashed into a chest like a rock wall. Hard arms reached to enclose her, holding her even as the man rocked back on his heels. She shoved away from him, used that momentum to spin out of his grasping hands. Two racing steps, three. She was caught from behind. She tripped, staggered off balance. Her legs tangled with the taut, muscular thighs of her attacker. A soft oath feathered in a warm exhalation over her wet hair, then they were both pitching forward into wet darkness.

He dragged her against him and twisted his body even as he fell. She landed in a rigid embrace, her cheek cushioned on a well-padded shoulder. For a stunned instant she lay unmoving, while the knowledge percolated through the fire in her brain that this man was not, could never be, her husband.

She drew a breath so hard it rasped with a harsh ache in her throat. In the same moment, she wrenched against the strong arms that held her.

"Be still," came the quiet and deep command at a level with the top of her head, "or I just may let you stay lost."

The timbre of his voice sent a ripple of alarm through her. She knew it, could hear it echoing, vibrating in her mind down long, aching years. How many was it? Nearly fifteen.

She had known this man was home again, everyone in Greenley knew it. He had been at his father's funeral, of course, but she had not attended. Of course.

"Reid Sayers," she said, the words no more than a whisper.

He was silent so long she thought he had not heard. Then he spoke in dry tones. "I'm flattered, or maybe stunned is a better word. I wasn't sure you would recognize me at the best of times."

"The last time we met was all too similar," she said, her voice tight. "Will you let me up?"

"No."

His answer registered in her mind as unequivocal, and with a slicing edge that had not been there the last time she had exchanged words with him. "You always did enjoy being mysterious," she said. "Unfortunately, I'm in no mood for it. Are you going to show me the way home, or are we going to spend the night here?"

He shifted, and the folds of a voluminous rain poncho settled across her. She shivered as she was enveloped by the heat of his body trapped under the waterproof material. His grasp tightened in reflex as he said, "Suppose I told you I intended to take up where we left off?"

"It's too late."

Did he hear the faint quiver of doubt in her voice? How could he, when she was not certain herself of that flash of reaction? She wasn't afraid of him. She had felt many things, from scorn to hate and embarrassing flares of sheer yearning, but never fear.

"Maybe," he said in pensive consideration, "and maybe not. A woman who has just tried to kill her husband could be capable of a lot of things."

"How did you know—" she began, then stopped as she saw how it could have been, must have been.

"I heard the first shot and came at a run in time to see the others. Yes, I did follow you. And you're right—I could have stopped you long before this."

His voice was a deep, disturbing murmur under her ear. She did her best to ignore the sound while she concentrated on the meaning of his words. She said, "But you didn't. You waited until you thought I was desperate, though what you hoped to gain is more than I can see."

"Is it now?" he asked, settling her closer against him. "Actually, I thought I might not need to intrude on what looked to be a successful escape. However, letting you wander around all night soaking wet seemed to be carrying noninterference a bit too far."

"Besides which, the opportunity to crow over me was too good to miss."

"The thought," he said deliberately, "had not occurred to me, but now you point it out, I don't mind if I do."

The tone of his voice sent alarm jangling along her nerves. She pushed against him, trying to lever herself out of his hold.

It was a mistake. In an effortless flexing of muscles, he rolled with her, turning her onto her back within the confining poncho. He allowed his weight to settle upon her, pinning her in place. One of her arms was caught under him. He captured the other at the wrist in a painless but unbreakable hold.

She shuddered as she felt his male heat drive the chill from her body. In the space of a moment the wetness of her clothing seemed to steam against her skin. Her breasts were pressed against his chest, his thighs held hers apart, and the ridged hardness under the zipper of his jeans nudged the softness at the apex of her legs.

She strained upward, digging in her heels as she tried to throw him off. The movement brought their bodies into closer, more fervent contact. She felt him stiffen, heard the soft, abrupt intake of his breath. She went still.

From inside her there rose a sweet, piercing ache that she had not felt in years. Fifteen years, to be exact. With it came an emptiness that was all too familiar, one that Keith had never been able to fill.

It was infuriating. It was astonishing. It was frightening.

Caught in the vortex of her own emotions, she lashed out at the man who had forced her to face them. "You always were good at taking advantage, you and all the other male members of your family."

His sigh lifted his chest, and she could feel the definition of his taut muscles. It did nothing to help her concentrate on what he was saying.

"Still harping on that old tale? I would have thought you were old enough by now to have a little tolerance."

"For your Yankee great-grandfather's misdeeds?" she inquired tartly. "But I would have to extend it to you, too. And you know what they say about falling acorns."

"Good thing my great-grandfather wasn't a tree," he answered in dry amusement.

"He still cheated my great-grandmother, and took advantage of her in other ways."

"I never heard that she complained. Only her husband—and her descendants."

Reid Sayers's great-grandfather had, nearly a hundred years before, been a lumberjack new to the South, looking for opportunity. He had found it when he met Cammie's great-grandmother, Lavinia Greenley. Justin Sayers had enticed the poor wife and mother into a torrid affair. Before it was over, Justin had finagled three hundred acres of prime land from Cammie's ancestress, and Lavinia's husband was dead.

It had been a scandal whose echoes still sounded in

Greenley, not the least reason being that Justin Sayers had stayed in the community, had prospered and left descendants. To call the division between the Sayers and Greenley families a feud would have been melodramatic, but the coolness and lack of social contact was real.

"Lavinia Greenley was not the complaining kind," Cammie said stiffly.

"Apparently not. I've often wondered about that." His tone, as he went on, was pensive and a little rough. "I used to wonder sometimes, too, if she was at all like you. And what you would have done in her place."

Her breath lodged in her throat. She had never dreamed that Reid Sayers thought of her at all. It was disarming, and oddly painful, to know that he had pictured her as Lavinia. Without stopping to consider, she said in stifled tones, "Did you see yourself as Justin?"

"Who else?"

The taut sound of his voice reverberated in the rain-drenched night that surrounded them. His face, as he hovered above her, was scant inches from hers in the darkness. She could feel the brush of his warm breath across her cheek. His scent surrounded her; it was compounded of fresh night air, a whiff of some woodsy after-shave, and his own warm masculinity, yet with an undertone of wildness that stirred an answering fierceness.

The muscles of his abdomen hardened. His biceps, under her neck, knotted. He drew breath with a soft, hissing sound of tightly leashed control.

Above them the wind sighed in the treetops. Raindrops pattered on the leaves and also on the glazed material of the poncho that covered them. They gleamed darkly in his hair and dripped in a slow warmth from his face to her forehead. Their touch was like a caress.

Cammie knew with abrupt and shocking clarity that if she moved so much as a finger, if she drew too deep a breath or allowed an eyelash to flicker, he would lower his head and press his lips to hers. If she did more, if she lifted her arms to circle his neck or opened her legs even a fraction farther, he might take her there in their nest of wet leaves.

Drifting through her mind, not quite formed but compelling, was the urge to shift, to move, to press against him in wanton invitation. Appalled by it, yet unbearably enticed, she held her breath.

Somewhere behind them a dead tree limb, made heavy by the steady rain, released its hold with a crack. It fell to the ground with a soft thud.

A shudder ran over Reid. He breathed a quiet imprecation, then abruptly levered himself up and away from her. Surging to his feet with lithe ease, he reached down and pulled her up to stand beside him. He whipped his poncho from around his shoulders, swirling it around her and pulling it closed over her breasts.

"Let's go," he said in a toneless command, "before I do something we'll both regret. Again."

Their passage through the woods was swift and sure. The man at Cammie's side never hesitated, seldom slowed, never stopped except to help her over a fallen log, a shallow branch or creek. He could not have been more at home, it seemed, if he had been moving across his own living room.

The poncho Cammie wore was so long that it nearly dragged on the ground. She tripped over it several times before she snatched up the excess material and bunched it in her hands.

Reid Sayers caught her each time she stumbled, almost as if he could see in the dark, or else had a sixth sense about her progress. He released her just as quickly.

Cammie was uncomfortably aware of him as he moved beside her. In some deep recess of her being she anticipated his touch when she faltered and missed its support when he removed it. She didn't want to feel that way, didn't want to feel anything except, possibly, a decent gratitude for his rescue. It was disturbing.

There had been a time, long ago, when she had mooned over Reid Sayers with a secret passion as intense as it was foolish. She had watched him from a distance, enjoying the way his sun-bleached blond hair grew from a peak on his forehead, the sense of fun that leaped so easily into his face, and the crinkles that appeared around the rich blue of his eyes as he smiled. She had liked watching him move, the play of the muscles under the brown skin of his shoulders and arms, the strength of his legs exposed by cutoff blue jeans.

He had been some three years older, and impressively more mature than the boys she went with to the movies, skating, or picnicking. To her, he had seemed sophisticated, experienced. Above all, he had the inevitable allure of things that are forbidden.

There had been moments when she had seen Reid and herself as the star-crossed lovers of some ancient fable. She had imagined that the two of them would come across each other one day when they were alone, and would know in an instant that they were meant for each other. They would be united in marriage, putting an end to the discord that had been festering between the families for nearly a hundred years. Such silly daydreams.

It had not happened quite the way she pictured. She had been swimming off the end of the boat dock at her family's camp house on the lake. Reid had been staying with friends at the camp next door, a fact she had known very well. She had not expected him to surface in the water beside her, however, or to close in on her so they were treading water with their noses practically touching and their legs brushing together in the warm currents of the lake.

"What are you doing?" she had gasped, like the startled virgin she was then.

His answer had been simple. "I saw you down here and couldn't resist joining you. Or this."

His arms had closed gently around her. The sunlight gleamed like molten gold in his hair as he bent his head, brushing his lips over the drops of water caught on her eyelids. Then he kissed her, his mouth warm and sweet on hers, caressing, questing, questioning.

For an instant she had flowed toward him in a response as strong and natural as breathing. Their bodies had melded, fitting together with precision and grace, like two sculptures carefully constructed by a master craftsman for the express purpose of being joined.

His hold tightened as his chest expanded in a breath of wonder. His lips brushed hers, learning their smoothness, their gentle contours, their delicate edges and moist, innocent corners. He tasted her, the tip of his tongue gently abrading; sweetly, tenderly invading. He sought the sinuous, guileless touch of hers. Finding it, he applied gentle suction. Blindly he brushed his hand over her breast beneath the thin, wet material of her bathing suit. Settling with exquisite care around that firm globe, he tested its tender fullness, its fit in his palm.

Pure, unrestrained desire jolted through her with the force of a lightning bolt. She was unprepared for it, unaware that such internal heat and upheaval was possible. In that same instant, she felt the firmness of his arousal against her thigh, sensed his barely controlled need.

She panicked.

In unreasoning fear she pushed away from him. She shouted something at him, though she was so upset that she didn't know then, and never remembered afterward, what she said. Swirling in the water, she turned and struck out for the dock, reaching it in a few short strokes. She scrambled up the ladder on the side and ran for the camp house as if the hounds of hell were after her.

Her parents and their guests were gathered for drinks on the screened porch on the north side of the camp. Cammie had been able to slip in on the east side unnoticed. In her room, she had stripped off her wet bathing suit and wrapped a towel around herself. Then she flung herself down on her bed, crying out her humiliation, bewilderment, and utter, soul-wrenching despair. She hated herself for exposing her inexperience. She hated what

Reid must think of her for running like a rabbit. She hated him for making her lose her cool. Most of all, she hated him for destroying her half-formed fantasies.

Reid had remembered; his words back there proved it. The thought was not a comfortable one, even now. Somewhere inside her the consternation and humiliation of that day lingered.

Did he really regret kissing her all those years ago? But why should he? It had, perhaps, been a natural enough impulse for a young man at the height of his sexual drive. She was the one who had created a scene and turned the episode into a tragedy in her mind.

Before today there had been no opportunity to even guess at what Reid had felt then. He joined the army almost immediately afterward. She had heard that he qualified as a Ranger, that elite troop of near-superhuman soldiers whose job it was to infiltrate enemy positions ahead of the advancing army. Later there had been rumors of the CIA and some form of covert operations in Central America and then in the Middle East. Then, just a few weeks ago, Reid's father had died, and he came home.

Cammie had been so preoccupied with thoughts of the past that she didn't notice the light shining through the trees until she was close enough to see that it came from the windows of a house. She halted, standing with the rain spattering down on the poncho that covered her.

As Reid paused, turning back to face her, she said in accusation, "This isn't my car."

"It was closer." The words had a clipped edge of impatience, as if he had expected her objection but was still irritated by it.

"I can't go in there."

"Don't be ridiculous. You need dry clothes and something hot to drink. I promise I won't molest you."

"I never thought you would!" There was anger and a trace of embarrassment in her tone.

"No? I'm amazed. What then? It's just a house; it won't contaminate you."

It wasn't just a house. Lavinia Greenley, so the story went, had been seduced within the walls of the dark, solid structure. No other Greenley had ever stepped foot in it.

It was a rectangular log pile of two full stories topped by a dormered attic. Built of virgin yellow pine, each great log was more than a foot thick. Chimneys of hand-made brick flanked it on each side, and there were high, narrow windows that could be closed off by heavy shutters on the inside. With narrow eaves and a flat front, minus the protection of porch or portico in the tradition of homes farther north, it had the look of a place that could be held against all comers.

The house had been built in the early 1890s by Justin Sayers. He had lived in it like a recluse behind an eight-foot-high stockade made of logs. The tall fence had fallen into ruin and been removed years ago, but to the townspeople of Greenley, the place came to be known simply as the Fort.

Every log in the house had been taken from the land Justin Sayers had stolen from Lavinia Greenley. Every board in it had been cut and planed in the sawmill that he had established a few short miles away.

The sawmill operation had been immensely profitable; it made him a wealthy man. Then, some years after the turn of the century, Justin had taken on a partner, a man named Hutton. Hutton worked up North in a paper mill and knew the fledgling industry. Sayers had the land, the timber, the backing, and the contacts. The two men brought in the machinery, and the paper mill replaced the sawmill.

The paper mill, greatly expanded, still squatted at the edge of the town, jointly owned by the Sayers and Hutton descendants. Now, Reid Sayers and Cammie's husband, Keith Hutton, along with Keith's older brother, Gordon, shared the ownership of the mill. Because Reid had inherited the land and his great-grandfather's original stake in the partnership, he had the majority interest, and was therefore the controlling partner.

Cammie glanced at the man beside her, at the bulk of his body in what appeared to be a shirt of tree-bark camouflage worn with faded jeans, at the angles and planes of his face, picked out by the faint glow of light from the house. She moistened her lips before she spoke.

"If you could just drive me back to my car—"

"As soon as you're warm and dry," he agreed in tones of calm reason. "It's a promise."

She shook her head. "I would rather go now. I'll be fine, really."

He stood watching her for long moments while rain plastered his hair to his head and tracked slowly down his jaw to his neck. He took a slow breath and shifted his shoulders, as if abdicating responsibility. Then in a single, smooth movement, he bent to thrust one hand under her knees and the other behind her back. Lifting her high, bracing her against his chest, he strode with her toward the house.

"No!" she cried, but it was too late.

She struggled, bucking and twisting. He clamped his arm around her so tight that the breath went out of her lungs and her face was pressed into his neck. Suffocating, feeling the bite of his fingers, she was made aware of how carefully he had handled her earlier under the trees.

She stopped fighting, allowed her taut muscles to relax; there was nothing else to be done. By degrees his hold eased to no more than a firm embrace.

Reid pushed inside the back door and made his way through a wood-paneled kitchen and along a wide hallway to the foot of a rustic but carefully crafted stairway. As he paused at the bottom, she said, "If I'm supposed to be impressed by this red-necked macho force, you've misjudged me. I prefer finesse in a man. I also prefer one who asks before he grabs."

"Are you going to undress yourself," he said through set teeth, "or shall I do it for you? You will note that I'm asking, though I could always do it for you."

Cammie searched her mind for something more annihilating to say. "And against your worst inclinations, too. Now I'm the one who's amazed."

"I've never forced a woman in my life, but there's a first time for everything," he said in rough tones.

"Oh, yes," she said, "and then you can go back to mistreating animals and children. That should suit you just fine."

She felt the shock of what she had said shudder through him like the unexpected lash from a whip. He would have dropped her if she had not been clinging to him with one arm around his shoulders and a hand clutching the placket of his shirt. As it was, her feet struck the lower stair step with such force that the sting burned all the way up to her knees. She wobbled, only just catching her balance by reaching for the newel post when he wrenched backward from her.

As he stepped free, his gaze was blank, turned inward upon some horror only he could see. His face drained of color, leaving the bronze of the sun on the surface like a stain. A white line appeared around his mouth. His voice rough, almost unrecognizable, he said, "The bathroom is at the head of the stairs, a robe is behind the door. Come down when you're ready."

He met her gaze for a single, searing instant, then turned and strode away, back toward the kitchen.

It was a retreat, fast and definite. Cammie stared after him until her eyes burned and her fingers, pressing into the newel post, were numb.

She had wanted to hurt him. She had succeeded, though how, exactly, she was not quite certain. Of one thing she was positive: the blow had been a direct hit, a hammer strike to the heart. In his eyes, turned up to hers and revealed by the light shining down from the stairwell above them, there had been such unrelieved agony that she felt sick remembering it.

And she never wanted to see it again.

Chapter Two

▨ ▨ ▨ *The temperature in the kitchen was several* degrees warmer than it had been earlier, and the smell of brewed coffee was strong on the air. Two dessert plates had been set on the work table of time-polished wood, along with forks and napkins. A generous piece of pound cake lay in the exact center of each plate. In the middle of the table, next to the sugar bowl and cream pitcher, was a bottle of Courvoisier.

Reid sat at the table staring at his knit fingers. His hair seemed darker than Cammie remembered it, though a part of the darkness was because it was still wet. Since her own long mane was more than half dry, he must have waited to have his shower until long after she had drawn her bath. He had changed into a soft, faded chambray shirt and a pair of jeans that were even a lighter blue. In comparison, his eyes were the color of fresh-mined turquoise, and were just as hard and opaque.

He got to his feet as she entered, drawing out a chair and holding it for her before he walked to the cabinet to fill two ironstone mugs with coffee. Returning to the table with them, he set hers in front of her, then reached for the brandy bottle.

"None for me, thanks," Cammie said in haste.

"Don't let's start that again, please."

He spoke without looking at her and without a pause in his task. There was the striated sound of a limit reached in his voice. It held her silent while he poured a generous measure of liquor into her coffee. She reached for the cream, stirring it into the concoction while she waited for him to sit down.

Difficult tasks, she knew, should be plunged into without waiting. She caught the inside of her bottom lip between her teeth for only an instant before she spoke. "I'm sorry if what I said earlier touched a nerve. Going for the jugular with words has become a habit with me."

"It always was," he said with a wry twist of his lips as he resumed his seat. "You were fairly lethal at sixteen."

"You mean— I don't remember much about that day." A flush for the half-truth burned across her cheekbones.

He gave her a direct look with a faint glint in its depths. "Don't you? I'd like to give you a direct quote, but I've managed to block out most of it. Finally. You insulted my ancestors, said I was a conceited jackass, that my kiss was too wet and I had bad breath."

"I didn't." The words were blank.

"You did," he answered with certainty. "You also said that if I ever touched you again, you would scream bloody murder—or be sick."

Cammie looked down at her coffee. Her hands shook a little as she picked up the cup. "You caught me by surprise."

"You surprised me, too, something I vowed never to let happen again. Which is why I may have been a little rough earlier."

"I see. Mere self-protection."

"I've already joined the army once to get away, or rather to escape the things you said that day and the way you looked at me. It turned out to be a bit drastic. I prefer not to have to do it again."

"You're joking," she said, her eyes wide. "Aren't you?"

"Am I?" he said, his gaze steady as it held hers.

She couldn't tell, which was almost as disturbing as the thought of how she might have affected his life. She took a deep breath. "If you expect another apology, especially at this late date, I'm afraid you'll be disappointed. You—You moved in on me too fast."

"And got what I deserved. Let it go. I had other reasons for getting out of Greenley, and none of it matters anymore anyway." He reached for his coffee mug, his eyes shielded by his long, golden-brown lashes as he sipped.

It mattered to her; the shock was, how much it did. She could not press it, however, not after his dismissive words. She drank another hefty swallow of her coffee, shuddering at the bite of the brandy. Its potency ignited a glow of warmth in her stomach that began to spread. She drank again before she finally spoke.

"The other reasons, did they have something to do with the paper mill?"

His gaze was considering. "I don't think it's any secret that I never wanted to work there."

"What about now, with your father gone? Will you be taking his place?"

"It seems to be expected."

"Not by everyone," she said dryly. "Keith was hoping you would stay away. You know he stepped up to assistant manager while his brother has been filling in as manager?"

Reid nodded. "Gordon hasn't said anything about either of them keeping the jobs."

"He wouldn't. Keith's brother is nothing if not diplomatic."

"Smooth," he agreed.

"A good businessman, of course," she said in grudging tones. "I expect he's waiting to see what you decide."

Cammie had never cared for Gordon Hutton. He seemed to think his doormat of a wife was perfection in the species, and he'd always done his best to tell Keith how to handle her, too, so she'd fit the same mold. At times, when Cammie was especially outspoken, it seemed to her that Gordon could barely restrain himself from demonstrating his ideas.

"Keith used to be a good kid," Reid said, "back when we played football together. Lisbeth wrote me about you two getting married. And when you separated."

His assessment of Keith was generous; Cammie remembered those football games well. Her husband had played tailback to Reid's quarterback. Keith was fast and slick, but he was also a grandstanding jerk who had done his best to steal the glory.

"Lizbeth?" she asked, her voice tentative.

Reid indicated the buttery-rich pound cake that neither of them had touched. "Cook and housekeeper for the Sayers these thirty years, the closest thing to a mother I had after my own died. She kept me up to date on everything worth knowing in Greenley."

Cammie knew whom he meant, had seen her around town. Lizbeth was a statuesque black woman with long hair she wore braided around her head, and skin the tobacco-gold shade of brown known as bright by those of African blood. She glanced at Reid, to find him watching her closely.

He looked away, rubbing his fingers along the handle of his cup. His voice neutral, he said, "So what happened?"

"With the marriage?" A small, derisive smile curled her full mouth. "It was a mistake from the beginning. Keith and I started going together my last year at college. Everybody seemed to think we were the perfect couple. One day he gave me a ring, and I couldn't think of a good reason not to take it. The next thing I knew, I was brushing rice out of my hair and popping birth control pills."

Cammie gave Reid a quick look, but his expression had not changed. There was more to the story, of course. She sometimes felt as if she had lived for years in limbo, waiting for her life to begin. Marrying Keith had been a feeble attempt to jump-start it. It hadn't worked, which was not entirely Keith's fault.

She went on, "Then I found out that I was expected to

melt quietly into the background and never be seen or heard again."

"And you didn't do that." It was a statement rather than a question.

"Our fights over it have become town legends. Keith's skin is thicker than yours." She hadn't intended to refer to that again; it must be the brandy loosening her tongue, she thought, and hurried on to cover the lapse. "But what about you? How is it you never married?"

He moved his shoulders as if the muscles of his neck were tight. "I did. In Colorado, just after I left the army. It lasted exactly a month."

"A whole month?"

He acknowledged the irony with a grim smile. "I tried to warn her that the Ranger training I'd been through, the uses it was put to in Central America and the Caribbean, was designed to dehumanize, to turn men into animals that act on instinct. She thought she could change all that. We had been married two weeks when she came up behind me in the bathroom. I was shaving with an electric razor, didn't hear her. She put her arm around me at the throat. Instinct kicked in. She was in the hospital two weeks; it was pure luck that she didn't die. She started divorce proceedings the day she got out."

"How terrible," Cammie said slowly. "I mean for you."

"It wasn't too great for her."

"You never tried again?"

He gave her a steady look. "I'm barely housebroken, not fit husband material for any woman."

For just an instant she saw him as he must appear to other women, the rugged physique, the broad forehead and firmly molded mouth, the straight nose with a slight bump at the bridge as if it had been broken. There was an old-gold-tinted shadow of beard on his lean cheeks and jaws, a scar half hidden in one eyebrow. His hands were big and sun-brown, but were well-made with neat, close-clipped nails. His self-assurance was bone deep, accepted and forgotten. Then there was his eyes. Clear, steady, they held self-derision and half-hidden pain, but they were not the eyes of an animal.

"You underestimate yourself, I think," she said finally.

"You're wrong."

The words were flat, with the heavy sound of denied emotion. Was there a warning in them? If so, it had nothing to do with her.

"That isn't all, is it—your marriage, how it ended?" She tilted her head to one side in careful consideration. "There was something else that happened to you."

He came to his feet so abruptly that his chair skidded on the waxed linoleum. "Finish your coffee. I'll take you home."

"To my car, you mean," she said, veiling her eyes as she felt warm color surge into her face. She was not used to being dismissed, though it was possible she had asked for it. She had forgotten, for a moment, who he was.

"I mean home," he answered. As she raised a questioning gaze, he moved to the cabinet, where he picked up a wallet and keys, her wallet and keys, and tossed them on the table. "I went back to check on Keith, just in case, and to drive your car around here to save time. It was no go. Somebody had slashed your tires."

The thought of him making that trek through the woods and cold rain again just to save her a little trouble gave her an odd feeling inside. She disregarded it as, in tones of disgust, she said, "Keith."

Reid nodded as he reached for his coffee cup and drank the last swallow. "His tracks were there. I take it he isn't happy about the divorce."

"You could say that," she said, and told him briefly about the way she had been hounded.

"Someone should have a talk with him." There was an edge of carefully repressed ferocity in Reid's voice.

Cammie gave him a sharp look as she pushed back her chair and stood up. His face was shuttered, with no clue to what he was thinking or what he intended. She said, "I hope that won't be necessary, after tonight."

A wry smile came and went across his face, but he said no more.

There was a Jeep Cherokee and a Lincoln Town Car in the garage at the Fort. Since there was a stretch of muddy road to be covered, Reid backed the Jeep out.

Cammie, sitting stiffly beside him, pulled at the faded and shrunken robe of navy flannel she still wore, trying to cover her knees. The robe had to be a relic of Reid's high school days, she thought, since it was so short and worn. It gave her an odd feeling to think it might be a favorite piece of clothing, carried with him around the world.

Still, she hated to think what people would say if they saw her in it; the busybodies would have a field day. She had not been worried enough about it, however, to struggle back into her clammy underwear or wet shirt and jeans. If she didn't give people something interesting to talk about, they would make up something worse.

She and Reid spoke very little during the short drive. The pecking of the rain on the Jeep's roof and the swish of the windshield wipers were loud in the silence. Once she saw him glance at her, look back at the road, then turn his head toward her again. The planes of his face were tinted soft emerald by the dash lights, though his eyes remained in shadow. His gaze rested on her hair, spilling over her shoulder; they skimmed over her breasts, where they pressed against the soft flannel, and touched the opening at the bottom of the robe where it had fallen away from her knees again. As he lifted his eyes, they locked with hers across the width of seat that separated them.

Cammie felt the brush of heat like an intimate caress where his gaze had touched her. She wanted to look away from him, but it was as if her regard was caught in an invisible snare. Never in her life had she been so aware of a man, of the powerful shaping and contained strength of his body. There was something elemental about him, and as enduring as the pineland hills of the game reserve itself. At the same time, he had internal barriers like thick and impenetrable second-growth timber, barriers that could be used for protection, or as an ambush for the unwary.

It also seemed, watching him, that he could be right in describing himself as animalistic. There appeared to be an untamed and dangerous side to his nature, like the rare tawny cougar known as a swamp panther. And yet, she felt no fear of it. Rather, she recognized in the soft singing of the blood in her veins a perilous need to discover whether, if she came close, he would turn and attack or permit her to touch him, to share his wildness.

Wrenching her head around, she stared out into the darkness. She clenched her teeth as she waited for that instant of insanity to pass.

The house where Cammie lived loomed dark and still as they turned into the drive and wound their way up the hill toward it. Older than the Fort by several decades, it was identified in the public records as Evergreen, though most people called it the Greenley place. Georgian in concept, it rose two stories high, with fanlighted center doorways, evenly spaced windows, and upper and lower porches grafted on in the style typical of pre–Civil War homes built by Louisiana planters. Modernized and added on to over the years, it had a gracious aspect left over from a quieter and slower time.

During its antebellum heyday the place had been surrounded by several thousand acres of cotton land. The more distant fields had gradually been allowed to go back to woodland, while closer acreage with road frontage had been sold off to pay mortgages or for ready cash. There was less than eight acres kept clear around the house these days, though to Cammie's mind, that was plenty to mow and trim in the summer.

Keith had hated living in the old Greenley mansion. He had called it drafty and musty-smelling, and complained that something always needed repair. He wanted to sell it and build something contemporary and convenient, with lots of glass and open decks, preferably out on the lake east of town.

Cammie had refused. She had inherited Evergreen when her parents died, and she loved it. She had to admit he was right about repairs; the house seemed to chugalug money. Still, the spacious rooms, the generations-old furniture, and the garden with its huge old plants, which had been put into the ground by Greenley women long dead, were constant joys. She couldn't imagine living anywhere else.

Reid strode with her through the light rain toward the back door. Cammie saw his appraising glance as it moved over the house looming above them. She wondered if he was comparing it to the Fort.

She also noticed, as they neared the steps leading up to the back porch, that his narrowed gaze raked the dimness beyond the house and behind the glow of the security light at the end of the drive. Though she looked also, she could make out nothing in the dark and swirling mists of rain. No doubt his watchfulness was a habit, another of those instincts he had talked about. It was oddly comforting.

Turning as they reached the shelter of the back porch, she spoke with brittle politeness. "I'm afraid I never did thank you for—for coming to my rescue this evening. I want you to know that I do appreciate it."

"My pleasure," he said, the words low and deep and as empty as her own.

She smiled, a mechanical movement of the lips. "Well, then, I guess I'll see you around."

He put out a hand to catch her arm as she turned from him. There was a frown between his eyes. As she stiffened and raised a brow in inquiry, he nodded toward the dark side garden. "Keith is over there. Watching you."

"You mean he's out there—now?" She flung a quick glance over her shoulder.

Reid nodded. "His Land Rover is a half mile down the road, angled in behind the church; I saw it as we passed. He's about fifty yards to the right, back behind the camellias."

The idea of Keith skulking out there, spying on her, looking for some way to sneak back into her life, brought the rise of anger and a shadow of apprehension. Her voice tight, she said, "I can't believe this."

"The sheriff, Deerfield, is a cousin of yours, isn't he? Maybe you should call him." Reid's voice carried a tentative edge that suggested he was less than satisfied with that solution.

Nor was Cammie satisfied. If she made that call, the news would be all over town by morning. On top of that, Keith might well spread a biased version of the events of the night in his own defense. There was no telling what kind of lurid fiction would come of it all by the time both stories had made the rounds.

She gave a quick shake of her head. "Maybe it won't be necessary. Anyway, I don't know what action the sheriff or anyone else can take, since all Keith has done is threaten me."

Reid's voice as he answered was uncompromising. "You can't let it pass, not if you want to stop him."

"There must be another way," she said unhappily.

The look he gave her was steady. "There are only two things. You can fight, or you can give in."

"I tried using a gun, remember?" she said with acerbity.

"A show of force was a mistake, since you apparently didn't intend to follow through. If you won't call the police, then the only tactic left is subversion."

"You mean stall? Trick him into thinking I may go back to him until after the divorce is final?"

"I had in mind inviting your cousin to dinner tomorrow and telling him to come in his patrol car," he answered in frowning concern. "Or something like bringing a pair of Dobermans into the house, maybe renting a room to a tae kwan do instructor."

"I have a better idea," she said slowly, as alarming, half-formed impulses swirled in her brain.

"Such as?"

She didn't stop to test the origin of her solution, or its implications. As it settled, becoming a firm idea, she simply set it in motion.

Moving toward Reid, stretching on tiptoe, she slid her arms around his neck. Her gaze wide and appealing, her lips tremulous, she whispered, "Kiss me."

He was fast on the uptake. His instant of stiff amazement was barely perceptible before he bent his head and closed his arms around her. She pressed her lips to the smooth and firm contours of his mouth and settled against him until the nipples of her breasts nudged into his chest and her lower body molded to his pelvis.

Reid drew a ragged breath. His hold tightened, and abruptly he took the initiative from her.

Her lips parted under the onslaught of his kiss. Pleasure spiraled up from deep inside her, tingling along every inch of contact between them. Her pulse leaped to a frantic tempo. Heat invaded her body in waves. She accepted the bold and warm sweep of his tongue between her parted lips, and returned it with fervent grace.

Lost, she was lost in half-remembered sweetness, in the revival of sensations she had thought were only imagined. They shook her heart so that it expanded, aching in her chest. With a soft sound deep in her throat, she pushed her fingers through the thick silk of his hair at the base of his skull and tightened her arms around his neck.

He smoothed his hand over her back, with its soft flannel covering, gliding lower to the gentle swell of her hip. His light grasp lingered there, learning the texture and resilience of her, drawing her closer until she could feel the heated hardness of his body, sense the tenuous control that allowed him to trespass just so far and no further.

Sanity returned with unwelcome suddenness, rippling through her on a shudder. She couldn't believe what she had done, could never have conceived a few hours before that it was remotely possible. It had to be caused by the peculiar events of the evening and the careless raking up of the past.

That wasn't all. With painful honesty she faced the fact that there was another element involved. Somewhere inside she had a need to find out once and for all whether what had happened so long ago between this man and herself was just a fluke or as startling as she remembered. And, yes, a desire to stroke the panther.

She caught her breath on a small gasp, and drew back with care. Her voice a little hoarse, she hurried into explanations.

"I thought—it seemed that if I could make Keith think there's another man in my life now, he might give up and leave me alone."

"I figured as much." Reid's response was soft and not quite even.

She had thought he understood, but needed to be positive. She went on quickly. "That it's you makes it even better. You're intimidating, though Keith would deny it with his last breath. He was always jealous of you—and it's worse now that you may be coming into the mill."

"I see."

She could feel her courage receding, being replaced by confusion. Before it could slip away entirely, she hurried on. "The—The trick might be even more effective if you would come inside. There will be no obligation, I promise. And it will be just for a little while."

She realized as she spoke that she was taking a lot for granted. The fact that Reid was no longer married didn't mean he didn't have a woman somewhere.

"For a little while," he repeated, the words abrupt, almost mechanical.

She swallowed hard as she turned with him toward the back entrance under the shelter of the porch. Her hands shook as she put the key in the door. She grasped it hard, hoping he wouldn't notice.

Inside the house, she flicked the lights on while Reid closed and locked the door behind them. She turned then, and saw him watching her with the same careful, measuring expression she felt on her own face.

Reid exhaled with a short, hard breath. He felt as if he had been handed a bomb and it had detonated in his hands. The concussion had shaken him to the center of his being, had taken his wits and his strength and turned his insides to hot mush. And he was not yet certain he had survived the blast.

His voice less even than he would have liked, he said, "You're full of surprises."

"I don't mean to be."

She gave him a swift look, then swung and moved ahead of him through what appeared to be a sitting room located at the end of the long hallway through the house. His gaze rested an instant on the bronze shimmer of her hair hanging down her back, on the sheen of the skin on the calves of her legs, and the slight sway of her hips under his old robe. The knowledge that she was naked under the worn flannel was a white heat in his mind; he knew she was because he had felt it. Dizziness and disbelief caught at him. He gave his head a hard shake before he moved after her.

They entered a big, airy kitchen with white-painted cabinets topped with yellow tile and a long bank of plant-crowded windows that faced toward the back of the house. It was so much larger and brighter and more open than its counterpart at the Fort that he felt exposed, and that was before she switched on the fluorescent strip lighting. The height of the room from the ground made it unlikely that Keith could see in from outside; still, it made him wary.

Over her shoulder Cammie said tentatively, "Since I'm taking up your time, I'd like to offer you something for dinner. Will a steak and salad do?"

"Fine," he answered through stiff lips.

She was trying to give herself something to do, he thought, and trying to make the situation seem natural. The least he could do was help her out. Walking deeper into the room, he leaned against the end of the one cabinet and put his hands in his pockets.

Cammie moved back and forth, taking steaks from the freezer against one wall and putting them into a microwave to thaw, searching out lettuce and tomato, broccoli and carrots from the refrigerator. He watched, thinking how unreal it was that he was there in her house.

It was funny, in a grim fashion, that it was his background with the mill—and possibly the reputation of his sordid past in covert operations—that made him useful to Cammie all at once. These were the very things he would have expected to repel her. Beyond that, the uppermost emotion he could sort from among those that crowded his chest was gratitude.

It had been a long time since he had been close to a woman, any woman. They were far too fragile and easily hurt. He didn't trust himself with them, hadn't for a long time.

Cammie had responded to him. He had felt the slow, sweet burning where their bodies had touched, had tested the frantic pulse in the tender curve of her neck and tasted the sweet tang of desire on her tongue. It struck him as nothing less than a miracle.

He should leave, he knew that beyond a doubt. To stay was dangerous, for both of them. If he should hurt her, this woman of all women, he might never get over it.

He couldn't go. Not after what had happened out there on the porch. He owed her something for that, for letting him feel for the space of a few quick breaths that he was not the pariah he thought, not just a machine with bestial instincts. He would do, and be, whatever she wanted, if she would allow him to pretend just a little longer that he was a normal man.

He was staring at her, at the way her hair shifted across her shoulders, catching the light in individual red-gold strands; studying the curve of her mouth, the slender turn of her waist as she moved here and there. He knew he was, but couldn't help it. It was that irresistible. Though the effect on him would very likely disgust her if she noticed it.

He needed a distraction, needed it in the worst kind of way.

"What can I do to help?" he asked.

She flung him a quick look, as if she had never heard a man say such a thing. "Nothing. I can do it."

He moved toward her, picking up one of the carrots that lay beside the sink. His voice even, he said, "Do you have a potato peeler?"

She turned to a drawer and took out the utensil, handing it to him. She watched him as she might a child with a sharp knife while he sliced a long, paper-thin peel from the carrot in his hand. Satisfied, apparently, that he knew what he was doing, she went back to washing lettuce.

"Keith doesn't do kitchen duty?" he asked as he worked.

Her lips twitched in the wry smile he was coming to expect. "Like you, we have a housekeeper who comes in by the day. Keith always considered paying her wages his contribution to household chores."

"He might have been more willing to pitch in later, when the children came. Most men come to it then."

"Maybe."

"Was there a reason you didn't have any? Children, I mean." It was a question that had been in the back of his mind for some time. He had been expecting off and on for years to hear that she was a mother.

She glanced at him with a frown between her eyes before she tore paper towels from the roll to drain the lettuce. "At first, Keith thought we should wait; he didn't want to be tied down. I decided later on, for different reasons, that he was right."

He wondered, abruptly, what she would look like when

she was pregnant. Nothing less than bewitching, he suspected, much as she was now, but more so. He liked the
shape of her mouth, generous, made for smiling, and
he thought he could spend quite a while getting used to
the way her brows arched. Her witch's eyes with their
layers of blue and green, gold and gray, fascinated him;
he would like to move in nose to nose, to study them. Her
cheeks were a little hollow, and there were shadows under
her eyes; she could use a few more pounds and a lot more
sleep. Still, she was beautiful, no doubt about it. Pregnancy could only add to it.

He put down an extremely well-peeled carrot and
picked up another one before he spoke in an abrupt
change of subject. "I meant to tell you before, I'll check
out your car tomorrow and put new tires on it. Will you
be home if I bring it by around nine?"

"There's no need," she said with a startled glance. "I
can send a man from the garage."

"I'd rather see to it; Keith may have left you another
little surprise."

Her movements stilled and doubt invaded her eyes.
"More damage? You don't really think so?"

Did he? He wasn't sure, but it made a nice excuse. He
said, "I can tell more about it when daylight comes. In
the meantime, I can leave the Jeep here, in case there's
somewhere you need to be in the morning."

"How would you get home?"

"Walk," he said with a shrug. "It isn't far through the
woods."

The microwave oven chimed as its cycle ended. There
was a silence as she moved to take the steaks out and tear
open their plastic wrapping. She turned them out onto a
platter, found Worcestershire sauce and set it out, then
reached for a pottery garlic jar. Holding a garlic bulb in
her fingers, she said, "There's another solution."

He looked up, alerted by a shading of strain in her
voice. "Such as?"

"You could spend the night here."

He put down carrot and peeler and stood with his arms braced and his hands spread flat on the countertop. The tile was cool under his palms, but did nothing to ward off the sudden furnace heat in his brain. As he turned his head slowly to look at her, it felt as if every bone in his neck grated and snapped with the tension that gripped him.

"Do what?" he asked in toneless disbelief.

She moistened her lips with the tip of her tongue. "You heard me."

He had. That was the trouble.

Outside, the rain had begun to pour down again in a steady drumming. He counted his pounding pulse, which made a counterpoint to the soft noise.

"In one of the spare bedrooms, of course," she said hurriedly.

He looked away from her, fastening his gaze on his own pale face reflected in the window over the sink with the dark night behind it. His voice like cracking ice, he said, "I can't."

"Why? It's only one night, not a lifetime commitment. There's no obligation involved."

"I realize that." At least he had assumed it.

"So where's the problem? Unless— I see." She turned her back on him.

"I doubt it," he said, the words measured, louder than he intended, though he couldn't help that. "I don't give a damn about being used—there's nothing unusual in that. It would give me great satisfaction to act as a buffer between you and Keith, if that's what you need. I don't care what the gossipy neighbors think, as long as you don't. And I have no need to deny what you ask out of some misplaced retaliation for the bad blood between our families."

"What is it then? Do you walk in your sleep? Or are you afraid I'll be consumed with lust in the middle of the night and crawl into bed with you?"

A short, hard laugh left him. "That's the least of my worries."

"Well?" She turned back to stare at him.

"Suppose," he said, switching his gaze to her reflection there beside his own in the rain-speckled glass, "that I hurt you?"

"You wouldn't. You couldn't."

The look on her face was so certain. She didn't understand, even after what he had told her.

He moved almost before the decision was made; that was the way it worked. Before she could make a sound, before she even began to guess what he intended, he locked his arms around her in a death grip, one of many he had learned too well. He wasn't hurting her, but she could not move without causing herself pain. Nor, given her lesser strength and lack of knowledge, could she possibly break free.

In those fleeting seconds as he settled his hold into place, he felt the unaccustomed thrust of doubt. His motives for this demonstration, he suspected, were far from noble. To feel the soft delicacy of her body pressed against him again—to know that she was inescapably in his power, however briefly—for these things any excuse would do.

He shifted slightly to place his fingers on the tender curve of her neck behind and below her ear. His voice no more than a whisper, he said, "Do you realize that I could kill you in seconds, without a sound, by applying pressure just here?"

"I don't doubt it at all," she said, the words astringent.

"Do you understand that I could do anything at all to you, and there is no way on God's green earth you could stop me."

The pupils of her eyes dilated, and her breasts rose against him with the depth of the breath she took. She searched his face for a brief instant before she released the air in her lungs. She said, "I can see how it might be possible."

"Then you realize why I can't stay?"

She stared up at him with irritation seeping into her face, collecting in her eyes. "I realize that if you don't turn me loose this minute, I'm going to kick you where it hurts, just like I did Keith."

He grinned; he couldn't help it. And he had meant to be so menacing. The only way she could manage to hurt him was if he let her, but that wasn't what tickled his sense of humor. It was her spirit, her sheer, uncaring defiance.

If there was a woman who could survive whatever vicious instinct he might have, whatever brutal act he might inadvertently commit against her, it was possible she was the one.

Possible, yes, but not likely.

Chapter Three

🔲 🔲 🔲 *They ate their steak and salad in virtual* silence. Cammie, all too well aware that Reid had neither agreed to her proposal nor completely refused it, was reluctant to say anything that might swing his decision the wrong way.

She glanced up once, to find his gaze resting on a spot a foot or so below her chin. The belt of the robe she wore had slipped, she discovered, letting the neckline fall open, exposing the pale curves of her breasts.

She should have changed clothes, she thought; she would have been more comfortable. It had seemed awkward and rather coy, however, after wearing the robe in front of Reid at the Fort.

In a gesture as casual as she could make it, she reached under the napkin on her lap to draw the edges of the robe tighter, closing the gap. When she looked at Reid again, he was giving his steak his undivided attention, and the tops of his ears were pink.

Her attention was caught by his hands as he sliced off a bite of meat. She had noticed them earlier. They were big and square, but well-shaped. The fingers were long and marked by small white scars. There was precision and controlled strength in the way he used them. She wondered what it would be like to feel them upon her, inside her.

She drew a sharp, sudden breath and was not surprised to feel heat rising through the lower part of her body.

Reaching for the glass of burgundy she had poured to go with the meal, she took a hasty swallow.

She must be losing her mind, having a mental break-down; there was no other explanation for the things she had done this evening, beginning with firing her pistol at Keith. It wasn't like her, it wasn't like her at all.

It would be easy to say her husband had driven her to it, but she wasn't sure she could accept that excuse. It was as if she had stepped over some invisible boundary within herself and now, somehow, was speaking and behaving with primitive intuition. It was frightening, yet exhilarating at the same time. Perhaps it was like the dangerous instincts Reid had been trying to describe to her. There was something seductive in the thought of being controlled by something other than pure reason.

It was possible, of course, that she was making too much of the situation, Cammie told herself. What had she done, after all, except invite a man into her house, then ask for his protective presence for the night? Surely there was nothing so unusual in that.

Except that it wasn't just any man. It was Reid Sayers.

So she was attracted to him, so what? She wasn't some teenager with more hormones than self-control. That Reid was in the house, if he decided to stay, would make no difference in how well she slept.

And even if it did, the problem would not be insurmountable. She would stay in her bed, and he would stay in his. The male body held few mysteries for her, and no great enchantment. How much difference could there be between two men?

How much indeed? Exactly?

She would not think of it. Whatever happened, would happen.

They cleared away the dishes, leaving them in the dishwasher for the housekeeper to deal with in the morning. Afterward, Cammie left Reid drinking coffee in what had been the front parlor, now known as the living room, while she excused herself for a few minutes.

Upstairs, she quickly put fresh sheets on the bed in the blue bedroom that was usually used for guests, and checked the towels and the soap situation in the connecting bath. There was no guarantee that Reid would use any of it, but she had found that Keith would sometimes accept a *fait accompli* if it was sprung on him.

She paused as she was taking a new toothbrush still in the package from the closet. She thought she had heard a door close, the back door. The sound was quiet, but she was used to every creak and click in the old house.

Had Reid left? She could not imagine that he would without a word of good-bye. Then again, he was still a stranger to her, in spite of everything.

Cammie found Reid in the sun room, a cozy place with tall windows and a southern exposure. Furnished with wicker cushioned in a pink-and-gray-striped material, with a huge cut-leaf philodendron in a tall terra-cotta pot and African violets on the windowsills, it was her favorite room. She spent most of her free time there, reading, stitching, crocheting, or working on her watercolor paintings of flowers.

He was standing in front of the gray-veined, marble fireplace that centered one wall. With his hands jammed into the back pockets of his jeans, he was staring up at the portrait of her that was centered above the mantel.

Cammie paused in the doorway, watching the look of absorbed contemplation on his face, before she came forward. Her tone neutral, she said, "It was done from a photograph; Keith commissioned it for our fifth anniversary. A bit too lady-of-the-manor, don't you think?"

"Maybe," he said, his face relaxing in a smile as he turned, "but it still suits you."

She refused to acknowledge the pleasure his comment gave her. She said instead, "Your room is ready when you are."

He didn't move, though his face hardened to the same texture as the polished marble behind him. In the soft tones of a man issuing a warning, he said, "I haven't agreed to stay."

"I know." She added baldly, "Will you?"

Appreciation for her frankness, and something more, glinted in the blue of his eyes. It was possible that the saving grace, if there was to be one, would be his sense of humor.

He turned back to the mantel, taking something from the shelf above it. When he faced her again, her magnum pistol was in his hand. "I meant to give this to you earlier, but it—slipped my mind."

She accepted it, weighing it in her hand as she looked up at him. His shirt was splattered at the shoulders with damp spots of rain, and droplets sparkled on the gold-brown hair of his forearms below the rolled sleeves. The handgun must have been the reason he had left the house just now, she thought; he'd gotten it from the Jeep.

She said, "You had it all along."

He acknowledged it with a brief nod. "I saw it when you dropped it in the woods. It seemed you might have a use for it."

"I might at that," she said.

There was a pause. Then in trenchant tones, he said, "About tonight . . . discouraging Keith is one thing, but what about the effect on your divorce? What if he decides to use you having a man here against you in court?"

"He wouldn't dare," she answered. "His own adultery has been so public that documenting it would be ridiculously easy. Beside, I asked for nothing from him, so there's nothing to contest, nothing for him to gain. The community property we've accumulated is so mortgaged, the only thing left to divide is the debts."

"Even this house?" he asked with a quick frown.

Cammie shook her head. "Evergreen is heir property and mine alone. Actually, Keith wanted to put it up for cash. He even went so far as to arrange it behind my back, but I refused to sign the papers."

Reid said tightly, "I heard about your father and mother. It's a little late, but I'm sorry."

Her father had been killed in a head-on collision with a log truck less than a year after her marriage. Her mother, who had been fighting breast cancer at the time, had simply stopped struggling and let it take her. Cammie accepted his sympathy with a slight inclination of her head before she went on. "Anyway, the communal property consists of our two cars and the silver and china we were given as wedding gifts."

"I know his interest in the mill is tied up, so he can't draw on it directly, but he makes a good salary. Is he that bad at managing his money?"

Reid's manner was intent, the question personal. It was possible, however, that he had a right to ask. Any assistant manager who could not handle his personal business could hardly be considered a good choice to control the finances of a company like Sayers-Hutton Bag and Paper Company. Still, going into detail about Keith's spending habits felt wrong to her.

She said after a brief hesitation, "Let's just say Keith enjoys the good life."

A smile indented the corner of Reid's mouth. "I had almost forgotten that such discretion existed. I suppose your mother taught you it's impolite to talk about money problems."

"Something like that."

"You must have been the perfect wife. Keith's an idiot."

She turned sharply away from Reid, moving to where a half-completed watercolor of a wild purple flag, or iris, sat on an easel. Putting the handgun down on a nearby table, she reached out to touch the silky paper, feeling for dryness.

Over her shoulder she said, "I tried to be perfect. I took gourmet cooking lessons and studied books on home decorating and table presentation in order to be a good hostess. I joined all the right clubs and groups to improve our social life. I exercised and ate right to stay in shape; I spent hours on my complexion, my hair, and my nails. I read to broaden my mind, and drove out of town to buy sex manuals to find out what was wrong with our love life. I studied all the magazine articles that said I was supposed to be endlessly understanding, never talk about my problems or pains, but encourage my man to tell me his. And do you know what happened?"

"I can guess," Reid said. "Keith didn't appreciate it."

She turned to face him, her eyes dark. "He took it for granted. He thought I was supposed to do all these things. In his mind, he deserved perfection."

"And now he thinks you have no right to deny him his perfect world since he's decided he wants it back."

"It's more a matter of pride than anything else. He thinks if he calls and begs and pleads and follows me around, making my life miserable, that I'll believe he loves me and give in. He's wrong. But the six-month waiting period before the petition for divorce goes into force will be up soon. If the usual conditions exist, no reconciliation, no cohabitation, then the decree can be handed down immediately."

"You think he's getting desperate, then?"

She was grateful to Reid for putting it into words for her. She said, "I'd like to convince him it's no use, that I can never go back to him."

"Which is where I come in."

"If you don't mind."

As she met his gaze, she recalled some of the things she'd said to him, just now and earlier. It struck her that she had never even thought of saying such things to Keith. In all their six years of marriage, her husband never guessed that she had read a sex manual, never dreamed that was where she'd found some of the subtle suggestions she had put to him. Not that it had done any good.

Reid Sayers was different. She had the feeling that she could say anything to him, that he would never be shocked or contemptuous, or even surprised. There was a bedrock of tolerance within him, perhaps beyond that of most men; the things that had happened to him, that he had seen and done, had ensured it. He would not presume to judge a man, or a woman, but would accept them as they were with all their flaws. He had lost his belief in perfection.

"Do you have a job?" he asked in serious tones.

She smiled a little as she saw that his mind ran to practical matters, unlike her own. "You're asking how I'll live? I have a small inheritance, plus a half interest in an antique shop. Neither allows for wild extravagance, but I'll get by. Also, I have a degree in French, and I've worked on a number of CODOFIL projects—the Council for Development of French in Louisiana—at the state level. As it happens, I'll be leaving tomorrow for a weekend CODOFIL conference in New Orleans. I could probably get a job teaching French through that connection, if need be. And if all else fails, I suppose I can turn Evergreen into a bed and breakfast place."

A corner of his mouth tugged in amusement. "Somehow, I can't see you welcoming tourists and getting up at six in the morning to set out croissants and coffee."

"I'll manage. I'm not one of those helpless females who has never paid a bill or bought an insurance policy. As a matter of fact, I always took care of those things."

"Perfect, like I said. So the only thing you need right now to ensure a decent future is a man in your—spare—bed."

His voice was even and not at all encouraging, still she felt a sensation inside very like elation. Her face warm, but her expression as serious as his, she said, "Yes."

He watched her for long moments. Turning from her slightly, he took his hands from his pockets. He raised one arm to rest a wrist on the mantel, his fingers curling slowly into a fist. His chest swelled with the depth of the breath he took, and she heard its rush as he released it. Finally he said, "If—and I do mean if—I should happen to agree, there will be ground rules. Do you think you can abide by them?"

She didn't care for the sound of that. Tilting her head, she said, "Such as?"

"They're simple, really, but important. Don't ever walk up behind me. Don't move too fast in my vicinity unless I'm watching you. And don't, for the love of God, approach me in the dark without fair warning. Forget even one of these, and we may both be sorry. But by then it could be too late."

She stood listening to the echoes of warning and desolation in his voice, and she wanted to cry. For any man to be so terrified of human contact—not for himself, but for others—that he would cut himself off from it with such ruthless determination, was tragic. The urge to help him was inescapable.

"How is it," she said quietly, "that you can go among people and think about working with them at the mill, if you can't trust yourself any more than that?"

"I'm not sure I can. I expect to take it nice and easy, and to keep my back to the wall."

"You tackled me out there in the woods without hurting me. I don't remember it being a problem for you."

His jaw flexed so that the muscles stood out in relief. "That was what you might call a planned attack. I knew exactly what I was doing. I was in control."

She certainly could not deny that. She tried again. "What about out on the porch. I approached you in the dark, or very near it, and you didn't harm me."

"I was facing you at the time, I saw you coming. There was no element of surprise."

"I think there was a little," she said in dry tones. She hesitated, then went on. "Anyway, just for my own protection, I'd like to clarify a point. As long as you realize what's coming at you, there should be no problem. Do I have that right?"

"Generally speaking, yes. There is no—reaction, usually, if there is no surprise, no apparent threat."

"There are many different kinds of threats." The words were spoken in low tones, almost to herself.

"I meant in physical terms," he said in caustic explanation.

Her eyes were wide as she met his dark blue gaze. "So did I."

A visible tremor ran over him, leaving a prickle of gooseflesh along the surface of his arms. He looked away from her. His voice rough, he said, "Well, then. Where is this bed?"

Cammie lay awake sometime later, staring into the dark and watching the constant flicker of lightning around the edges of the curtains at her bedroom window. The wind was rising, whining around the eaves of the old house. It appeared to be blowing up a spring storm to go with the rain.

She wondered if Reid was asleep, two doors down the hall. Or was he lying there in the old four-poster bed wide-awake, wondering why he had let her talk him into staying?

There had been no men's pajamas in the house. Her father's things had been donated to a charity drive long ago, and she had packed Keith's belongings and had them delivered to his girlfriend's trailer. Not that Keith's clothes would have fit Reid. Her husband had put on weight around the middle over the years, and was at least two inches shorter.

She found herself wondering if Reid was sleeping in his briefs or if he preferred the nude. He didn't seem like the kind of man who would accept confinement of any kind.

Cammie shifted in the bed, sliding one arm above her head as she rolled to her side. Her own nightwear, a gown of peach silk, felt heavy and binding against her skin. She thought of discarding it, but that seemed too much like discarding a restraint.

Restraint from what? That was the question.

But no, that was dishonest. She knew perfectly well the confusion of desires that tempted her. Her problem for most of her life had been that she understood herself too well. Ignorance of her inclinations and impulses had never been an acceptable excuse.

Was it some peculiar need for self-immolation that drove her to consider rising from her bed and making her way down the hall in the lightning's flare? Was it sheer female contrariness, a craving for something that had been deliberately placed beyond her grasp? Or was it the ancient feminine need to offer compassion?

Was it the simple lust of a woman who had been without a man for months? Or was it an urge toward mutual healing?

Was it, perhaps, a need to extend recompense for past injuries?

It could be any or all of these things. It felt, however, like a homing instinct.

Reid Sayers was nothing to her. How could he be? She hardly knew him, and the little she had learned of his activities over the last decade and a half was not encouraging.

He was not someone she would have seen much of if he had remained in town; the family differences meant they would seldom have met in a social way. Even if they had seen each other from time to time, the incident at the lake might well have kept them apart.

If these things were not enough, there was his background and obvious inclinations. He might own the mill, but his education had probably been neglected while he was in the army. His clothes seemed to consist of jeans and camouflage. He lived in the game reserve and drove a Jeep. All that added together made him the King of the Red-Necks. He was, in fact, everything that she most despised in a man.

Why, then, did her body respond to him as it had to no other?

She kicked at the sheet that covered her as she flung herself over on her back. This was a passing moment of insanity. She would get over it.

The last thing she needed was another complication in her life. In any case, a woman didn't throw herself at a man.

She wanted him with a deep internal ache that had nothing to do with physical need. It was as if something of her essential self reached out to him.

He would think she was crazy, or possibly depraved. Maybe she was. Why else would she even think of risking the pain and danger he might bring her?

She sat up and slid out of bed, walking to the window, where she pulled the curtain aside and looked out. The trees in the garden were silver-green in the lightning flashes, the undersides of their leaves showing pale gray as their branches tossed in the wind. Thunder rumbled a warning, then detonated with a solid boom.

Grasping the window sash, she pushed it up. The sound of the rain and wind blew into the room on a gust of fresh, moist air. The rich, wet smell of it was like inhaling an aphrodisiac. The thunder was louder, the lightning's glow more intense. As she leaned on the sill, a silver trident streaked down the sky above the treetops. Hard on its singeing crackle came a shattering explosion of thunder that shook the floor under her.

And yet, the greater storm was inside her, a violent conflict between values and instinct.

There had been a great deal of thought and discussion about the last this evening. Why should she be concerned about following its lead now?

She straightened from the window and, leaving it open to the rain, moved across her bedroom and out into the hall. She hesitated, closing her eyes tight, then opened them wide and turned toward the bedroom at the end of the long corridor.

As she took one deliberate step after the other, it seemed that she was somehow outside herself, watching what she was doing in mingled approbation and disbelief. It was eerie, as if she had little to do with the legs that moved forward or the feet that trod the soft, Oriental runner stretching down the hall. She felt compelled, or perhaps drawn by some force outside herself.

Was it true, or only an excuse? Either way, she couldn't seem to stop herself. She wasn't sure she wanted to try.

She was not quite without self-preservation, however. Reaching out toward the blue bedroom door, she grasped the knob with delicate precision. She turned it slowly to prevent the quiet metallic noise it might make. As she pushed on the door panel so that it swung inward, she called the name of the man inside in soft warning, trying not to startle him if he was asleep.

He wasn't.

His sigh was so ferocious, and so close beside her, that she felt it like a warm wind brushing her face. In the same instant, a hard grasp fastened on her wrist and pulled her forward. It was a small jerk, almost gentle, but it carried enough force to send her spinning into the room. She caught the post of the bed and sat down, abruptly, on the mattress.

Reid pushed the door closed with a snap, then swung toward her. "Testing my reflexes?" he asked in quiet rage out of the darkness.

His window, like her own, was open to the storm. Beyond the curtains that billowed with the wind, lightning stitched its way down the dark night sky. In its fading blue glare she saw the stalwart masculine beauty of his naked body. And the torment in his face.

"No," she said in quiet answer. "Rather, tempting them."

"Pity the poor beast. Is that it?"

His voice recoiled from her, drifting away toward the

room's blackest corner. With his back to the wall there, he stopped.

"More like mutual consolation," she said, when she was sure he did not intend to leave the bedroom.

"And to hell with the rules."

She shook her head, and her hair slid forward, half concealing her face. "This isn't a case of forever. Consider it, if you like, simple human contact. For that, I've followed procedure."

"Coming here in the middle of the night?" he asked incredulously.

"You weren't asleep, or you would never have heard me. I tried to approach you from the front. I gave you fair warning by calling out. I moved as slowly as possible. And I don't think, if you're fair, that you can call my being here a threat."

"That is a matter of opinion," he said succinctly.

"Maybe I misunderstood," she said, rising to her feet and moving toward him with gliding steps. "Tell me, if I come toward you now, like this, if I reached out to touch you, would I still be within the rules?"

The wind sweeping into the room molded her gown to her every curve and hollow. It took the folds of silk, the ends of her long hair, and sent them flying toward him. As they swept out to brush him with feather strokes, she stopped. Lifting a hand, she placed the tips of her fingers against his chest one by one. Slowly, carefully, she trailed them through the golden brown tangle of hair on his chest.

"Don't!" The word was harsh with command.

She ceased all movement. She had been sustained until this moment by bravado and desire and an odd sense of rightness. They were beginning to desert her.

She drew back her hand and clasped her arms around her upper body, holding tight. In tones freighted with need and despair, she said, "I don't pity you; you do a good enough job of that yourself. But you might consider, before you sacrifice both of us, that other people have problems that require human contact as much as you reject it. And they, too, feel pain."

He listened, it seemed, to the truth that decorated her words. He said quietly, "The only thing I'm hurting is your pride. Pride mends."

She considered that, and also the faint shiver she saw in his arms, which were pressed behind him as if he would push the wall aside to give himself room for retreat. Her voice was tentative, but without the sound of defeat: "Tell me you don't want me, and I'll go."

"That would be an obvious lie."

It would indeed. The glimmering lightning confirmed the evidence of his arousal.

She said, "Why is it so complicated, then?"

"Oh, it isn't," he answered in challenge, "not if all you want is plain sex. I somehow thought you would expect moonlight and flowers. And promises for tomorrow."

"I had that," she said, her eyes wide in the dark. "It didn't last."

"Nor will this. And I will hurt you," he went on, the words fretted with desperation. "If not now, then in some moment when you most need kindness, when you are least ready."

Her voice aching, she whispered, "I only need tonight."

The wind blew around the house. The rain washed it. The lightning glimmered with the steady pulse of old, worn-out neon.

His answer, when it came, carried the biting edge of defeated anger. "So," he said, "do I."

He reached for her as if he meant to break every bone in her body, or make her regret her daring. She didn't flinch, still she could not prevent the shiver that ran over her as he closed his hands upon her. He swept her up in arms like the hard, enclosing branches of trees, and stepped with her toward the bed.

She expected to be flung onto the mattress. Instead he sank down upon it, holding her close as he settled with

her upon its yielding surface. His fingers, as he touched
her, drawing her close against his long body, were
careful not to bruise. His kiss, as his lips found hers, was
tender beneath its demanding force.

The ache of released tension and gladness crowded
into her throat. Cammie swallowed hard and placed her
hands on his shoulders, curling them around his neck.
Endlessly accepting, deliberately pliant, she moved
against him in accommodation.

It was her last conscious decision. His mouth on hers
destroyed thought, and the caresses of his hard hands
pushed aside the barriers of polite social usage between
them as he stripped away the silk that covered her. If they
had ever been strangers, they were no longer.

His warm breath grazing her nipple caused it to contract. He laved the sweet, crinkled nub with his tongue in
pensive pleasure, circling the dusky coral aureole and the
pale, soft-skinned mound that trembled with the beating
of her heart. Arriving at the peak once more, he took it
into his mouth with gentle suction, delicate abrasion.

Cammie smoothed her hands over his shoulders,
pressing the sensitive palms to the ridged muscles while
rich, triumphant pleasure rose inside her. With it was
mingled an immense, spreading lassitude. She wanted
this moment, this night of storm, never to end.

Alive, she could not remember ever being so alive.
With deep drawn breaths, she reveled in the burgeoning
responses of her body. She was aware with every mol-
ecule of her being of the man who held her, the formidable strength of his lithe form, the fresh, heated male
scent of him, the silken curl of his hair at the base of his
neck, the taut resilience of his skin.

He trailed a row of kisses, moist and heated, down the
valley between her breasts, to her navel, then lower. He
brushed the flat surface of her abdomen with his lips,
made wet arabesques with his tongue, then blew warm
air across the sensitive curls at the apex of her thighs.

The rapture of it spiraled through her, sending a shudder of intense longing deep into the lower part of her body.

It was a craving that he tended with refinements so consummate and drawn out that they bordered on torture. Inhaling her scent like the fragrance of an exotic flower, he delved into its heart, tasting her, laving the most sensitive and delicate portion with his tongue, drinking the nectar that she released for him.

The muscles of her abdomen convulsed, and a soft moan sounded in her throat. He paid no attention, but gathered her hips in his hands and lifted her closer.

The rain fell. They never noticed. With eager mouths and questing hands, searing want and fierce restraint, they sought each other on the mattress. In lightning's silver outlining, they handled the springing hardness and liquid softness of each other's bodies, learning texture and tone, the shaping of the bones underneath, the sites of utmost response.

They did not speak above a whisper. With concern and carefully gathered signals, they dredged their hearts for grace and the gifts of transient pleasure, and spread them before each other. And in the process they wove a fabric of desire, mutual and immutable, that had in its strength some emotion so much greater than mere lust that it might substitute, for this one night, for a minor form of love.

She brushed a hand along his side, caressing the faint ridges of one of several old scars. Moving her fingers farther down, to the line of his taut flank, she clenched them, letting him feel the light scrape of her nails. He shivered, a gasp catching in his throat. She kissed his shoulder and raked it gently with her teeth, then licked the tiny sting away, tasting the salted essence of him. He pressed into her with the long, hard fingers she had wondered about, had needed. With an incoherent murmur, she tensed against him, around him, undulating in the grip of fierce, annihilating wonder.

He needed no other sign. He placed his knee between

her smooth thighs, spreading them wide, fitting his hardness into her wet, tender depths.

Cammie shuddered with the intensity of the delight brought by that fevered joining. She wanted him deep, and with the need, opened herself completely to him in trembling demand. He met it, pressing slowly in and out, teasing, taking her higher and higher into rarefied heights of effort.

She surged to meet him, lifting, rocking. He increased his depth and speed. She took his thrusts, feeling herself softening with them like malleable clay, reforming, molding herself to a perfect receptacle for his tumultuous hunger. Their skins glowed with heat, grew slippery with moisture. In the black and silver world of the storm, they stared into each other's eyes with wild, near desperate yearning.

Surcease took them unaware, in sudden, blinding reward. With it, they soared: released, windblown, pulsing with the consummate splendor that is the beating heart of life. They clasped it to them and rode it to its inevitable end.

For long moments they lay stunned, with panting breaths and fused, trembling bodies. Finally Reid shifted his weight, easing from her. He drew her long hair from under his shoulder, brushing it away from her face. Drawing a silken strand down her back as if testing the length, he left his palm resting in the center of her back, where the strand ended.

Outside, the rain fell with a ceaseless drumming that echoed the throbbing of their hearts. The lightning was only a dim, distant flicker.

Reid spread his fingers, smoothing his palm in a slow circle. "I'm sorry," he said. "I didn't mean to rush you."

"Did you?" she said in husky doubt.

His low laugh feathered across her breast, making the nipple contract. "A little," he admitted. "It's been a long time for me."

"For me, too," she said. Shifting, she placed a forefinger on the flat coin of his pap and rubbed, watching the shadowy movement through eyes that were slumberous with remembered rapture. Her movement stilled. "At least, it's been more than a year since—but for the rest, the best, not ever."

He lifted his head. His voice taut, he said, "Never?"

She moved her head in minute but position negation. "Keith—"

"—was a selfish bastard," he finished for her. "And stupid."

"He thought he knew what he was doing, but he didn't. You did." She turned her flushed face into the curve of his neck, hiding it. This was one more secret that she had never breathed to anyone.

"Next time will be better," he said quietly.

"Will it?" she said in muffled incredulity.

"I think it's possible," he said, humor and wonder threading his tone. He cupped the gentle turn of her cheek in his long fingers and lifted her mouth to meet his. "Shall we see?"

Chapter Four

▦ ▦ ▦ *Reid woke within seconds of the time he* had set himself, two hours after he'd closed his eyes. The rain had stopped. All that was left of the storm was the uneven splatter of water dripping from the trees outside.

He lay still for long moments, consciously recognizing the coolness of the air after the rain, the feel of the smooth percale sheets under him, the softness of the mattress, the silken tickle of the swath of hair that strayed across his arm. Cammie lay against him, her hips nestled against his belly. God, but it felt right.

He was motionless, impressing the feel of the woman in his arms deliberately, indelibly, upon his memory while his mind wandered back through the night. The sweetness of her, the way she had responded to his slightest touch and least urging, the small sounds of pleasure and need she had made, all these things shifted in his mind like a dream of glory. There was nothing coy, nothing vulgar in the woman he held, only grace and caring and frank sensuality. He had been honored that she had come to him, and he knew it. That he had taken as much advantage of it as he was able in the space of time given to him was something he could not help.

He was sure that never, even when he was a wrinkled, wobbling husk of a man, would he forget how he'd felt when he knew he was the first to help her reach orgasm. It affected him so profoundly that he'd tried to give her double that pleasure for every time he took his own from her. And in doing it, had increased his own many times over.

The memory would warm him on cold nights for a long time. As it warmed him now. Incredibly.

Self-control was an absolute necessity, even if it was a bit late for it. He closed his eyes as he fought the stirring of his body. It took longer than it should have to conquer it.

Easing away from Cammie, he drew the sheet and blanket closer around her, then slid from the bed. He had left his clothes on a chair near the door. He picked them up on his way out.

Moments later, dressed except for the boots he carried, he descended the stairs in the dark and made his way along the hall. As he passed the sun room, he paused, then swung inside.

The portrait over the marble mantel had squares of light flung across it from the outside security light near the driveway on that side of the house. One square illuminated the painted eyes. He walked closer, tilting his head back to stare up at it.

The painting was life-size, showing Cammie seated in a chair of dark green brocade. Her dress was soft gray velvet with a wide lace collar that had been delicately reproduced in silvery, cobweb strokes. The painted hair was lustrous, cunningly back-lighted for a near halo effect. The face was beautifully captured; its oval shape; the determined chin and straight, aristocratic nose; the delicately molded mouth, with its confident smile. It was the eyes, however, that captured his attention. They were large, a delicate blending of green, blue, and brown with a gray outer ring; and they were secretive, mysterious.

It came to Reid as he stood looking up that there was in them the sensitive sadness of the conscious dreamer. They were the eyes of one who prefers the imaginary world she has built for herself, even knowing its falseness, to ugly reality.

It was a part of Cammie that she hid remarkably well. He might never have recognized it, he thought, if he had not seen it firsthand, as she tried to avoid accepting his help, as she talked about her marriage. Her most lethal verbal barbs were brought out to protect that inner self. She allowed no one to trespass.

He wanted entry there more than he wanted life itself. And was as unlikely to find it as he was certain of eventual death.

He wondered if Keith Hutton had ever penetrated his wife's defenses. Or if they had been erected, primarily, to keep him out.

It seemed, looking back, that they had always been in place. Teenage girls were notorious for tender hearts, but Cammie's had been more sensitive than most. She was the girl who could cry on demand, not as a simple parlor trick, but from the mental pain of living in a world where others were carelessly cruel. She was the girl who could be depended on to recognize poetic allusions, who walked around flowers in the grass instead of stepping on them, who always rescued lame ducks and rooted for the underdog.

She had changed very little from those days.

He had.

He didn't like the idea that he might qualify as either a lame duck or an underdog in her eyes. If he did, however, it made him even more dangerous to her. He would never become a part of her inner world, even if he could. He would tear it down from the inside; it could be no other way. That was how he had been trained: to destroy.

It was possible that he had already given her the greatest injury that could be inflicted. He had shown her, without intending it, even trying his best to avoid it, that the walls of her inner world could be breached. She had invited him in, it was true, but he could have, should have, refused. At least he had enough integrity left, and strength, to leave quietly, and to close the door behind him as he went.

Or maybe it was only self-preservation, after all; he couldn't stand it if he hurt Cammie. It would never be of his own will, but things had a way of happening, intended or not. He had learned that the hard way.

His wife had been a lot like Cammie, or so he had once thought: the same rich hair color, the same eyes, even if Joanna's had been more green than hazel. But what he had taken for sensitivity in the woman he married had turned out to be timidness. Her concern and loving attachment had only been used to make him feel guilty for not caring more, while her passion was counterfeit, a camouflage for desperate neediness.

Joanna, focused on her own feelings, her own limited vision of what marriage should be, had never even begun to understand him. She had been incapable of accepting what had really happened when he turned on her that morning in the bathroom. She wouldn't believe it was the result of simple animal reflexes, but insisted on taking it as a violent rejection. He could not love her, she said, could not really want to be married to her, if he could hurt her like that.

Maybe she had been right; he didn't know. If she'd been able to forgive him, he would have lived with her and tried his best to make some kind of life. It hadn't happened that way. And when she was gone, when the divorce was final and her belongings no longer cluttered his life, he had been embarrassed at the relief he felt. Joanna, it seemed, hadn't been the only one willing to accept any substitute for love and a normal life.

He wondered what Cammie would have done in Joanna's place. He wondered, but the last thing he wanted was to find out. The answer might be too dangerous, for both of them.

He couldn't stand the thought of anyone else coming close enough to be a threat, either. Even her husband, especially her husband.

What she needed was a guard. Someone outside who

could keep watch from a distance—a great distance—and make certain she wasn't hurt any more.

He had nothing better to do.

There was no sign of Keith Hutton outside the house. Reid wasn't surprised. Neither Cammie's husband nor his Land Rover had been in sight when he'd gone back out in the rain to get Cammie's wallet and the pistol.

He had not told her that, of course. He should have, certainly would have, if he had known it was going to matter. He had been certain that nothing could persuade him to act against his better judgment, but hadn't been prepared for a frontal assault.

He wasn't proud of his surrender, no matter the reasons for it. But neither did he feel regret.

Less than a half hour after he had reached the Fort, Reid was ghosting through the wet woods, covering the few miles that separated the old log house from the Greenley place. The woods dripped and the creeks and branches he crossed were high with runoff from the rain, but he made good time. He should. He knew every hill and gully, tall pine and fallen oak along the way, had since he was ten and first began to notice Camilla Greenley.

It had been a sappy thing to do, sneaking around the back way to lie hidden in the woods, watching her house and hoping for a glimpse of her. Nine long years he had kept vigil, nine years in which she never noticed he was alive.

Once, he had seen her at her bedroom window dressed in frilly shorty pajamas. He had lived on the memory for weeks. Hopeless. But even now, recalling it had the power to make him smile.

A lot could be overlooked in a boy with a crush on the prettiest girl in school. Judgment would not be that lenient toward a grown man. He would have to be careful.

He would be, not that he cared. The only person who

had any right to question his motives was Cammie, and she, of all people, would never know.

So involving were his thoughts that he came upon the house almost before he was aware of it. It was still and insubstantial in the gloom that was just turning from black to dark gray. He could see the glow of the security light on the other side of the house, but the windows were dark.

His gaze rested on the rectangles of black glass where the spare bedroom was located. He thought of Cammie lying where he had left her, in soft, warm nakedness, and the ache that he carried inside throbbed into insistent life. He suppressed it as he had earlier, turning it off as ruthlessly as he had turned off nearly every other soft emotion in the past twelve years and more.

How would she feel when she woke to find him gone? She might be angry, might feel betrayed. Or she could be relieved. It was entirely possible she could be glad. He wondered if he would ever know. It seemed suddenly intolerable that he might not.

There was a dark shape moving in the deeper black at the base of the house. Reid watched it with his senses tingling. There was nothing natural about the movement; it was no trick of the light, no tree shadow moving in the wind or shrub shaken by the flight of a bird.

The dark figure was a man. He was trying windows.

A soundless grunt vibrated in Reid's chest. His gut feeling had been right.

He eased from the tree line, ghosting in a wide, intercepting circle. As he moved in soundless pursuit, he felt a surge of rage that Keith would try to break into her house. What right had he to go near her?

The right of a husband, for a week or so more. That was an uncomfortable thought, uncomfortable and inescapable.

Frowning, Reid moved with dogged purpose. At the same time, he was puzzled. He had been so certain Keith had left early, just after the kiss on the porch; he could have sworn he'd heard the Land Rover as it revved away. One of the reasons he had left the house while Cammie slept was to be certain. Why, then, was Keith skulking like a burglar, trying to get at Cammie again? Was he that upset over Cammie taking up with another man?

There was something more going on here than the attention of a repentant husband. Reid meant to find out exactly what it was. To do that, he needed to catch Keith, not just scare him off.

The man disappeared around the corner of the house, heading toward the back door. Reid sprinted forward.

Inside the house there was a sweep of pale light, then darkness again. It appeared that Cammie had been roused by the fumbling sound of the attempted break-in, that she had found a flashlight. Reid braced himself for an outcry, even a scream.

The solid report of a magnum pistol ripped into the night. The sound crackled, traveling, echoing back from the woods.

The man let out a curse of surprise. It was followed by the thud of heavy footfalls.

Reid rounded the house. He came to a jarring halt as he saw Cammie on the back porch with a long housecoat of clinging white pulled around her. The shape of the magnum pistol was clear against the pale cloth.

Admiration and rage in equal parts rose up inside him. She had protected herself without his help, but to do it she had left the security of the house, exposing herself to danger. She'd chased off her prowler, but had also prevented him from catching the man.

He might, with an extra effort, still chase down whoever had been sneaking around the house. To do it, he would have to pass through the trees and shrubs directly in front of Cammie. It was a risk he couldn't afford.

A moment later the chance was gone. Somewhere down on the highway a car roared into life and squealed away.

The vehicle did not sound like a Land Rover. Reid stood with a scowl between his brows, wondering if he was losing his mind or if the early morning mist left by the rain had done strange things to sounds.

Cammie turned and went back into the house. The kitchen light came on. Reid circled until he could see through the kitchen window. She was moving between the cabinets and the sink; he could just see her head and the tops of her shoulders. Once, she stopped and put her hand to her temple, rubbing it before she pushed her fingers through her hair to comb it back away from her face.

Her face was pale and there were shadows under her eyes. Her lips were deep rose and a little swollen. She looked tousled and rumpled and heavy-lidded, as if she had had a hard night.

"Sorry," Reid whispered. And stood perfectly still while he quelled the aching need to break into the house, to take her in his arms and soothe her soreness. Or add to it.

She had never been more beautiful.

The smell of brewing coffee seeped out into the fresh, early morning air. There was the faintest sheen of dawn beyond the trees. In just a little while it would be light enough to see, and to be seen. Cammie would be all right, she had to be.

It was time he was going. Time and more.

Cammie was breathless and in no welcoming mood as she opened the back door. Persephone was out in the laundry, where it was impossible to hear a knock. Cammie had been packing for her trip to New Orleans, trying to get ready to leave in the next hour. She had been forced to run downstairs as the quick rapping sounded for the third time.

The young woman who stood on the porch was tall and rangy, with a rather plain face that might have been improved considerably if she'd bothered with makeup. Her blond hair was fine and straight, and worn with a center part in a look popular during the seventies. Her jeans were faded almost to white and ragged at the cuffs, and with them she wore a man's chambray work shirt with the tail hanging out. She was noticeably pregnant.

Cammie had seen the girl before only from a distance, but still recognized Keith's girlfriend without difficulty. Her voice rising in surprise, she said, "Yes?"

The girl's pale lips stretched in a nervous smile. "You're Cammie—Mrs. Hutton, aren't you? Keith always said you were gorgeous. I'm Evie Prentice."

The compliment and the smile were disarming, and perhaps meant to be. "I know who you are."

"I don't mean to make trouble," the girl went on quickly. "It's just that—well, there are things going on I don't understand, and I thought from the way Keith talks about you that you wouldn't mind if I asked a question or two."

"I'm surprised he mentioned me."

Evie Prentice shrugged. "Well, there's just so much time you can spend making out, isn't there? And I'm good at listening. I think maybe that's what men like about me."

Cammie thought they might also go for her utter simplicity and her long-legged figure, which in better times must bear a strong resemblance to Wonder Woman. She refrained from saying so, however. Being unkind to this girl would be like running over a deer in foal on the highway. She stepped back. "I expect you had better come inside."

Cammie led the way into the kitchen, indicating a chair at the worktable. She offered coffee, but Evie declined it, asking for water instead. Cammie set it in front of her and took the chair opposite. The girl picked up the glass and sat it in her hands. When she looked up at last, her pale blue eyes held a look near desperation.

"You don't want Keith, do you?" she said, her voice tight. "I mean, you're not trying to get him back?"

Cammie was not sure what she had expected, but it wasn't this head-on approach. She said, "Not so you'd notice."

"I knew it, I knew he was telling a story." The girl let her breath out in a rush. "I told him you wouldn't do that because you've got too much pride."

"I would hope so," Cammie answered quietly, tilting her head to one side.

"But I had to find out, don't you see? I had to be sure so I could figure out what he's up to with his talk about getting married and all one day, then claiming the next that he's got to go back to you. I lit into him about that, and finally he said it was because he felt sorry for you. You missed him so much, he claimed, you were about to die. I didn't believe him because I heard him talking to you on the phone, and it sounded like he was the one begging you to be his wife again. I told him that, and he cussed at me."

"He tends to get a bit touchy when you catch him in things," Cammie said dryly.

A troubled smile came and went across Evie's face. "I still don't understand what got into him, though. I mean, I want him to be happy, and if he was tired of me, I think I could take it, but that's not it. Still, here he is, aggravating you at all hours. It makes no sense."

"I have to agree with you there."

"I tried to tell him all he was doing was making things worse. He said I didn't know what I was talking about, but that's not so. There was a man I got mixed up with a while back, a fine, upstanding pillar of the community type. When I broke it off, he near drove me crazy trying to make me come back to him. The more he pestered me, the madder I got, till finally I threatened to call his wife."

"And that stopped him?" Cammie said curiously.

"It sure slowed him down."

It was odd to sit there discussing the situation with this girl, and also to have such a sense of kinship with her. With a wry grimace Cammie said, "Too bad that won't work for me."

"Yeah," Evie agreed. "I don't suppose you could come right out and tell Keith to quit acting the fool?"

"I've tried that."

"Figures. What is it with him? You think maybe he's being plain contrary because you didn't fall apart when he left? Some men really can't stand it when they see you can get along without them."

"Could be," Cammie said doubtfully, "though I would hate to think he would go to so much trouble for such a pitiful reason."

"Right," Evie said with a sigh. "So would I."

Any answer Cammie might have made was lost as a strident clanging jarred through the house. The sound was the antique twist-type door bell at the front door.

"You got company," Evie said, her eyes wide as she pushed back her chair and got awkwardly to her feet. "I'd better be going."

"There's no need, really." Cammie rose but remained where she was, since she saw Persephone pass in the hall on her way to get the door.

"It might be Keith, and I'd rather he didn't find out I've been talking to you."

"I suspect it's just my uncle; he's the only person I know who comes to the front," Cammie said, then went on at Evie's look of inquiry. "The Reverend Jack Taggart. It doesn't suit his dignity as a man of the cloth to use the back door like everybody else."

Evie edged toward the hall. "Then I'll only be in the way. I'll slip out the back—"

It was too late. A ponderous tread sounded, then the large form of Cammie's uncle filled the kitchen doorway. His smile was unctuous and his greeting for Cammie familiar and hearty before he looked toward the other young woman.

"Evie," Cammie began automatically, "this is—"

"No need for that," the reverend said, moving forward with his hand outstretched. "I thought that was your car I saw in the drive out there, Evie. We've been missing you in church, especially in the choir."

"Yes, well, I've been a little busy," the young woman said, an acutely uncomfortable expression on her face.

"That's no excuse, you know." The reverend's gaze slid over Evie's figure, pausing on her waistline before he released her and stepped back. "We'd like to see you again."

"Sometime, maybe," the other girl said. "Now I've got to run." Swinging so quickly that her pale hair swirled around her, she headed for the door. The reverend was forced to step aside to prevent a collision.

Cammie slipped past her uncle, following Evie as far as the back porch. "I wish I could have been more helpful," she said quietly.

"Never mind," the other girl replied in compressed tones. "I shouldn't have come. I knew it was a mistake, but I thought—well, anyway, I'm sorry I bothered you."

"Don't worry about it, please." Cammie paused, went on. "I hope things work out for you."

"I appreciate that. Really."

The other girl held her gaze an instant, then turned and walked quickly down the steps. Cammie watched her until she reached the beat-up Honda on the drive. There was a frown between Cammie's brows when she turned back inside the house.

Her uncle stood waiting for her in the kitchen with his hands on his hips. His voice was heavy with censure as he said, "What in the name of Heaven was that girl doing here?"

Cammie felt the familiar rise of irritation. His interference in her life since the death of her parents, well-meaning as it might be, was becoming increasingly hard to take. Walking past him to the coffeepot left on the warmer, she poured a cup and pushed it toward him along with the cream and sugar. She said over her shoulder, "Evie wanted to talk about Keith, that's all."

"Why? To find out his favorite recipes or how he likes his shirts ironed?" Her uncle took his coffee to the kitchen table, then remained standing, pointedly, until she pushed away from the cabinet and seated herself.

Watching him settle into his chair, Cammie knew it was unlikely that he would budge from it until he had the full story. She told it as simply as possible.

Her uncle pursed his full lips. "That's all very well, but I don't think you should encourage this girl to hang around you. It doesn't look right."

His attitude was typical; he was a self-righteous man. Straying sheep returning to the fold of the Church were one thing, but in the home they were something else again. "I doubt Evie wants to be my bosom buddy," she said, then added before he could say anything to irritate her further, "Anyway, tell me what brings a preacher out so early?"

Her uncle's fleshy face tightened. "Really, Camilla, you know I prefer the title of Reverend."

"Sorry," she said, but she wasn't. The slip had been accidental, but she thought he might be a better man if his self-importance were punctured a little more often.

"Actually," he said with deliberation, "your aunt sent me. She was concerned over some tale she got at the grocery store."

"Was she? Why didn't Aunt Sara come herself?"

"You know how teary she gets when she's upset. Besides, she claims it isn't our place to stick our noses into your business. I told her that was nonsense, that we are your closest kin. Who better to look after you now that Keith is—that is, now that you're alone."

Cammie felt her temper rise another notch as she began to see what was on her uncle's mind. With an effort, she kept her voice even as she said, "Aunt Sara was right. There's no need for you to bother with my problems."

"Not bother? It's nothing less than our duty to check on you, especially when there were shots fired from this house at three o'clock in the morning."

"That was because of this little problem with Keith I

was telling you about. He can't seem to get it into his head that this isn't his home anymore."

"So you shot at him?" The disapproval was plain in his voice.

"It seemed the thing to do at the time."

"You could have talked to him, tried to work things out." Her uncle's rooster comb of white hair above his domed forehead shone silver in the morning light as he dipped his head to drink the lukewarm brew in his cup.

"I don't want to work things out," she said in grim tones.

"Marriage, you know, Camilla, is a sacred institution sanctioned by God, not just a contract to be broken. You should search your heart and seek the forgiveness that will let you return to your rightful place as a wife."

"Thank you for your concern," she said, "but I don't need forgiveness. And I've discovered that I prefer being single to having a husband who doesn't know the meaning of the word faithful, much less 'sacred.' "

He was not immune to sarcasm. There was a flush on his face and his prominent gray eyes flashed as he said, "You dare mock me, after running around all over town half dressed? After spending the night with Reid Sayers?"

"I don't think—" she began.

The Reverend Taggart overrode her defense with the booming voice he usually reserved for sermons. "No, apparently you don't think! The man's vehicle was sitting in your driveway until all hours, Camilla, for all to see. You had better take care, or you'll find yourself in deep trouble. Sayers is not to be trusted. You wouldn't believe the things that have been going around about him."

"I'm sure you would, and you're going to tell me all about them."

"Given your lack of sense, not to mention repentance, I feel it's my duty. Sayers is dangerous, a psychotic personality. He was trained to kill in the Special Forces; I was in the service myself, so I know what that's like. He's taken the lives of any number of men and half killed a woman out West somewhere. He's been over there in the Middle East, up to his neck in that mess with the Israelis and who knows what else. Now he's holed up out in the game reserve in that old house with no friends, no visitors."

She gave him a scathing glance. "I'd think you would want to see someone help him, then. What happened to Christian kindness?"

Alarming color rose into the older man's fleshy face. "Don't try to tell me my job, Camilla. Sayers is past earthly help. They say he has electronic equipment, guns of all kinds, hand grenades, a regular arsenal. There's no telling when he may decide to use it."

"That's ridiculous," Cammie snapped. Even as she spoke, she remembered her own impression of Reid as a man who could be dangerous. At the moment she was too angry with her uncle to care.

"You'll think different about it when he turns on you one day. You may remember then that I tried to warn you." He drank the rest of his coffee in a single swallow and set the cup down with a bang.

"I doubt it will be necessary," she said. "Now, I have to finish packing, if you don't mind. Tell Aunt Sara not to worry, I'll be fine."

Cammie surged to her feet, forcing him, with his punctilious manners, to stand also. Swinging from the kitchen, she turned toward the back door at the end of the hall.

He stepped past her where she held the door open, pushing the screen door wide. Pausing, he turned back with a heavy frown. "I realize that you aren't a young girl anymore, Camilla. But I also know you've had a nice, simple life up to now. You're too trusting, you don't know a thing about men like Sayers. I just want you to be careful."

She frowned as she realized it was possible that at least a part of his concern was real. It was also possible he couldn't help his habit of sermonizing, any more than he could control his self-important attitude. He and her aunt had no children, which was, Cammie had often thought, a pity. If they had managed to have a half dozen or so, her uncle might have had less time for her.

"Yes, well," she said, "I'll try to keep it in mind."

"Do that. And I wish you would give Keith a chance. He's made mistakes, but most of us have." Seeing the stiffness returning to her face, he hurried on. "I would be happy if you would let me guide you in this trying time, if you would come and worship with me."

Cammie smiled without answering, other than to repeat her message to her aunt. It was a source of embarrassment to her uncle, she knew, that she and her parents had never attended his church. The Greenley family had been active for generations in the small church just down the road on what had once been Greenley land. She saw no reason to change now.

She watched her uncle's portly figure as he took himself away down the steps, walking quickly to his car. It was only after he had driven off that she looked toward the garage.

Her Cadillac sat inside. On it were four perfect tires with thick new treads and pure white sidewalls.

Reid. How had he managed to get it done? It was just now time for the service department of the local tire store to open. He was an amazing man. In a lot of ways.

I only need tonight.

The echo in her mind made her wince in sudden mental pain.

He had taken her at her word, and why shouldn't he? She had meant it at the time. Or so she thought.

It had been, after all, a dumb thing to say.

Heat climbed into her face as she thought of other things she had said to him in the night, other things she had done with him.

What had gotten into her? What must he think of her?

He had been so very different from Keith. It wasn't

just the hard perfection of his body, or even his experienced skill, though these things had been a part of it. Rather, it was the concentration he brought to what he was doing. It was as if nothing existed except the two of them and the moment. Nothing mattered other than the pleasure he took from her body, and that he gave in return. She had felt so many things, wondrous, unimagined things, but most of all she had felt . . . cherished.

She needed more of that. Like some dangerous drug, she could easily become addicted to his touch, his presence beside her in the dark.

Persephone appeared from the direction of the laundry with a stack of freshly folded dishcloths in her hand. Her eyes shrewd in her brown face, she said, "You didn't offer the preacher any of my peach cobbler?"

"I didn't think about it," Cammie said.

"Right," came the dry answer. It was quickly followed by another probe. "He sure was in a hurry."

Cammie smiled with a weary shake of her head. "He has a lot of other people's business to mind."

"Don't you know it," Persephone said with a chuckle. Her dark eyes were bright as she went on, "Mr. Reid, he sure was up late last night."

Cammie looked at her housekeeper with resignation. "How do you know?"

"Lizbeth, who does for him, she's a cousin of mine."

"I never knew that." It seemed a failing, somehow, that she had not. The two women, now that she thought of it, shared the same bright-colored skin, the same long hair. Persephone was more slightly built, however, with a wiry strength in her short frame. Her hair was streaked with gray and tightly drawn back in a knot on top of her head.

The housekeeper lifted a shoulder as she replied, "I've got near as many cousins as you, maybe more. Anyway, Lizbeth said he was out till all hours, then after he come in, he went right back in the woods again. He had more clothes wrinkled up and wet than she had seen him use up since he was a boy. He's mostly as neat a man as a body ever come across."

Reid had few secrets from Lizbeth, that much was clear. Cammie thought in resignation that she probably had no more from Persephone. She was reluctant to end the conversation, anyway. It gave her an odd pleasure to hear some of the intimate details of Reid's life.

She said, "But he made it home without any problem?"

"Oh, yes indeed. He was looking kind of low, though. And Lizbeth said he started making phone calls as soon as it got daylight. Seems like he may be going on a trip."

"Oh?"

There was a shadow of sympathy in Persephone's dark eyes. "He didn't say where he was heading, but he was hell-bent on making sure he got there."

For the first hour of the five-hour drive to New Orleans, Cammie worried the information she had discovered about Reid like a cat with a toy mouse. He had said nothing to her about going out of town. There had not been a lot of opportunity, of course, but it seemed he might have mentioned it in passing when he heard she was going to be gone for the weekend.

Was there some reason he hadn't told her? Was he seeing another woman? Did he have business with some group of right-wing crazies who wanted to take over the country using his arsenal? Had he been recalled by the CIA for some dangerous mission in Eastern Europe or China?

She was being as ridiculous as her uncle, the reverend, she told herself. Reid had a perfect right to go anywhere he wanted, stay as long as he pleased. She had no claim on his time, nor did she want any. He owed her nothing, especially not a detailed itinerary of his days. Or his nights.

She was going to the Crescent City, and she was going to have a good time. She was going to forget Keith and his unwanted attentions, forget Greenley, forget Reid and the gossips and everything else. She was going to eat good food, drink a little wine, maybe dance a little. Or a lot. She needed to get away, to try to relax. If she couldn't do it in the City that Care Forgot, it couldn't be done.

She felt better by the time she reached Alexandria and shot from narrow, two-laned 167 onto Interstate 49. She began to smile as she sailed over the great Mississippi River bridge at Baton Rouge and knew she was on the east bank. By the time she crossed the Bonne Carré spillway on Interstate 10 and looked out over the vast brown expanse of Lake Pontchartrain, she was exuberant.

New Orleans was, and always would be, special to her. The air was softer there, the rhythm slower, the music hotter, the atmosphere looser. The sweet olive bloomed sooner in New Orleans, perfuming the streets with its old-fashioned sweetness. The rich miasma of cooking seafood shook the taste buds and urged them to wake up. The wild cross-mix of colors and races, classes and types, was a constant and fascinating puzzle. The old buildings like Beauregard House and the Cabildo gave her a sense of wondrous permanence, as did the river that wound like a giant snake around the town. New Orleans was both a challenge and a rest cure. She was more herself, less a Greenley of Greenley there. She loved it.

The hotel where the CODOFIL conference was being held was that most French of New Orleans hotels, the Royal Orleans. Built on the site of the famous old St. Louis Hotel favored in pre–Civil War days by the aristocratic Creoles of the Vieux Carré, it was located in the heart of the French Quarter at Royal and St. Louis streets. Cammie would not be staying there herself, but would be within easy walking distance. She had been offered the use of an apartment owned by a family friend, an attorney from Baton Rouge who kept it as a pied-à-terre for business or pleasure trips to the city.

The caretakers for the apartment, an elderly man and

his wife, who had been with the attorney for years, let Cammie in. Pressing a drink into her hand, they sent her out to the courtyard to rest from her drive while they unpacked her bag.

The sun had set and evening shadows were beginning to gather between the ancient brick walls. Cammie sat sipping her chilled white wine and enjoying the soft, warm air and the stir of a gentle breeze from the river. The noise of the traffic in the streets beyond the thick walls was no more than a distant murmur. By slow degrees she felt some of her tension begin to slip away, banished by the drifting fragrance of Confederate jasmine from the vine that climbed one wall, by the soft clatter of banana leaves and the musical spatter of the corner fountain, which was surrounded by impatiens in shades of red and coral-pink.

If she closed her eyes, she could almost feel Reid beside her. If he were there, the two of them might sit in just this kind of restful silence. Or perhaps they would talk quietly of little things while the knowledge of the long night that lay ahead of them, a night of loving, flowed between them. He might take her hand and fit it to his until the spaces between every finger was filled with him. Perhaps he would raise it to his lips and press a kiss into the palm, flicking it with his tongue. . . .

Daydreams.

She thought she had outgrown them, that she was too old to need them. Apparently, she had been wrong. And what harm was there in them, so long as she knew where they ended and reality began?

It was a wrenching effort to drag herself from her chair and go inside. There was no help for it, however. She had to get ready for the cocktail party that was to open the conference.

Cammie's mother had been distantly related to the Barrows of southern Louisiana, who were in turn descended from the Barrows of Virginia. Her mother never made much of the connection, but she still had

inherited certain immovable ideas along with the blood-
lines. It had been a maxim with her that Old Money did
not follow fashion's trends. Quality, according to her
mother, was the only important criteria, whether it was in
cars, in furniture, in clothes, or in something so mundane
as garden clippers.

She did not believe in designer labels. For clothing,
there were a few classic styles, a few soft, natural fabrics
that were suitable for everything from evening wear to
raincoats. Anything else was trendy nonsense suitable
only for the new rich who felt it necessary to show off
their wealth, or else teenagers with a need to be different.

Cammie tended to follow her mother's reasoning
because it was simple and easy. Her dress for the cocktail
party was a classic black sheath in silk crepe that fastened on her left shoulder and had a flowing pleat down
the side.

Her jewelry had also come from her mother. It consisted of a gold-and-diamond pin in a fleur-de-lis design,
a pair of classic diamond earrings, and a set of combs set
with pave diamonds that she used to hold her hair in a
shining cascade down the back of her head. The long
pleat of her dress opened to several inches above the
knee for a provocative glimpse of slender leg as she
walked, but the look achieved was basically one of elegant simplicity.

She was just spraying the sides of her hair to hold the
escape of wisps to a minimum when the doorbell rang. It
startled her; there were one or two people from the conference who knew where she was staying, but she had
made no arrangements to meet with any of them before
the party. Rising from the dressing table and smoothing
her dress into place, she moved through the antique-
crowded bedroom into the living room.

The caretaker, standing erect and formal, had opened
the door to the new arrival. He bowed the gentleman into
the room, then made a discreet departure.

The man turned with casual ease toward where

Cammie stood. He brushed aside the black satin lapel of the jacket of his perfectly cut evening suit and pushed one hand into his pocket. The movement brought into prominence the soft white of his shirt front, with its gold studs, and the black cummerbund that wrapped his flat waist. There was appreciation in the dark blue of his eyes as they rested on her, and also the stillness of waiting.

All men looked good in evening dress; attractive men were often stunning in it. Few, however, wore it with real ease. This one did.

As he inclined his head in the briefest of greetings, the light of the chandelier overhead caught in his dark blond hair with the sheen of old gold. A slow smile curved his mouth as he saw the disbelief that rose in her face. "I came," he said quietly, "to see if you were in need of an escort. Only for tonight."

It was Reid.

Chapter Five

▦ ▦ ▦ *In keeping with the French theme of the* conference, arrangements had been made to hold the cocktail party at an old French Quarter mansion located just off Jackson Square. Decorations were primarily in French blue and included the tricolor of France paired with the Louisiana state flag, with its nesting pelican on a blue ground.

The French ambassador was there with his charming wife, both looking bored but consistently gracious. The governor moved here and there in quick succession, flashing his charismatic smile and spilling bon mots with a Cajun flavor around him like largesse. A number of senators and representatives where shaking hands and whispering in the corners. The Neville Brothers were circulating, enjoying themselves hugely. Harry Connick, Jr., was holding court near the windows and not far from the door, in case of the need for a quick getaway. The familiar faces of local television luminaries were scattered here and there. Ann Rice was rumored to be coming, and a somewhat inebriated society matron was taking bets on whether she would or would not be wearing black. The CODOFIL people, most of them state officials and schoolteachers, or else city people with ties to the old French emigrés, were conspicuous by their inconspicuousness.

Being New Orleans, the food was a major attraction. It consisted of the usual enormous and beautifully piled fruit trays, the silver dishes of crudités with accompanying dips, and the chefs in tall, fluted hats slicing bits of meat from huge haunches of roast beef and stuffing them into minute rolls. There were also boiled new potatoes cut in half and spread with sour cream dotted with caviar, oysters on the half shell, bacon-wrapped broiled oysters, spicy boiled shrimp, bite-size crab rolls, plus a dozen other such substantial delicacies.

Wine and spirits were dispensed with flare and dispatch by white-coated waiters. A jazz band played a combination of mellow and uptempo pieces outside in the courtyard, while inside a string quartet scraped out Verdi and Mozart.

There was little to distinguish it from a hundred other parties Cammie had attended in New Orleans. The most astonishing development was the way Reid adapted to the occasion. He moved about the room with her without self-consciousness or any apparent inclination toward fading against the nearest wall and holding it up, that habit of most southern men faced with an uncomfortable situation. Smiling and at ease with whatever person or group he happened to find himself with, he initiated conversations and expressed his views with assurance. The bits and pieces of French that were tossed around as an inevitable part of the evening were not only comprehensible to him, but on several occasions he was able to add to them.

The change was unsettling. Cammie kept turning to look at him again and again, comparing him in her mind to the man in the woods. She had been so certain he was a total red-neck, not precisely ignorant or socially inept, but certainly without the most remote interest in or acquaintance with the language of diplomacy.

Reid, catching her sidelong glance as they stood alone for a change near a set of French doors that were open to the night air, returned it with startled inquiry for a second. Then a slow grin curved his mouth.

"Embassy parties," he said with a shrug, as if reading

her mind was nothing at all. "I was in and out of Washington for several years. And a good friend of mine is a Frenchman from Tel Aviv, now in New York."

"You worked with him during the intifadah?" she said.

His grin faded. Stillness gathered in his face while his eyes took on the blue-gray sheen of polished steel. When he spoke, his voice rasped like a weapon being unsheathed.

"Where did you get that?"

"The rumor mill," she said at once. "Is it wrong?"

His gaze slid away from hers. "No," he answered after an instant, the words toneless. "No, it's just that I sometimes forget its accuracy."

There was something in his voice that stirred her curiosity. She tilted her head to one side as she said, "Were you in Israel long?"

"Long enough."

It was as if there were shields going up in his mind, clanging into place one after the other, closing off access. To probe further would be useless; he was going to tell her not one single thing more than he wanted her to know.

In some peculiar fashion, those internal barriers, that hard inner core where she was forbidden to enter, evoked respect. If she also felt the urge to test them, she at least still had the good manners to refrain.

Abandoning that touchy subject for another, she said, "Why did you come tonight? I mean really."

He looked at the glass of bourbon and soda in his hand as if he had just discovered it. "It seemed as good a way as any to spend a weekend."

"I still don't understand how you managed an invitation."

"Contacts."

That much seemed to be true. She had seen him nodding across the room to one of the female liaison officers from the French embassy, another acquaintance, no doubt, from his Washington days. And Senator Grafton from their district, an influential man on Capitol Hill, had waylaid Reid when he went to freshen their drinks, keeping him in close conversation for a good fifteen minutes.

The implication that he had shown up in New Orleans to be with her was flattering, of course. It also made her nervous. Did he expect to continue with the arrangement of the night before? Did she want it herself, after all?

"I don't think you said where you're staying." She hadn't thought to ask, either. She had been so astounded by the way he had turned up, and that he had known where to find her, that she'd gone with him to the party as docilely as a lamb to the slaughter.

"Windsor Court," he answered with quiet humor in his eyes. "I didn't, you see, take my welcome for granted."

Her smile in return was perfunctory. Sex without strings, without expectations, between two virtual strangers. That was what she had offered, and what he had accepted.

There was a deep-down eroticism in the idea, especially when the man was as attractive as Reid Sayers. She had never in her life been so aware of herself as a woman. The heat of his gaze, now and then, when he forgot to guard it, was like a caress. She had seen him inhale deeply as he stood near her, then smile as if he enjoyed the fragrance of her gardenia perfume, and her. She could feel her body tightening in places, softening in others under the silk of her dress when he brushed against her. It was, in its way, frightening. But exciting, also. And tempting.

Still, she was not sure a relationship would work beyond their one stupendous night. There were too many pitfalls, too many unknowns, too many differences between them. There were too many people involved, and not enough privacy.

She had no doubt whatever the news of the two of them spending the weekend in New Orleans was already circulating back in Greenley. She could just hear the telephones ringing, see the carts pushed close together at the grocery store. The rich imaginations of those who were dependent on prime-time television for excitement had few bounds. The gossips probably had them naked in bed in some hotel suite at that instant, sipping champagne and doing wicked and lascivious things with what was left in the bottle.

"What are you thinking about?" Reid asked, sounding intrigued as he surveyed her flushed face.

She turned a wide, considering gaze on him. Her voice husky, she said, "Human nature."

The evening advanced. Cammie's feet, in black silk shoes that matched her dress, began to protest against so much standing. Her smile felt strained. The female liaison officer, ultrachic in a YSL dress of yellow silk cut several inches above her shapely knees, had taken Reid away to introduce him to friends. The two of them had wound up in a corner talking and laughing in such quiet voices that Reid apparently had to bend his head within inches of the woman's lips to hear her.

The Frenchwoman wasn't the only female in the room who had noticed him. There was a pair of young schoolteachers who had paraded past him with over-bright smiles at least three times. A woman in red with a cloud of hair dyed an unlikely shade of midnight-black was eyeing him with hunger in her face. And a red-haired female in a dress covered with glittering aqua beads was sending him sultry signals over the shoulder of her balding husband.

It was funny, in its way. It might have been more entertaining to Cammie had she not been certain that Reid missed nothing of what was happening. It was possible that there was such a thing as being too alert.

It was time to go.

There were couples she had seen, most of them long married, who could communicate with a glance across a room, letting each other know infallibly when they had had enough. Such a convenient method was unlikely to suffice with her and Reid, but she was willing to give it a try. She turned her gaze in his direction.

Reid looked up, glancing toward her with a smile and

an almost imperceptible nod. She felt a small catch in her breathing.

At the moment, there was a light touch on her elbow. "Mrs. Hutton, I've been anxious to have a word with you all evening, but you've been surrounded every time I looked your way. Could I persuade you to give me a moment now?"

Cammie swung to see Senator Grafton beside her. Tall and a little stooped, he had the long face, the lank hair, and melancholy air shown in the later portraits of Jefferson Davis. He was, in fact, distantly related to the former Confederate president, a fact he downplayed with considerable skill, since he was a Democrat dependent on the black vote. She gave him her hand and a pleasant greeting, then stood waiting to discover what he wanted of her. It wasn't long in coming.

"As a prominent member of the younger set in Greeley, I'm well-aware of the influence you have there," the senator began with a somber smile. "I wanted to ask your support in pushing through this arrangement with the paper mill. The Swedish conglomerate is anxious to get into the American market, but they don't want a lot of trouble. I know the old guard in town is fairly nonprogressive and may move to try to prevent the sale, but I'm sure you'll agree that the prospect of two thousand new jobs outweighs tradition by a considerable margin."

Cammie stared at him. "You mean—are you saying there's a Swedish company negotiating to buy the mill?"

"You didn't know? I assumed, since you were with Sayers—" The senator hesitated, plainly uneasy with his mistake.

"No, I didn't," Cammie said candidly, "and I'm not sure I like the idea, not if there's going to be an expansion of any size."

"The benefits for the area will be enormous. I'm speaking of the financial aspect, of course."

Cammie's father had been a conservationist of sorts.

She was no stranger to discussion about industrial land use versus ecological needs. Her own affection for the woodlands around Evergreen had sharpened her interest in the problems. She tilted her head, her hazel eyes sober, as she said, "But the mill, running at its present capacity, maintains a good balance with the surrounding timberland and watershed. What will happen if the capacity is increased?"

Senator Grafton touched the knot of his tie, an expression of acute discomfort on his thin face. "I'm afraid that's not my department, but I feel sure every effort will be made to satisfy regulations."

"Regulations are fine, but they don't always control the quality of the water people drink and the air they breathe. Then there's the wildlife. Two thousand new jobs would, I think, mean almost double the present production. That will call for twice the number of trees being cut, twice the wildlife habitat being cleared. Have there been any plans drawn up to show the effects of that kind of harvesting?"

"I'm sure I couldn't say. My part, as you must know, is to persuade industry, foreign or domestic, to move into the state of Louisiana to increase revenues and improve the quality of life for people." The senator, catching sight of Reid moving to join them, saw his way out. In sonorous tones he finished, "People, that's my concern, first and always. For the rest of it, I suggest you talk to Sayers here. As the man who holds the major interest in the mill, he's the one who will have to make the final decision."

The senator divided a stiff nod between the two of them, then moved off toward an aide who waited for him. Reid watched him with a considering look in his eyes before he turned back to Cammie.

"I suppose you can guess what that was about," she said.

"I'm afraid so."

Her voice low, yet shaded with anger, she said, "Why didn't you tell me?"

It was a long moment before Reid answered. "I had other things on my mind. Besides, there isn't a lot to tell at this point. I'll be glad to go into it as much as you like, but not here. Maybe over dinner?"

A restaurant, she thought, would be neutral ground, and as such, much better than her borrowed apartment. To be alone with him did not seem like a good idea at the moment. She said simply, "Where?"

He pushed back his sleeve to glance at the flat gold watch on his wrist. "We have reservations at Louis Sixteen, just about now."

The Louis XVI, somber and elegant in red and gold, was one of the city's many bastions of French Continental cuisine. Their waiter belonged to that professional, definitely nonservile, tradition found in only two places on the North American continent, New York and New Orleans. Cammie appreciated the thought Reid had obviously given to the evening. She also enjoyed, in a distracted fashion, the various courses of the superb meal as it was put before them. Regardless, her greatest concern was the paper mill.

What Reid had said was apparently the simple truth: nothing had been finalized about the sale. Representatives from the Swedish conglomerate had toured the mill as observers and had driven through the countryside looking at the reserves of timber acreage that were owned outright by Sayers-Hutton Bag and Paper, plus the vastly greater holdings held on ninety-nine-year leases. They had made arrangements for an independent accounting firm to check the financial operation, and a date had been set for that in two weeks. However, no formal offer had been tendered and no firm commitment made by either side.

Cammie listened to Reid's version of the events, concentrating not just on what he said, but the sound of his voice as he spoke. When he was finished, she sat back in her chair. Quietly she said, "This is why you came home, isn't it? To sell the mill."

"I came home because my dad called and asked me to come, period. He had his massive heart attack the same night, and I have to wonder if worry about the sale didn't contribute to it. I won't say that the prospect isn't appealing, however, because it is. You must know that."

Yes, she knew. She also knew that he could have mentioned the possibility of the sale when they had spoken about his taking over active management of the mill. He hadn't. Why? Was it because he wanted to keep it quiet until the business was completed, so that there could be no opposition? Or was it only that he had considered the sale his private business?

To be perfectly fair, the whole thing was none of her concern. Other than the interest controlled by Keith and his brother Gordon, the mill belonged to Reid. He could dispose of it as he saw fit. He had no real obligation to discuss it with her even as much as he had this evening. Regardless, there were larger issues at stake, other lives and livelihoods involved.

Placing her fingers on her wineglass, twisting it and watching the candle on their table make golden gleams in its depths, she said, "Have you thought at all about how this will effect Greenley and the rest of the parish?"

"I've thought of little else," he answered at once. "Greenley is a dying town—or haven't you noticed? Half the shops along main street have closed. Two out of three of the local car dealerships had folded. There used to be three movie houses, seven or eight cafés, three or four barbershops. Now there are none. Where have they all gone?"

Cammie made a small shrugging movement of her shoulders. "A lot of places closed after Wal-Mart opened—the five-and-dime, the dollar store, some of the department stores—but Wal-Mart hires twice as many people as the combined payrolls of the stores that went out of business. The cafés closed when the fast food places came in, the barbershops turned into hairdressers catering to both sexes. Other than that, the problem seems to be that people are more mobile these days, they go out of town to the bigger cities where there's more choice to buy cars and clothes and to eat out. It isn't just a case of people leaving."

"But they are going," Reid insisted. "With the best will in the world to save jobs, the mill has had to automate to stay competitive in the paper business. That means fewer jobs than there were ten years ago."

"There are also fewer children being born," Cammie pointed out.

"True, but it isn't a factor, except that there's more money to go around, more to spend on college. Kids graduate with degrees, and they see there's nothing for them in Greenley. They go to New Orleans and Baton Rouge, to Atlanta and L.A. It doesn't have to be that way."

"Maybe. What we need is different industry, not more of the same kind. Greenley has been a one-horse town, a paper mill town, for too long."

"I agree," Reid said seriously, "but it isn't going to happen until we have better access to national markets, which means a four-lane highway down the center of North Louisiana. That won't come about until there's more money in the state treasury. The treasury can't be helped a lot until the economy turns around and there's more money coming in. We're talking years. The Swedish takeover is now."

Cammie's lips tightened as she leaned toward him. "They'll take out too much timber, even if they don't clear-cut it, which they easily could. Without the tree roots to hold the soil, the runoff from the rains will fill the creeks and branches, the bayous and rivers and lakes with silt. A lot of these waterways are just now recovering from the pollution of the forties and fifties; they won't be able to take on a new threat. The parish will lose as much from recreational spending as it will gain from expanded jobs."

"The forestry service monitors the waterways," Reid

said with a trace of impatience. "Conditions would never be allowed to deteriorate that far."

"Possibly not, but they never seem to mind losing a little stream or two here and there. It adds up."

"In the meantime, two thousand jobs will be created. That's two thousand families that will stay put or move in, several thousand people with a better standard of living."

"There's another thing," Cammie persisted. "The only place this expansion can take place is behind the present mill. That land is virgin timber, some of the last tracts left in the state. There's never been development or improvement back in there, nothing cut except to open it for hiking trails and a few picnic and camping areas."

Reid's mouth thinned. "I'm well aware of that, since my dad, and his granddad before him, went to great lengths to save it as a wilderness park."

"Are you also aware it's one of the most important nesting areas for the red-cockaded woodpecker in the northern part of the state? Did you know that the red-cockaded woodpecker is an endangered species?"

"It isn't the only site."

Cammie heard the defensiveness in his tone. Her voice was firm as she said, "No, but it's the best one. All woodpeckers need old timber that's allowed to decay naturally, but especially the big red-cockades. They can't make the size nests they need in young, strong-growing trees like those in the stands planted by the forestry service, nor can they find high-density insect populations there. They also require hardwood trees, not the endless forests of pulpwood pine that we have now—certainly not the expanded pine-tree farms that will spring up if old forests are cut and the land put to timber use."

"Since when," he said irritably, "did you get to be an expert on woodpecker habitat?"

"I've watched them all my life. My dad was an amateur bird watcher. He used to call the big red-cockades Indian head woodpeckers."

"So did mine," he said. "And I have every sympathy for the woodpeckers, and every intention of protecting them where it's possible. But I have to tell you that people are more important to me than birds."

"You're quoting the senator," she said in exasperated disparagement. "You might at least be original."

He gave her a level look. "You might consider whether the senator could have been quoting me."

She stared at him for a long, considering moment. Her hands were shaking with her anger and distress, and she clasped them beneath the edge of the table. "It doesn't matter who said it first," she said on an uneven breath. "It's still an excuse to do what's best for you—and let what's right go hang."

"Right in this case, it seems to me," Reid said evenly, "is a matter of opinion."

"Oh, very good. That should make it easy to satisfy your conscience while you take the money and run."

Anger leaped like blue fire in his eyes. "There's nothing easy about it!"

"No, there certainly isn't going to be," she said bitterly, "because I'm going to see to it. I'll form committees, organize petitions, call on the press. I'll create so much noise and opposition that you'll have to listen. You just may wish you had never heard of Sweden, much less a Swedish buy-out of your mill."

He pushed his plate out of the way, sitting forward in his chair. He reached out as if to touch her, then drew back as she flinched from him. "Listen to me, Cammie," he said earnestly, "if you're doing this because of what happened between us last night—"

"It has nothing to do with that!"

"Doesn't it?" he shot back at her. "I think you're scared. I think you've decided you want me out of your life, and this is as good an excuse as any."

She sat with her back straight and her nails digging into her clasped hands. Her voice tight, she said, "If I wanted to be rid of you, I wouldn't need an excuse!"

"You might find it harder than you imagine. But there's no problem; I'm gone."

"I told you—"

"So you did," he interrupted. "I just don't happen to believe that anybody likes woodpeckers that much!"

The waiter, approaching from behind Reid, was unfortunate enough to choose that moment to ask if he could bring them anything else.

"Yes, the check," Reid said, the words so deadly quiet and his eyes so opaque that they could only be shields for impulses too violent for civilized company.

His face whiter than the napkin draped over his arm, the waiter skimmed away to do what he could to speed them out of the restaurant.

Reid took Cammie back to the apartment, but he did not come in. He was not invited, though Cammie wasn't sure a gilt, deckle-edged invitation would have tempted him. She was glad, she told herself with fierce emphasis. She was not the kind of woman who was sexually aroused by anger. On top of that, she had no use for a man who cared more for money than for the natural beauty around him. She had been married to one of those.

As her anger seeped away, however, it was replaced by depression. She had thought, for a few short hours, that Reid was different. It hurt to be wrong.

The remainder of the CODOFIL conference passed in a blur. She attended meetings and served on committees, but she hardly knew what was discussed or decided. She met people and had drinks with friends, and could not recall afterward what she had said to whom.

She walked in the French Quarter, admiring the art work displayed by the itinerant artists around Jackson Square, stopping for café au lait and beignets at the Café du Monde, and buying a garnet bracelet at a store selling antique jewelry on Royal Street. She introduced a friend who had never seen them to the old houses of the Garden District, and shopped for a summer suit at Canal Place. She spent an evening at Pat O'Brien's doing her best to find the bottom of the enormous glass holding a drink known as a hurricane. All of it was pleasant; none of it absorbed more than the surface of her thoughts.

Her free time was spent scribbling notes about the things she would do when she got home, giving form and structure to her threat to Reid. Her's would be an opposition campaign like nothing he had ever seen. She might not change his mind, but when it was over, he would understand that he'd been in a fight.

It was a relief when the conference came finally to its end and she could begin the long drive home.

The last thing she wanted, when she pulled into the driveway at Evergreen late on Sunday afternoon, was to see Keith's Land Rover parked there. Annoyance mixed with trepidation washed over her. His vehicle was blocking her way to the garage. He had apparently let himself into the house.

He was in the kitchen. He was standing with the refrigerator door open, eating peach cobbler out of the pan with a serving spoon and drinking milk straight from the carton.

"Hey, I got hungry waiting for you," he said, flashing his little boy grin as he saw the look of distaste on her face. "Besides, nobody makes peach cobbler like Persephone."

Cammie set her overnight bag down against the wall. She tugged the strap of her shoulder bag of soft black leather from her shoulder and placed it on the nearest countertop. Her voice carefully controlled, she said, "How did you get in?"

He set the cobbler pan back on the refrigerator shelf, took a long swallow of milk before he answered. "I happened to see Persephone's husband turning in here, bringing your supper. I told him I'd put it in the house."

He meant that he had cajoled and intimidated Persephone's husband, a veteran twice his age with an artificial leg, into giving up the housekeeper's key. She wondered how long he had been waiting and watching before Persephone's husband had come along.

She said, "The locks on the doors of this house are well over a hundred years old or I would change them. Since I'd rather not do that, I want Persephone's key back."

He reached into his pocket, then hesitated, his eyes on her face. Jangling the big metal key on its ring, he said, "I'll trade you."

"What do you mean?"

Removing his hand from his pocket, he took a last swallow of milk, then closed the refrigerator door and tossed the spoon he had been using onto the countertop. Taking a yellow paper from his pocket, he sent it skidding across the counter toward her. "I brought the estimate for the damage to the Rover."

Cammie made a mental note to throw out the rest of the cobbler and buy a new carton of milk. Without touching the piece of paper, she said shortly, "Why is it I have the honor of seeing it?"

"Now, don't be like that, baby. You know you cost me a pair of headlamp assemblies, not to mention a new hood."

She was not in the mood for this. She said distinctly, "I'm not your baby, I was never your baby, and, as you know perfectly well, I despise men who call women childish names. If you have problems with your Rover, it has nothing to do with me. I'm not responsible in any way for your debts."

"But I don't have the money!" he protested, throwing his arms wide.

"And I do, is that it?"

"And besides that, you did it, you know you did."

"For good reason."

Crafty self-righteousness surfaced in his face. "Hey, I'm the one who should be mad here, the one who got shot at. And all I was doing was riding down the road."

"You were harassing me. You threatened me."

"You made me so mad that I may have gone a little overboard. Any man would. You'll have to overlook it."

She gave him a straight look. "I think, instead, that I'll go out to the pistol range and work on improving my aim."

"I'd be worried," he said with a lifted brow, "except I know you wouldn't hurt a flea, much less me."

Her voice carrying quiet warning, she said, "I wouldn't advise you to bet on it." And it was at least two seconds before she recognized where she had suddenly acquired that particular tone of voice. Reid. Reid's soft and devastatingly effective warnings.

Keith's eyes widened, then he reared his head back. "You must have had one hell of a weekend to put you in such a foul mood, honey. What happened? Didn't Sayers measure up?"

She had known Keith was a shallow, small-minded, egotistical man; she had just not realized quite how lacking he was until—until she had spent time with Reid Sayers. That bit of knowledge did nothing to soothe her temper.

Her voice soft with menace, she said, "Get out."

"Don't be that way, honey. I was thinking while I was waiting on you about your little episode with old Reid. I mean, I know you were just curious since you never had another man, nobody except me. I can understand, really I can."

"Is that the reason you went looking for something different? Curiosity?"

"Well, hell, a man needs variety. So maybe a woman does, too, I don't know."

"I suppose it makes no difference who gets hurt in the process, either? Such as people like Evie Prentice?"

A grim light came into his face. "We'll leave her out of it, if you don't mind."

"I don't mind at all. Go on back to her. It's where you belong."

"You don't mean that; it's just jealousy talking. You want us to get back together, I know you do. If you didn't, you'd have changed your will."

His-and-her wills, naming each other as beneficiaries, had seemed logical and practical in the early days of their marriage, a matter of estate planning along with the health and life insurance. She hadn't thought of them in ages. With a sardonic look in her eyes, she said, "That's really straining it, Keith. But thanks for the reminder, I'll see about it tomorrow."

"Come on, Cammie," he said with a scowl. "What do you want me to do? Get down on my knees and beg?"

"No, thanks, though it might be a nice change."

"I'm trying to be big enough to overlook your little fling with Sayers. Doesn't that prove how much I want you back?"

The soft laugh that shook her surprised even her with its cynical edge. "Maybe. But it also shows that you still don't have the faintest idea how I feel. I want you out of this house. Now. Or I call the sheriff."

"You wouldn't." As she swung from him and toward the wall phone, he said hastily, "All right, all right. Wait a minute." He stood chewing his lips while her hand hovered over the receiver. Finally, he shrugged. "All right. Give me the money for the bill and you get the key. We'll call it even."

It might just possibly be worth it, she thought. But she wasn't a big enough fool to turn the money over to him. He would be back in a week with the money gone and the bill still due.

"Give me the key and the estimate," she said, "and I'll take care of it."

"God," he said, "you used to be such a sweet, trusting little—"

"That was before I married you."

A sneer twisted his face. "I hear Sayers is a lady killer of a different kind. You had better watch your step around him."

She looked at him, suddenly reminded. Her movements slow, she took the key he held out and then reached to pick up the estimate. "Tell me, did you know that there was a company wanting to buy out the mill?"

A wary look stiffened his face. "How did you find out?"

"Never mind. You knew, yet you never said a word to anybody—if you had, it would have been all over town. I wonder why you kept so quiet."

"It was mill business. Besides, nothing was settled; it was just a preliminary offer. I'd have looked a fool if I had talked it up, then it turned out to be nothing."

That had just enough of a self-serving ring to be true, though she still thought there was something he wasn't telling her. "I suppose," she said dryly, "that you think it's a good idea."

"Why not? Gordon and I wouldn't get as much from it as Sayers, but it would still be a nice piece of change."

A thought struck her. "But if there's a reconciliation between us, if we're living together at the time of the sale, I would be entitled to half of what you get. I would have thought you would hate that."

He took a hasty step toward her, stopping only as she retreated. Holding out his hand, he said, "I wouldn't mind, honest to God. It would maybe make things better between us, since you wouldn't be the one with the most money anymore."

"Yours would be gone in a year," she said with a shake of her head. "We'd be right back where we started."

"Oh, Cammie," he said, his voice low and his eyes wide, "would that be so bad a place to be?"

Chapter Six

▦ ▦ ▦ *The smell of the paper mill, that raunchy* odor like a combination of boiled cabbage and sewage gas, had been an embarrassment to Reid when he was growing up. He had felt personally responsible for it, since his family owned the mill. His dad, a practical man, had always said it smelled like money to him. That had certainly been true; most of the currency circulated in the town carried the stench.

Reid, standing in his father's office, exhaled with a soft snort. Everything in the room was marked by the familiar smell: the leather office chair, the papers in the file cabinets, the pictures on the walls of the mill buildings in their different stages over the years, even the drapes at the window where he stood. He still didn't like it, though he would get used to it again, he supposed, given time. The office also harbored a faint hint of tobacco from the cigarettes his father had smoked until five years ago, and the Cuban cigars that had been his grandfather's indulgence. That scent was a reminder; he could live with it with no problem.

Leaning against the window frame, looking out over the complex of buildings, he felt an undeniable stir in his chest. There were bigger paper mills in the South, but few more efficient. Sayers-Hutton Bag and Paper had its own steam-generated power plant, so it was not dependent on local utilities. The wood yard was a model operation, from the wide, well-guarded gates where the wood trucks lined up to discharge their heavy loads of logs and pulpwood lengths, to the great portable crane that fed the wood into the de-barking and chipping machines. The digesters, where potent chemical mixtures were added to the shredded chips, belched their environmentally regulated but still noisome fumes into the atmosphere to a strict timetable. The great paper machines rumbled and roared at a steady pace, gulping the malleable and purified pulp that came out of the digesters and boilers, drying it and rolling it out in continuous sheets of brown Kraft paper. The bag division took some of the rolls and turned them into bags and sacks, but the vast majority of them were shipped out in the truck-and-trailer rigs that waited in line like disjointed gray freight cars.

There had been a time when most of the paper had gone out on freight trains, when the mill had owned its own railhead and rolling stock. That had been in the early days; the paper mill and the railroad had put in their appearance at the same time, one dependent on the other. The old tracks still snaked through the mill yard as a reminder of another era.

The mill had grown, expanded, changed with the times. It still would, Reid knew, even if nothing came of the Swedish deal. Still, he looked on the possible change of ownership, the huge expansion, as another form of progress. The only difference was that he and the Huttons would no longer be directly concerned with it.

It would be a shame, he supposed, if the family mill tradition ended with him. His dad and his granddad, and old Justin Sayers before them, had been proud of what they had accomplished, and of their contributions to the industrial growth of the South and the increase in the standard of living of the people of Greenley. So was he, in his own way. He just wasn't sure he wanted to live his life for brown paper.

Before the paper mill was put in operation, the area around Greenley, like so much of northern Louisiana, had been farming country. Settled in the late 1840s, there had been a few big places like Evergreen, but most had been subsistence farms. Life on them had been close to the earth, fair during the good years, when the rains fell right and disease and insects were kept at bay, but hard during the bad ones.

Cattle and hogs had ranged free in the woods, people had raised milk cows and chickens, fruits and vegetables; had ground their own cornmeal, boiled their own cane syrup, carded cotton and wool, spun it, wove it, and made their own clothes. Cotton was the cash crop, but the only thing it stretched far enough to buy was flour by the barrel, leather shoes, rifles, knives, patent medicines, and an occasional length of fancy piece goods for a Sunday dress.

Few of the area farmers had ever owned slaves. Those who did were seldom able to afford more than a couple of hands to help out in the field, with maybe a female to help the woman of the house with her endless chores of sewing and cooking and preserving food—and to watch after the babies that came every year or two as regular as clockwork.

The War Between the States, as it was known locally well into the 1950s, changed matters very little. Its main result was to take the promise out of the Promised Land for people who had still been first and second-generation immigrants from the slums and rocky farms of England and Ireland, Scotland and Wales. Afterward, farmers and former slaves alike had scrabbled for a living from soil that had never been very rich to begin with, sinking deeper and deeper every year into a spiritual and economic depression that never really lifted. And still hadn't, not entirely.

The paper mill had made things easier. Farmers had quit the land for the steady wages that would buy store-bought clothes, automobiles, washing machines, Christmas toys. People had moved to town, to be closer to the job. And all the acreage that had once been rolling farmland had been taken back by the woods so completely that it was difficult for even the old-timers to point out where the big old places had been.

The land that had always needed special pampering to make a good cotton crop grew trees without effort. The long growing season, with active growth nine months of the year and root growth the other three, produced more board feet of timber per acre in less time than nearly any other place in the world. In the last twenty years, timber had become Louisiana's main natural resource, providing sixty-one percent of its agricultural income. The state actually produced seventeen percent more wood than was harvested every year. It was no wonder the Swedes wanted to locate there.

Behind Reid the office door swung open. Gordon Hutton, a hefty man with heavy jowls and thin, brownish-gray hair in retreat from a narrow forehead, stepped into the room. With the briefcase in his hand, his three-piece suit, and his air of bland pomposity, it appeared he might have been born in a boardroom.

He came forward, hand outstretched, as Reid turned. His voice jocular and a bit bland, he said, "My secretary told me you showed up this morning. I've been expecting you every day for the past month. I'll have them move my things out of here right away."

Reid's first impulse was to tell the man not to bother. That wouldn't do. He needed to take hold and settle in sometime, and it might as well be now. Besides, it had given him a jolt to see somebody else's belongings on his dad's desk, to realize that somebody else, somebody heavy, had been sitting in his chair. Curious. He had never been the possessive kind, but he was beginning to show the signs. It had been coming on since he got home, he thought. Maybe since he tackled Cammie in the game reserve.

"I'd appreciate that," he said. He smiled, and kept on smiling as he braced himself against the other man's attempt at a bone-crushing handshake.

"I have a number of problems that need to be cleared

up first thing this morning," Gordon Hutton said. "As soon as I'm free, I'll take you on a tour of the place, show you what we've been doing while you've been gone."

There was condescension behind the other man's affability. It scraped across Reid's nerves. He said in dry tones, "Don't rush, I expect I can find my own way. I was practically raised here, you know."

Gordon Hutton's smiled faded. "So you were. My old man never let me or Keith near the place until we were in college, didn't want us underfoot while he was working. Shortsighted of him, I always thought."

"But here you are, enjoying the job, and here I am, dreading it."

Gordon Hutton pushed out his lips in a judicious pucker. "Since you mention it, I have to say I never thought I'd see you back here. Everybody expected good old Greenley would be too small to hold you after all your globe-trotting."

Reid looked at the other man, his gaze steady. "Funny how things work out."

"It is indeed," Gordon said without expression. "Well. I'll leave you to get on with your homecoming." He heaved himself around and walked from the room, snapping the door shut behind him.

Cammie had been right, Gordon Hutton did resent his return. Staring after the man, Reid wondered if he would have noticed if she hadn't alerted him. Probably not.

Gordon had never been a particularly likable person. Big even as a boy, he had used his weight to push the smaller kids around, and his position as one of the boss's sons to intimidate most of the rest. It had been his cross to bear that Reid, though younger by several years, could not be daunted by either tactic. That hadn't kept Gordon from trying. It seemed he was still at it.

Reid waited a few minutes to see if anyone was going to appear to clear the office. When no one did, he raked the papers on the desk together, bundled them up with everything else he didn't need, and dropped the lot on the floor. Digging a pen and a legal pad out of a drawer, he laid those ready, then walked to the corner, where a huge, black steel safe, a relic from the twenties, sat. He knelt on the floor in front of it, putting out his hand to touch the ornate red and gold lettering around the door.

The safe had been the most fascinating thing about the mill to him when he was a kid. He had been no more than four when his grandfather had let him open it for the first time. There had been a box of caramel all-day suckers inside. Big surprise, or so his grandfather pretended. They had smelled like cigar smoke and the mill, but tasted fine. After that, it had been Reid's special privilege when he was around to take the business records from the safe in the morning, then put them back in the afternoon.

A smile curved Reid's mouth as the combination sprang into his mind the minute he touched the dial. Feeling the same heavy spin, hearing the tumblers kicking over, it seemed for the first time that he just might belong after all.

The financial and operating statements were there, just where he expected them to be, where the Sayers men had always kept their accounts. The only difference was that they were now computer printout sheets in plastic binders instead of leather account books. Removing the statements with dates going back six months, Reid closed the safe, then sat down and spread the printouts across the desk.

Two hours later he was still leafing back and forth, frowning, taking notes, and running his fingers through his hair. He had known the operation had grown in the last decade and a half, but had not known the extent of it. He was amazed.

The only way to make sense of the figures was by comparing percentages and ratios. Still, he was a little puzzled by some of what he found.

He dug deeper, checking back and forth. He was beginning to think he might one day get a handle on the operation when he heard the quick tread of footsteps coming toward the office. The door swung open with such force it banged against the wall.

Reid was on his feet in less than half a second. Ready. Poised with his back to the nearest wall and the closest weapon to hand, a letter opener, in his clenched fist.

Keith Hutton strode into the room. He grabbed the door panel and slammed it shut again. His voice rough, edged with a sneer, he said, "I've been wanting to talk to you for three days, Sayers! It's about time you showed up."

Reid eased his stance, rolling his shoulders to remove some of the tension. Tossing the letter opener on the desk top, he moved around the desk to rest one hip on a corner. Bracing his hand on his thigh, he said, "If you'd really wanted to see me, I think you could have found me."

"You'd have liked that, wouldn't you," Keith scoffed. "Well, I'm not fool enough to run you down at the Fort. Too many men have accidents out in the game reserve to suit me."

He was talking about fall hunting accidents and other assorted homicides that showed up in the vast stretch of deserted woods from time to time. The idea didn't warrant comment. Reid said evenly, "I have nothing against you."

"Well, I've got plenty against you. I know you've been sleeping with my old lady. Hell, everybody in town knows it. But I want it stopped, here and now. You got that?"

For a brief instant Reid wanted nothing so much as to push the other man's teeth down his throat for the tone of voice he used toward Cammie. It would not be hard. Keith Hutton's once handsome face and athletic body were both going soft. His eyes were bloodshot, and his hand, propped on his hip, waggled back and forth as if he couldn't hold it steady. The smell of liquor was strong around him.

He wasn't worth the effort it would take to flatten him,

Reid thought. In contempt laced with pity, he said, "I think Cammie is capable of making her own arrangements. And choosing her own friends."

"Some friend. You got no business being anywhere around her," Keith stabbed a finger at Reid. "She's still my wife until the divorce is final."

"The way I heard it, you left her."

"Anybody can make a mistake." Keith's eyes shifted.

"With a woman like Cammie, you don't always get a second chance." Reid's tone was bleak. He had his own regrets where she was concerned, some of them going back years, some as new as this past weekend. He should never have allowed her to make him lose his temper. He wouldn't have, of course, except that he was afraid she might be right about his motives and the mill. None of which mattered now.

Keith narrowed his eyes. "You telling me you're taking over?"

Reid rose slowly to his feet. "I'm telling you," he said, "that you were an idiot for letting her go. I'm also telling you, since you brought the subject up, that you should be the one leaving her alone. I don't care for men who hound women."

"I'd like to see you stop me," Keith said, thrusting his chin out like a teenager in a schoolground fistfight.

"Keep it up, and you will."

Something in Reid's voice, or perhaps it was something in his eyes, made the other man blink rapidly. He took a quick step backward. A scowl drew his brows together. "Cammie tell you to warn me off?"

Reid smiled with a faint twist to his mouth. "It was my own idea."

"Yeah, I thought so. I think you don't look too happy, either, like maybe you don't like this mess she's stirring up. Like maybe I don't have to worry too much, after all."

"Cammie may not like the idea of the mill being sold, but nothing she does can change the way I feel."

An odd expression crossed Keith's face. "You think not, huh? You think you'll sell and everything'll be fine. Just like that. Well, old pal, funny things happen."

Reid studied the man with every sense alert. "Is there a problem in the mill? Do you expect the workers or the unions to oppose the sale?"

"You're the boss now. You figure it out." Keith gave a sharp crack of laughter. Stumbling a little as he turned, he left the office.

Reid stood still for long moments. His thoughts moved in swift precision, though he didn't like the conclusions he reached. Smoothing a hand over his hair and clasping the back of his neck, he finally turned back to his desk. Picking up his pen again, he looked down at the computer printout. The neat tabulations ran together without making any sense.

The pen bent in his hand, creaking as his grasp tightened. Flinging it down, he strode from the office. Maybe being out in the mill yard would be better. It was unlikely to be worse.

At seven o'clock that night, Reid was standing under what had become his favorite pine behind Cammie's house, leaning against the trunk while he watched cars fill up the drive. She was having her organizational meeting for the group opposed to selling the mill. He knew some of the men and women arriving, but many he didn't. It made no difference, his information service was firmly in place. Persephone had given Lizbeth a fairly complete rundown on the guests.

The owner of the weekly newspaper, who acted as his own reporter, would be there, also the lady owner and manager of the radio station. Whatever their views on the subject, the meeting was news, besides which, they were friends of Cammie's. The speaker for the evening would be the lanky and bearded type who headed the low-key environmental group in the area. Also present would be Frederick Mawley. Mawley was the lawyer in town who specialized in nuisance suits, spite divorces, and bankruptcy cases. His practice was lucrative, though he was cordially despised by the business community.

Surprisingly enough, the sheriff was supposed to be on hand. Most elected officials would have run a mile before becoming embroiled in the controversy. Sheriff Bud Deerfield, however, was not only Cammie's cousin, but was apparently concerned about the increase in crime that might be caused by the influx of new people into the community with the expansion. More than that, he wasn't new to liberal causes. He was rabid about gun control as a means of crime prevention, an unpopular stance for a part of the country where most households had at least one gun and usually more. People overlooked it because they knew his youngest daughter had been killed while playing with a shotgun, and his wife had become an alcoholic because of the tragedy.

The rest of the guests were mainly society matrons, young and old, women who were active with the DAR, the garden club, and a half-dozen other organizations. They were the group who handled most of the charity work in the community, funding the "pink lady" volunteers at the hospital, keeping the parish museum in operation, collecting for the Heart Fund, the March of Dimes, and all the other good works. They might, if a person cared for such things, be called the blue blood of the community. Most didn't consider themselves in that light, and the few who did probably didn't qualify. The majority could be depended on to resist change on general principles, unless it happened to have a direct effect on the lives of their children or grandchildren.

The night was clear and damp, neither warm nor cool. Reid could smell the elusive fragrance of wild azaleas in the woods, and also of the pale orchid George Tabor azaleas just coming into bloom under the tall pines in the side garden. He thought he caught, too, a wafting of sweet olive from the tall shrub growing near the side door leading out of the house on the same side as the gazebo.

It occurred to him, after a time, that he could watch and be comfortable at the same time under the cover of the semi-enclosed gazebo. The wrought-iron table and chairs inside would suit him just fine.

From the octagonal structure with its railings shrouded with budding clematis vines, he could smell the coffee that would be served with the refreshments. The kitchen window was open to the night air, and also one or two of the living room windows.

He lounged at ease on a cool, white wrought-iron chair, wondering about what kind of pie or cake Persephone might have made and listening to the rise and fall of voices from inside. He felt left out. And he was bitterly envious of all those who were welcome, free to come and go at will, in Cammie's house.

He had also been envious of Keith Hutton earlier. Her husband.

The easy way Hutton had claimed her still set his teeth on edge. The idea that the man had once actually had the right to do it, yet had thrown it away, amazed him. If he had been in Keith's place, if he had ever been granted the privilege of seeing her as she bathed, holding her as she slept, burying himself in her softness whenever he chose, he thought he might kill to keep from losing it.

Reid scanned the windows of the house, and also the side door. He would check all points of entry when everyone had gone, when Cammie had turned out the lights. It was a fairly useless exercise; the old locks were no great barrier. It would take him all of fifteen seconds to get inside anytime and anyplace he chose. Still, it would make him feel better to know everything was as secure as possible.

He had considered waiting until Cammie was asleep, then taking up a post inside the house. She would never know he was there, he could see to that without any problem. From the standpoint of defense, the position would be much more effective.

Unless, of course, he might be considered one of the

dangers Cammie should be protected from. Then it became a chancy tactic.

He was used to those.

He should never have gone to New Orleans. He had faced that fact and accepted it in the last two days and nights. He himself had set the parameters for what had passed between them, and Cammie had accepted and used them. Afterward, he had tried to change the rules. It had been the wrong move.

Why had he done it?

Lust? Yes. God, yes.

The need to test the undeniable physical attraction between himself and a woman who understood the drill required in order to be safe with him? That, too.

But it was also something more. The answer he had found, after considerable soul-searching, was ego. He knew how she saw him—rough-cut, without finesse— and he'd wanted to show her a different man.

He had only demonstrated that he wasn't different at all.

And he'd discovered that she didn't trust him. No matter what kind of man he was.

There was absolutely no reason for him to be dumbfounded by it. Not when he didn't trust himself.

The meeting seemed to go on forever. Reid utilized the time by taking one or two of the five-minute naps that allowed him to keep going when he was spending most of his time on guard duty. He roused as the first guest to leave let the back screen door slam behind her. Soon a general exodus was under way and the driveway began to clear.

The last to go was Mawley, the lawyer. He stood at the door for what seemed like ages, spouting some guff that required him to reach out and touch Cammie's arm now and then. Reid, who had left the gazebo and circled around to the back side of the house, stood watching from the shadows of the garage. The man was tall, with silver-black hair and a thin aristocratic face. He wore black-rimmed glasses and the easy air of a man who lives well and thinks he deserves to live better.

He looked as if he should be called Frederick instead of Fred. Reid had never been introduced to him, but he disliked him on sight.

As the conversation on the porch continued, Reid wondered if Mawley was handling Cammie's divorce. That would account for part of the long-winded discussion. It didn't account for the way the other man leaned over her or the too familiar note in his voice.

Cammie, perhaps in an effort to move the lawyer along, walked ahead of Mawley from the porch and down the steps toward his car. The lawyer still had things to say, however, and he went on about them at great length.

Cammie's voice took on the dismissive note of someone trying to break away from a conversation without being actively rude. She said something about Mawley calling her when the new will was ready, then began to edge back toward the house. The lawyer reached to catch her arm, holding her in place.

Reid's patience snapped. He pushed away from where he leaned on the corner of the garage. Whistling a little under his breath, he strolled from the shadows and across the backyard, toward the drive.

Cammie saw him over the lawyer's shoulder. Her lips parted for an instant before they snapped shut. Her face took on an ominous stillness.

"Nice night," Reid said as he came within hearing distance.

The lawyer spun around. His expression, in the glow of the security light, was startled and none too pleased.

Cammie's voice sounded stiff as she spoke. "What are you doing here?"

"Walking," Reid said, keeping his voice nice and easy.

"You're trespassing."

He made no reply, but stopped at her side and stood looking expectantly at her guest.

Manners took precedence over annoyance, as he had suspected they would. She made the necessary introduction.

"Yes, of course," Mawley said, extending his hand. "I thought I should know you. It's a pleasure to finally meet."

Reid accepted the gesture, but concealed the sardonic humor that went with it. It would not be wise for a lawyer with ambition to be impolite to the owner of the largest industry in the parish.

The man turned back to Cammie. "I'll call you later in the week, shall I? And we can go into this further. In the meantime, do keep me posted on what you're doing."

She agreed with firmness and without so much as a glance in Reid's direction. The lawyer got into his gray Porsche and drove away.

"You were spying on my meeting," Cammie said, turning to him with her hands on her hips before Mawley was halfway down the drive.

Her abrupt movement and the faint night wind brought to Reid the scent of gardenias mingled with warm, clean female. The desire that welled up in him was like a blow to the solar plexus. His eyes watered with it, his every nerve and muscle clenched in spasms, and he felt the beat of his heart like a jackhammer against his ribs. He wondered, in consternation, if she could feel and smell the sudden animallike heat of him.

"Me?" he said as innocently and naturally as he could manage. "Why would I do that?"

"You're afraid I'll throw a monkey wrench into your precious machinery, and you would like to stop me."

He watched her for a long moment before he answered in quiet tones. "If I decide to sell the mill, Cammie, I will. What you're doing has no bearing on my decision. I don't bow to pressure."

"We'll see about that," she said, crossing her arms over her chest. "But you were still spying."

He allowed his gaze to rest on her face, then wander down to the smooth curves of her breasts pushed up by her crossed arms. The inclination to tell the truth and shame the devil uncoiled and stretched, flexing its muscles inside him. Distracted by the view, he could see no reason to refrain.

He spoke on a low laugh. "I'm only surprised you just now discovered it."

"You admit it!" She lowered her arms, her eyes widening to dark pools in the dim glow given off by the security light.

"I've spied on you for years," he said, his voice taking on a husky undertone. "I used to watch you for hours while you played in the woods back there, wading in the creek, picking violets and catching crawfish, or swinging on the same grapevines that I had cut and left dangling. Once I lay within six feet of you for a whole afternoon while you sat on a pallet reading your book. The only thing that separated us was a patch of pine saplings, sedge grass, and brier vines, but you never knew I was there."

The intrigued confusion and stain of color that flitted across her face did much to restore his equilibrium. The question stiff, almost reluctant, she said, "Why?"

He should have been ready for that. He wasn't. Nor, he thought, was she ready for the whole truth. He lifted a shoulder. "Why do boys that age do anything? To see if I could. To see if you would notice. You were invading my woods, my haunts; you had to be studied."

"Your woods?"

"I was there first. After a while, watching you got to be a hobby or a sport, like studying the habits of the squirrel or the deer you hunt."

"A sport," she repeated, her voice taut as an odd shiver ran over her skin at his choice of words. "You mean you watched me for the fun of it, because you got a kick out of it? That makes you no better than a voyeur!"

The anger that descended on him pushed icy splinters of pain into his brain, yet did nothing to cool the heated need of his body. He wanted to take her down on the grass, to make her retract the words that besmirched something that had never had the dirty, indecent cast she gave it. He wanted to force the words back down her throat with mouth and tongue, and wring an apology from her using every sexual wile and sensual trick he had ever learned. Fighting the urge with a force that brought perspiration to his forehead, he made no reply.

"Well, I hope you enjoyed it," she went on in scathing fury, "because now that I know, I'll call the police if I ever catch sight of you around here again."

She swung from him, leaving him standing there as she marched away back into her house. The door slammed behind her.

His voice soft, reflective, Reid said to himself, "Oh, I did. I enjoyed it a lot. And I enjoy it more now."

Chapter Seven

▩ ▩ ▩ *The media coverage given Cammie's cause* in the week following the meeting was, in her opinion, good on the whole. The local paper had taken a somewhat tongue-in-cheek attitude since the owner was a rampant right-wing conservative, but she had expected that. What was more important was that the dailies in the larger towns and cities surrounding them had picked up the story. People were always more impressed when a local happening made headlines outside the area.

There seemed to be a weather change in the state toward environmental issues. For decades such concerns had taken a backseat to progress and big business. In the past year or two, however, there had been growing attention paid to questions of water pollution, chemical dumping, and the loss of the wetlands that were the habitat for a large portion of the migratory birds of North America. Cammie thought her championing of the woodpeckers, and the reservations she had expressed about selective water and land use, had tapped into this trend.

Another indication that she was making a difference had been the telephone calls in the last few days. There had been a half-dozen from people applauding her willingness to take a stand, and four from people who wanted to get involved and help her make a difference. There had also been four from men and women anxious to let her know how shortsighted they felt she was being with her campaign, plus a couple of heavy breathers who sounded more angry than turned on.

Cammie wondered, as she left the house for a gathering of the Pine Tree Festival Committee downtown, if Reid had seen any of the papers or heard the comments on the news. She hoped he had, and that he choked on them. He would find out how serious she was about fighting him on this issue.

She still seethed at his nerve in showing up the night of her meeting. It was nearly as upsetting as his suggestion that she was using her opinions on trees and birds as a shield against him. Where did he get off, hinting that her convictions were a mere personal convenience? She had been concerned about the place where she lived long before she ran into him in the woods at night.

As for hiding behind the mill issue to avoid him, why should she? She had practically seduced him, hadn't she? There would have been no relationship, however impersonal, if not for her.

She wasn't afraid of him. If she had wanted to steer clear of him after their one-night stand, she could have done it without resorting to such an elaborate ploy.

And if he thought she was disappointed that their contact was entirely physical, that she objected to the limitations he had set, he was much mistaken. She didn't want anything more from him or any other man. There was no room in her life just now for emotional involvement.

She liked the idea of being free, of doing exactly what she wanted, when she wanted. She enjoyed being able to come and go without questions or snide comments. She was ecstatic that she didn't have to worry about someone else's mealtimes or clothing or ideas of what she should do with her evenings. She felt as if she was beginning to take control of her own life for the first time in years.

She didn't need a man. She certainly didn't need Reid Sayers.

Cammie frowned as she stared through the windshield of her Cadillac. An older man in a pickup lifted the fingers of his hand from the steering wheel in a wave as he passed. She flicked her own in automatic response, though a second later realized she had no idea who the man had been.

All right, she told herself with unflinching self-knowledge, she had missed Reid. She found herself thinking of him at odd moments, of things he had said, expressions that had passed across his face, the way light and laughter had caught in his eyes. There were times when she could almost feel the pressure of his mouth on hers or the touch of his hands. It was a wrenching effort not to think about the hours she had spent in his arms.

Another thing was the recognition that there was a sense of security missing from her days and nights. While he was with her, she had felt absolutely safe. With him in her bed, she'd slept better than she had in years, since she was a child.

It was strange. Evergreen was dear and familiar, and she had seldom been actively afraid, and yet somewhere inside she must have been constantly on guard. Even when Keith had been around, she'd been uneasy. Her husband had seldom thought to check the doors and windows to see if they were locked, and was such a sound sleeper that he never heard the strange noises that disturbed her. With Reid it had been different. She'd been able to let down her guard, knowing it was not necessary. It had felt good.

Missing a protector, however, was not the same thing as longing for a lover. Not the same thing at all.

Oh, she could admit that the heights and depths of physical satisfaction she had reached might have had something to do with the soundness of her sleep. Certainly Reid had been far more considerate in that area than Keith had ever thought of being.

There were a great many other things that Reid had been: strong, generous, caring, accomplished. There had been both gentle and rough magic in his arms.

The sudden deep, pulsating ache of longing caught her

by surprise. She pushed it aside with an effort. What point was there in giving it free rein, or in remembering?

It was better to concentrate on her anger. The very idea of spying on her meeting—as if she was one of his terrorists or some other subversive threat. Where did he think he was, back in Israel? He had no right to invade her privacy and that of her guests, nor to trespass on her property.

All the same, she could not deny that there had been a split second when she'd been relieved to see him.

Fred Mawley could be encroaching in his smooth, persistent way. It had been all she could do to get him out of the house after the others had left. He seemed to think he was the Good Lord's special gift to Greenley's divorcées, and that she should be delighted to take off his wrapping paper. Rumor said that he could always be persuaded to take a part of his fee out in trade if a female client was even semi-attractive. From the veiled hints he had let fall, she didn't think the rumors lied.

Conceit in a man was fast becoming a deadly sin to her. That was one thing she could not accuse Reid of. Not that she was interested in cataloging his good points. He had more than enough bad ones to keep her busy.

She could not get the thought of Reid watching her so long ago in the woods out of her mind. She'd been so sure she was alone back then, so certain that the silly games she had played, singing to herself, flitting here and there with a piece of bed sheet tied to her shoulders like a cloak, had been unobserved. To know that he had seen her took some of the innocence from it, and yes, much of the pleasure.

Like most only children, she had been imaginative. Possibly she had been lonely, though she was so used to it that it never occurred to her. She had made up playmates as she was growing up, sometimes using children from school, or else cousins she had seen at family get-togethers, sometimes creating wholly imaginary human and animal friends. The summer she was thirteen, she had pretended that there was a boy, tall, strong, blond. They had played chase, picked blackberries. She shared her lunch with him, and he lay with his head in her lap while she sat with her back to a pine tree. She had told him about her dreams and ambitions, and how much she loved the woods. He had listened and been endlessly understanding.

Was that the summer Reid had come so close while she read? Was it possible that she had sensed his presence? Or had she caught a glimpse of him somehow without recognizing it, and incorporated him into her make-believe world? Had he heard all those silly, stupid things she had said, the plans she'd made for the future?

It gave her cold chills just to think of it. Someplace in the back of her mind there was a slow, seeping dread that he might one day tell her he'd been there then, and overheard.

She'd stopped going into the woods in quite that same way when she was around fifteen. Her mother, always concerned about her explorations, had sat her down and talked to her about the danger for a young woman. After that, her time in the woods had been limited to an occasional walk.

It was probably a good thing, when all was said and done.

No, she didn't really believe that. Despite her outrage, she couldn't believe that Reid would have harmed her.

What would have happened if he had shown himself? Would she have accepted his company and been glad of it? Or would the old enmity between their families have made her too wary, so she took to her heels as she had at the lake? She honestly didn't know.

Voyeur.

The word she flung at him haunted her. She didn't actually think there was anything salacious about his watching. She had just been so disturbed to learn of it that she needed to strike back at him. That accusation had been the first weapon she could find.

It had been effective, she thought. She'd felt his anger flowing toward her, around her, like a hot wind. There had been an instant when the skin of her neck and arms had prickled with the brush of danger. She was certain he meant to lash out, but her own fury had been so great that she hadn't cared if he did. Almost, she had wished that he would.

And what had she done when he hadn't? She left him standing on the drive while she ran away from him again.

Maybe, just maybe, she was afraid of him after all. Or if not of him directly, of what he might do to her life if she allowed him into it.

She shook her head, trying to banish such thoughts. As she did, she realized she was sitting in front of the restaurant where her dinner meeting would be held. She'd been talking to herself and gripping the steering wheel as if it was a life preserver. A man and his wife had just given her a funny look, while an elderly black man had walked thirty feet out of his way to keep from passing too close to her car. With a wan smile and a sigh, she reached for her purse and climbed out of the car.

The food served at the dinner was no better and no worse than was to be expected, consisting of mystery meat, soggy vegetables to which sugar had been added to help the taste, and a cream custard for dessert that had the consistency of library paste. At least the tea was drinkable.

The business meeting afterward was short and effective. The chairwoman, Wen Marston, put forth several suggestions for the festival coming up in two months. Nobody objected, but nobody volunteered for the work, either. The chairwoman ran a gimlet eye over the gathering, choosing her victims. As soon as these had been strong-armed into agreeing to head the various job committees, the meeting was adjourned and the socializing began.

Cammie stood talking and laughing for several minutes with Angelica Emmons, the attractive black woman who was principal for the middle school, and who happened to be Persephone's daughter. When Angelica left to pick up her son, who was practicing with the school play, Cammie moved to the sideboard where the urns and pitchers holding the extra coffee and tea had been set up. Refilling her coffee cup, she was just taking a swallow when a rich contralto voice spoke behind her.

"What's this I hear about you developing a sudden love for peckers?"

Cammie choked and coughed, only just preventing herself from spraying coffee by clamping her hand over her mouth. She turned accusing and watery eyes on the woman who had spoken.

Wen Marston was Cammie's fourth or fifth cousin on her father's side. Her name was actually Gwendolyn, but she hated it with a passion and threatened bodily damage to anybody dumb enough to use it. Tall, rotund, and round-faced, she wore her hair twisted in a bun on top of her head. She was loud, pushy, and sometimes ribald, and she had a heart like warm butter. Wen knew everybody in town, in part because she was active in local affairs, but mainly because of an intense interest in people as subjects of conversation. She was Cammie's partner in the antique shop. She was also a superactive member for whatever group she happened to join, usually bulldozing her way into office. She ran the Pine Tree Festival Association with an iron hand.

Cammie, trying to make herself understood between coughing and the other woman's hearty wallops between her shoulder blades, said, "Woodpeckers, Wen, woodpeckers."

"Ah, rats. I guess I should have known it was nothing so exciting, not you, not in Greenley. Now in New Orleans—"

"Nothing happened in New Orleans," Cammie said in haste and with emphasis.

"Did I say it did? Lord, but you're touchy." Wen's voice dripped insinuation and she opened her eyes wide.

"I hear old Keith's fit to be tied about your little escapade Way Down Yonder in the Big Easy. That'll teach the son of a gun to go chasing after sweet young things—and getting caught."

"It's nothing to do with him," Cammie protested.

"No? Then I'm all confused. If you didn't go to New Orleans with Reid Sayers to get back at Keith, it must have been because you fancied the guy. And if that's so, why the devil are you taking the woodpeckers' side against him now?"

"I didn't—it isn't like that."

Wen rolled her eyes. "Right. Keep your secrets, then; see if I care."

"There's nothing personal between me and Reid," Cammie said firmly. "I'm simply opposing him about selling the mill."

"Come on, Cammie, don't give me that; this is old Wen you're talking to. You're gorgeous, and a free woman— well, almost—and he's an unattached male of better than average looks and prospects. It's a natural."

"A natural what?"

"Bedtime story. What do you think? And I wouldn't blame you one bit. I got myself a good look at him again at the meeting last night, first time since high school. He was quite a hunk back then, but honey, let me tell you—I have to say he's something else now. He can park his boots under my bed anytime."

For a single moment Cammie felt a jarring tremor of something remarkably like jealousy. Then it was wiped from her mind. "Meeting?" she demanded. "Did you say meeting?"

"You didn't know? Reid invited all the mill employees and their families to a big fish fry at the mill camp on the lake—my baby brother Stevie let me tag along; he works in the instrument department, you know? Well, Reid got up in front of everybody and really leveled with them, just like his old man used to do."

Cammie clenched her hands on her coffee cup. She

took a quick sip before she asked, "What did he have to say?"

"Just that he knew everybody had been hearing rumors and he wanted to set the record straight. He admitted that an offer had been made for the mill, but said a decision was still a long way off. He mentioned feasibility studies, comprehensive audits, and a lot of paperwork to be done before anything concrete happens. In the meantime, he promised that he's doing his best to keep everybody's best interests in mind, and that everybody's job will be safe, no matter what."

"That—That rat!" Cammie exclaimed.

Wen stared at her an instant. "All right, come on. Give. What did he do? I know he spent the night at your house, because Keith told Steve, and Steve never kept a secret in his life, not from his big sister. Did he run out on you?"

Cammie put a hand to her forehead, then pressed her eyes where a headache was beginning. "Is that what everybody thinks, that this is some sort of woman-scorned thing?"

"I never said that, honey," Wen objected, reaching out to touch Cammie's arm in reassurance. "For all I know, the man took advantage of you and you're too nice to get back at him any other way."

"Oh, God," Cammie moaned in wry distress for the community imagination. "That isn't the way it was, either. Why in the world can't people mind their own business!"

"So all right, I can take a hint," Wen said with a pretense of huffiness. "Changing the subject, I wanted a word with you about this business with the meetings and the press and all. I am hurt to the quick that you didn't wait till I got back to go with it."

Wen had been away for several days on one of her regular jaunts to antique jewelry shows, buying and selling in a segment of the antique business she used to cover her personal finances. Cammie searched the other woman's face, trying to decide if she was serious, or if she should wait for the joke. "I might have, if I had known you were really interested."

"I'm always interested, you know that. Nothing sends me up like making trouble. I hear you've got things stirred up pretty good."

"Have I?" The taste of the coffee was suddenly bitter. She looked around for a place to put her cup.

Wen took it from her and plopped it unceremoniously on the seat of the nearest chair. "You've got the town fathers wetting their pants, honey, afraid you're going to screw up the deal that will bring them in all the lovely moola—they can just see themselves collecting the check for all the extra taxes a bigger operation will have to pay. I heard one of them call you a crazy bitch yesterday. That means they're scared."

"Of me?"

"Why not? You've got it all together: money, connections, background, looks. Hell, you could run for mayor and probably get it."

"I don't want to run for mayor."

"I do, but no matter. Actually, I'm still of two minds about this mill deal. Sometimes, I think it would be a good thing if Greenley didn't get too big. In a case like that, some man's always gonna want to be the boss. If it stays piddling-size, the menfolks may decide it's not worth it, that I'd be a shoo-in for mayor."

"I'm not trying to keep Greenley small," Cammie said, a frown between her brows.

"Aren't you? Well, that's sure what's going to happen if you have your way."

"Besides," Cammie went on, "you don't have to wait until a man fails to run before you try for mayor. You've got my vote any day."

Wen's smile was dry. "Right, well, I'd rather have your support. Instead of seeing you waste it on this woodpecker thing."

"I see," Cammie said slowly, her gaze on the other

woman's face. "All this was a roundabout way of telling me I would be better off doing something else."

Wen sighed with a sound like a steam engine dying. "See, sweetie, the bigger the mill gets, the bigger the town gets. The bigger the town, the bigger the Pine Tree Festival. The bigger the festival, the bigger I get—well, I'm big enough already, but you know what I mean. I do, for sure, want to be mayor, but mayor of something, not mayor of nothing. Which is what Greenley's going to be if we don't watch out."

"And what if Greenley isn't a fit place to live anymore?" Cammie's voice was tight. She hated being manipulated, especially by someone she had expected would understand.

"It'll survive."

"Nothing's indestructible. Don't you read the papers? Haven't you seen the data on how much we need trees, on the effect of the destruction of the rain forests? The trees right here count just as much as those in South America. And so does the wildlife."

"I'm not denying that, but what we have here isn't a bunch of exotic trees and birds that will be lost to the world if we don't save them; it's just pine trees and peckers—I mean woodpeckers."

"You're hopeless," Cammie said.

"I'm a realist. What you are is a romantic. Only there's not much call for romantics in Greenley. There's something else people are hungry for, something they haven't seen enough of lately."

"And that is?"

"Money, honey."

"There are more important things." Cammie could not keep the defensive tone from her voice.

"Yeah, power for one. Which money can buy; let nobody kid you about that. You're standing in the way of both of those things for a lot of people, sweetie. Be real careful, or you just might get hurt when push comes to shove."

There was not much that could be said by way of an answer to that. They went on to talk of other things, an upcoming estate auction they needed to attend for the shop, also the family reunion that would be held that weekend. It was officially the Bates family gathering, a branch of her mother's side of the family, but half the people in Greenley would be there, since family connections were an endless interconnecting circle in the parish and surrounding area. As the meeting began to break up, Cammie and Wen talked their way out the door and into the parking lot.

The words of warning Wen had spoken lingered, however, as Cammie drove homeward. They sprang loud and clear in her mind when she found the raw egg splattered on her front door.

The smell of it struck her in the face as she opened the back door. Nauseating, it swept toward her in waves on the draft coming down the long, open hallway. It was all she could do not to gag as she moved with mechanical footsteps toward the front of the house. She turned on the porch light and swung the main entrance door open with gingerly care.

A dozen eggs at least must have been lobbed at the door, and another dozen at the ornate fanlight in the shape of a rising sun above it, and the glass panes on either side. Only the thickness of the old glass and the smallness of the panes had kept the fanlight and side lights intact. Still, the thick yellow ooze covered everything in a primitive glue. Drying fast, it clung in globules and slimy sheets to the deep grooving and moldings around the glass.

Standing there in the light of the electrified lantern that swung on a chain in the center of the front porch, Cammie felt the hair rise on the back of her neck. That someone could dislike her and what she was doing so much that they would cause this kind of nasty damage made her sick to her stomach. She felt, too, as if she was spotlighted for all to see in her distress, as if there might be someone out there in the darkness watching, laughing.

She lifted her chin. Let them laugh. She wouldn't be defeated by a little egg. No, and not by friendly advice or broad hints, or subtle threats. She had just begun to fight.

Greenley hadn't seen anything yet.

Nor had Reid Sayers.

Chapter Eight

▦ ▦ ▦ *Reid was at the Bates family reunion. So* was Keith.

Cammie, catching sight of the two men standing some distance apart as she climbed out of her car, almost got back in again and left the park. What kept her from it was pride; that, and the certain knowledge that half the people standing around were watching her from the corners of their eyes and waiting to see what she would do.

Neither man had any connection with the Bates family, as far as she knew. Keith had most likely come for the free food and because he knew it would irritate her. It was possible, of course, that Reid was there for the same reasons, but she doubted it. Someone had invited him, no doubt, but the question was, who? And why?

Reid stood under a spreading oak, leaning with his back against the trunk. A shaft of sunlight falling through the tree leaves struck dark gold gleams from his hair and made a brilliant blue dazzle of his eyes. His stance was easy and relaxed as he lounged with one hand in his pocket. He looked at home, blending effortlessly with the men around him in his tan dockers and a yellow shirt with the sleeves rolled to his elbows. As he met Cammie's gaze, she thought she saw a challenge in his face.

The family reunion, she saw with bleak appearance, was not going to be the pleasant gathering she had expected.

Keith gave her a cocky salute as he saw her. Leaving

the man he'd been talking to, he ambled toward her. As he came close enough to be heard, he said, "I always did like that dress on you."

She was wearing a dusty rose shirtwaist with a striped belt in rose, green, and aqua-blue, and paired with matching espadrilles. She had bought the whole ensemble only a month before. So far as she knew, Keith had never seen it. She turned from him to open the back door of her car, taking out the baked ham she'd brought. Over her shoulder she said baldly, "What are you doing here?"

His smiled faded. His lips tightened before he answered, "Protecting my interests."

"Meaning?"

"I saw Wen at the Dairy Queen. She said she invited Sayers. It seemed like a good idea for me to show up, too."

Cammie gave him a scathing look as she handed him the ham to hold. "You must be the last person to find out that Reid and I are on opposite sides of this mill business."

A short laugh left him. "I heard it, but thought I'd see for myself. What did he do wrong?"

"Not a thing."

"You don't say. You got something against Swedes, then?"

"It's the expansion that bothers me, not who owns the mill, though I'd prefer that the policies Reid's father operated under stay in force."

"Pollution controls? Emission tests? Sending out scouts to find out where the woodpeckers are nesting? Cordoning off whole sections of land until after nesting season?"

"He did all that?" She paused as she brought out the coconut cake she meant to add to the feast.

"Sure," Keith said with a shrug. "The mill workers and wood haulers thought he was crazy, but he was the boss."

"I didn't know." She looked to where Reid was

standing. He was watching her, though he glanced away, avoiding eye contact, as he saw her turn in his direction.

"There's a lot of things you don't know," Keith replied in bleak tones.

"I'm not sure I want to, either," she said sharply. Seeing Wen arriving in her GMC Suburban across the park, she gave her cousin a wave, but didn't go to meet her. Instead she retrieved her ham from Keith and left him standing as she turned away toward the food tables.

It was a beautiful day; the sun was shining, the breeze was warm, the grass was such a brilliant green it hurt the eyes to look at it. There were children playing on the swings, older women sitting under the pavilion in lawn chairs exchanging news and verbal genealogies, and older men standing in groups under the trees talking politics and sports. The food was laid out in the shade on long stretches of narrow wooden planking. The heaped platters and covered bowls and trays crowded every inch of surface, along with gallon jugs of tea and fruit punch and enough Styrofoam plates and cups to feed an army. The smells that rose from the tables wafted warm and luscious on the air.

Cammie found a place for her contributions to the bounty. Then, seeing her aunt Beck across the way, she moved in the direction of her favorite relative.

The elderly woman, pine-splinter sharp mentally at nearly a hundred, but about as substantial as a dandelion puffball, had come with her widowed daughter. The daughter had unloaded a huge pan of chicken and dressing and was carrying it to the tables. Aunt Beck was doing her best to lift a plastic dish of potato salad nearly as big as she was from the trunk of the car.

Cammie called a greeting as she approached, then folded her great-aunt in the quick, obligatory hug extended to family and close friends. She turned then and reached for the potato salad.

The covered plastic bowl was warm to the touch.

"Shouldn't this be on ice?" she said dubiously as she looked from it to the elderly woman.

Her great-aunt, black-eyed and with her short white hair brushed back in waves as fluffy and light as the feathers on angel's wings, turned on her. "Who do you think you're talking to, girl? I've been carrying potato salad to reunions for seventy years, and I've not poisoned anybody yet. I made this with new potatoes in their skins and good onions and pickles, but no eggs and no mayo. Yogurt, that's what's in it. Good for you. You taste it, see if it's not the best you ever ate."

"Yes, ma'am," Cammie said meekly, though with amusement rising in her eyes. Aunt Beck was and always had been able to take care of herself. She never forgot anything, and you couldn't put much over on her. Getting around wonderfully well, she raised orchids and bromeliads in her small home greenhouse in winter, and raked her yard, dug flower beds, and planted slips and seedlings every spring. She was confidently planning her hundredth birthday party, and there seemed no reason to suppose she wouldn't make it.

"What's this I hear about you and the Sayers boy?"

The dark old eyes were quick and bright. They made Cammie feel as if she were about seven again. "Nothing much," she said self-consciously.

"Humph. His grandfather was a fine man; Aaron, was his name. I walked out with him once or twice, before I settled to marry my Henry."

"Aunt Beck!" Cammie said, pretending shock.

The elderly woman tilted her head as she watched Cammie. "You thinking of that family nonsense? I never did put any stock in that. Besides, telling young people they can't look at each other is pure silly, like fencing off catnip from a kitten. On the other hand, Aaron's grandson is different, a throwback to old Justin Sayers. And they used to say Justin was as sweet a man as ever lived, until you crossed him. Then he was a plain devil."

"Was he now?" Cammie said in dry tones.

"What I'm saying is, you be careful." Aunt Beck gave a sharp nod.

"I don't think you have to worry."

"Humph," the elderly woman said, her dark gaze skeptical.

The morning advanced. More and more cars arrived, disgorging more laughing men and women, more yelling children, more food. A band consisting of two guitars, a keyboard, and a bass fiddle assembled itself on a makeshift bandstand and began to play country and western favorites. A volleyball net was set up and the teenage set began a game. A few charcoal grills were lighted, and barbecued chicken and ribs that had been cooked at home were laid out on them to reheat and improve their flavor. The savory smoke and fragrance drifted in a blue haze over the gathering.

Cammie wandered here and there, talking to first one person and then another, renewing acquaintances, exploring relationships. Someone had worked up a computerized family tree, and she looked at it, ordering her own copy like everyone else.

Reid, she noticed, had hardly moved out of his chosen place, a spot under a big oak, at the edge of the group of men and as far from the women as possible. Several of the matrons and most of the younger women cast glances in his direction, and it was easy to see he was the subject of quite a few conversations.

Keith mingled more; he had attended many such reunions in the past and was easy with the big group. Every time Cammie saw him coming toward her, however, she changed positions, either surrounding herself with kids or burrowing deep into the group of older women. The last proved most effective; few men wanted to risk being trapped among the conversations about hysterectomies and hot flashes, who was sleeping with whom, and who had been mentioned on the prayer list with terminal illness.

There was one person who had no qualms about

wading into the hen party. As a minister, he was used to
dealing with the clannish and autocratic females who ran
most churches, and most families.

"Well, Camilla," the Reverend Taggart said in a low,
confidential tone as he came up behind her, "I'm glad
you saw the wisdom of my advice."

"What advice—" Cammie began, then stopped as her
uncle nodded in Reid's direction. "Oh, I don't think it
was your advice so much as circumstances."

"Whatever it was," the minister said firmly, "I think
you'll find it's for the best. I can't say I approve entirely
of what you're doing about the mill now, but at least
you're on the right path in avoiding extramarital affairs.
Chastity is the right and proper course for a woman. Now
you must search your soul for guidance toward a reconciliation with Keith."

Cammie gave the heavy, silver-haired man a clear
look. "I told you I don't want a reconciliation. And I'm
not so sure about chastity."

The reverend's eyes popped open. "Camilla! Watch
what you're saying. I understand that you're joking, but
other people don't know you that well."

"Thank Heaven for small mercies."

"Don't blaspheme," he said severely. "I tell you again
that divorce is an abomination. Nothing can sunder what
He has joined."

Her uncle's censure gave Cammie an almost irresistible urge to go and flirt outrageously with Reid. It
didn't seem such a good idea, however, when she
glanced in Reid's direction. He was taking note of the
exchange, even as he gave most of his attention to the tall
and earnest man standing next to him.

"Fudge, Jack!" came a sharp voice from behind them.
Aunt Beck, seated upright in a webbed plastic and alu-
minum chair nearby, leaned as she spoke to poke the
minister in the back with a sharp and bony forefinger.
When he swung to face her, she went on. "You show me
where it says in the Bible that divorce is an abomination.

And while you're at it, tell me what business it is of yours what Cammie does or who she does it with."

The minister's face tightened so abruptly that his jowls quivered. "It's my duty as a man of God—" he began.

The old woman gave a derisive snort. "You just like to meddle, always have, since you were old enough to walk. Used to come to my house with your mama and daddy. If they didn't keep an eye on you, you'd be going through my dresser drawers and peeking under the bed and in the icebox. Meddlesome, that's what you were."

"I think," Reverend Taggart said with barely concealed annoyance, "that you have me confused with some other child."

"No, I don't. It was you." The sharp brown eyes inset in fine crepelike wrinkles crackled with enjoyment. "And when you weren't meddling, you were listening to things you shouldn't. Never did know why you decided to be a preacher, unless it was curiosity about other people's sins and carryings on."

Sara Lou Taggart, the Reverend Taggart's wife, moved with hesitant steps from where she had been quietly talking to a friend. Brushing at her silver-streaked brown hair with a quick, nervous gesture, she said, "Why, Aunt Beck, what a thing to say to Jack. He's just trying to guide Cammie in the way he thinks she should go."

"What does he know about Cammie and her doings?" The old lady's lips twisted. "Or guidance, either."

Color that might have been from anger or embarrassment rose in Jack Taggart's face. His wife threw him a quick, anxious glance. "He's a man of God. What else is he supposed to do?"

"Mind his own backyard and preach the gospel, that's what," Aunt Beck said positively. "And let other people be."

"Come along, Sara," the minister said. "You know there's no use arguing."

The censure in his voice suggested that his wife had started the imbroglio. It also implied that the elderly woman was too senile to be worth the time it took to argue with her.

"Turkey," Aunt Beck muttered, casting a narrow and resentful gaze after him.

Cammie, hiding a smile, wondered which of her great-great-grandchildren the elderly woman had picked up that phrase from. She touched her aunt's fragile, bony shoulder. "Thanks for sticking up for me."

"Ha," the silver-haired woman said. "I've no patience with fools, even well-meaning ones."

Cammie, uncertain just who the old lady considered foolish, and afraid she might learn, felt it was wisest to remain silent.

Just when everyone was beginning to think that starvation in the midst of plenty was at hand, the women still arranging bowls and platters of goodies glanced at each other, murmured among themselves about who else might be coming, then decided it was time to eat. Someone began to prepare plates for the younger children. Another woman lifted her voice, calling to the men to come and get it. Brother Taggart graciously accepted an invitation to give the invocation. Immediately thereafter, everyone fell upon the feast.

It might have appeared to an outsider that the men and children were all served first, while the women were forced to wait. Things were not quite as they appeared. The fact was that the women controlled the day, the gathering, and distribution of the food. They decided when everyone ate, and what, and no man dared touch food until given the signal.

The proceedings were also more orderly than they looked. A great many men had already had their plates heaped up by their wives. For them, it was a case of walking forward to get the food and drink, then wandering off to find a quiet place to eat it. Any man who had no woman to pile his plate with the best selections usually waited until the women had been served before he joined the line winding around the long tables. The well-brought-up southern male, chased out of his mother's kitchen from the time he was old enough to become demanding, learned early that if he wanted to eat, he had to wait until he was invited and take what he was given.

Reid hung back, turning his shoulder to lean against the oak tree. Several other unattached men nearby waited, too, while they finished a long and involved tale about bass fishing. Sheriff Bud Deerfield was among them, out of uniform but still carrying his handgun on his hip. Keith was also in the group.

Cammie, helping to dole out coleslaw and chicken and dumplings, watched Reid from the corner of her eye. Even after the other men began to ease in the direction of the good aromas, he still kept his place.

There was a small girl, perhaps five or six, moving slowly past him toward where her mother, big with pregnancy, sat. The child was carrying a laden plate with a fork balanced on top of it in one hand, and an over-full glass of punch in the other. As the little girl neared Reid she began to lose control of her load. Her plate tipped. She gave a despairing cry.

Reid moved swiftly. He caught the plate, then lifted the drink in a smooth movement just as it began to tip toward the front of the little girl's white pinafore. The smile the child gave him was beatific, the look in her eyes worshipful. She could not have been more impressed if he had been her own personal guardian angel.

Cammie was too far away to hear what the little girl said. But she saw Reid's face.

His eyes turned to liquid pools of pain. An instant later every expression, every nuance of emotion, vanished as if wiped away by a total exercise of will. Taking exquisite care not to touch the child, he transferred the plate and glass back to her as carefully as if they were living things. He recoiled from her then, backing away as swiftly as he had moved toward her in the beginning. Regaining his place under the tree, he pressed his back to the rough bark of the oak as though he meant to hold up the trunk by main strength.

There was a tightness in Cammie's throat, an aching constriction like the desperate need to cry, though she wasn't sure why. She swallowed hard against it. Reaching for a foam plate, she began to fill it. When it would hold no more, she poured sweetened tea over ice in a plastic glass, then picked up both plate and glass and turned toward where Reid stood.

Keith, moving with one or two other men to join the line in front of the tables, saw her coming in his general direction. He began to smile. As she came nearer, he put out his hands as if he thought the food she held was for him.

Cammie saw Keith and realized she should have given him a wider berth. It couldn't be helped. He had no right to expect her to feed him, no reason to think she might. With a lift of her chin, she sidestepped him, walking on to where Reid stood. She knew Keith jerked around with his hands on his hips, scowling at her back, but she didn't care.

"What's this?" Reid asked with a slight frown between his brows, though he automatically took the plate she thrust at him.

"It looked as if you were going to wait until everything was gone before making a move."

"But you haven't eaten." He attempted to press the plate and cup back into her hands.

"I will, in a minute."

His gaze lost a little of its bleakness. His expression turned considering. "I'll wait for you."

She hesitated. "All right, but only because I have something to prove."

Surprise and doubt flickered in his eyes. He opened his mouth to question her, but she moved away before he could speak.

He was sipping his tea and surveying her return with fixed concentration as she joined him once more. He had somehow commandeered a pair of lawn chairs in her absence. As he steadied the back, she dropped down into one of them. He took the other. They set their tea on the ground beside their chairs as they settled their plates on their laps.

"Well?" he said.

She had had time to think of what she meant to say. She answered with composure. "I wanted to demonstrate that our disagreement isn't personal."

"I see," he said. He paused. "Isn't it?"

"Not as far as I'm concerned," she answered, sending him a quick glance from under her lashes.

"That's nice to know."

There was an undercurrent of irony that made her uncomfortable. She eyed him uncertainly. "You don't mind, do you?"

"Being used to squash nasty rumors, especially about being tried and found . . . lacking? Feel free anytime. Or use me any way, for that matter."

"I think," she said with a haze of color riding her cheekbones, "that the talk ran more along the lines of a woman found lacking."

It was an instant before he spoke. "And that bothered you?"

She picked up a piece of fried chicken, looked at it, then put it down again. "Let's just say that I prefer to keep people guessing."

"That's easy," he returned. "We could always disagree in public and have a private affair."

Her lips compressed before she forced them to relax. Her voice not quite even, she said, "Or vice versa."

"A private disagreement and a public affair? I'm amazed, but not unwilling. Would you like to start right here with a passionate kiss, or shall we just wander off down by the lake and grope each other in plain view?"

She met his gaze for long seconds, and was not sure whether what she saw there was mockery or audacity, or a combination of both.

"Neither," she said on a sharp breath.

"No? Too bad."

"Will you please be serious?"

"Oh," he said dryly, "but I am."

She closed her eyes, then opened them again. Her voice tight, she said, "All right, I can see you aren't going to listen until you have your pound of flesh. I'm sorry I called you a voyeur. Does that make you happy?"

"No," he said, the word vibrant with annoyance.

The man was totally unreasonable. And ungrateful, since he hadn't tasted his food. Cammie gathered her feet under her, getting ready to rise.

Reid shot out his hand to hold her in her seat. "It doesn't make me happy," he said, "because I've decided after careful consideration that you may be right."

It was the last thing she had expected. She stared at him, snared by the rich blue color of his eyes and the candor of his gaze. His fingers pressing warm and firm into her skin were such a vital reminder of things she had tried to forget that she felt disoriented, not quite certain what to say next. It was a relief when he spoke into the silence.

"I hadn't thought of how it might seem to you, my— call it spying, for lack of a better word. I shouldn't have sneaked around like that. Or else I should have kept my mouth shut about it."

She laughed, she couldn't help it, as she heard the wry note in his voice, saw the downward tug of his mouth. He was so obviously without regret for his activities. "And you wish you had not let me know."

"You might say that," he agreed.

His gaze as it rested on her face was intent. His hold on her arm had loosened. It was a moment before Cammie realized that his thumb stroked her wrist, feathering back and forth over her pulse, noting its swift beat.

How easy it would be, she thought, to slip into an affair, private or not, with Reid Sayers. She would never have believed it. How had it come to this so quickly?

How had it happened that she could be so easily moved by this man out of all others.

It wouldn't do. He had told her flat out that he had nothing to offer her. She believed him. Sex without strings was fine for one night, but she was going to need more than that one day, someday when she was finally free.

It was a shame.

She removed her arm from his grasp with firmness, but without haste. He didn't try to hold her, and she appreciated that. Summoning composure and what she hoped was a look of polite interest for the sake of their audience, she embarked on the kind of small talk that she could carry on in her sleep.

It was not one-sided. Reid asked questions, and actually listened to the answers. She found herself telling him about the first-place ribbons she had taken in judged shows with her watercolors, of the rose-covered arcade she wanted to build from the house at Evergreen to the gazebo, of a porcelain holder for hat pins she had sold that morning at the antique shop, and of her ambition to travel around the world on a freighter.

In return she discovered that he liked lasagne, but didn't care for spaghetti, that his French friend in New York was Jewish and the two of them played computer chess on weekends, that he despised cellular phones but had one anyway, and that he had always wanted brothers and sisters. She found out, too, that he had a special interest in music. He collected 78-speed classical jazz records that he played on an ancient Motorola phonograph, but used a state of the art stereo for his favorite classical composer, Haydn. And he often used a midi-interface system with a keyboard attached to his computer for his favorite pastime of writing country music.

"You mean beer-drinking music?" she asked with a faint smile.

"Songs about heartache, and also about the love of a good woman," he said. "Don't you care for it?"

"How can I not? It's the only music with a recognizable melody line and words that aren't an assault on good taste, not to mention decency. Besides," she added flippantly, "there are so many new, good-looking male singers."

"Modern-day troubadours, telling stories in song and rhyme—poetry for the working man, and the only outlet he's allowed for his feelings."

"He might try sharing them with the woman in his life," she said wryly.

Reid shook his head. "Too risky. What if she doesn't understand? Or understands too well and despises him? Or pities him?"

Cammie met his dark gaze, caught by the unexpected sensitivity. Or perhaps it was not so unexpected. She gave a slow shake of her head. "You're a surprising man."

There was a sudden flash of something bright and hot, like spring lightning, in his eyes. It lasted only an instant before he turned it off, turned away. Still, she had felt its glow, and felt the shift of her heart in her chest.

Reid Sayers, she realized, was a man who kept much of what he was, what he thought and felt, well-hidden. He was firmly armored within himself, immune to probes and wayward curiosity. She wondered what it would take for him to open up and allow someone to touch his essential self. It did not seem likely that she would ever find out.

It really was a shame.

Chapter Nine

▒ ▒ ▒ *"You probably don't remember me,"* the young woman said. She perched nervously on the edge of the living room sofa with its soft pattern of salmon, aqua, and yellow flowers on a cream background.

She was right, Cammie didn't, though she searched her mind diligently for some connection. The girl's last name, Baylor, was one of the old family names in and around Greenley, but Janet Baylor didn't ring any bells. The other woman's face was vaguely familiar, with its pale skin and softly molded features topped by ash-brown hair that just missed being mousy. The impression might, however, have come from no more than a family resemblance.

"Really, there's no reason you should," Janet Baylor said. "I was four years behind you in school. You know how it is, the younger kids remember the older ones, but the older ones hardly know anybody more than a year younger is alive? But I remember you most of all because when my little dog my daddy had just bought for my birthday got run over, you were in your car right behind the truck that did it. You stopped and picked Rocky up, and took my dog and me to the vet."

"Oh, yes," Cammie said as a flash of memory returned. "That must have been years ago. Did everything turn out all right?"

Janet Baylor smiled as she gave a nod. "Rocky's ten, getting on up there for a dog. But he wouldn't be around if weren't for you, and I've never forgotten it, nor how kind and concerned you were that day. That's why when I found out about the stuff at the courthouse, I was disturbed in my mind. They told me to keep it quiet, but it seemed wrong. Finally, I knew I had to come and tell you about it."

Persephone came into the living room just then, bearing a small tray holding the glass of water that was all Janet Baylor had requested. Cammie had offered coffee or soft drinks with cake, but it had been refused. She thanked the housekeeper and passed the other woman her water and the linen napkin edged with Brussels lace that Persephone had considered appropriate. It was only when these formalities were out of the way that she spoke.

"I don't understand what you're saying. What did you find at the courthouse?"

The other woman swallowed a sip of water. She looked at Cammie, then away again. "Well, it's like this. I work in town as a paralegal with Lane, Endicott and Lane. Mostly, it's routine: filing mortgages, checking judgments, chasing probates and successions, that kind of thing. Then a few weeks back, we had a request from the mill to do a title search, looking up the old lease agreement with Justin Sayers, and also the original land deed for the property where the mill sets."

Cammie felt a tremor along her nerves of something that could only be called excitement. Janet Baylor was talking about the land supposedly deeded to old Justin by her great-grandmother Lavinia. She had always known there was something odd about that transaction.

"I'm with you so far," she said, giving the other woman a smile of encouragement.

Janet Baylor nodded. "I found the lease from Justin Sayers to Sayers-Hutton Bag and Paper, ninety-nine years, all signed and notarized; no problem. But I couldn't find hide nor hair of the deed from Lavinia Anne Wiley Greenley to Justin Sayers. Nothing. Zilch. It should have been listed or filed in three different places. There was no sign in any one of them."

"Are you suggesting that it was misplaced sometime in the last hundred-odd years—or stolen?" Cammie's gaze was narrow with cogent thought.

"No, no nothing like that," the woman said, looking alarmed. "I'm thinking that it was maybe destroyed back in the twenties, when they had the big fire in the courthouse." She frowned. "Even then, some notation of it should have been in the register for the latter part of the 1890s—that old book is still in good shape. There are two other possibilities."

She paused, passing her tongue over her lips as if they were suddenly dry. Cammie had begun to suspect what Janet Baylor was going to say. Cammie watched her closely as she said, "Yes?"

Janet Baylor took a deep breath, held it a moment, then let it out in a rush as she squared her shoulders. Lifting her chin, she said, "The first is that the deed was never filed for some reason, that it's floating around somewhere, or buried in some safety deposit box. The second is that there never was a deed."

Never was a deed . . .

Cammie, staring at the marble mantel across from the sofa, heard the echo of the words in her head. If there was no deed, then the mill land—and perhaps the buildings on it—belonged to the Greenley heirs, the descendants of Lavinia Greenley and her husband Horace. It would mean—

"There was something else."

Cammie turned her head sharply as the girl's stiff voice jolted her awareness. "Yes?"

Janet Baylor twisted the glass in her hand, then reached out to set it on the tray that had been placed on the low table in front of them. Her fingers were trembling so badly that the water sloshed over, puddling like liquid crystal on the silver. "Oh, I'm sorry."

"It doesn't matter," Cammie said. "Go on."

With her long, thin lashes quivering, shading her eyes, the other woman clasped her hands in her lap. "Well, I was digging into the old Greenley succession, thinking maybe the deed had been misfiled, or maybe there was some complication, such as a previous mortgage or maybe a connection to another, larger land transaction. It was in there that I found the divorce papers."

"What? Mine?" Cammie asked, her brows drawing together in puzzlement.

Janet Baylor shook her head. "Horace and Lavinia Greenley's."

"You must be mistaken. There was no divorce. That would have been a terrible scandal in those days."

"But there was, in 1890, two years before Horace Greenley passed away. I saw the paperwork with my own eyes. It was signed by Horace as plain as day; the signature matched a half-dozen other examples in the file. But the papers were in a sealed envelope, and Lavinia Greenley had never signed them. I think it's possible that—" She stopped, then tried again. "There's nothing to show that Lavinia ever knew about it."

Cammie shook her head. "That can't be right. The two of them were living together as man and wife when Horace died, they had a child just a few short months before then."

"I know," the other woman said, nodding, "I looked it up."

"But that would mean—" Cammie began, then stopped. The thought in her mind was of her own great-grandfather, Jonathan Wiley Greenley, firstborn child of Horace and Lavinia, and nearly five years old when Horace had died. There had also been the daughter born to Horace and Lavinia after their reconciliation following Lavinia's affair. There were quite a few descendants to the second child, people she had called cousins for years—including Wen Marston and the sheriff, Bud Deerfield. If there had been a divorce in 1890, then that later child, the daughter, was illegitimate. Her descendants were still related by blood, of course, but not in the full legal fashion they thought. They had never had a true claim on the Greenley estate, it seemed.

Strange. Not that it made any difference. It was all so long ago, and straightening out the legal complications would cost more than it was worth, even if anybody cared. She certainly didn't.

"What it means," Janet Baylor said, "is that it doesn't matter whether there was ever a deed to the mill land or not. What it means is that Lavinia Greenley, when she deeded the land, if she deeded it, had no legal right to make the transfer. She had no widow's usufruct of her former husband's property. The most she could have done, legally, was to hold it for her minor son, your great-grandfather, Jonathan Wiley Greenley."

Janet Baylor was now watching Cammie expectantly. Cammie stared at her, trying to understand the significance of what the other woman was saying. She saw the faint outlines of it, but her mind would not quite encompass it.

The pale, brown-haired woman leaned toward her. "Don't you see? Horace and Lavinia's son and only legal heir, Jonathan Wiley Greenley, had two sons and a daughter. The daughter died young of polio. The oldest son married at twenty-three, during World War Two, but was killed at Guadalcanal; he never had children. The only surviving child was your father. You are his only child, the only legal descendant. The mill land belongs to you. And the ninety-nine-year lease expires in less than two years."

Hers. The mill land, and by extension the mill itself, were rightfully hers. The words recurred in Cammie's mind, slowly gathering force.

She said, "The Swedish company isn't interested in renewing the lease. They want to buy outright."

Janet Baylor gave a quick, hard nod. "If you want to prevent the mill buy-out, all you have to do is refuse to sell."

The exultation that swept through Cammie was fierce. She could save the trees, save the land, save the red-cockades. The battle was over before it had begun. As the owner of the mill, she could structure the ecology of the parish as she saw fit. Nothing and nobody could stand in her way. The relief, the sheer, glorious gladness of it, bubbled in her veins like champagne. The smile that curved her mouth shone brilliant in her eyes.

Then slowly, surely, the effervescent joy began to go flat.

If the town died, she would be solely, completely responsible in a way she would not have been before, when there had been other people acting with her in opposition to the buy-out. It was a sobering thought.

"There's another angle," Janet Baylor said. "It just came to me last night—and is a big part of the reason I decided to see you this morning. If you own the land, and are the only heir, then you should have been getting the money for the lease all these years. On an annual basis, the lease amount Justin Sayers agreed to doesn't amount to much, a dollar per acre per year. But if you add it up over a hundred years and compound it at an average interest rate—as a court might order after litigation—the total comes to a considerable amount. That's money the mill owners would owe you, whether you decide to sell or not."

Cammie stared at the other woman while what she had just heard revolved in her head along with a burgeoning suspicion. She hesitated, then said with care, "I think you mentioned that you discovered all this several weeks ago. Does that mean that the results have been passed on to whoever requested it at the mill?"

"Yes, it has."

"And do you mind telling me—or do you know?— who it was who contacted Lane, Endicott and Lane?"

Janet Baylor nodded once. "The way I understand it, the request came from Gordon Hutton."

Cammie had not known she was holding her breath

until it left her in a soft rush. Reid had hardly been home long enough to have authorized the work of the paralegal, but it still might have been done by his father. In that case, it was unlikely that he would not know the results. With Gordon behind it, the same thing did not necessarily follow.

There was one person, however, who almost certainly had known. That person was her ex-husband.

Contempt gathered inside Cammie, spreading as it grew. The reason for Keith's sudden interest in nullifying the divorce petition and taking his old place as her husband was glaringly apparent. Under Louisiana's community property laws, half of everything she gained during the course of their marriage was legally his. If the mill was sold, and she was awarded ownership by the courts, he would collect half. Even if the sale fell through, he stood to rake in a share of the huge sum that might come from the old lease.

But if the divorce petition was granted before everything was settled, then he would miss his honey-fall. He would get nothing. Nothing at all.

She would see to it, Cammie thought, that he got exactly what he deserved.

Bringing her mind back to the woman beside her with difficulty, she said, "I can't tell you how grateful I am to you for coming to me. But you won't get in trouble for it, will you?"

Janet Baylor pressed her lips together before she answered. "I don't exactly know. You'll want to use what I've told you, I expect, otherwise there's no point. But when you do, do you think you could—forget how you found out about it?"

"I'm sure I could do that, yes," Cammie agreed, reaching out to touch the other woman's hand.

They both smiled with understanding at the same time.

Late the next day Cammie decided to talk to Reid. She had mulled the things she had learned over in her mind

for more than twenty-four hours. Yet the more she
thought about it, the more angles she found to consider,
the more possibilities and unanswered questions. She
was tired of what she had come to feel was a useless
mental exercise. Most of all, she was tired of the doubts.

Regardless, the new aspect that had been placed on the
contention between Reid and herself was not the only
thing on her mind. There was another suspicion that had
gradually crowded out most considerations.

It had to do with Reid's confession that he had
watched her the night of her meeting, and also as she was
growing up. No matter how many times she went over
what had been said that evening, she could not remember
him saying those were the only times that he had
watched. Nor could she recall any hint of a promise that
he would never do it again.

Those lapses, she had come to believe, were signifi-
cant. She intended to test the idea.

She made her arrangements early. It was not that there
was that much to do, rather that she didn't trust leaving
anything until the last minute.

She laid out a costume consisting of a dark gray windbreaker, black stirrup pants, long-sleeved knit shirt,
socks and shoes. Stripping off what she wore, she
dressed quickly in the dark clothes. A few minutes later,
while there was still a faint glow of daylight in the sky,
she let herself out of the house.

She paused for a moment in the side garden to lift her
head and sniff the fragrance of sweet olive and azaleas on
the night air. She thought she caught a whiff of honey-
suckle, too, plus the faint, acrid odor of privet. There was
none of the pesky privet shrubs around the house itself
now, but there had once been a hedge planted by her
grandfather in the thirties. It had been pulled up and
destroyed, but its remnants grew wild in the surrounding
woods, established by seed scattered by birds. Her steps
light, she moved on, heading toward the smell.

She chose a huge, old privet for her refuge. It was

thick enough for cover, but had no thorns or prickly foliage. The interior limbs were low enough to make a good perch, and stout enough to hold her weight. The greatest advantage, though, was that the scent of the blooms would cover any lingering hint of her own perfume.

She was taking no chances. She remembered Reid's demonstration of his reflexes and his abilities too well.

Waiting was not easy. There were a thousand tiny rustlings and creaks, chirpings and calls as darkness slowly thickened in the woods. The fine, soft leaves of the privet shifted with the breeze and her slightest movement, brushing against her with the same delicate touch as tiny spiders and other crawling things. Gnats found her, blowing around her eyes, and there came, now and then, the insistent whine of a mosquito in search of bare flesh.

She had left several lights burning inside the house. As the night darkened, the long beams shining from the windows made squares of brightness on the grass, and sent their gleams into the edges of the woods. She watched the open spaces between the trees, adjusting her eyes to the natural shadows that shifted in them as an aid to spotting what was unnatural.

The tree branch she was sitting on began to cut into her legs. She shifted a little, and reminded herself to be patient.

She saw the moving shadow perhaps a half hour later. Her breath caught in her throat, and she strained her eyes to follow it through the trees. It was low to the ground, small and gliding, totally silent. Keeping to the undergrowth just out of range of the light from the house, it moved swiftly and with purpose.

It was a cat.

Cammie relaxed, leaning her head back against the privet's trunk. A spiderweb attached itself to her cheek and became tangled in her lashes. She wiped it away and sighed.

One moment the opening she had been watching between a sweet gum and a cedar was empty. The next it was filled by the width of a man's shoulders.

Cammie blinked to be certain she wasn't seeing things. The image, broad, bulky, and powerful, blended with the shadows, disappearing then appearing again.

Reid.

She hardly dared to breathe as she watched him reconnoiter the house, moving soundlessly in a wide circle around it. He might have been a ghost, or a larger version of the cat she had seen earlier, or even the panther to which she had once compared him. Satisfied, apparently, that all was as it should be, he returned to a place some thirty yards away, in a direct line with her bedroom window. Hunkering down on his heels, he took up a post. An instant after he ceased moving, she had to rub her eyes and focus with care to tell he was there.

She had been right. That knowledge did strange things to her. She wasn't certain what she felt most, threatened or protected, afraid or gratified.

The one thing she didn't feel was indifferent. She was aware of a giving sensation, as if her primitive female self was responding to the night and the quiet strength of the man who watched. It wasn't what she wanted, but she could not seem to help it.

So what now?

She had a few choice things to say to him. If she could get near enough to do it without him massacring her. She opened her mouth to call out to him in warning. Abruptly, she closed it again.

There was something about his shape there in the gray-blackness of the night that bothered her. Was it too large, too compact? Had there been just a suspicion of awkwardness in the way he settled to his heels?

It had to be Reid; who else could it be?

Unless it was Keith.

It seemed so unlikely. Keith had never been much for

hunting. Besides, he was too thin in the body to cast that much shadow.

Yet it had to be one or the other. Didn't it?

The soft night breeze was in her face. That meant she was downwind from whoever was sitting there. It was possible that any slight sound she made would be carried away. She could try to get closer before she made her presence known.

She eased from her perch with exquisite care. Holding the branches aside to keep them from brushing against her, she ducked under them, then stepped carefully from the privet. She had been forced to take her eyes from the place where Reid had been resting. When she looked back, she could no longer see him.

Had he moved, or had she changed her angle of vision, losing him in the shadows? She couldn't tell. She clenched her teeth as a nervous shiver ran over her. Halting with one foot barely on the ground, she hovered in indecision.

It was impossible to stand where she was all night. In any case, there was no guarantee that it was safe, not if the man she had seen was on the prowl—whoever he might be.

She took a slow step, placing her foot just so, putting her weight on it a little at a time to avoid the crackle of fallen leaves. Bit by bit she shifted deeper into the woods, circling away from the house and the man who watched there.

It might have been an hour later, it might have been two hours, when Cammie saw the faint glimmer of the lights of Evergreen through the trees once more. She stepped among the lower limbs of a young pine while she stood straining her eyes at the shadows, turning her head this way and that to listen.

This was crazy, even stupid. She couldn't imagine what had made her think that discovering if Reid was out here was worth risking her neck. She was tired of playing this high-stakes version of hide and seek, tired of straining every muscle to keep from making a sound. If she could just get anywhere near her own back door without being maimed, she was going to hightail it inside faster than a cat could blink.

There was nothing to be seen except trees and dew-silvered grass and shadows that were cast by the rising moon, moving gently in the breeze. She was going to go for it. She stepped gingerly from her cover.

A strong arm snaked around her waist, snatching her back against a body as hard and firmly planted as a hickory tree. Her gasp of shock and terror was smothered by a warm hand clamped across her mouth.

"If Keith or anybody else starts wearing gardenia perfume," Reid growled at her ear in weary exasperation, "I'm in big trouble."

Chapter Ten

🔲 🔲 🔲 *"How long have you been out here, right* here?" Cammie said the minute she could peel his fingers from her mouth.

She felt the stillness that came over him. "You saw someone else?"

"That's what I'm trying to find out."

His decision was immediate. "Stay here," he said, the words so low she was barely certain she heard them. "Put your back to the big pine right behind us. Then don't move a finger, not even so much as a millimeter. Don't cough, don't sneeze, don't make a sound, not even a whisper. I'll be back."

He was gone before she could answer. She stood exactly as he left her for long seconds, trying to control the tremors that suddenly affected her knees. Dear God, but this man could get to her. And the irritating thing was that she wasn't sure whether it was fear or unbridled female yearning. Whichever it was, she didn't like it.

She moved after a moment to do as he said, however. It wasn't a question of obedience, but rather of self-preservation. She didn't intend to give him any excuse for making a mistake about just who it was he was scouting.

The only reason she was aware of his return, she thought, was because he intended it. One moment there was only darkness, the next he was silhouetted against the light from the house. He made no sound, but stood an instant until he knew she saw him. Then he took her hand, drawing her with him away from Evergreen. It was after they had stopped, deep in a section of tall pines a good half mile or more away from the house, that she recognized how trustingly she had followed him.

It was infuriating, when she had so little reason.

The pace he had set had been more sure than swift, but she was still breathless as she stood so close beside him. Her hand in his felt extra warm, as if she touched pure energy. His stance was alert, intent, his attention focused on the way they had come. She waited until he turned to her with an easing in his bearing before she spoke in soft tones.

"You didn't find anything back there?"

"Some sign," he said with a slight movement of his shoulders. "It might have been yours; it was hard to tell in this light."

"There was someone there, unless you were playing games." She did not trouble to hide her suspicion.

"I wasn't," he said evenly, "but I'm willing."

"I'm not! I've had more than enough sneaking around."

"Fine. You can find your own way back any time."

A chill feathered down her spine. Her voice taut, she said, "I could, believe it or not. But since I came out here because I wanted to talk to you, it would be self-defeating."

"I thought you were going to yell for the police the next time I came near your place."

"It seems like a better idea all the time," she said in exasperation.

"But not so long as you have a use for me," he suggested, his voice uncompromising. "Why feel around in the dark? Why not just pick up the phone?"

"I didn't think you'd be home, since you had very kindly told me where I might find you." She waited, not quite breathing, for his answer.

"Maybe," he said softly, "I told you too much."

"Or not enough," she shot back at him as she heard the evasion in his voice. Recognizing also its troubling intensity, she hurried on. "You could have mentioned, for instance, that there is no record of Justin Sayers ever owning the mill land."

He was silent for so long that Cammie was certain he was weighing excuses. When he spoke, however, his tone was quietly searching. "You want to run that by me one more time?"

Without revealing the source of her information, Cammie told him what Janet Baylor had said in as much detail as she could remember. When she was finished, she paused, then added, "I'm not sure of all the legal complications, but the gist of it seems to be that I own your mill."

"Congratulations," he said.

Cammie, hearing the irony in his tone, and his lack of anger, felt her joy slipping further away. Frowning to herself in the dark, she said, "Aren't you going to contest it?"

"Why? I've always been a little uncomfortable with the idea of a family fortune based on a woman's generosity."

There was something here she didn't quite grasp. In an effort to understand, she said, "What if my information is wrong?"

"In that case, the hard decisions will be mine again."

"I don't understand you," she said, the words stark.

"It's no great problem," he answered. "I'll fight to the death to protect what's mine, but I refuse to raise a single drop of sweat over something that isn't."

A tight smile curled one corner of her mouth. "I doubt your partners will feel the same."

He was fast, she had to give him that. There were scant seconds between the time she finished speaking and his short laugh.

"Keith knows? And Gordon?"

"So it appears."

"I don't think," he said deliberately, "that it's just the money Keith's after."

She wondered briefly if he had said that because he thought she needed to hear it. "No," she replied, "it's the power. It would give him great pleasure to control both you and his brother, even if it's only through me."

"I never said that I wouldn't fight Keith," he said.

There were rods of steel buried in the set concrete of his voice. She sent him a long glance, but the shadowed planes and hollows of his face were unreadable in the darkness.

He spoke again, almost at random. "You haven't told Keith you know, have you?"

She shook her head, then realizing he could barely see that movement, if at all, she said, "Not yet."

He was silent, while far away an owl called, a lonesome sound. He turned his head finally, as if he could feel her speculative gaze. His voice abrupt, he said, "Are you sleepy?"

"Not—really." She hesitated because she wasn't sure where her answer might lead.

He turned from her, shrugging his jacket from his wide shoulders. He leaned to spread it on the ground, then touched her shoulder with a slight gesture, pressing her down toward it. When she had seated herself, he dropped to the ground beside her.

In the quiet that descended, Cammie could hear the whisper of the night wind above them, feel its damp coolness against her face. The pine needles under them were springy, a resilient bed. The musty, yet resinous scent of them rose around them, mingling with the green freshness of spring. She and Reid sat without touching, yet she could sense his warmth, and just catch the wood fragrance of his after-shave. She thought of what he had said about her perfume, and wondered if he could smell it still.

"Yes," he said, and gave a low laugh as she turned her

head sharply to stare at him. "It's in your hair, I think. What do you do, shampoo with it?"

She looked away, as if he could see the color in her face. "I spray it in the air and walk under it."

He nodded, as if a mystery had been solved. "After you bathe, and before you dress."

"What?"

He looked away, or so she thought from the faint rustle of sound. "Never mind. I wanted—I'm curious about this great affair between Justin and Lavinia. Nobody ever talked about it in my family."

"Too disgraceful?"

He considered that. "It was more that Justin was a private man, I think, and his wife, my great-grandmother, did her best to pretend it never happened. She married Justin, so I gather, only a few months after the break-up of the big affair, as if Justin was caught on the rebound. I heard my mother and her friends talking about it once or twice, but they always changed the subject when they thought I was paying attention."

"I'm not sure I know all of it myself," Cammie said slowly. "It came my way in bits and pieces, too. My grandmother, my father's mother, was always defensive about it; she was a good Christian woman, duty bound to be disgusted by such goings-on. My mother was more tolerant, but then it wasn't her side of the family. Anyway, the general gist of it seems to be that Lavinia wasn't happy in her marriage. She was ten or twelve years younger than Horace, and liked to dance and sing. He thought hard work was the sole measure of a man—or a woman—and that church was a sufficient social outlet for anybody. They had a baby son that Lavinia loved dearly and treated like a favorite doll. That was the situation when the logging crews came into the area."

As Reid nodded his understanding, she went on. "The timber companies were from the east, where they knew the value of the wood. The farmers around here were glad enough to have somebody else do the back-breaking labor of cutting down the huge trees and removing them with oxen teams—as far as they were concerned, the timber was in their way. People like Horace Greenley offered hospitality to the crews; it was the neighborly, traditional thing to do, since there were no hotels of any size and the boardinghouse filled up fast. Justin Sayers was one of the men who stayed at Evergreen."

"I think I begin to see what happened," Reid said.

"I suppose it was natural enough," Cammie agreed. "Greenley treated the logging crews like royalty. There were square dances, box socials, candy pulls, and even brush arbor revivals; everybody got in on the fun, you see, even the preachers. The loggers were so different from the farmers all the young women knew. There were one or two unplanned pregnancies and shotgun weddings. Then the big trees were all gone, except for those in the swamplands that were hard to reach and scattered tracts that people like Horace held on to for their own reasons. The loggers moved on. When they went, Lavinia left town with Justin."

"Just like that."

Cammie frowned. "Oh, I doubt that it was easy or that she had no regrets. Well, I know she did have them, because after nearly a year of traveling with Justin to New York and Chicago and Saratoga and staying for a while with his people in Vermont, she returned to Greenley. Horace took her back, which everybody thought was extremely noble of him. Though it turns out it was a sneaking kind of revenge, since he had already divorced her in secret."

"And then Justin came back, too," Reid said when Cammie stopped.

"Yes," she agreed. "I've always wondered why he did."

"For Lavinia, of course. He had persuaded her to go away with him once, he must have thought he could do it again."

It was interesting, Reid's certainty, Cammie thought. Was that what he would do if he wanted a woman?

"Anyway, Justin never left again," she said, "even afterward, when he was married to someone else."

"Now that was a subject that did come up, why he stayed," Reid said. "Seems he liked the mild climate and easy Southern ways. Besides, there was, all in all, quite a bit of timber still left standing, and he was a sawyer, not to mention coming from good Yankee merchant stock that had nothing against making money."

She stared at his shape in the dimness. "I never meant to suggest there was anything wrong with it, or with seeing an opportunity when it stares you in the face."

A soft sound left him. "Justin was a touchy man, or so I've always heard. So is his great-grandson." He paused. "Where were we?"

It was a moment before Cammie went on. "This is where everything gets murky. Lavinia was pregnant when Justin got to Greenley, and apparently people were counting on their fingers to figure out who the father was. Maybe she refused to leave her toddler again, or was trying to do what she thought was right. Anyway Justin turned to another woman, and they were married. A few weeks later, Lavinia gave birth to a little girl."

"And the finger counters, what did they decide?" Reid said. "I only ask because of wondering if some of your cousins might not really be my cousins."

"No one knows," she said dryly. "I suppose it must have been too close to call. Anyway, what happened next put it out of most people's heads. When the baby was only a few weeks old, Horace was found dead out in the cotton field with a bullet in his head. There was a pistol in his hand, but everybody said he was too God-fearing a man to take his own life. Most thought Lavinia had shot him."

Reid let out a soundless whistle. After a moment he said, "She was never arrested that I heard."

Cammie drew up her knees, clasping her arms around

them as she shook her head. "She was a grieving widow and a new mother, her family was socially prominent, and there was no proof. Women of her kind, it seems, could sometimes get away with murder back in those days. Maybe because they so seldom acted without good cause."

"Do you think she did that, get away with it, I mean?" Reid's voice was curious, yet reflective.

"I'm not sure," Cammie said slowly. "It seems so unlikely. And yet, what if she found out what Horace had done? What if she knew that when Justin came back for her she was already free, but Horace hadn't told her. I think in her place I might have been ready to commit murder."

"Maybe Justin killed Horace for some of the same reasons," he offered. "Maybe Lavinia found out he did it, but couldn't live with it, and that's why they never got back together."

"You think she took the heat for him, because she knew she wouldn't be prosecuted?"

"I don't much like the sound of that, but I suppose it's possible," he said.

"But it doesn't explain the land deal. Why did Lavinia sign the acreage over to Justin?"

He swung his head toward her. "You don't doubt that she did that?"

"Not really. Justin apparently thought it belonged to him all those years ago, or he would never have put his sawmill there."

"Maybe the two of them were silent partners?" he suggested. "Stranger things have happened."

"Or if Justin did shoot Horace, maybe Lavinia felt guilty because she was afraid she had driven him to it."

Reid went stiff beside her. "No great-grandfather of mine ever took a payoff, if that's what you're suggesting."

"Not exactly," Cammie said in tentative tones. "But what if the two of them, together—"

"No. I don't believe he would have killed in cold

blood, either. Maybe during some blowup over the whole situation, yes, but not just to be rid of the husband. Justin was your regular Victorian patriarch, upstanding, proud, stubborn, not too flexible—"

"Rather like Horace, except younger and better-looking," Cammie said in wry amusement. At the questioning motion of Reid's head, she added. "I've seen pictures of Justin in the town history. You're a lot like him."

"I'd say thanks, but I'm not sure it's a compliment."

She was, but it didn't seem a good idea to admit it. As she looked away from him, she rocked off balance, her shoulder touching his. She could feel the warmth of him through her windbreaker, and also the firm ridge of muscle that ran down his arm. It seemed he was returning the pressure, supporting her without comment or effort.

She shifted to regain her position, then released her knees to sit forward. Moistening lips that were suddenly dry, she said, "Anyway, I don't suppose we'll ever know all the details. Lavinia might have been trying to keep Justin around, or maybe she traded the land to him in exchange for cutting timber for her. Or possibly she did it for Greenley out of the goodness of her heart, because she thought the town needed the industry. She did, apparently, have an altruistic streak. She donated the first three hundred acres of land to the state for use as the beginning of the game reserve, you know, several years later."

"And Sayers-Hutton Bag and Paper has been adding to the reserve as it acquires land ever since. Did you know that?"

She frowned. "I never realized."

"A family tradition to the tune of thirty thousand acres—less Lavinia's three and whatever was acquired from other landowners, of course." A short laugh shook him. "The state may have no title to the land, only jurisdiction over management of the wildlife, but I'd like to see anybody try to take even an inch of it out of the program."

"I wouldn't, even if I could. Nobody's trying to kill woodpeckers back in the reserve."

"I am not," he said with soft distinction, "trying to kill woodpeckers."

She barely glanced at his still form. "You could have fooled me."

"God, Cammie, you make me want to—" He stopped, drawing a harsh breath.

The tension that stretched between them had been there all along. In the sudden quiet, it seemed to take on a life of its own. Cammie could feel it shivering over her skin, insinuating itself into her veins. Her stomach muscles tensed and her thighs tightened. Her mouth throbbed, as if with the rush of blood that might come with a kiss. She knew, abruptly, that if she moved, if she said a single word, Reid would reach for her. The shock was how much she wanted to break his tenuous control, how hard it was to keep from it.

His voice, when he spoke again, seemed to come from far away and to carry a ragged edge. He said, "I would like you to do me a favor."

"What is it?" The words were husky, not quite steady.

"I want you to let me talk to Keith about this business with the deed before you let him know you've found out about it. It's asking a lot, I know, but I'd like to see what kind of excuse he comes up with for not letting me know."

"Why should I do that?" she asked, tilting her head.

"No good reason except my own satisfaction," he said with a trace of wry humor. "Will you?"

If he had argued or demanded, she would have refused. As it was, the quiet nature of his request made it seem not unreasonable after all.

"Why not?" she said.

Reid arrived at the mill an hour early next morning. It was becoming a habit; he had learned that he got as much work out of the way in that first hour as he did in the rest of the morning. More and more often, the mill supervisors and other personnel were coming to him with problems and suggestions as they learned he was approachable as well as being his father's son.

He was proud of their growing confidence and trust in him. At the same time, it made him feel guilty, since he was thinking of selling them out.

That wasn't precisely correct, of course. There would be guarantees in place, the mill would go on just as before only bigger and better. Still, he sometimes wondered, as he sat looking at the pictures of his father and grandfather and great-grandfather, Justin himself, if they would have seen things his way.

He wasn't getting much done this morning. He had dragged the profit and loss and operating statements out of the safe again, going over them for the tenth time or more. There were still one or two sets of figures that bothered him. Bookkeeping wasn't his field, but he had traced the problem to procurement. That was Keith's area of responsibility. As soon as his secretary made it in for the day, he was going to send for copies of the checks issued for supplies, as well as the invoices for the past six months.

He couldn't concentrate for thinking of the night before. The way he had found Cammie in the woods, waiting for him, tapped much too directly into his fevered dreams for comfort. He was tormented by his fantasies of what could have happened, might have happened. He could not stop himself from wondering what she would have done if he had pulled her down on the pine straw with him in the dark, baring her soft skin to the night, and to his touch and taste.

He should be getting used to the aching pressure of desire she brought to him on sight, much less from sitting with her shoulder pressed against him in the dark. He wasn't. If he closed his eyes, he could conjure up the scent of her, of gardenias and clothes dried in sunshine.

God, he wasn't even safe from wanting her in his own office.

He sometimes felt like a starving man allowed only a single taste of a banquet before being forced to stand guard over the forbidden richness. That it was his own circumstances that caused it made it no better.

There was a bittersweet pleasure in it, regardless. Cammie was coming to accept him as a part of her life, even if not an important part; the night before proved it. She had believed he'd known nothing of the legal problems with the mill land, he was almost sure of it. Not that it was possible to be absolutely certain of anything with her. Cammie was good at hiding her feelings. Too good.

At least she hadn't ranted and raved, hadn't delivered one of her verbal assaults. He felt he'd come away from that hour or two of closeness with relatively few bleeding wounds. Who could tell? Unless something happened to spoil the rapport, the two of them might manage one day to have an entire conversation without insulting each other. Not that he was holding his breath.

His early morning work time was gone; he could hear other people arriving in the offices down the hall. Somewhere there were even raised voices, somebody letting off steam. He might as well see if Keith had made it in, have his talk with him and get it out of the way so he could concentrate on other things. If the opportunity presented itself, he might even ask him a question or two about the huge amounts of certain supplies, ink for instance, that the mill was suddenly using as if there was a direct pipeline to the distributors.

As he left his office and started down the hall, a door opened near the far end. Two men emerged.

Reid slowed, with every well-honed instinct tingling. The hard, compact look of the two men, the assessing stares that they turned in his direction, bordering on insolence, tightened his stomach muscles. He felt, in that instant, the absence of a weapon at his side. It was the first time he had thought about that kind of thing in weeks, the first time since he had returned to Greenley.

The two men, strangers as far as he could tell, nodded politely in his direction, then walked quickly away down the hall in the direction of the mill entrance. Reid frowned after them as he realized the office they had been visiting belonged to Keith. His face hardened as he moved on down the hall. Knocking once on the door, he pushed inside without waiting for an answer.

Keith sat hunched over his desk with one arm wrapped around his belly. He pressed a blood-smeared handkerchief to the red wetness that trickled from the corner of his mouth and inspected the result. As the office door clicked shut, he looked up, exposing a bloodshot eye that was rapidly turning a vivid bluish-purple.

"What do you want?" he said thickly.

"Nothing that can't wait. Do you need a doctor, or somebody to take you to the hospital?" The damage, Reid thought, looked more painful than life-threatening, but there was always the possibility of internal injuries.

"I don't need anything—especially from you," Keith muttered, the words compressed and difficult as he squeezed his ribs. "Get out, leave me alone."

It was plain to Reid that Keith didn't intend to discuss what had happened. The reason wasn't hard to imagine. He'd been worked over, and the men who'd done it weren't social acquaintances. Reid pegged them as professional strong-arm boys. Cammie's complaints about her husband's spending habits, and the conclusions he himself had reached, were beginning to make an interesting kind of sense.

Keith's color was improving, probably the effect of temper. Reid stared down at the weak, self-indulgent man who had been married to Cammie, and was amazed at how little sympathy he felt for him. He wished, for reasons that he didn't much care to examine, that he could have been behind a few of the punches that had redecorated the other man's face.

After a moment he said in hard tones, "If you're in good enough shape to shoot off your mouth, Hutton, maybe you'll be able to understand one more warning, painful or not. Sneaking around Evergreen can be a dangerous occupation. A man could get hurt seriously, if he isn't careful."

Cammie's husband gave him a snide look. "You're a fine one—to talk."

"You could say that," Reid said, giving the words a different meaning from the one intended. "And I would advise you to pay attention."

"Cammie's—my wife. She would have come back to me if—you hadn't come sniffing around."

"If you think so, you're a bigger fool than I figured. Speaking of which, maybe you can answer a question for me. I'm interested in hearing just why I wasn't informed about the problem with the title to the land this building is sitting on."

Keith Hutton stared at him with wide, glassy eyes before he snapped them shut and let out a groan. "Jesus, what a time—to spring something like that."

"You did know about it, then; I thought so. What was the idea? I had to find out sometime."

"You—You ought to talk to Gordon. Yeah, that'll get it. He can tell you all about it."

"About what?" The question, peremptory, sharp with worry, came from the open door. Gordon Hutton stepped into the room. As he took in his brother's condition, his lips pressed together in a tight line. He swung around, closing the door behind him with a snap. As he turned back, he said, "What's going on here?"

Keith watched his brother with a shadow of fear in his watery eyes. Dropping the handkerchief and wrapping both arms around his ribs, he said, "Sayers is pissed because—because nobody told him about the missing title."

Gordon Hutton's face was pale and his eyes cold as he turned on Reid. "And you took your fists to my brother?

If that's the way you conduct business, it looks like a good thing you're getting out of the mill!"

Reid raised a brow, but before he could speak, Keith said in gasping haste, "Let it go, Gordie. I—I probably said a few things I shouldn't. Anyway, Sayers does have a stake in the deal. You can tell him how it was, can't you?"

It was obvious that Keith didn't want his brother to know what had actually taken place in his office. Reid's first inclination was to set the record straight. After a second's consideration, he thought that there might be more advantage in having Keith indebted to him, at least until he found out why he'd been elected as the heavy.

With his gaze on the older brother, he said, "Maybe I directed my questions to the wrong man, anyway."

Gordon Hutton grunted. "I have a meeting in half an hour and a lot of paperwork to get through beforehand, but I can give you five minutes. Come along to my office."

The peremptory command might have been a bid for time, but Reid thought it was primarily a power play, an attempt to dominate the issue by forcing him to face Gordon on his turf. He'd seen that game played by experts in the military, had weathered enough of it to last a lifetime. His voice perfectly polite, but his gaze unyielding, he said, "My office is closer. I won't keep you any longer than necessary."

Gordon swung with stiff movements and strode ahead of him down the hall. It was plain, as he entered Reid's office, that he had to fight the urge to walk behind the desk and take his usual chair there. He compromised by standing behind the visitor's chair and bracing his hands on its back.

Reid, rather than taking the seat that would have given him most control, moved to rest one flank on the corner of the desk. He made no effort to initiate the discussion, but waited, allowing his silence to force Gordon into an explanation. He thought for a moment that Gordon was going to call his bluff. The other man's face was set, his manner overbearing. Then his features took on a purplish tint and his light brown eyes, deep-set and almost lashless, turned feral. He pressed his lips together, the corners turned down, before he spoke.

"This title business has been going on for some time, too long, to my way of thinking. We had a preliminary report, but it seemed best to double-check it. I wanted to be certain the whole thing wasn't some idiot mistake made by this girl hired to do the leg work. You have to understand that we can't move on this until we're certain of the facts."

The sound of the other man's voice grated on Reid's nerves. "You were the one who contacted the law firm, authorized the title search?"

"As a part of normal routine when the possibility of the sale came up, yes."

Reid nodded. "But you didn't report the results to my father."

Gordon smiled with a tight movement of his lips. "What was found was so unlikely that it would have been stupid to go off half-cocked over it. Good business practice required a thorough evaluation before any decision was made, and then a slow and careful assessment—"

"Don't patronize me, Hutton," Reid said in trenchant tones. "I'm well-aware that the legalities must be observed and normal care taken to prevent errors. But I also realize that the preliminary report could, and should, have been presented weeks ago. What interests me is why it was suppressed."

Hutton clenched his jaws. "What I want to know is how you found out about it. I will not tolerate leaks in my operation—"

"Our operation," Reid corrected. "And how I found out isn't important; I'm extremely grateful for this particular leak."

"All right, all right, but all I've done is protect your interest as well as mine and Keith's. I don't think you want to let go of a multimillion dollar operation like this on the say-so of a silly legal aid who doesn't know a deed from her right tit. You wouldn't have come home, wouldn't have interfered in mill operations you've ignored for years, if you weren't interested in protecting what you have here."

Reid felt his temper heating, though he kept it under rigid control. "You think you have me figured, do you?"

"That's right," Gordon said, his expression coldly contemptuous. "You're tired of risking your neck in god-forsaken hellholes for peanuts. You thought you'd come on back here where the living is easy, just step in and take over where dear old dad left off. The timing is just dandy, with the sale that's pending; you can draw your share, kick back, and never hit another lick at a snake. Fine, I don't care. But just don't give me any bullshit about what happens between now and when the sale is final."

"Suppose," Reid said in even tones, "that the mill turns out to belong to Cammie?"

"Too bad. We aren't ready to turn it over to a damned female who never had a thing to do with it just because of a missing piece of paper."

"Why not, if the problem with the land is legitimate?"

Gordon Hutton stared at him a long moment, then swore under his breath. "That bitch. I might have known. She has you under her spell like all the rest, like she had Keith until he was man enough to get out from under her. I can't begin to understand what it is she has between her legs that turns grown men into weak-kneed patsies, but it must be some hot stuff."

Reid came to his full height with lithe strength. The space between him and the other man was not wide; he crossed it in two even strides. Skirting the chair between them, reaching out with casual force, he caught Gordon Hutton's shirtfront in his fist. He twisted it, pulling the heavyset man up on his toes.

"The lady," he said with soft emphasis, "is a beautiful

and intelligent woman. It disturbs me to hear her spoken of in the terms you just used. I sometimes have an uncontrollable urge toward violence when I'm disturbed. Do you think you can understand that?"

Hutton's eyes were glassy and staring from their sockets. He tried to speak, but only made a coughing, choking sound. Reid eased his grasp a fraction.

"Yes. All right, I see," the larger man wheezed.

"Good." Reid released him, giving a brush to the wrinkles in the other man's polyester and cotton shirt. "Maybe you'll understand, too, that you don't know me as well as you think. You don't have the slightest idea of how I feel or what I want. And you aren't equipped, mentally or morally, to guess."

He stepped back, since remaining close was too great a drain on his self-restraint. He continued with measured precision. "I will tell you one thing, and I expect you to remember it. I don't want anything underhanded going on with this sale. I don't want Cammie bothered in any way, shape, or form. And I want to be informed every step of the way through the legalities. I think, in fact, that you had better have Lane, Endicott and Lane report directly to me. I'll feel better, less disturbed, that way."

The look Gordon Hutton gave him burned with hate and injured ego, but he made no reply. Jerking his clothing back into place, he squared his shoulders. "You will live to regret this."

"Maybe," Reid said, "but I doubt it. And you may find that watching your language pays—when we get hit with a suit for reimbursement for the hundred-year lease, plus interest."

"She wouldn't dare."

Reid's smile held an edge. "You think not? I don't claim to know the lady well, but I don't think she has much affection for any of us. That being so, I'd say nothing is more likely."

Chapter Eleven

▓ ▓ ▓ *The country club sprawling over its hill with* a view of the lake had once been a family mansion. The columned portico still made an impressive entrance. What had been a ballroom served now as a fine setting for dinner and dancing. The bank of tall windows and French doors that opened out onto the lakefront, and the flagstone terrace descending in easy levels to the water's edge, gave the place the prerequisite air of grace and privilege.

That was all that was right about the club. The house itself needed painting, the drapes inside were threadbare, the food served was barely adequate. The pool and golf course were maintained after a fashion, but it had been years since the tennis courts were resurfaced. Membership had been declining for some time, and no one seemed to care. The days of belonging to the club as a status symbol seemed to be over.

It was possible the country club mentality was dying out with the WW II generation that had spawned it. More likely, the slow demise was just another symptom of a stagnant economy, a dying town.

Cammie stood on the screened porch of the old family camp house across the narrow neck of the lake from the club, watching the activity around it. She could see the lanterns strung along the dock, hear the music drifting across the water. There was a wedding reception in progress over there. She had attended the ceremony and

171

stopped in for a little while at the reception as a courtesy. She slipped away early. The affair had been nice, but she hadn't been close enough to either bride or groom to make staying for the departure of the bridal couple a necessity. Since she was going to be out at the lake anyway, she decided to pack a bag and stay overnight at the camp.

She and Keith had held their own wedding reception at the club. It was one of her nicer memories of their marriage. The music had been sentimental, the champagne heady. Her gown was a drift of candlelight-colored silk and lace sprinkled with spangles, and Keith looked like a wedding cake groom. He'd seemed so proud, so happy. There was the excitement of a new beginning. Or so she'd thought at the time.

Upon ending a marriage, she reflected now, not everything you discarded was terrible. The good times, few and fleeting as they might have been, still tugged at the heart, still caused discomfort.

There was the golden topaz ring Keith had bought her on their honeymoon in Mexico. He knew she liked it when they saw it in the shop, and had waited until she was taking a nap to go back and buy it. He gave it to her in the bottom of a margarita glass. She wasn't fond of the drink; she sipped at it a few times, then started to toss the rest over the balcony railing of their beachfront room. Keith nearly had a heart attack.

Then there had been the day a year or so later when Keith sold his fishing boat to make the down payment on the sports car he thought she wanted. They couldn't afford it; she had only admired the thing because he expected it. Still, it had been sweet of him to want to give it to her. She'd despised the car, with its stick shift and seats that practically skimmed the ground, but it had been months before he found out.

Keith had needed a different kind of woman, she thought, one more frivolous, less prosaic, less emotionally demanding—someone who would have had a fit over the sports car or rhapsodized over a ring hidden in a margarita as the height of romance. Someone who could have accepted material gifts as the only expression of love and affection Keith had to give. She'd never been that kind of woman, though she had tried hard for a long time.

Cammie swung to stare out over the lake as she caught a movement from the corner of her eye. It was a fiberglass bass boat ghosting over the water, the driver sitting in the stern. The low hum of a trolling motor reached her. Moments later she saw the craft turning toward the camp's boat house and dock.

Glancing down at herself, she realized the white T-shirt and cream-colored skirt she'd pulled on when she got to the camp made her easily visible there under the overhanging porch. She took a step backward, ready to retreat into the house. A visitor was the last thing she wanted just now.

"Don't go running off, sweetie, it's just me!"

The hail coming over the water stopped her. Wen Marston. That rich, humor-laden voice was recognizable anywhere.

The tension left Cammie in a rush. Smiling, she pushed the screen door open and walked down the gravel path that lead to the edge of the lake. As the boat bumped the dock, she caught the line Wen threw to her, then stepped back as her cousin clambered up the ladder.

Cammie spoke over her shoulder while she tied off the line. "What are you doing out at this time of night?"

"Visiting, honey. I skipped the wedding and was late for the reception over yonder—old Mrs. Connelly called me out to appraise her grandmother's diamond bar pin again, which is a big tease because the woman's never gonna sell it. Anyway, somebody said they thought you left for the camp. I figured I'd come tell you this great story I just heard."

Cammie hid a smile for Wen's unselfconscious rattling

as she turned toward the camp house. "Come in and let me fix you a drink."

"Now you're talking."

Cammie poured a stiff bourbon and Coke for Wen and white wine for herself. They took their glasses back out onto the porch since the night was so pleasant. Settling into a pair of Adirondack-style lounge chairs made of cypress, they leaned back, breathing deep of the soft air. Their faces were barely visible in the light shining from the kitchen.

"I don't know why you don't just move out here," Wen said as she swallowed a large part of her drink. "I would if it belonged to me."

"I think about it now and then," Cammie said.

The camp house, with only two bedrooms and a great room that encompassed kitchen, dining room, and living area, was compact and convenient. The bungalow roof that spread over wide-screened porches on four sides, and the cathedral ceiling and soaring fireplace faced with dovetailed pine, helped give it a more spacious feeling than its size indicated. There was a restful quality about it also, a sense of long, drowsy summers, quiet winters, and unrelenting comfort. But it was nearly fifteen miles from town, and it wasn't Evergreen.

The two of them exchanged a few more bits of banter. Finally, Cammie said, "So what's the story? Don't keep me in suspense."

Wen gave Cammie's relaxed form a skeptical look before she tipped up her drink again. "All right," she said, after she'd swallowed and wiped her mouth. "There's this girl who works for Arthur Lane—quiet little thing, bit on the mousy side. She was a Reese before she married the Baylor boy. They got a divorce last year, you might remember?"

"Janet Baylor." There was a chilled feeling at the back of Cammie's neck that had nothing to do with the glass of cold wine in her hand. Janet was the paralegal who had found the problem with the mill title.

"Right," Wen said, giving her a stabbing stare in the dimness before she went on. "Seems she's been living in the apartments out on the old cemetery road since she broke up with her husband. Well, yesterday morning, she didn't come in to work. One of the other girls at the law office called, but there was no answer. Nobody thought too much about it until she didn't come in again this morning. When they still couldn't get hold of her, they called her mother. She went over to check. Janet was gone."

"Just—gone?"

"Closet empty, nothing in the bathroom, purse and car nowhere in sight. It looked like she threw everything into a suitcase and took off. Left her breakfast dishes, stuff in the refrigerator, picture albums, cedar chest full of the kind of souvenirs girls keep—dried-up corsages, empty valentine candy boxes, the toasting glasses from her late, unlamented wedding. Everything was helter-skelter, like she was in a tearing hurry. But she didn't stop to tell anybody where she was going, or when she'd be back."

"Nobody saw her leave?"

Wen shook her head. "They found her car late this afternoon in the parking lot at St. Francis Hospital in Monroe. They thought maybe she walked to the bus station from there, since it's nearby, but nobody remembers seeing a woman like her. Far as anybody can tell, she just disappeared."

Cammie frowned as she stared out over the lake. The moon was coming up, edging cautiously above the trees. She watched it lay a shifting, silver-gilt path across the water. "Why would she do a thing like that? Anybody have any ideas?"

"There's nothing much to go on," Wen said with a shrug. "Janet wasn't the kind of girl who had a lot of men friends. She didn't drink or go out of town to make the rounds of the lounges. The only thing at all unusual, apparently, is that she had a male visitor the night before she left. But there's only the word of a widow lady down the street on that. It was almost dark and the widow's eyesight isn't what it used to be; she couldn't put a name to the man."

"Was there sign of a struggle?"

"Not so you'd notice. It appears Janet left the apartment under her own steam. Some think she took off with this visitor of hers, then maybe her car was stolen later. Either that or the two arranged to meet out of town so they wouldn't be seen together, then caught a cab to the airport for some romantic getaway. On the other hand, there's also the possibility she might have been duped into going off with some maniac, and her body will turn up in a ditch."

Cammie was silent as she sat thinking. Maybe Janet Baylor's disappearance had nothing to do with the girl's discovery at the courthouse, but the possibility was there. If there was a connection, then it was important that the sheriff's office should know what they were dealing with. It bothered Cammie that her business would have to be made public, but there was no help for it.

"Janet came to see me last week," she said. Sighing, she set her wineglass down beside her chair. Pushing her fingers into her hair and resting her head on her hand, she told the story of what the paralegal had found at the courthouse.

"That explains a few things," Wen said in grim tones when Cammie had finished. "Nancy Clemens, one of the women in the Clerk of Court's office, was telling me that somebody took an Exacto knife to the record books a couple of days ago. She said several big folio pages are gone, though they aren't exactly sure when they were taken."

"It makes sense if it's the divorce records that are missing," Cammie said, frowning. "But I can't believe Janet would do that. She just doesn't seem the type."

Wen gave a cynical snort. "People will do a lot of things you wouldn't believe for the right amount of money."

"But everybody knew she worked with the records; they must have known when she came and went. It would be so obvious."

"A person who's always there might be the last one anybody would notice. Of course, it could also have been somebody after what she found, somebody who hoped it would be a long time before the missing pages were discovered. It might have been, too, except Nancy Clemens is a neat freak. She picked up a giblet of paper from the floor and recognized that it came from the old record books."

"I'll have to go back to the house to call Bud," Cammie said. There was no phone at the camp house, never had been. That was one of its many benefits.

"He'll be glad to have the lead," Wen said in agreement, "though I'm not too sure I'll be thrilled if he tracks down Janet and the papers. You realize my side of the family just got made illegitimate retroactively?"

Cammie turned toward her in the dimness. "I know it does, and I'm sorry. But surely it can't matter, not now."

"Not to you. You've got the name and the big house—and maybe even the mill." The undercurrent of envy, faint and coated with humor though it was, sounded plain in the other woman's voice.

"By accident of birth only," Cammie objected. "I can't take any credit, so I don't see why I should have to take the blame."

"Nice, too," Wen moaned, "and so gorgeous you've got men fighting over you. I can't stand it."

"Don't be ridiculous," Cammie said, reaching for her wineglass.

"You didn't know? My ever-humming grapevine tells me Keith and Reid had it out in Keith's office a few days back. Keith got the worst of it."

"What do you mean?" Cammie said sharply, pausing with her wine suspended halfway to her lips.

"A black eye, a bloody nose, and two cracked ribs," Wen said succinctly.

"Reid wouldn't—" Cammie began, then stopped. He had mentioned something about talking to Keith. Maybe the discussion had got a little out of hand. When she spoke again, she said, "Who was out spreading this story? One of the mill secretaries?"

"Actually, I think it was Vona Hutton. Gordon came home raving about it, and poor Vona caught the fallout. Naturally, she had to tell somebody, just to relieve her hurt feelings. She was due to help decorate the church down at the First Baptist. That did it."

The source seemed unimpeachable, but still Cammie sat frowning. The whole thing didn't fit with what she knew of Reid's formidable self-control. It was always possible, of course, that he hadn't wanted to control himself.

Wen stayed until she'd finished her drink and the lights inside the club across the way began to go out. As they rehashed the news Wen had brought, Cammie thought that her friend would have liked to delve a little deeper into what was behind it. She wasn't sure what held Wen back, but she doubted it was discretion.

Cammie walked Wen down to the dock. They said good night, then Wen climbed down into her boat and started the trolling motor. Cammie released the line holding the boat and tossed it into the stern. Then, just before Wen reached back to put the motor in gear, she stopped.

"So what are you going to do if the records don't turn up and there's no way to prove you own the mill?" she asked.

"I don't know," Cammie answered. "I never saw anything to show that I owned it in the first place."

There was a slowly widening gap of water between the boat and the wooden dock. The idling motor made a low hum. Wen spoke across both. "Yeah. Well, I can think of a lot of people who would like to be sure no proof ever shows up, not with you wanting to stop the expansion. Also, a lot of people besides me who won't like having their family tree chopped up for kindling wood. You be careful, now. You hear?"

Cammie lifted a hand without answering. The trolling motor changed its pitch from a rumble to a muted whine. Wen swung the boat in a wide circle in the water, then headed out across the lake, back toward the country club.

Cammie watched until the boat faded into the darkness. She thought she saw it nose into the club landing in the dim light, then heard the dying gasp of the trolling motor. Still, she stood on the dock with Wen's words playing over and over in her brain.

Could someone actually have harmed Janet Baylor because of what she had found at the courthouse? And if Janet Baylor was that much of a threat, what was she?

Cammie wished she was back at Evergreen. It felt like escaping from a goldfish bowl when she left; she'd begun to dread walking through the house at night, feeling as if someone might be lurking in the dark halls, or nervous at passing an uncurtained window where she might be watched from outside. Now the big house seemed like a refuge.

The moon had arched higher into the sky, washing the night with its pale light. There was a night breeze off the lake, a hint of coolness in its damp breath. It carried the smell of the water, a blend of fish and vegetation and decaying things. Just along the shoreline, a bald cypress lifted its moss-draped arms toward the heavens in mute supplication. Far off, there came the cry of a night bird, a mournful counterpoint to the chorus of peeper frogs and singing insects.

Her gaze moved over the shining paillettes of moonlight that lay on the dark water, following them to where the lake lapped gently against the pilings of the dock under her feet. It was just there, some five or six feet out from the end of the dock, that Reid had appeared in front of her all those years ago. It seemed possible it was that memory, as much as anything else, that had brought her out to the lake. The moment came back to her at odd times, as intrusive as an old, unsettled grief. She had the feeling there was something about it she was missing, something she should have known.

Whatever it was still eluded her. She turned away in irritation, walking back up toward the camp house.

A shadow moved near the corner of the squat building. Cammie stopped abruptly. She strained her eyes in the darkness.

The movement did not come again. It might have been a shrub waving in a stray breeze. It could have been a prowling cat or dog that had slunk away, nervous of strangers.

It might have been, could have been, any of those things, but it wasn't. Cammie was almost sure of it.

Fear coursed through her veins with the burning pain of corrosive acid. Her heart beat in wrenching surges. She could hear her pulse like a hot, feathery whisper in her ears.

The urge to lift her skirt and strike out for the back door with legs flying and arms pumping, as she used to do when she was a frightened child, was so great that repressing it made her shudder. The light from the kitchen was a golden beacon as it shone through the open door under the porch, but it only served to make the rear of the house darker. She hadn't thought to shut or lock the door as she and Wen moved outside; there had seemed no earthly reason.

It was possible, of course, that the moving shadow was Reid.

Her anger uncoiled at the thought. The heat of it gave her the power to move. She forced herself to keep on, placing one foot in front of the other, drawing closer to the house. If he was shadowing her again, if he dared show himself after giving her such a scare, she might kill him. Or throw her arms around him and never let go.

Yes, or maybe run like hell after all.

The person who had the most to gain from seeing the courthouse documents destroyed—and the woman who had found them gone—was Reid Sayers. Cammie had been avoiding that logic for the past hour. She could avoid it no longer.

The narrow wash-gravel path worn into the slope by years of footsteps going up and down to the lake seemed to stretch for miles. The grating crunch of it under her feet was noisy. She could feel the brush of ragged spring grass, wet with dew, against her ankles. Through the trees she could catch the pale glint of an outside light from the next camp house along the shoreline, but it was too far away to think of running there for safety or calling for help.

The angular patch of dark shade cast by the house roof reached out and covered her. A few steps more and her hand was on the screen door. She opened it with a quick swing, catching it as it was closing behind her so it wouldn't slam.

The dim length of the porch was empty. The inside doorway was a black hole. It took a strong act of will to move toward it.

She stopped just inside and reached for the light switch. The room, its rustic country rocking chairs draped with quilt throws, the tables flanking the overstuffed couch piled with books, sprang into glaring relief.

There was nothing, no one there. She reached for the door, snatching it shut, turning the dead-bolt lock. Leaning her head against the solid wood, she sighed in relief.

Cammie's hands were still shaking when she straightened. She thought about the glasses she and Wen had used, which were still out on the porch. They could wait until morning. She turned toward her bedroom. A hot bath to relax tense muscles and take away the chill inside her; that was what she needed.

It helped. In fact, it worked almost too well. She was overheated, her face flushed and her hair damp at the hairline by the time she climbed from the tub. She blotted the water from her skin with a towel, then smoothed moisturizer over her face. Reaching for a brush, she dragged it through her damp hair, giving herself time to cool off a little before she slipped into her nightgown of batiste with its white-on-white embroidery.

The material of the gown had once been crisp and smooth and opaque. Age and wear had made it as soft and thin as a rag, and washing had drawn up its hem from floor-length to just above her ankles. It drifted down over her with a cool, gliding motion as Cammie pulled it on. Settling it around her, she moved into the connecting bedroom.

She stopped, alerted by some half-recognized instinct. An instant later she realized what was wrong. The light was off. She knew she'd left it on.

She turned toward the bed. There was a long, dark shadow lying across the turned-down sheet. It stirred.

"Lord, baby, I thought I was going to have to come in there and get you," Keith said as he sat up.

Shock rippled over her in a searing wave. It was followed by cold rage.

The light switch was on the other side of the room, next to the door. Cammie started toward it. Her ex-husband rolled from the bed, blocking her way.

She came to a halt. Crossing her arms over her chest, she said, "What is it? Another bill you can't pay?"

"You got any extra cash lying around, it would come in handy, but no, that's not what I had in mind." He eased his stance a little, propping one hand on his hip. "I thought maybe you were lonesome out here on the lake, thought you might want a little company."

"You were wrong." The words were clipped, a reaction to the suggestion she heard in his voice. His eyes glittered in the glow of light from the bathroom, but she couldn't tell if it was from malicious pleasure in making her nervous or lascivious intent.

He cocked his head. "What happened to you, Cammie? You used to be so soft, so reasonable."

"I married you."

"All right, all right," he said, moving a slow step closer. "Maybe it is partly my fault. Sometimes men do dumb things; they just can't help it. But I'll make it up to you, if you'll only let me."

She watched him closely, listening to the timbre of his voice instead of what he said. When he stopped speaking, she said, "I can't believe you would try this, not again."

"Why not? I just want to make things right between us." He eased toward her again.

"You don't have to, you know," she said, shaking her hair back from her face. "Janet Baylor's gone and so are the records. There's no percentage in trying to hang on."

The confusion in his face seemed real enough, though it lasted only a second. His voice dropping to a husky note, he said, "I don't know what you're talking about, and I don't care. This is between you and me. Don't give up everything we had, Cammie, please. Don't give up on me."

The bathroom light glanced across his face as he moved toward her, picking up the yellow and purple bruising just fading from under his eye and the thickness of swelling across the bridge of his nose. She barely registered these signs of the beating he'd taken as she fought the impulse to retreat before his studied advance. He reached for her, wrapping his hand around her neck to draw her toward him for a kiss, the way he used to do, and she brought up her wrist and knocked his hand away.

"Don't!"

"Damn it, Cammie, quit being so stubborn. You've got to come back to me!"

"Oh? What about the girl who's going to make you a father any day now? Do you think you can keep us both happy—or do you intend to dump her?"

His face twisted with his frustration. "She has nothing to do with it."

"Funny, I thought she did," Cammie said, turning a shoulder to him as she began to edge away. "I thought she was the reason you wanted your freedom."

He grabbed her arm, swinging her back around. "She was a mistake, all right? She made me feel big, like an important man, but she could never hold a candle to you."

Seeing the angry guile in Keith's face, Cammie was suddenly sorry for the young woman who was going to have his child. Her anger drained away. Her tone quiet, she said, "Go back to her, Keith. She wants you. I don't."

He cursed, and his fingers tightened into cruel hooks. He jerked her against him, his voice dropping to a rough, hot rasp against her ear. "I tried to do it the easy way, but you wouldn't have it. Now we'll do it like I started out in the game reserve, the hard way."

She felt the thrust of his body against her hip, felt the hot, turgid length of him, and knew with sick certainty what he intended. If marital relations were resumed, forced or not, the divorce petition would be nullified. Keith had only to declare in court that they had been together as man and wife. If she could not deny it under oath, then he would have won.

Her options were few. Screaming would do no good since there was no one near enough to hear. She had no weapon. That left talking her way out of it or fighting.

"Rape is an ugly word," she said in hard tones, "but I will report it."

He gave her a hard shove so she stumbled in the direction of the bed. "Go ahead. It'll be my word against yours. We'll see who the guys at the sheriff's office believe."

"I think Bud will listen to me." He gripped her arm again, and she tried to jerk away from him, but his hold tightened, his fingers biting into her.

"Maybe, maybe not. I'm not too sure he'll want to get involved in a sleazy domestic quarrel. And I sure don't think you want everybody in town smacking their lips over the details."

The bed was against the backs of her legs. He bent over her, his breath fetid with halitosis overlaid by the bourbon he had used to give him boldness and the breath mint he'd chewed to cover it.

Cammie swallowed hard on nausea. Her voice strained, she said, "Maybe the person I should call is Reid, then. You may not be so anxious to face him again."

It was the wrong thing to say. His face twisted with rage and he muttered an obscenity. He grabbed the front of her nightgown, his knuckles gouging into the soft valley between her breasts. Grunting with effort, he slung her across the bed. He threw himself across her, bringing his knee up over her legs.

She twisted, punching at him. Bracing one foot, she heaved him backward a few inches, enough to try to bring her knee up between his legs.

He blocked the move with a shift of his body, then dropped his weight on her, driving the breath out of her lungs, locking her knees. Before she could recover, he levered himself up and straddled her hips. He caught her forearms, holding her immobile while he ground himself against the soft mound above her pubic bone.

Fury and disgust rippled over her. She set her teeth, wrenching one arm in a sudden backward move, yanking it free. She drew back her fist and struck hard for his nose.

Keith howled, grinding out a curse as he bent forward in pain. Then he snapped erect. His face turned savage as he whipped out a hand to seize one wrist, then snatched the other. He twisted them, grinding the bones together. She gave a choked cry. Dragging both arms above her head, he pinned them with one hand. He swung his hand back and brought it around in a vicious slap.

Crackling pain exploded against her face. It streaked along her jaw, then throbbed in her cheekbone. Her breath lodged in her throat. Tears sprang to her eyes. Her ears rang. Before she could make more than a single strangled gasp, he drew his hand back again.

The blow never landed.

Keith's weight suddenly lifted, dragging across her. A

hoarse yell ripped from his throat as his feet hit the floor and he staggered across the room. He struck the wall, bounced off it, then sagged against it again. Cursing and crying, holding his injured ribs, he slid to the floor.

In the darkness of the room a shadow moved, lithe, powerful, with danger in every tense line. It glided toward the fallen man, bending over him.

The shadow was Reid.

Chapter Twelve

▓▓ ▓▓ ▓▓ *Reid recognized too well the cold enmity* that held him as he stared down at the man whimpering on the floor. It was the detachment that allowed him to kill, if need be, without an excess of regret. There was an added element this time, however. He was watching in quiet anticipation for an excuse.

His contempt for men who used their superior strength to terrorize women was virulent. A man who would do that to Cammie deserved whatever came to him. He waited with a silent prayer that Keith Hutton had a weapon and would try to use it.

"Reid?"

He heard Cammie's voice as if from a great distance. She came toward him, approaching with slow steps in the dim light, using every care to remain in his line of vision. Her caution and apparent fear of him touched him with remorse, penetrating his defenses as nothing else could.

His gaze traveled slowly from the tumbled silk of her hair to the shadow made by the vivid patch of color on her cheek, and lower, to the gentle shape and movement under the thin white cotton of her nightgown. Like a fog lifting, he felt his sense of being separate from his soul leaving him. He regretted it. He didn't want, didn't need, the acute, driving sensual awareness that took its place.

She put out her hand, barely grazing his shoulder with her fingertips. He felt each single touch like a series of stabbing electric shocks. The urge to take her right then and there, to bury himself in her seductive softness and blot out the world, ripped through him with hurricane force. It stopped his breath and left him with every muscle rigid in the effort of containment.

"Don't," she whispered.

Don't kill Keith?

Don't take her?

Don't control himself, so that he might do both?

The need to be positive of what she wanted—and why—cleared his brain. He relaxed with consummate effort and in minute degrees, easing his stance over Keith, retreating a fraction from her so that her hand fell away from his sleeve.

There were some things he would not relinquish. He was not sure when the decision was made, but he would not fight it. He did not intend to let the woman in front of him out of his sight again soon, not for hours, at least not for the rest of the night.

Bending, Reid dragged Keith to his feet. He ignored the other man's groans and curses as he frog-marched him from the room with strength fueled by brutally repressed urges. He knew Cammie followed after them, but it made no difference. Shoving her husband through the great room and out onto the porch, he used the man's body to thrust the screen door open, then ejected him into the night.

Keith stumbled forward, then caught himself. Slewing around, he planted his feet and knotted his fists. "Just who the hell do you think you are?" he yelled.

"The man who will kill you if you ever try a stunt like this again," Reid answered evenly. He took a step forward, and was not surprised to see Keith flounder back a matching pace. In a voice suffused with hard promise, he went on, "I know where you left your Rover. I'd better hear it leave in the next five minutes, or I'll come after you."

Cammie's husband wanted to fight, wanted passionately to prevent Reid from staying behind in possession of the field and the woman. But the man knew his limitations, and he didn't have it in him to ignore them and attack anyway. Keith Hutton stood for a moment while his face took on a distorted grimace, as if he was about to cry. Then he whirled and disappeared into the darkness.

Reid waited. After a short time there came a powerful roar as the Land Rover sprang to life. The engine was slammed into gear. Tires squealed a protest as the vehicle tore off into the night.

Reid turned then, stepping back inside the porch and latching the screen. Cammie had flipped on the light in the great room. As he turned, he saw her standing in the door, watching him. Her face was still, her eyes huge and dark. He kept his gaze fastened above her collar bones with an effort. Still he saw, with a peripheral vision that was entirely too accurate, the perfect silhouette made by her body in the white nightgown with the light behind her.

He was not fool enough to destroy his pleasure by commenting on it. Moving forward enough to improve the view but not enough to disturb it, he said in neutral tones, "I'm sorry I couldn't get here before you were hurt."

"You were following Keith, weren't you?"

He heard the tremor, quickly stifled, in the words. He was touched by that sign of inner fortitude as by nothing in recent memory. It was his fault. If he had not been so enthralled with watching her in the moonlight earlier, he would not have lost sight of Keith. If he had kept her ex-husband in view, he would not have been forced to circle the camp house trying to find his trail, or to pick a deadbolt lock after he realized Keith was inside with her.

He looked down at his hand, which was still curled into a fist. Concentrating on relaxing it, he said, "I saw him at Evergreen. When he discovered you weren't home, he lit out like he might have some idea where to find you. So, yes, I followed him. It wouldn't have been necessary if you had told me where you were going."

"I didn't know I was supposed to report my movements," she said, spinning away from him and taking a few agitated steps into the great room.

His gaze, resting on her back and hips, was intent as he followed her into the house. Closing the back door, he locked it and flipped the dead bolt into place. He thought Cammie was aware of what he was doing from the stiffening of her shoulders, but she didn't object. It was, to his mind, a victory of sorts.

"You weren't," he said as he moved past her into the kitchen area. "And it won't matter after tonight. I've decided to stick a little closer to you from now on."

"Am I supposed to be honored?"

He paused while taking a handful of ice cubes from the freezer compartment of the refrigerator. The expression on her face, he saw, was half annoyed, half intrigued. He said, "I'll accept mildly grateful," and watched with grim appreciation as a flush moved slowly upward from under her scooped neckline.

"Oh, all right," she snapped with a gesture of capitulation, "I thank you very much. I'm glad to see you. I don't know what I would have done if you hadn't come charging in like the gang busters. Is that what you wanted to hear?"

He made no reply, but smiled a little in rueful self-knowledge as he searched through drawers for a plastic bag, found one, then dropped the ice cubes into it.

"If that's for me," she said, momentarily distracted by his actions, "I don't need it."

"Whatever you say, but you'll have a bruise to explain," he replied, his attention on sealing the bag's zip strip.

Her lips compressed an instant, then she abandoned her resistance. She said, "You are the most infuriating man. You'd have run a mile, I swear, if I had fallen on your neck crying my thanks the minute I saw you."

"You're probably right." She was exactly right, though there was no point in total honesty.

"And you don't even have the decency to deny it so I can be mad."

"Maybe I don't want you mad."

Her eyes glittered between narrow lids. "I think you do. Or did. I think you like raising my blood pressure. Well, if you're doing it now because you consider I need distracting from a little thing like almost being raped, you can think again."

"I think," he said as he moved toward her and pressed the ice pack he had made to her reddened cheek, "that you're sensible enough to figure out why I do most things. And to respond accordingly."

Her gaze somber, and centered somewhere near the second button of the camouflage shirt he wore with his jeans, she said, "I get so tired of being sensible."

In the stillness that gripped him, he felt the soft trip of his pulse. "Are you by any chance," he asked with care, "feeling generous in your victory?"

She lifted her gaze to meet his, and he saw her witch's multicolored eyes darken. Her lips, as they parted for her softly drawn breath, were smooth, delicately tinted with natural color, infinitely inviting. Her breasts lifted against the soft draping of thin fabric, peaking it with the slow tightening of her nipples. His every tendon contracted with response, and he steeled himself against the drawing pain.

Abruptly, she reached to take the plastic bag of ice from him, holding it to her face as she whirled and moved away. Seating herself on the couch, she crossed her other arm over her chest.

She had just proven that she understood him very well, Reid saw. It was perverse of him to wish that she hadn't. He would have liked an excuse for making love to her, any excuse. It wasn't just simple desire—if desire was ever simple—but a need to comfort, and to ease her pain. Which was the height of ego, he knew, to think his masculine essence had the power to heal.

Her voice stiff, she said, "What victory am I supposed

to have won? The paralegal who found out about the divorce has left town, and the evidence that might give me the mill is missing. You're the one who's ahead now."

"I heard; Lane, Endicott and Lane called me. You think I had something to do with this girl disappearing?"

"Who else is there with as good an excuse?"

"Any number of people, I would imagine," he answered.

"Keith didn't know about her, otherwise he would have had no reason to come here, no reason to do what he did."

"That's a matter of opinion," he said, his gaze steady. "He might have been driven by something other than money."

"I somehow doubt it."

"Believe me," he said, "it's possible."

Her eyes widened a fraction as she watched him, then she looked away. "You don't seem worried that people will think you're the one who got rid of Janet Baylor—the paralegal."

"People—or you?"

"Either one," she said, refusing to accept his attempt to make the question personal.

His thoughts moving in another direction, Reid answered with only half his attention. "Why should I care?"

"Why shouldn't you?" Cammie replied astringently.

He met her gaze, holding it. "I have as much stiff-necked pride as the next man, maybe even more. I'd just as soon be thought guilty as to be forced to prove my innocence."

"You expect to be taken at your own evaluation? That's all very well, but most people require something more."

"Do you really think I'm so desperate I would do away with this woman to gain title to the mill?" he demanded. It was so long before she answered, that he felt a tight, gripping sensation in his chest.

Finally she said, "No. But I don't know why I don't."

He was powerless to stop the slow smile that curved his mouth. "You trust me."

"Only to a certain point," she said quickly.

It was far enough for now. Or was it?

Standing there, watching her, he felt as needy as a small boy, yet there was nothing boyish about the desire that crashed through him in waves. There was something dark and desolate in her face as she returned his gaze, an unconscious yearning that was a reflection of the well-spring of passion trapped inside her. He had released it once, and was obsessed by the memory. He knew there were more subterranean depths he had not reached, that no man had, or perhaps could. Yet the compulsion to try was a constant ache, one he thought he would carry to his grave, and beyond.

It was possible that something of his thoughts was in his face. Her gaze flickered, falling away from his. She surged to her feet and moved away from him.

He took a quick step after her before forcing himself to stop. His words soft, and freighted with much more of what he felt than he intended, he said, "Don't be afraid. There's no need."

Her hair shifted across her back, catching the light in iridescent gleams as she turned her head. "You prowl around my house, invading when you please. You pull strings. You want to destroy the things I hold dear. You beat up people. You appear out of nowhere in the middle of the night. Afraid? I should run screaming through the woods. God knows why I don't."

"Courage." After a moment he added, "Fairness."

"I don't think so," she said with a quick shake of her head.

"What then?"

A crooked smile tugged at the delicate curves of her mouth. "Curiosity. Isn't that the sin Eve was banished from Eden for when all is said and done?"

He felt an arrested expression congealing his features,

but could not prevent it. He swung from her and began
searching through the cabinets once more. Finding what
he sought, he took down two glasses and poured a measure of twelve-year-old scotch in each one. He drank a
hefty swallow of his before walking toward her and
pressing the extra glass into her hand.

Only then did he dare ask, "Are you satisfied? Your
curiosity, I mean?"

She didn't answer at once. It wasn't that she didn't
know what to say, he thought, but that she was suspicious
of his meaning. And well she might be. He was, against
all decency and reason, testing the outer limits of what
lay between them.

She drank, her throat moving in a smooth glide as she
swallowed. A small shudder shook her as the liquor hit her
stomach. Abruptly, she said, "I have a few reservations."

"Such as what I hope to gain?" He swirled the amber
liquid in his glass, watching the agitation that matched
his own.

"That sounds like a good place to start."

"You don't believe it's your beautiful body?"

A soft laugh left her. "Hardly."

"Good," he said, and drank the still-turning liquor
before setting the glass on the nearest table and moving
closer. "Then you won't think I'm collecting a
reward. . . ."

She watched him come and stood statue-still, though
the pupils of her eyes dilated and her lips parted. He bent
his head with slow deliberation, holding her gaze, being
careful not to intimidate, alert for the slightest sign of
resistance.

Her mouth, as he pressed his own to the warm and perfect contours, had the heady sweetness of whiskey combined with the lingering mint of toothpaste. He felt her
jerk of reaction as his arms closed around her, then she
was quiescent. Her lips under his slowly warmed and
molded to his own. The tension eased from her, and he
drew her closer until she rested against him, every warm

and scented curve passing into him like warm clay adhering to a mold.

He brushed his mouth over hers, enjoying the tactile sensation and her small movements in response. He touched his tongue to the sensitive line of her lips' joining, tasting the moisture there, probing the dainty indentations of the corners. The skin was so delicate, so fine, that he thought he could feel the soft pulsing of her blood under it.

With an inarticulate murmur, she eased closer. He felt her fingertips as they began a warm slide from his shoulders to the back of his neck. A prickling of pleasure tingled along his spine, and he increased the pressure on her mouth, probing deeper.

The touch of her tongue was subtle. Ladylike. It suggested a conscious effort toward restraint that was more enticing than the most blatant of hot, thrusting passion. It invited exploration, promised rich wonders of wantonness if he were patient enough to discover them. He was enchanted, possibly meant to be, and didn't care. He had seen the wanton once before, and needed desperately to find her again. Blind, deaf, without conscious thought, he followed the lead of his spinning, seeking senses.

Until he felt her grow still, then begin to withdraw as insidiously as she had advanced.

Seconds, short seconds. That was all it had taken for her to destroy his defenses.

He was, he knew, dangerously close to the edge. There was a deep trembling at the center of his being as, one by one, he began to close down his responses.

She drew back, her eyes liquid, not quite focused. Her voice was husky as she said, "I don't like you."

"You never did," he agreed, his voice not quite steady.

"I hate what you're going to do to this town, this parish."

"I know." He touched his lips to the space between her brows, to the fragile curvatures of her eyelids.

"But I understand now, since I thought the mill might be mine, how hard it could be to disappoint people."

He tried to collect his thoughts, to hear what she was saying as well as the murmurous seduction of the tones that were produced in her throat and the feel of the gentle vibrations that her voice set off in his own chest. It wasn't easy when he was trying at the same time to fight back rampaging inclinations. "Do you?" he said, and was uncomfortably aware that the comment was less than articulate.

"So, even if the proof that I had some interest in the mill is gone, you don't have to feel responsible for me."

He leaned away from her, his gaze searching her face. "Is that what I'm doing?"

She frowned. "You said I could figure it out for myself."

"It was a dumb thing to say."

She slid from his arms. She didn't push or shove—he didn't remember releasing her of his own will—yet one moment she was there, and the next she was standing six feet away. "It made perfect sense," she said. "And still does."

He watched her as she turned and moved toward the bedroom door. When she was almost inside, he said, "Does that mean you're going to stop fighting me—and the sale?"

She gave him a smile that did not quite reach her eyes. "Never."

"Good," he said. "You had me worried."

She braced one hand on the door frame, looking at him over her shoulder. "You can go home now."

"You know better than that." His smile was twisted.

Was it relief that crossed her face, or resignation? He would have given much to know. She turned away before he could be sure, and disappeared into the dimness of the room.

Reid stood for long, endless minutes where she left

him. Finally, he shuddered with such violence he felt the ripple of it to his toes. Swinging around with a slicing movement, he left the house.

He prowled the outer perimeters of the property, skirting the house, walking the edge of the lake. Near the dock he stopped. He took deep breaths as he stood staring out over the water. Turning squarely toward the silver-gold path of the moonlight that streaked the glassy black surface, he accepted its glow on his skin like a caress. And he tried not to remember.

He couldn't help it. It was there at the end of the boat dock that he had first tried to close the distance between Cammie and himself. It hadn't worked; he had been too aggressive, too abrupt, too much at the mercy of hormones gone wild at the slightest touch of a particular female. Even now he winced at his clumsiness.

He wasn't that boy anymore. Or was he?

Maybe he was still trying to redeem himself, at least in his own mind. Maybe he had something to prove, a festering wound to be lanced before it could mend.

Sex as a knife to cut out old poison, old pain? Now there was a weird concept. It didn't say much for him or for the woman who might be the weapon. Yet what else was there, for him?

Reasons.

Was he so desperate that he would accept anything as an excuse for holding Cammie one more time? Could he ignore tomorrow for the sake of tonight? Even if he could, would it be fair? Or right? Or even halfway intelligent?

Taken in turn, the answers were: Yes. Yes. And no. No. God, no.

Was he going to do it anyway?

He set his shoulders, standing with his feet braced and his hands on his hips as he faced the flooding, passionless glare of the moon. His features hardened. As if drawn, he pivoted slowly to gaze up at the dark camp house. He lowered his hands to his sides. With deliberate steps he began to walk up the slope.

What he would do depended a great deal on Cammie. But not entirely.

Chapter Thirteen

⬛ ⬛ ⬛ *Cammie watched from her bedroom win-*
dow as Reid made his way back up to the house from the
lake. His long-legged stride, the swing of his arms and
set of his shoulders, gave her an odd feeling of vulnerability. His face in repose was dark and even intimidating.
The moon touched his hair with the sheen of silver-gilt,
and the wash of it across his features made him appear as
implacable and set on his private course as some ancient
knight on a desperate quest.

She had little compunction about studying him while
he was unaware. It should by all rights be her turn.

She released the breath she had not known she was
holding as he passed from view and entered the house.
Still she stood, thinking of the easy strength and quiet
assurance of his movements, thinking of the way he
smiled and the flashes of acute understanding that
gleamed in his eyes.

She wished she knew what she believed of him.
Instinct and logic, habit and justice, anger and attraction
warred inside her, and she was left hovering, distracted,
in the middle of them all.

She didn't hear him, didn't sense him, didn't know he
was there until she felt the slide of strong arms around
her and the warmth of him at her back. She gasped and
tried to turn, tried to yank herself out of his hold. He
shifted, and abruptly her arms were caught and clamped
to her sides. She couldn't bend, couldn't turn, couldn't

free a hand, couldn't move. The quick, short breaths that lifted her chest pressed her breasts against his hard forearms, crossed in front of her. His close clasp was neither tight nor hurtful, but there was no weakness in it.

The urge to fight swept through her. She subdued it with an effort that brought the dampness of perspiration to her forehead. Struggling would not only be undignified, it would be useless against this man. That was a lesson she had already learned.

Recognition of her helplessness sent a strange flutter of sensation through her stomach and into the lower part of her body. Her voice tight, she said, "Let me go."

"I don't think so." The words were low and without inflection.

"What are you doing? You just got through annihilating Keith for this."

"I don't intend to force you, if that's what you're afraid of."

She gritted her teeth against a wave of dizziness that had nothing to do with fear. "No? What, then?"

"Friendly persuasion."

"I don't feel friendly!" she snapped.

"No?" He moved his arm so that it brushed across her nipples. The response was immediate, and obvious to them both.

"Don't," she said, the single word quieter, with a ragged undertone.

"Then listen to me."

There could be no harm in that. She gave a reluctant nod.

He settled his hold more firmly, so she was drawn even closer against him. "I was wondering," he said against her hair, "if you could consider me in the light of an endangered species? I'll pretend to be a woodpecker, and you can pity me."

"I never knew a man who needed pity less," she answered in low tones.

"Compassion, then. I'm not proud."

But he was, and she knew it. And so knew, too, the effort required to make his plea, and also to keep his voice even and leavened with humor as he did it.

Around the tightness in her throat she said, "Only for a single moment, a single night?"

"It's the way they come, one at a time and with no guarantees." His lips brushed the hair at her temple, as if in apology.

She didn't trust him, no matter what he thought. There were too many things that were unexplained. And yet, her body was tired of fighting the unbridled attraction that lay between them. It overwhelmed her with sensations that could not be ignored. It made her think that doubts and suspicions were frail things compared to the magic of the desire spilling into her blood.

"What do you want me to say?" she asked, the words shaded with distress.

"Yes, that's all," he answered quietly. "Just—yes."

She stared straight ahead, out into the night. It was a moment before she answered. "Will you kiss me first?"

"Turn your head," he said, as if he suspected a trick and was wary of loosening his hold.

She did more. Leaning her head back into his wide shoulder, she relaxed, allowing her body to rest fully against his taut form. She shifted a little, tilting her head back as she turned her face toward him.

He bent to touch her lips with his, feathering their satin surfaces with light strokes of his tongue, tasting her surrender. He took his time, as if there was nothing but time left in the world, or as if this one kiss might be all that time allowed.

With gentle care he laid the length of his mouth along hers, fitting upper and lower lips together, matching edges and corners. Brushing his head back and forth, he used delicate friction to increase the heat between them, then flicked along the line of the joining with moist pressure that allowed him to slip inside. He skimmed the fragile inner lining, flicked across the sleek porcelain smoothness of her teeth, and plunged in abrupt, velvet penetration to engage her tongue in his play.

She could not escape, but it was the last thing she wanted. Rapture vibrated along her nerves with the sweetness of a chord struck by a master musician. She felt it swelling, invading her every pore with its sensual melody. She met the sinuous heat of him, twining, following his lead. The flavor of scotch and heated male melted on her tongue, assaulting her senses. Indulging every whim and need, she explored the silken sleekness of his mouth in her turn, returning incitement for incitement.

Shock and delight rippled through her as his hand cupped her breast. She felt the firm globe tighten, straining into his palm with a rush of escalating sensation. He rubbed the ball of his thumb across the nipple, teasing it to beaded firmness with care and close attention. His hard hand and her yielding flesh, his vital strength and her defenseless hunger, made point and counterpoint of a passionate melody. She shivered with the piercing rise of it inside her, with its clear, vibrant harmony.

His heart throbbed in his chest; she could feel it against her shoulder. He tested the corner of her mouth, then blazed a trail of kisses to the point of her chin and along her jaw to her ear. He flicked her earlobe with his tongue and drew it between his lips. She felt the gentle nip of his teeth, the suction, and her breasts tingled while pleasure writhed along her nerves.

"Take off your gown for me," he whispered, his warm breath fluttering over her ear.

She would have liked to comply, but she wasn't sure she could stand alone. "You take it off," she said with an ache in her voice. "Please?"

His breathing was deep and not quite steady. His hands were sure, however, as one by one he released the small pearl buttons that held her scooped neckline. Tilting his head to watch over her shoulder, he spread the edges of the opening wide. His chest expanded as he exposed the smooth curves of her breasts to the light of the moon falling through the window glass. Tucking the extra material out of the way, he drew his fingertips over the twin satin-smooth rises, outlining them, fitting them slowly and completely within the cages of his long fingers.

For long moments he held her, gently plucking her nipples to tender, elongated peaks. Then he turned her in his arms, brought her to face him. He brushed his lips across her brow, the tip of nose, her lips, her chin, then lowered his head to moisten first one nipple, then the other, with his tongue. Settling on one, he took it into the hot wetness of his mouth, drawing on it with wickedly gentle adhesion.

Desire ran with the effervescent glide of liquid moonlight through her veins. In it also flowed an element of enchantment for his consummate skill and the courtesy that caused him to exercise it. Some close-held fastness within herself that had never succumbed to force, that was held fast against crudity, crumbled soundlessly under the onslaught of his intuitive caresses.

"Reid . . ." The broken whisper was involuntary, a soft plea rather than a protest.

He lifted his head. Doubt and passion were dark in his eyes as he searched her flushed face and heavy eyelids. His voice hardly more than a rough whisper, he said, "You want me to stop?"

She shook her head in a violent negative. What she wanted was impossible to put into words.

The smile that rose in his eyes was strained, yet luminous with satisfaction, before he shielded it with his lashes. He pressed his face into the valley between her breasts, exploring it with lips and tongue. His warm breath drifting over her skin brought prickling sensitivity to the surface.

He pushed the cap sleeves of her gown from her shoulders and down her arms. The neckline caught for a moment low on her hips, leaving her like some living nude statue with the gown's draping fullness in folds around her calves and ankles. He drew back, his gaze tracing the curves highlighted in moon glow and the hollows left in shadow. Slowly he followed with his hands. As his palms smoothed into the slender curvature of her waist and down over the swelling of her hips, he dislodged the clinging gown. It whispered down, settling in a crumpled pile around her feet.

The expression on his face was almost like pain. It did strange things to her. She felt some deep tenderness ripple through her while she stood unmoving, with her hands held with palms out at her sides. She had never been worshipped before, never felt exalted, never in her life known the incredible sense of infinite giving that pervaded her. She wanted him, wanted to do and be whatever he needed of her. In that moment the giving seemed the reason she had been created, the ultimate answer to her own intolerable craving.

There was urgency in the grasp of his hard fingers as he knelt and drew her toward him. She rested her hands on his shoulders and closed her eyes, letting her head fall back, her hair hanging in a shining, tapering mass below her shoulder blades. The wet heat of his tongue swirling around her navel took her breath. The tracery he made across the flat surface of her belly enthralled her. The nuzzling of his face in the triangle of fine curls where her thighs joined caused her legs to tremble. The feel of his warm breathing there at that most secret entrance to her body, sent her mind tumbling, rootless, into uncharted realms of sensation.

Thorough and without inhibition, he followed the fluid creases, testing their petal-smooth texture, seeking her essence. He drew out her response, encouraged it, reveled in it. While her hands tangled in his hair, clenching and unclenching, he found the dainty protrusion nestled at the apex of her being, and lavished his most exquisite care upon it.

The low sound she made had a fretted edge of desperation. Her hands curved into talons indenting his skin under his shirt before some last vestige of recognition made her relax them. His hands gripped her hips tighter in response. He kneaded the firm curves, as if he would mold them to fit his hands alone. Then he freed one hand, sliding it forward between their bodies and upward along her inner thigh. With his fingertips he parted fine curls and moist, tender flesh, probing with one finger into her soft depths.

The pleasure was so abrupt, so ferocious, it took her breath, her voice, the brightness of the night. She arched over him, her hands loosing their grip, the fingers flexing wide with the sudden, uncontrollable release of tension. She felt herself collapsing, but could not prevent it.

He supported her as he lowered her to her knees before him. His eyes burned with intense blue fire as he gathered her close. He took her mouth with hungry force, demanding that she meet it. She gave way, acquiescing, murmuring in wordless gratification. He thrust his tongue deep, withdrawing it, plunging again. Holding that intimate invasion, he skimmed downward over her body once more to the heated softness spread open for him. With unremitting skill he pressed into her.

Her body welcomed his touch, beckoning with rhythmic internal pulsing. He followed that heartbeat cadence, insinuating a second finger as her muscles relaxed enough to accept it, as her own hot wetness eased the way.

Mad, she was going mad with the paroxysms of feeling that rampaged through her in waves. She could not bear it, could not contain it in body and mind and remain sane and whole. Release had to be found; he had to join her in it or she would explode. Groping blindly for the front of his shirt, she tore at the buttons.

He came to her aid, ripping his shirt open with a single hard wrench, dragging it from his jeans while she reached for his belt. He brushed her faltering fingers aside while he unfastened it with one hand, then released the snap of his jeans and skimmed down the zipper.

He didn't halt her questing fingers as she found the heated length of him that lifted from his briefs. Still, his indrawn breath sounded hard-pressed, especially as she gauged his thickness and springing rise with intense gratification.

As if to distract himself from her careful ministrations, he weighed her breasts in his hands. And he watched, barely breathing, as the dusky rose nipples with their flaring aureoles contracted into puckered sweetness under his kneading touch.

"You are so beautiful," he said in low wonder, almost as if to himself.

"And you." The whisper was so soft it was like the sough of a night breeze.

His hold tightened. Her hand clenched.

Abruptly, he dropped his hands to her waist, lifting her even as he unfolded his long legs and lowered himself to his back on the floor. She was pulled between his hard thighs, drawn upward to lie on his chest. She rested there a moment, pressing her cheek into the crisp gold mat of hair on his chest, rubbing her face against the hard thud of his heart.

"Whenever you want it," he said, pulling her higher, positioning her so that his probing, slightly wet hardness nudged at her softness.

She raised herself a little and settled upon him, watching his face as she took an inch or two of him into her body. His expression was so open, yet so fierce in his concentrated pleasure. His ragged breathing and the jarring of his heart signaled the turmoil he concealed, the quiver of his eyelids the only indication of his faultless restraint.

The need to return to him some measure of the ecstasy he had given her was an ache inside her. It pressed higher, bringing the rise of tears to her eyes. They pooled there as she sank upon him farther, taking more of him.

She felt his shudder of reaction. "God," he said, his

voice rasping. Bracing himself, he lunged upward, reaching her depths with a single, hard twist of his hips.

She cried out with the onslaught of bliss. Clutching his hard-muscled shoulders, she squeezed her eyes shut and undulated her hips, taking him into the final, unconquered fastness of herself. She wanted him deep, fixed, embedded.

He raised himself to answer her need, giving her the friction required. Until it was no longer enough.

They moved in concert then, gliding together in a rapport that went deeper than two fitted bodies, deeper than heated skin against heated skin, deeper than soft gasps and whispered entreaties and low sounds of near unbearable pleasure.

Nothing had prepared her for the grandeur of what flowed between them. Always before, she had been too conscious of the ridiculous indignity of physical coupling. She had never known this transcending grace that touched the joining of bodies with intimations of the sublime.

They rose higher, mounting toward the far off crescendo they both anticipated, moving, ever moving to the ageless and elemental music of loving. It was, instead, a silent meshing of souls, two parts of a whole meeting in perfect balance, finding the delicate symmetry of motion and emotion. She held nothing in reserve, nor did he. Breathless with effort, feverish with longing, they strove.

And crashed suddenly into a single note of ecstatic, piercing clarity. It rang through them both, one so fine, so powerful and near impossible, that it swept them together and left them clinging with desperate hands.

One that could, if they were not careful, shatter their very hearts.

Chapter Fourteen

■ ■ ■ *Cammie had always considered that women* who went straight from one troubled relationship into another lacked common sense. She was beginning to understand that emotions didn't lend themselves to tidy concepts of correct time and place.

She had never been at the mercy of what she felt before. During her marriage, she had maintained a detachment that made her stand back and judge her actions and adjust her behavior to keep her from becoming too involved with other men and risky situations. She had always thought it came from a moral upbringing plus semi-intelligent choice. Now she had to wonder if it had not been fear. Or simply that the temptation had never been quite so compelling.

These thoughts rambled across the surface of her mind as she lay in bed in the bright light of morning and watched Reid come toward her with a towel wrapped around his waist and a cup of coffee in each hand. Common sense should have told her to run from him like a rabbit.

"Cream, no sugar, right?" he said, as he placed her cup on the bedside table. His expression was warm as his gaze rested on the soft skin exposed above the sheet, but his voice held nothing more than polite inquiry.

He missed little. She had no doubt he was as aware of how uncomfortable she was with him as he was of her coffee habits. She nodded her agreement without quite meeting his eyes.

He left the room again, returning moments later with a stack of buttered whole wheat toast on a plate. Setting the plate in the middle of the bed, he climbed in beside her and leaned back on the pillows. He crossed his long legs at the ankles and reached for a piece of toast, biting into it with obvious enjoyment.

As her gaze rested on the contours of his arm with its coating of hair that glinted gold in the morning light, Cammie was reminded of how she had come to be in the bed. He had picked her up from the floor where she had lain half stunned when their loving was done. Placing her on the mattress, he had begun again. It was done without fanfare, without permission, with a kind of insistent beguilement that made protest impossible.

It wasn't that he was insatiable, but rather that his need was more than surface deep. It was as if he had years of deprivation to make up for. Thinking of it now made her stomach muscles flutter in reaction.

Was he as amazing as she thought, or had there been more wrong with her marriage than she had guessed? Her limited experience made it impossible to know.

She reached for her coffee and sipped it. Perfect. She should have known.

Her voice neutral, she said, "What do we do now?"

"What would you like?" he asked, his eyes bright blue, the firm curves of his mouth tugging in a wickedly reminiscent grin.

It was a question she had answered more than once during the night before. She gave him a look of scathing reproach, though she could not prevent the flush that highlighted her cheekbones.

He tried to look thoughtful, but it wasn't easy with impudence lingering in his eyes. "We could have lunch and dinner in bed, with a snack or two—or something— in between."

"You know what I mean!"

"Yes, but the only answers I have are the ones that interest me," he said, sobering slightly.

"We can't stay in bed forever."

"There's something radically wrong with the world then."

"You would be bored stiff," she asserted, taking another swallow of her coffee.

His grin returned. "Lord, I hope so."

She choked and coughed to clear her throat before she could speak. "You're impossible!"

"A little unlikely, maybe, but not impossible."

She fell silent. She was trying to face the future, while he was denying it. She had no idea whether his evasion was from a momentary unwillingness to make the effort or because he knew there was nothing ahead for them.

She hadn't expected promises. She preferred not to think of them.

He released a long sigh, and tossed what was left of his piece of toast back on the plate. "I would like to take you back to the Fort with me and keep you there. At least you'd be safe."

Safety. No other consideration.

She said, "I doubt Keith will try anything again. All he wanted was to nullify the divorce." When Reid only watched her, making no comment, she added, "That is what you were talking about?"

"I think you'll have to explain it to me," he said, his voice deliberate.

The whole thing would have been less embarrassing, she thought, if she could have claimed that Keith was inflamed by passion. She gave the simple facts and fell silent.

"I should have killed him." The words carried an undertone of suppressed violence.

The news that Wen had given her, that Reid had beaten up Keith in his office at the mill, flitted through her mind. It must have been true; she had seen the signs the night before in the discoloration around her ex-husband's eye and the way he favored his ribs. She had also seen the ease with which Reid had dealt with him. And Keith's fear.

"It's a great temptation," she said with astringency, "but I don't much want it on my conscience."

"Then we go on exactly as before."

"Is that a suggestion or a question?"

He gave her a direct look. "Think of it as an attempt to find out what you have in mind."

"Nothing," she said in exasperation. What she had wanted, she well knew, was to know what he intended, what he expected from the future. Whether from caution or cunning, or some male instinct of self-protection, he was not giving that away.

"Then," he said with a faint smile, "nothing is what we'll do."

It wasn't quite that easy, of course. They read month-old news magazines and ancient *National Geographics* while shifting back and forth in the bed to use various parts of each other's anatomies for pillows. They listened to a Mozart collection on Cammie's portable CD player. They padded back and forth in the kitchen in their bare feet, getting in each other's way as they made tuna salad and boiled eggs and iced tea for a late lunch. And they made love slowly, then showered, took each other fast and hard, and showered again. Then had a light dinner—consisting of apple pie and ice cream—in bed, food not being a priority.

It was only as morning came again that the awkwardness between them returned. They remembered they had to be back in town early; both had jobs and obligations. As they finished their breakfast and got dressed, the stilted awareness of their differences grew slowly to elephantine proportions. No amount of humor or common sense could make their association seem normal, much less lasting.

Reid suggested that he see her back to Evergreen. She agreed, since it was easier. She had no desire to linger at the camp house. There had always been uncomfortable memories there. Now there were too many by far.

Still, when they reached the big house on the hill, she didn't want him to go. Watching him drive away, she felt deserted and desolate. It was as if he took her security with him.

The morning advanced. In an effort to distract her thoughts, she put in a call to Fred Mawley. He seemed to take it as a personal compliment and was inclined to chat. It was long moments before she could put the question on her mind to him. No, he hadn't gotten around to revamping her will just yet; he hadn't known she was in any particular hurry—she was a lot younger than most of his clients who troubled to make a formal division of their estates. She knew most women didn't bother, didn't she, especially in Louisiana, where bequests were fairly cut and dried? Yes, he had the joint will he'd drawn up for her and Keith somewhere there on his desk, along with the changes she wanted. He'd get right on it. And how about dinner on Saturday night? They could go to the Tower Club in Monroe. It was quiet, very exclusive. Since he had invested in membership, he needed to show up often to get his money's worth.

She refused dinner, with all due appreciation. There was, thank goodness, another meeting of the group opposing the mill that night. They were to map out further plans for free publicity for the cause.

Thinking about the upcoming meeting, Cammie realized she needed to get on with her plans for the day. She was behind on her personal effort to solidify the organization.

She got out her address book and placed several calls to the state capital, to men and women who might have ideas to offer or an interest in helping. She was proud of the level of interest expressed by various people, from the well-known photographer of Louisiana wildlife to the widow of an oil man from Shreveport, who occupied her time with worthwhile causes. Cammie also got in touch with a longtime friend at the Wildlife and Fisheries Department, inviting him to come and speak to their group on the effects of timber harvesting on the watershed. It didn't take a lot of arm-twisting to get an agreement.

She was less successful when she turned to making local calls to remind people about the meeting or to ask them to join the group. Women she had known for years were extremely rude; one even hung up on her. A man called her several uncomplimentary names, and told her she needed a houseful of kids to keep her busy so she wouldn't meddle where she didn't belong. The last person she spoke to, an elderly friend of Aunt Beck's, told her she was a disgrace to her parents and grandparents.

Cammie sat for a long time after she replaced the receiver, staring into space with her hand still on the phone. She'd known that some in town were upset with her stand on the mill, but hadn't realized how high feelings were running. The thought of so much ill will directed against her made her feel sick. That friends and neighbors, people she'd known all her life, could turn against her so quickly left her stunned.

It was hard for her to understand how little the average person cared about the land. They seemed to think nothing could or would change it. A part of that, she thought, was the character of the land itself in Louisiana. It was so rich, so fecund and endlessly replenishing.

The rains filled the branches and creeks, the rivers and the swamps that were the catch basins for the overflow. Soil that wasn't held in place by terraces or trees and plant roots shifted and moved, but seldom went far since the terrain was too level for it to gain much speed or distance. Heat and rain caused rampant growth; just keeping the roadsides clear was a major headache each year, as saplings and shrubs and tall grasses leaped into view-distorting obstacles at the curves. Tree saplings that seeded in old flower beds around abandoned houses could shoot up almost overnight. If not cut back, they became trees that supported vines, sheltered briers, and gave shade for the fungi and lichen, mold and mildew that destroyed roofs, walls, and foundations. An abandoned house could, in a few short years, be literally pulled down by the weight of the vines, dead leaves, limbs, and the organisms that ate into it.

The cycles of life and change were constant, and always had been. Most people seemed to think that a little destruction by way of control was a good thing, and a lot of it couldn't hurt much. They were wrong, of course, but there seemed no way to make them see it.

The phone rang under Cammie's hand. She jumped as if she'd been slapped, then shook her head in irritation.

"Cammie, is that you? I've been trying to get hold of you for ages. Are you all right?"

The voice, with the querulous, die-away sound of a personality stunted by being constantly overborne, belonged to her aunt, Sara Taggart, her mother's sister. Cammie answered with as much easy pleasantness as she could manage.

"Your uncle suggested I should call you, and really, I can't help thinking he's right this time," her aunt said when the usual commonplaces had been exchanged. "I don't know what to make of it, truly I don't. But I couldn't see keeping it from you, not after everything that's happened."

"What is it, Aunt Sara?" Cammie asked. She tried to keep the impatience from her voice but wasn't sure how well she succeeded.

"It's about this young woman who's turned up missing, the Baylor girl. One of the ladies in our congregation has a brother with cancer. He's been going over to St. Francis Hospital for his radiation treatments. His sister drives him, since his wife has to work—"

"What about the girl, Aunt Sara?" Cammie said in stringent tones. Her hand, gripping the receiver, had a sudden cramp from the tightness of her hold.

"I'm getting to it, Cammie. Seems the lady from church saw the young woman get out of her car and into another one driven by a man. She recognized her because she used to live by the family before Janet was married. She swears the vehicle was a Jeep, and the man driving it was Reid Sayers."

That someone in Greenley would witness whatever a person might be trying to hide did not surprise her. There was no place within a reasonable driving distance that was safe for any kind of clandestine activity, from making a shady deal to indulging in an afternoon's delight. People from the town were too mobile, too active, and too eternally interested in their friends and neighbors. Someone always saw. Someone always told. Word got around.

What had Reid been doing? Cammie wondered. Putting the paralegal up at some motel in Monroe? Taking her to meet a bus? Had he driven her far enough away to rent a car to drive out of state? Had he sent her away with enough money to start a new life?

Or just possibly, her body would turn up somewhere in a year or two in a shallow grave.

No. Cammie couldn't believe it; she wouldn't think such things.

"Cammie? You still there, dear? I didn't mean to upset you."

"What did you mean to do, then?" She heard the anger in her voice, but couldn't help it.

"Jack felt you had to know the truth. It wouldn't do, he said, for you to be taken in by this man. I mean, you know what Reid Sayers is—the family he comes from. And he's been gone from here so long, has turned into such an outsider. You hear such odd tales—there's no way of knowing what he might do. You must not forget that."

"I doubt that's possible." Even if she managed it, there would always be somebody to remind her.

"Maybe I should send your uncle over to talk to you. You know, he's had disappointments and pain himself. His trial by fire in Vietnam, when the Good Lord tested him for the ministry, gave him a special understanding for the troubles that come to us all. He spends long hours, day and night sometimes, giving aid and comfort to people."

Cammie had heard about her uncle's call to the Church and his devotion to duty many times. "There's nothing to face, Aunt Sara. I appreciate the information, but you don't need to worry about me."

The tone of her voice signaled an end to the conversation. Her aunt accepted it without argument. "Well, then, I won't keep you. You let us hear from you, now, let us know you're all right. And come to see us."

Cammie agreed, issuing an invitation of her own that was as empty as the one she had received. Then she hung up.

The sighting was a mistake, it had to be. Or else a vicious rumor circulated by someone with an overactive imagination. Janet Baylor may have met a man—nothing was more likely—but that didn't mean the man was Reid.

Anyway, he'd told her point-blank he had nothing to do with Janet's disappearance. Hadn't he?

She couldn't quite remember his exact words. It was possible he'd only led her to suppose he had no connection.

No, it couldn't be. He wouldn't do something that underhanded.

Or would he?

What did she know about him, really? Going to bed with a man didn't guarantee insight into his character.

And yet, where else was a person so completely himself. If you couldn't judge someone by the degree of thoughtfulness and tender concern displayed in the act of love, then how was it ever possible to know what he was like inside?

She was so disturbed that she couldn't concentrate, couldn't settle in to any task. She needed to unpack her overnight bag, but couldn't bring herself to look at the clothes and nightgown she'd scarcely worn. Persephone had made a grocery list, but the last thing Cammie wanted was to go shopping. She thought of driving to the antique shop, but there seemed no point if she was going to be useless when she got there.

Working among her flowers had a way of calming her. She picked up a pair of well-worn gardening gloves and a set of clippers on her way out of the house.

She spent an hour or so in the yard, cutting bouquets of azaleas for the house while pruning them at the same time, fertilizing the camellias and pulling winter grass from the annual beds. The day was warm and pleasant. It was time to begin setting out summer bedding plants. She decided to see what the local garden center had available.

Cammie went inside for her purse. Heading out again, she noticed Reid's robe, which she'd worn home from the Fort days ago. Persephone had laundered it and left it lying on a hall table, ready for her to return to its owner. She could drop it off as she went; it would only be a little out of her way.

Reid wasn't at home but should be back in a little while, the housekeeper said. Lizbeth offered coffee and cake, if Cammie cared to wait, but Cammie refused, explaining where she was headed as she passed the robe over.

"I've been wondering where this thing got off to; it was Mr. Reid's favorite, rag that it is," Lizbeth said. The tall, brown woman, her hair in a coronet of braids, smoothed the soft flannel with long, graceful fingers.

"I didn't realize—"

"Now don't you worry. He knew where to go looking for it, I expect, if he'd wanted it that bad."

Cammie could only agree, accepting in resignation that Lizbeth was fully aware of what was going on. She made her excuses and turned to go.

"About this mill business, Mrs. Hutton . . ." The housekeeper's voice trailed away, as if she was uncertain of the wisdom of speaking.

Cammie swung back, searching the other woman's face, which was creased concern. "Yes? What is it?"

"I've been wishing I could talk to you about it. Mr. Reid is worrying and worrying, trying to do the right thing—which isn't always as easy as some folks make out. His daddy, you know, taught him early to look on all sides of a thing, and he's trying, but he's got this pain inside him, this worry about what's best for folk."

"Yes, I know," Cammie said in encouragement as Lizbeth paused.

"See, he knows my man Joseph and my oldest two boys depend on wood hauling for a living—they got two pulpwood trucks between them. My youngest, Ty, now, he's making his career in the Air Force, so he's all right. But the others got to cut wood while the sun shines, 'cause it's a real trick to get it out of the woods during the winter when it rains so. The way things stand now, the mill can't always take what they cut during the summer, so it cuts into their pay. Oh, they make enough to live, long as I do my part, but they can't build much of a nest egg to carry over the bad times. The only way they're ever gonna get ahead is if the mill gets bigger, so it uses more wood. They're proud not to be on the welfare; they feel like men. But it's sad not to see much future down the road."

"I'm sorry, but they would be worse off if there were no more trees out there to cut."

"Joseph and my boys, they're careful. They leave the seed trees standing, just like Mr. Reid's daddy always used to say. They know how to notch a tree so it falls without tearing up everything left behind. They're good woodsmen—Joseph's daddy and granddaddy worked on logging crews back before there was such a thing as a chain saw. They know their jobs depend on taking care of the woods."

"And what about the wildlife? The best time for cutting trees is the worst time for nesting birds."

"They watch out for owl and woodpecker nests, and

cut around them. Sometimes they make a mistake, and they hate that. It's sad, but these things are all through life."

Cammie met the housekeeper's soft, dark eyes. "Sometimes these things get to be more than people— and trees and animals—can stand any longer. Then something has to be done."

"The Good Lord knows that's true," Lizbeth said with a shake of her head. "But if good-hearted folks would just get together, they could work it out. Don't you think?"

"It would be nice if they could," Cammie said with a wry smile. "It would be more than nice, it would be wonderful. But not everybody has a good heart."

"Now that's the living truth, and I can't deny it."

The housekeeper had made her point, and did not try to keep Cammie any longer. As Cammie went on her way, however, the woman's words stayed with her. That personal glimpse into the problems of others was disturbing. It was one thing to know of such things in general, something else to come face-to-face with them.

Sympathy, in a case like this, was counterproductive. She couldn't let it affect her, any more than she could turn coward because not everyone approved of what she was doing. Knowing that didn't make it any easier to dismiss.

As usual, she found more than she needed at the garden center. She bought a half-dozen flats of impatiens, also a pink mandevilla vine for the gazebo and a pair of rose-colored hibiscus to go on either side of the back steps. It was growing dark by the time she pulled into her driveway again with her haul.

Persephone had left a plain dinner of a pot of fresh vegetable soup and a pan of corn bread. Cammie ate early. She wasn't really hungry, but knew she should eat; she'd skipped lunch without thinking about it.

She was putting her dishes in the dishwasher when the knock came. She turned on the porch light and glanced out around the door curtain before she opened the back door. The sheriff stood there, heavy and solid in the dimness.

"Sorry to bother you, Cammie," Bud Deerfield said, touching a finger to his hat brim. "We had a call about a man being seen sneaking around the house here."

"Tonight?" Her voice was blank with surprise.

"Just a few minutes ago. I was close by when the report came in, thought I'd check it out."

Reid, of course. Or was it? She had thought he was too skilled to allow himself to be seen. It could be Keith again, in which case she might yet be grateful for the concern of nosy neighbors.

She stepped back, setting the door wide for her cousin to enter. "I'll be glad for you to look, but I haven't seen or heard a thing."

"Count yourself lucky." Bud wiped his feet on the mat with a deliberate gesture and stepped inside. He moved ahead of her down the hall, talking as he went. "Seems there's been a rash of prowlers in this neighborhood lately. At least three different widow women have been making life miserable for us, seeing men coming and going at all hours. It's mostly in their own yards, though."

"Have you managed to find anybody?" Cammie frowned at his broad back as she followed him.

"Not so far. I'd have said it was this business with the Baylor girl has the widows upset, except it started before that happened." He stepped into the living room, glanced around, then turned back toward the sun room.

"You think there's a connection?"

"Who knows?" His voice echoed back to her with a hollow sound as he made the circle from the sun room through the doorway leading out into the hall again. Passing her, he continued toward the front of the house once more. He swung around the newel post of the staircase and started up.

He found nothing, though he looked through closets

and bathrooms, and, to be on the safe side, got down on his knees and peered under the beds. He went outside then, suggesting that she lock the door behind him and be sure and check her windows when he had gone. She saw him circling the house, skirting the edge of the lawn where it met the woods, poking his head into the gazebo and the garage.

Ten minutes later he was back at the door. Just because it had been a dry-water run didn't mean there was nobody around, he told her. All she had to do if she heard anything was give a holler. He'd have somebody out there again before she could get her foot back.

She waited until he was out of sight down the drive. Crossing her arms over her chest, clasping her elbows, she walked back down the hall. Standing in the foyer at the foot of the stairs, she called, "All right. You can come out now."

Nothing. She felt a little foolish, but that made no difference if she was really alone. Some instinct told her she was not. And she didn't know which was more disturbing, the unbidden knowledge or the implication that she was so attuned to Reid that she could sense his presence. She turned slowly around where she stood, listening for sounds from upstairs, staring into dim corners.

"Reid?"

He materialized from out of the sun room, a shadow emerging from shadows. His footsteps were noiseless on the old floorboards, his movements easy yet alert. He stopped six feet away from her and stood waiting, poised.

She swallowed on the sudden tightness in her throat that she hadn't known was there. "How long have you been here?"

"Long enough." The words were laconic. "I was coming to see you when the sheriff drove up and I saw you let him in the house. I thought I'd check into it before I showed myself."

"How did you—why didn't Bud see you?"

"You two were making enough racket to cover the

retreat of a regular platoon. All I had to do was stay a
room or two ahead of you."

"But if you could do that, then—"

"There's nobody else in here with us, take my word
for it." He smiled a little as he spoke, though the humor
quickly faded. "And whoever your neighbors may have
seen outside, it wasn't me."

"Are you sure? I don't mean to doubt your word, but
anybody can make a misstep."

"Missteps and mistakes get you killed where I've been
these last few years," he said flatly.

If it hadn't been Reid out there, then who was it? Not
Keith, surely; not after the night before. However, there
was that other figure she thought she saw last week.
She'd almost convinced herself it was Keith that time,
but had never been entirely sure.

At least she could accept that Reid was telling the
truth. There was no reason for him to lie, after all. It
wasn't like the disappearance of Janet Baylor. There was
reason and more for that.

His eyes, resting on her troubled face, were dark blue
and trenchant. "What is it? More of my past sins coming
back to haunt me?"

The urge to tell him what her aunt had said, and hear
what he had to say in defense, was strong. Instead she
said, "Have there been so many?"

"A few." His face was somber as he gazed down at
her. "Though if it's gory details you want, you'll have to
try somewhere else."

"No, thanks," she said in clipped tones.

Turning from him, she moved back down the hall and
into the kitchen. He hesitated, then trailed after her, but
she paid scant attention. In the back of her mind she was
trying to decide what she was going to do about tonight.

"Lizbeth told me you came by the house," he said,
propping against the counter with his hands in his
pockets. "You could have saved yourself a trip. I was
coming over anyway."

She barely glanced at him. "I couldn't remember to hand over the robe when you were around."

"That's encouraging," he said with a smile, then added, "actually, I thought maybe there was something special you wanted to talk about."

She paused in wiping the countertop. "Such as?"

Irritation crossed his face as he said, "I don't know, Cammie. Any number of things: Keith, the mill, the missing papers, anything and everything that's on your mind. Or nothing at all, if you just wanted to see me. Hell, I can be optimistic every now and then."

"I wouldn't advise it," she said, the corners of her lips firm.

He lifted a hand to rake it through his hair. "All right, what is it now? What have I done, or not done, to put you in a snit?"

"Nothing," she answered shortly, if without truth.

"No? Then why is it that everytime we see each other, we have to start all over from scratch?"

She swung to face him. "What did you expect, that I would fling myself into your arms? Drag you into bed?"

"It would have been a nice change."

"Forget it."

"But I would settle for a welcome kiss."

There was a firmness behind the steady light in his eyes that disturbed her. She said, "I'm not sure you're welcome."

"Too bad. I'm here, with or without."

"Why?" she demanded. "Why, when you know I don't want you?"

His smile was grim. "I am nothing if not constant."

There was in the inflection of his words, and in their deliberate choice, a hint of meaning she could not quite grasp. Nor was she certain she wanted to.

She watched him with measuring eyes, remembering the moment in the early hours of the morning when she'd wakened in his arms. She had been lying tucked into the curve of his body, with her back to his chest. He hadn't been asleep, might never have slept at all. He lay with one arm holding her firmly against him and the fingers of his other hand in her hair. He was carefully straightening the silken mass, drawing it strand by strand across the pillow.

She'd felt so protected in that moment, so incredibly content. There had been a rightness in it like nothing she'd ever known. She had wanted to lie like that, unmoving, for the rest of her life.

It wasn't going to happen; he had as good as told her he was incapable of it. What choice did she have except to believe him? And wasn't that for the best, anyway, when it seemed that in her foolish fancies she had turned him into something he'd never been, something he could never be at all?

A considering look settled over his face. He said quietly, "You may not have wanted to talk to me, but there's something I wanted to say to you. If I could show you a way we both could come out ahead on the mill expansion, would you at least think about it?"

"Certainly," she said in chill tones. "I'm not unreasonable."

A muscle stood out in his jaw, but he went on without direct comment. "It's entirely possible to insert clauses in the purchase contract of the mill that would guarantee environmental controls. The Swedes could reject the terms, but I think they're anxious enough to establish a presence in this part of the country that they'll agree. It was always my intention to include certain safeguards. If you would like to add your input, others could be drafted. That's supposing I retain ownership. If it passes to you, then you'll do as you please. But it would still be a way to protect what's important to you while benefiting the community at the same time."

Her gaze was wide as she considered his suggestion. Abruptly, she turned away. "What do I know about contractual clauses?"

"More than most, I expect, or you can at least learn. A

lawyer would be required for the finer touches, of course."

"Of course," she echoed before she turned back to him. "Why are you doing this? And why has it taken so long for you to come up with it?"

"I'm doing it because—because it makes sense. As for the rest, I wanted to talk to the Swedes, find out for myself how committed they were to the deal before I started making problems."

She laughed without amusement. "Meaning that if anything goes wrong with the contract negotiations, you can always snatch the clauses back out again for the sake of the money."

"I'll fight for the things you believe in," he answered without flinching, "but no, I won't jeopardize this town and the jobs of the people who live here for the sake of a few birds."

He seemed so sincere, so right, so trustworthy. Yet he'd been seen with Janet Baylor on the day she disappeared. Both things could not be right.

She opened her mouth to ask for an explanation. At that moment Reid frowned, coming erect. Following his gaze, she saw through the window the flash of headlights sweeping over the side garden. It came from a car turning into the drive.

Reid lifted a brow in inquiry. Cammie shook her head; she was expecting no one.

The knock, when it sounded, was at the back. It was Bud Deerfield again.

It crossed Cammie's mind to wonder, as she pulled open the door, if someone might have seen Reid entering the house and called the police. An instant later she dismissed it. There was no point in being paranoid.

"Heavens, Bud, what now?" She was acutely aware that Reid had remained out of sight, hovering just inside the kitchen.

The look on the sheriff's face was troubled, and he took off his broad-brimmed felt hat, turning it around and around in his hands. "Cammie, I hate like hell to be the one to have to tell you this."

"What is it?" She stepped forward, the better to see his craggy face. The silver star pinned on his shirtfront winked in the dim light that beamed out onto the porch.

"It's Keith, honey."

"Is he hurt?"

"More than that. He's gone, honey. They just found him back in the game reserve. Coroner says it happened sometime this afternoon."

She drew a quick, shocked breath before she said, "A car accident?"

Bud shook his head. "He was shot, a .357 magnum. They found it beside him."

"He didn't— It wasn't . . . suicide?" The disturbance in her mind seemed to have so many causes, to come from so many questions and fears that it short-circuited her responses, leaving her numb.

Her cousin's face closed in and his manner suddenly became official. "No way. It was murder, pure and simple."

Chapter Fifteen

⬛ ⬛ ⬛ *Cammie stood with her hand on the door-*
knob after Bud had gone. He'd wanted to find someone
to stay with her, or else arrange some kind of sedative for
her. She told him neither were necessary. Regardless,
she felt odd, disoriented. She couldn't think what she
should do.

Her first impulse was to go to Keith's mother's house.
Her father-in-law had been dead some years, but she generally got along well with her mother-in-law—and knew
the older woman would take this hard. Yet, it was possible that her own presence would seem an intrusion
now, and a painful reminder of things best forgotten.

Keith, shot. It seemed such a foreign thing to happen
in staid, ordinary Greenley.

Murdered. Keith. And Janet Baylor had disappeared.

What was happening here? The town had always had
its share of Saturday night disturbances, family disputes,
tragic accidents, and acts of desperation over fatal ill-
nesses. But nothing like this.

Shot. In the game reserve.

She swung from the door and walked down the hall to
the stairs. Mounting them, she moved into her bedroom
and crossed to the bedside table. She opened the top
drawer where she had put away the pistol she'd threatened Keith with so short a time ago, the .357 magnum
Reid had returned to her.

It was gone. Of course.

Reid had followed her out of the kitchen, his footsteps quiet and even as he paced behind her. Now he leaned one shoulder against the door frame, watching her. She lifted her head to meet his gaze across the room.

His voice had a fretted edge as he said, "No, I didn't take it."

She hadn't thought it. Or had she? Without conscious intent, she said, "Where were you this afternoon?"

"Scouting timber," he said in a flashing reply. "And where else did you go besides the Fort and the garden center?"

Suspicion. It was an ugly thing. And a double-edged weapon.

She looked away from him abruptly, lowering her gaze. She pushed the drawer shut again and turned toward the center of the room. Stopping there in indecision, she clasped her hands across her waist and hugged her elbows against the chill inside her.

Reid watched her for long moments. Finally, he spoke in soft consideration. "Even if you did it, something I find hard to accept, I wouldn't blame you. I would assume, after seeing Keith hit you, that you had your reasons."

She looked up, and her startled gaze was snared and held by the clear expression in his eyes. Her voice a little hoarse, she said, "You might have had your reasons, too."

"For which you absolve me?" He tilted his head, his features intent.

"I'm not sure."

"No," he said in acceptance. "Unlike you, I can have no claim to extenuating circumstances. For me, there would be no excuse."

"And what if your reasons had more to do with what you thought I needed than your own motives?"

"You think I might have killed him for your sake?" His eyes narrowed slightly at the corners as he asked it.

"It seems possible."

The quiet gathered around them, hovering, as they watched each other. Then he inclined his head in abrupt agreement. "I might have at that, if I'd known you wanted it."

Truth. She knew it when she heard it. But was it whole or only partial? Had he, or hadn't he?

The terrible thing was, the answer made no difference to the swift and primitive gratification that radiated through her. She stifled it the instant she recognized what it was, but she could only deny it. What kind of woman was she that she could be pleased by a man's willingness to kill for her? She did not dare think.

She said quietly, "It would have been easier for you than for most."

"Easier to accomplish," he said. "Harder to overcome the well-learned reluctance."

She watched him, watched the play of vulnerability and self-hatred across his features, and knew abruptly that he had just let her see a part of himself that he kept hidden from all others. It was not that she had destroyed his defenses, she thought, but rather that he'd deliberately lowered them for her, for reasons that she did not dare begin to guess.

"Then if you are guilty," she said in quiet acceptance, "I must share it."

"Only," he said, "if you'll let me share whatever guilt might be yours."

Mutual suspicion, mutual lack of belief, mutual willingness to look the other way. Stalemate. Why did it hurt so much?

Reid's face changed and he took a step toward her. "There's something you should know—something happened between me and Keith at the mill."

"I know already," she said hastily, turning away from him. "It—It makes no difference. I would really rather not talk about it anymore, if you don't mind. And I would like to be by myself tonight."

He paused, and there was concentration in his silence,

as if he was listening to echoes of meaning in the sound of her voice, which even she could not hear. Or weighing consequences and inclinations she could not name.

Finally, he said, "Sleep, then, if you can. Wipe it all from your mind. Don't think of anything at all. There's no point in disturbing yourself over things that can no longer be helped."

"You speak from experience with violent death?"

A shadow of weariness darkened his voice. "What else?"

She did not hear him leave, but when she turned a moment later, he was gone.

The funeral was held two days later. It might have been sooner if not for the delay necessary for the autopsy.

Keith's family was anxious to have the services completed in order to put an end to the sensationalism. The calls and visits of the morbidly curious had been incessant. The throngs circling around the funeral home had grown larger hourly. At least four newspapers had called for permission to be present at the services.

The information came from the usual source, common gossip, and Cammie was not sure how reliable it might be. She debated over whether to attend the funeral because of it, however; the last thing she wanted was to be cornered for a comment from the widow. In the end she couldn't fight duty and tradition. Besides, to stay away would cause more comment than appearing, and she felt she owed some gesture toward the years she and Keith had been together.

It was nearly as hard to decide what to wear. The black of widow's weeds might seem a mockery, but to wear color could look too much like a lack of respect or even a celebration. She settled finally on a suit of dove-gray with a white silk blouse, and hoped it would be ordinary enough to escape notice.

A funeral in Greenley was rather like a formal social

event. The deceased lay in state in the parlor of the funeral home before the services began, with close relatives in attendance to receive those who came to pay their last respects. Close bodily contact in the way of brief hugs and comforting pats along with soft words of sympathy were extended. Tears and lamentations were silent, though there was a plentiful supply of tissues ready. The number and variety of the floral offerings were seen as a measure of the standing of the one being honored, and much attention was paid to the heft and decoration of the casket.

The service for Keith was marked by a selection of his mother's favorite gospel songs. A brief eulogy was followed by a sermon, one so fervent it seemed an invitation for converts might be extended at any moment.

Cammie deliberately came late to the services to avoid having to mingle and talk. She could not evade the photographer who stepped in front of her as she left the chapel, however, nor could she get away from the hard stares turned in her direction, or the whispers. Keeping her face as impassive as possible, she endured the attention, hoping it would soon be over.

It wasn't. She saw the reason why when the cortege wound its way to the cemetery. Reid's Jeep Cherokee was parked near the fence gate. It was to be expected, of course; the Huttons and the Sayers had been business associates for long years, and he had known Keith in school. He had at least had the sense to avoid the main service, putting in an appearance only for the graveside rites.

Reid was nearby in the crowd as everyone gathered near the mound of raw earth and the fake grass carpet under the canopy. He did not approach her, for which she was grateful. Still, there was a narrow aisle left open between the two of them, and the buzz of comment had the sound of hovering blowflies.

At last the graveside ceremony was over. Cammie had declined sitting in the seats reserved for family, but as

Keith's mother emerged from under the canvas tent, Cammie moved toward her by instinct.

For a moment the older woman looked through her as if she did not exist. Cammie did not allow her sympathy to falter, nor did she draw back from the swift hug she intended to bestow. She could feel the stiff rejection in her mother-in-law's body, however, and see the baffled anger shining through the tears that welled into the woman's eyes.

"I'm sorry," Cammie said, since there seemed nothing else that came close to being adequate.

"Are you?" the older woman answered in half-strangled civility. "I find it hard to believe. But I have been meaning to speak to you about any of Keith's things that might still be at your house. I will expect you to send them—home."

Vona Hutton, Gordon's plump and awkward wife, stood just behind Keith's mother. "That's right," she said with a self-righteous nod. At the same time, she glanced for approval toward her husband, who stood talking with the minister who had performed the service.

"Yes, of course," Cammie answered, concentrating her attention on the older woman. There was nothing of Keith's left at Evergreen, she thought, except possibly a few rusty tools, an old bicycle, and odds and ends of discarded auto parts. She would clear out every last screwdriver and corroded spark plug.

"Then we—his brother and I—ask nothing more from you."

It was a dismissal, a final break. No doubt it was meant to sting.

Cammie said quietly, "Whatever you prefer."

The other woman turned away with her head held high and her handkerchief clenched in her hand. Vona put her pudgy arm around her mother-in-law, murmuring soothingly. Cammie let them go, and tried not to feel relief.

Someone moved in close at her side then, and she turned, half expecting Reid. It was Fred Mawley.

The lawyer smiled down at her with caressing concern and attentiveness. "I was hoping I might find a minute to talk to you."

Cammie murmured something appropriate, giving the man only half of her attention. Reid was leaving the cemetery. He joined a group of men, most of them mill personnel, who stood talking off to one side.

"I'd like to schedule an appointment about the will," Fred Mawley went on. "The sooner we get things started, the better."

Cammie gave him a glance of dry inquiry as she began to walk in the direction of the cemetery gate. "Don't you think it's a little late now?"

He lifted a brow, then gave an abrupt chuckle. "Not your part of it, Cammie, but Keith's. You're still his beneficiary, you know, since your mutual wills were never canceled, never superseded by other arrangements. His assets come to you—including his share of the paper mill."

She stopped short, her eyes widened in unbelieving dismay.

Mawley, unnoticing, moved on a half step before he turned back. Quizzical amusement gathered in his face. "I can't believe it never occurred to you."

"It didn't." Her lips snapped together as she regained her self-possession.

"Gordon Hutton thought about it. I had a call from him yesterday morning, wanting to know how things stood. It struck me as hilarious really, since he was the one who—" The lawyer stopped, biting off what he'd been about to say.

"Gordon was the one who what?" Cammie asked with care.

Mawley looked self-conscious, though his smile did not falter. "Nothing. Nothing that has any bearing. Anyway, how about discussing things over dinner this evening? I'd like to have plenty of time for the details."

It was possible this development was part of the

Hutton family's resentment toward her. Cammie said, "I don't think there's any real rush."

"Tomorrow then, or the next day? I'm available at your convenience."

Beyond his shoulder, she saw Reid leaving. There was a stiffness in the set of his shoulders that troubled her. Telling Fred Mawley that she would call him, she walked quickly away.

She reached the cemetery gate before it occurred to her what Fred had almost let slip about Gordon and the will. It seemed Keith's brother might have had something to do with the delay in restructuring the document with its mutual beneficiary clause. If so, it would be a fine joke. The question was, why would he bother?

She couldn't wait to tell Reid about it. She wanted his reaction, needed to know what thoughts he might have on it. But though she increased her pace in the direction of the parking area, he was gone by the time she reached it.

The disappointment was so strong, her throat swelled with the press of it. Standing there, staring at where his Jeep had been, she realized how strange it was that she'd been so intent on sharing her news with someone she suspected of killing the man they had just buried. It also came to her that Reid might not think her news amusing at all.

Back at Evergreen, she changed clothes, pulling on a pair of jeans and a coral-colored knit top. She ate lunch, then went out and stared at the flats of impatiens she'd bought. In a sudden flurry of energy, she pulled up the pansies and ornamental kale that were beginning to fade after blooming during the winter and early spring, and set the new bedding plants in their places. She even planted the hibiscus she had bought for the urns that always sat on either side of the back steps.

It was only surface motion. As she worked, her thoughts were elsewhere.

Keith's death, from all reports, had been a professional job, a single shot to the head. Yet, any person in his right mind who wanted to see him dead would have waited until hunting season. At that time the woods—even the game reserve—were full of men with rifles; a shooting could easily be made to look accidental. The way the killer had gone about it seemed to indicate a person who acted out of uncaring rage, or else was sublimely confident of getting away with it.

Neither category applied to Reid. Cammie thought that if he had wanted to remove Keith, he would have killed him cleanly and quietly, then buried the body so deep and in such a hidden spot that it would never have been found except by purest accident.

Then again, that might be what she and everyone else was supposed to think. It was possible he had made the killing crude, knowing a too-efficient disappearance or death would have been like an arrow pointing straight at himself.

Again and again, Cammie went over the stark assurance Reid had given her that he did not kill Keith. She wanted to believe him, but it was so difficult. It made perfect sense that he would rid her of Keith's harassment, so long as she accepted that he was the kind of man who operated from implacable will and within his own flexible version of morality.

The trouble was, her assessment of his character, combined with what he'd said to her, made it just as possible that she was misjudging him. And she could not decide which would be more devastating: to be proven completely right or completely wrong.

Going back and forth in her mind was driving her crazy, and had been for days. This morning was the first time she'd seen him since the night he was at Evergreen. His behavior at the funeral gave her no help in making a decision. There must be something that would aid her.

She decided that staying away from him, avoiding any extension of their relationship, wasn't going to help her understand Reid. In fact, she might have to get as close as possible to him, in order to break through his defenses, to

find out the truth once and for all. It was the only way she
would ever have any peace.

Cammie tugged off her gardening gloves and left them
lying on the back steps with her dibble and empty flower
flats. A short time later, she was pulling into the drive at
the Fort.

Reid wasn't in the house. Lizbeth gave her a long, considering look, then pointed out the direction he'd taken
when he went into the woods.

The trail led to the Big Woods, the tract of virgin
timber that lay behind the paper mill and was joined on
its north boundary with the game reserve stretching
around the Fort. It was rough going for a while, until she
reached the old-growth timber. There, the huge, towering
pines and oaks, bays and gums and ash trees, met overhead, closing out the sunlight so that the underbrush
thinned, then disappeared. What was left was a brown
forest floor where mushrooms, moss and thick layers of
leaves made a soft cushion underfoot. It was an open,
echoing space where bird calls and the distant chatter of a
squirrel had a ringing quality. They vibrated around her
in the still air as if she were in a giant sound chamber.

Cammie stopped to catch her breath. Not only had she
been walking fast, but she'd come quite a distance. The
dubious wisdom of chasing a man she thought capable of
murder into this kind of deep woods skittered across the
surface of her mind. She pushed it from her as she concentrated on finding him.

Somewhere nearby she heard a tapping, knocking
sound. She smiled as recognition came. Turning from the
dim path, she moved in the direction of the noise.

A moment later she saw its cause: an Indian head
woodpecker. The size of a small rooster, with a gray-
brown body and a red cockade that began at its shoulders
and covered its entire head, the bird was clinging to the
side of a pine dying from pine beetle damage. The sun
glinted with a copper flare across its feathers as it drilled
busily, making a series of holes around the tree trunk. It

stopped long enough to cock its head toward her approach. Discovering no imminent danger, it went back to its search for insects and larvae.

It had been a long time since Cammie had seen one of the rare birds. She felt a certain nostalgic wonder at the sight, a little like a medieval female coming upon a unicorn in the woods. The world would be poorer if such fascinating creatures become extinct. She watched it for some time, turning back to the trail only after the red-cockade winged away deeper into the woods.

It was the music that guided her to Reid. She heard it from some distance away, a soft and lovely melody in a minor key played on a guitar. It reminded her of old folk airs such as "Greensleeves" and "Scarborough Fair," yet with something added, an unexpected, upbeat strength.

He was sitting at the edge of a fern glade. A guitar was cradled in his arms as he sat against the thick trunk of an ancient white beech tree. Just beyond him the green whorls of ferns clustered around a seeping spring in the side of a low hill above a creek. They raised their new fiddle heads out of the greenery and the deep mulch of last year's brown leaves.

There was a shaft of sunlight caught in his hair, turning it to gold. It shifted in bright gleams as he bent over the strings of his instrument. His face was absorbed as he played, then stopped, went back and replayed several bars of his melody, changed it slightly, then played it again.

It was music that could, and should, be accompanied by words. It was the beginning of a song, a ballad, perhaps, of love and loss. Beer-drinking music. The only outlet, as he had said, for a common man's emotions.

She thought of backing away, of leaving before he knew she was there. She should have known better.

"Don't run away," he said without looking up. "Come sit down, and tell me what you're doing here."

Her voice was tart as she moved to a spot not far from

him and dropped down on a half-rotted log. "Looking for you, naturally."

He sent her a hooded glance before returning to his intricate fingering of the guitar strings. "Why? Do you need another killing done? Mawley giving you trouble already?"

"I thought," she said in constricted tones, "that you were sure I could handle that kind of thing myself."

The music ceased with a sudden, twanging discord as he ripped his fingers across the strings. He put the guitar aside. Staring straight ahead, he drew a deep breath and let it out again. Only then did he turn his head in her direction. "Forget I said anything. Just tell me what you need from me."

Whatever personal feelings he might have, it seemed, had been put aside while he attended to what she might ask. She said, "There was something you wanted to tell me the other night about the fight between you and Keith at the mill. I stopped you at the time. I think maybe I shouldn't have. Would you tell me now?"

A blue spark shone between his narrowed eyelids before he gave an abrupt nod. In succinct phrases he explained the visit of the two thugs to Keith's office, and also what followed with Gordon.

She sat in frowning silence when he finished. Then she said, "I see how it must have been. Keith and Gordon were trying to pull a fast one about the mill title, so you beat them to the punch?"

"Meaning?" His voice was stringent.

"You paid Janet Baylor to strip the courthouse records and get out of town. Without that proof, everything was back the way it was, as far as ownership of the mill. You and the Huttons were even again."

"And you were out?" he said. "Then I must have miscalculated by getting rid of Keith, since it puts you back in the game again."

"You know about the will." It wasn't a question. When he shrugged without replying, she went on. "With it, my stake is not so large as it might have been. You may not like Gordon Hutton, but the two of you apparently want the same thing. I'm outnumbered on the selling issue."

"You always were."

He meant, she saw, in the fight to stop the sale, and in public opinion. She said stubbornly, "The money hasn't been paid yet."

There was no rise to that bait. His voice even, he said, "It was Keith's activities that concerned me most; what he had been up to could have been serious. So far as I can tell, there's been something like a half million paid out from his department on bogus ink and chemical invoices in the last six months—and who knows how much before then. The discrepancies skew the mill's bottom line, could make it look like a high-risk investment."

"He was stealing?" she said in puzzlement. "But . . . why, when it was his own company?"

"Not quite his alone," Reid said dryly. "It was also Gordon's, and I don't think he was anxious for big brother to find out. Or me, when I stuck my nose into the operation. As for why, you said yourself he was strapped for money. The reason obviously has something to do with the visit paid him by the strong-arm boys. Did you ever suspect Keith of betting on the ponies? Or high-stakes gambling?"

"He was a regular at Louisiana Downs; it was entirely too close to Greenley," Cammie said with a crease between her brows. "And he enjoyed Vegas. I never knew him to go overboard either place, but I haven't been around him much in the last few months."

"It should be possible to find out, if you want to go that far."

She watched him a moment before she said bluntly, "How far?"

"To New York."

Her own laugh surprised her. "Oh, sure. Just like that."

"I told you about Charles Meyer, the friend of mine who lives up there," he said, sitting forward, his face serious.

"He's a genius—and I use the word in its exact sense—with computers. He still works for the Company, and even the Bureau at times, in a quiet way. His title is normal enough, but his real job is to infiltrate computer networks worldwide for the purpose of gathering information—and to see to it nobody can return the favor."

Cammie watched Reid for a long moment, hoping for enlightenment. It didn't come. Finally, she said, "I don't see the connection."

"There has been for some time a concentrated federal effort to keep tabs on organized crime. Louisiana has been a target area because of New Orleans and the Marcellos crime family, with its Cuban and South American connections. Surveillance has been stepped up since the introduction of racing in the state, also the more recent lottery and casino gambling. If Keith had a brush with that kind of operation, there will be a record."

"So why not just call and ask your friend to find out?"

"I would prefer to look at the data myself. It could be sent via modem over the phone lines to my computer setup at the Fort, but that's a little too sensitive to risk. More than that, I can't take the chance of exposing Charles's contribution."

"Yet you mention it to me," she said.

"Yes," he agreed, his gaze steady.

It was an indication of trust in her discretion, her integrity; it could be nothing else. She was warmed by it, and amazed. At the same time, she was wary of the complications there might be in venturing into such murky matters with Reid.

"There's no reason for me to go," she said.

He arched a brow. "Not even for the proof of your own eyes?"

"I will accept your word," she countered.

He held her gaze while his own turned slowly crystalline with pleasure, and something more. "Will you now?" he said softly.

Where had that ready assurance come from? Cammie did not know, but she would not deny it. "Why not?"

And with those words the moment shifted, stretching with aching tension between them while the woods around them grew breathlessly still.

He held out his hand to her. When she placed her fingers in his warm grasp, he drew her toward him with an effortless flexing of muscles. He encircled her waist with his arm and settled her against his side in the bed of ferns and cushioning leaves.

"I can't tell you," he said in soft satisfaction against her temple, "how many times I've thought of doing just this."

It was crazy. She should have kept away from him, retreated from his touch, should drag herself free this minute. It was depraved to come so close to a man who might be a murderer. Yet even as her mind clanged with the warning, her body settled against him, absorbing his warmth and hard strength, and the fresh masculine scent of him.

She tilted her head back against the firm muscles of his shoulder, watching the play of light and shadow across the planes of his face, the shimmer of sunlight along the strands of his hair, which shifted in the light breeze. She could see the reflection of her own features in the dark, widening pools at the centers of his eyes. As he leaned toward her, touching his mouth to hers, she allowed her lashes to flutter down with a sigh of completion.

Sweet, firm, giving, his kiss was all that and more. He invited her participation, teasing, encouraging with warm lip surfaces, the lap and play of tongue and the application of delicate suction. Unhurried, he traced every curve and ridge and indentation of her lips, every quilted-silk segment of the inner lining, every sleek taste bud and tracery of her tongue. It was as if his need to know her had no boundaries, no restraints, found no detail too small to be noted, explored, learned.

She was captivated by his pleasure. It set free her own

rich savoring, causing it to burgeon with swift, incredible fervor. She lifted her free hand to lay her finger along his lean cheek, enjoying its heat and the faint scrape of bristles against her palm. Trailing across his ear, she slid her nails through the thick hair at the nape of his neck before clasping the back of his head to draw him closer.

He drew a quick breath, then smoothed his hand from her waist to the neckline of her shirt. His fingers not quite steady, but without hesitation, he unfastened the buttons and spread the edges wide. He dipped his head toward the uncovered curves above her bra, heating the nipples under the satin with his breath so they contracted into tiny knots, feathering the lace edges that plunged to the center closure with the moist heat of his tongue. She arched her back to give him greater access, and felt the sun's dazzle on her eyelids and its molten warmth in the center of her being.

There came a distant crackling, like the scatter of dried leaves. Reid's grasp tightened with abrupt, bruising force.

Suddenly, Cammie was freed. Her shirt was whipped into place to cover her. Before she could do more than gasp in surprise, he shifted with lithe strength to place her behind him, then surged to a defensive crouch before her.

Cammie gathered herself, rising to one elbow. She shook back the thick swath of her hair so she could see.

There was a boy of perhaps seventeen or eighteen standing less than fifty feet away. He carried a .22 rifle in his right hand and had a pair of binoculars swinging around his neck. There was surprise and self-consciousness, and all too ready understanding on his face.

"Where in hell do you think you're going?" Reid said in grating tones edged with distinct menace. "This is private property. Get off it."

A flush burned its way into the boy's face. He stumbled back a step, then turned and moved off at a fast stride that changed quickly into a trot. His crashing progress through the woods could be heard for long minutes before it died away again into softly rustling stillness.

Reid sighed and relaxed his guard. Lifting a hand, he ran his fingers through his hair in a harassed gesture. His voice flat, he said, "That was a mistake."

"Yes."

Cammie was forced to acknowledge that it could have been handled better. A smile and casual greeting might have glossed over the incident. Ordering the boy away could only cause resentment and make the whole thing seem more clandestine than it was. If the tale wasn't all over town by dark, it would be a miracle. She didn't think she could stand it, not on top of everything else.

"I lost it, and there's no excuse." He glanced away from her through the trees. "I just—hated knowing I put you in a position where it could happen."

"You didn't do it by yourself," she said in compressed tones. She closed her eyes, then opened them wide again. As he turned toward her, she met his gaze with sudden decision in her face.

"About New York? When can we leave?"

Chapter Sixteen

Cammie always enjoyed New York against her will. She would have liked to be indifferent to it, from regional tradition if nothing else. There was actually much about it she disliked: the viscous air that felt as if it had been breathed a million times before; the grimy, soot-laden surfaces that made wearing any color other than black or gray an exercise in optimism; the stone and glass monstrosities that blotted out the sky. But she delighted in the seething immensity of it, and the promise. The wit and humor and impolite drive of people who were wholly themselves without apologies appealed to something basic in her makeup. Le Corbusier, she thought, came closest to catching what she felt when he described it as "a catastrophe which an unkind fate has brought down on a courageous and confident people, but a grandiose and magnificent catastrophe."

She and Reid gave themselves a free day. After taxiing in from LaGuardia, they checked into the Roosevelt, a hotel Cammie liked for its central location and because it had something of the same layout and faded grandeur as the Fairmont in New Orleans. They made reservations for a show, and for dinner afterward at Le Perigord. Then they simply walked, in part to stretch their muscles after the long flight, but also for the pleasure of joining the sidewalk hustle.

They window-shopped on Fifth Avenue and watched a bag lady feed pigeons on the steps of St. Patrick's. They bought a giant pretzel with mustard from a street vendor while rubbing shoulders with a would-be model, an Arab potentate and his bodyguard, and a Rastafarian. They stepped around a pride of toy lions stalking and growling all over the sidewalk in front of an enterprising teenage salesman, ducked through a construction site, and had coffee at Rockefeller Plaza while arguing over whether the shining bronze overlooking the Center was really Prometheus or bore more resemblance to Apollo.

The show was not as good as they expected, the dinner was better. Afterward they went back to the hotel, where they took a bath, then lay in bed making up outrageous stories about the wedding nights, afternoon affairs, and paid sexual transactions that had taken place over the years in their room.

Reid's were so inventive and so outrageous that Cammie sat up in bed and rounded on him. "I do believe," she said with a trace of disappointment beneath the humor in her voice, "that hotel rooms turn you on!"

"Wrong." The answer was unequivocal, his smile sensual.

"I don't think so."

His expression grew serious as he saw the challenge in her eyes. He gathered himself, sitting up with his back against the headboard. In an expansive gesture, he raised his arms and locked his fingers behind his head. The words low and deliberate, he said, "Let me tell you what turns me on."

"Besides hotel rooms?" she countered. There was an odd tightness in the lower part of her body.

He shook his head. His eyes grew slumberous, yet intent. "Rainy nights turn me on. And red sunsets. Deep woods turn me on, as you ought to know. So does some music, some poetry. I can be turned on by a woman's long, fine hair, especially the sight of it lifting, blowing in the wind."

"Typical," she snorted.

He paused, then reached out with casual strength to

catch her arms, pulling her toward him. Dragging her across his body, he turned her to her back and shifted to hover above her. His voice dropping lower, he continued, "I am turned on, more than I can say, by the way your hair touches the middle of your back. The soft look on your face just before I kiss you gets me going. The shape of your breasts can do it, and the way your shirt drapes over them—not to mention that vee-shaped shadow hidden between them. I am turned on by the habit you have of leaving your panties until last when you undress. Also, the totally efficient way you slide them off over your hips; no coy glances, without caring—or maybe knowing—that I'm paying attention."

"That isn't fair," she protested, her eyes wide and her voice not quite even.

He might not have heard. Releasing his hold, he moistened the tip of his finger with his tongue, then slid it over and around the nipple of her breast, which peeped through the long tresses lying over her shoulder. "I'm turned on by the little sound you make as you catch your breath when I touch you—like this. The feel of your skin against mine turns me on. The thought of you under me, and me inside you, turns me on." He stopped, said finally in ragged tones, "You turn me on. Mostly you."

The light in his eyes was steady as they met hers without evasion. She sustained it while rich satisfaction spread through her. She had gotten more than she bargained for, but not more than she needed.

Her soft sigh feathered over his shoulder, making gooseflesh bead in its wake. She lowered her lashes and lifted a hand to smooth that momentary roughness. "Me, too," she said. "Or rather, I mean that you—"

"I know what you mean," he said, only the slightest trace of complacency threading the gratification in his tone.

She slid her arm around his neck, drawing his head down until her lips were almost touching his. Against his mouth she murmured, "Are you through?"

"Just beginning," he answered, and proceeded to show her.

Afterward Cammie thought Reid drifted off to sleep while she lay with her head pillowed on his chest and the moisture cooling on her skin. She was still, staring at nothing in the room that was too bright from the light coming around the window draperies and the hall door. The problems she had managed to keep at bay rose slowly in her mind. Her fingers, spread over Reid's chest, tightened involuntarily.

"Don't think," he said in quiet reprimand as he reached to catch her hand, pressing it against him.

"How can I help it?" she answered.

"Let me distract you," he said.

It was, almost, enough.

Charles Meyer lived in Queens, in one of a long stretch of red brick row houses with identical entrance steps and railings. The front door was painted a forest-green so dark it was almost black, and centered by an antique Victorian brass knocker. A black marble urn filled with brilliant red tulips and white alyssum sat beside it.

Reid's friend was like his house, neat, pleasant, yet with an elegance that set him apart. With his long, narrow face filled in by a beard sparked with white, his spare form and competent hands, he looked as if he belonged on some Left Bank side street in Paris, rubbing shoulders with fellow artists in shirtsleeves and berets. He also sounded like it, given his accent, though his wife Michelle did not.

His four-year old son, André, was very like Charles, except that he had the enormous, liquid-brown eyes of a fifteenth century painting and the hands of a violinist. He was a walking example of the workings of genetics, since his mother was dark-eyed, graceful, and elegant in a practical New York fashion. Their baby girl, Reina, seven months old, seemed cast in the same mold as her brother, though at present with angelic overtones.

Cammie felt a little awkward in the Meyer house at first, afraid she would say or do something wrong. Religion was not a high priority for her. She had been reared a Methodist, but in her family, worship and belief were casual and rather private matters, nothing to stir public passion. There were one or two Jewish families in Greenley, but they were not exactly Orthodox; Cammie had been well into her twenties before she had realized they were different in any way. She'd looked into the difference then, from curiosity, but her knowledge of Jewish observances and protocol was distressingly vague.

She needn't have worried. Charles and Michelle Meyer took her into their house and their confidence with obvious goodwill. They laughed and teased; their lively conversation, with its rapid-fire questions and quick, witty comments, was a joy to hear and a challenge to join, and left no room for uneasiness.

Michelle Meyer, it appeared, worked on Wall Street, something to do with the management of a mutual fund. Her investment savvy supplied the financial cushion that allowed Charles to work out of the house. On the surface, his job appeared to be the creation of computer software, and he had developed and marketed a number of innovative business applications. However, his main occupation, as Reid had indicated, was with government agencies.

Infiltrating worldwide computer networks was a game for him, one whose appeal was the challenge. His greatest interest, however, was in testing government computer security. Staying one step ahead of all the hackers and other interested parties who might try to tap into the vast data files, confidential and otherwise, that were maintained by the various federal agencies was his joy, amounting almost to obsession.

As a result, there wasn't much Charles didn't know

about computer security; there were few systems that he himself couldn't tap, if he put his mind to it. He was perfectly willing to lend his expertise on Cammie's behalf, since it was Reid who asked.

Dinner was a great meal, with a runaway pace to the banter, and the warmth as free-flowing as the wine. Afterward, Reid and Charles helped clear the kitchen, then huddled together before the computer in the tiny study located through an archway from the living room. They seemed to be testing some sort of warning system, double-checking times and conditions. It sounded like something personal.

Cammie and Michelle sat talking. Cammie found her attention wandering from what the other woman was saying, however, to the low-voiced comments between the two men.

Michelle Meyer broke off what she was saying about the problems of commuting into lower Manhattan to follow Cammie's gaze. A smile curved her wide, mobile mouth. "You're right, they're both a little paranoid—being in covert operations seems to bring it on. That's their fail-safe system they're checking out. Reid told you about it?"

Cammie lifted a brow in inquiry even as she shook her head.

"It's simple, really. Both keep their computers going around the clock, both have access to them in their room of last resort, the place they expect to hole up in if attacked. There's a two-word code. If it ever comes up, the other instantly sends in the Marines—or the police at the very least."

"Long distance?"

"There's no such thing as distance when you're working with computer signals."

"You are joking—aren't you?"

Michelle gave a brief shake of her head. "Deadly serious. It seems to pay these days, with all the burglaries and drug-related crimes, not to mention the people who might like to pick Charles's brain for his specialized knowledge—or Reid's, for that matter. It's just another alarm system, really, one a little more innovative than most."

Cammie had to admit it made sense. She said, "I hope Charles won't get into trouble over this computer search. I'd feel terrible."

"There's no special risk, though Charles wouldn't do it for just anybody. On the other hand, he and Reid are far too used to covert operations, acting just that tiny bit above and beyond the law, to let it worry them too much."

"They seem to be enjoying the whole thing," Cammie commented.

"No doubt they are. They have the same kind of minds—meticulous, but free-ranging. It's a shame Louisiana is so far away," Michelle went on as she leaned back in the overstuffed couch, tucking her feet under her. "Charles has missed Reid; there aren't many people he can talk to about what he does, even fewer who would understand it."

It was unsettling, to catch this glimpse of the life Reid had been living while away from Greenley. She said in tentative tones, "Perhaps he'll move closer, if the sale of the mill goes through."

Michelle gave a quick shake of her head. "I doubt that; he seems content where he is. Charles would be ecstatic, of course. They go back a long way together. Reid saved Charles's life once, you know."

"He didn't mention it."

"I'm not surprised; he claims it was just one of those things men do in a fight. It was during a border clash, one of the daily PLO skirmishes that took place in Israel in the months before the Gulf War. Charles and Reid were working in a makeshift communications headquarters. The place was blown up by a bomb preset in a car parked outside. Four of the Israelis were killed outright, another had a concussion. Charles was trapped with a roof beam across his back and a bone smashed in his leg. Reid was bleeding from a half-dozen places, some of them inside. Then the place was attacked. Charles and Reid and the other man were surrounded for hours by the Palestinian infiltrators. Reid was the only one able to put up much of a defense, yet the Palestinians were down to four men from a total of sixteen by the time help arrived, or so I gather. I've never heard the full tale—deliberately, I think."

Her voice stifled, Cammie said, "Reid can, apparently, be very—lethal."

A quizzical expression touched the other woman's face. "He's also the most gentle man I've ever seen. It's a puzzle. I've often wondered if it has something to do with being from the South."

"The legendary southern gentleman?" Cammie said wryly. "I don't think so."

"It's personal to him, then; I might have known. He is more totally himself, more secure inside himself, than anyone I've ever met. He's so strong that he has apparently never wanted or required much in the way of emotional defenses. That makes what happened in Israel just before he left the Company so much more terrible for him than—"

The other woman broke off as the sound of a crying baby came from the room where little Reina had been put to bed. "Be back in a second," she said, and uncoiled from the couch to vanish into the nursery room.

She came back a few minutes later with the fretful baby on her hip. Michelle tried to soothe her, offering bottle and pacifier, joggling her on her knee, rubbing her back, offering toys and nibbles. Nothing seemed to help.

Charles came out of his absorption and turned his head to watch them across the room. After a moment he called, "How about bringing her to me?"

The flash of relief on Michelle's face was instant. She carried the baby to her husband, passing her over. The baby quieted instantly.

Michelle looked disgusted as she rejoined Cammie. "That kid is a man's baby. No surprise, I suppose, since Charles took care of her during the day, from the time I went back to work until she was six months old."

Cammie smiled, watching the bearded man return to his work, shifting the baby expertly to his shoulder while he pressed computer keys in a swift, one-handed hunt and peck rhythm. Beside him, Reid's gaze rested on the child before he looked away. He shifted his chair to give Charles more space.

Charles glanced at Reid with a considering look in his dark eyes and a tilt to his mouth behind his beard. His gaze steadied. Abruptly, he lifted the contented, thumb-sucking child and pressed her into Reid's arms.

Reid stiffened. His eyes were suffused with the same unbearable anguish Cammie had seen once before. An instant later they turned blank, and a harsh, inarticulate sound of protest sounded in his throat. Charles did not relent, but met his friend's gaze with fixed regard while he held the sleepy child's head against Reid's shoulder. Slowly, carefully, the baby's father removed his hold.

Beside Cammie, Michelle sat forward in alarm. Her sharp-drawn breath made a hissing sound in the tense quiet.

Reid brought up one hand with a jerk to catch the baby before she could fall. Then slowly, as if against his will, he raised the other and settled it gently upon the small, narrow back. The baby sighed, relaxing against the firm muscles, turning her face into the curve of his neck.

Reid closed his eyes while he drew a deep and difficult breath. He moistened his lips as if they were dry. His gaze, when his lashes lifted again, was without focus, with a clear shimmer between the lids.

"Oh, God," Michelle said, sagging back against the couch.

"What is it?" Cammie said in perplexity, even as she recognized the draining away of her own near unbearable anxiety.

"Coffee," Michelle said abruptly as she straightened and sprang to her feet. "I'll make some for us. And there's cheese cake if you'll help put it on plates, Cammie."

Cammie knew an excuse when she heard one. She followed the other woman from the living room into the kitchen. It was no surprise to see Michelle lean against the cabinet, clasping her arms around her upper body as if to still the visible shiver that shook her.

Her voice sharp, Cammie exclaimed, "Surely you didn't expect Reid to hurt your baby."

"No, no; it was just so—so miraculous, I can't stand it," Michelle said with an unsteady smile.

Cammie stared at her for a taut second. "What is it? What really happened in there?"

"For just a second, I half expected to see Reid pitch my baby daughter back at Charles like a ticking time bomb. He was here in New York just after she was born, you know. When he came to visit, I made the mistake of giving her to him to hold. I thought he was going to faint; he turned whiter than her undershirt. I didn't know then, Charles hadn't warned me."

"About what? I realize there's something, just—not the details."

Michelle's gaze held hers for a long moment before she looked away. "If Reid hasn't told you, I don't think I should. You'll have to ask him."

"And if he won't talk about it, what then?" As there was no relenting in Michelle's expression, Cammie added in urgent tones, "Please. I have to know."

The other woman furrowed her brow in thought as she turned toward the refrigerator and took out a cheese cake, then set dessert plates beside it. Moving to the coffee maker on the cabinet, she pulled it forward and filled it with water, then reached for a sack of gourmet coffee and an electric coffee mill. The smell of the fresh-ground beans rose in the room as the beans were added and the mill did its noisy work. The other woman dumped the coffee into the maker and turned it on.

Finally, she turned back to Cammie. "I may regret it, but . . ." She shrugged. "It's just that he—well, this thing with children has nearly driven him to the edge. It was the reason he quit working with covert operations, the main reason he went home and buried himself in the woods down South the minute he had an excuse. He—He killed a little girl, you see."

Cammie put the knife she had picked up to cut the cheese cake down again. Disbelief shuddered through her, leaving blank distress in her mind. "No," she said in low tones. "No, I don't see it at all."

"It was in a little settlement in the Golan Heights. Reid was working with the Israeli elite forces as an adviser, commanding a task force of a dozen men. It was their job to prevent PLO infiltration and to keep the town quiet. There had been rioting among the Palestinians in the area, but things had stabilized. The task force spent their days with routine patrols, readiness drills, jawboning local leaders. There was also a lot of free time. Headquarters was in the middle of the town, near the market. There was a couple of Palestinian families living down the street. One of their little girls, hardly more than five or six, played around the front door, hung around most of the day. Everyone made a pet of her, especially Reid. They gave her candy and gum, made toys for her, taught her a little Yiddish, a little English."

Cammie put a hand to her lips in the beginning of pain and distress as she saw where the story was leading. She could picture it all so well, too well.

"You may know something of the Israeli-Palestinian problem," Michelle went on, her voice weighted with weariness, "the endless, bloody fighting over a narrow strip of sandy land, the deep hatred that has been festering now for generations, the violence of the intifadah. You may have heard or read, too, about how little human life counts for in the Middle East, especially female lives."

"That little girl—" Cammie said with difficulty.

"Her father had been a leader in the intifadah, and was killed in an uprising. The girl, her baby brother, and her mother were living with the father's brother. This man, the girl's uncle, was fanatic about the movement. Fight to the death, no sacrifice too great, that kind of extremism. He had sent the girl, of course."

"You mean . . ."

Michelle stared straight ahead, her gaze bleak. "When the task force became used to seeing her playing around them, when they took her in among them, then she was sent one last time. She was sent with explosives wired for detonation and strapped with heavy tape to her chest."

"No," Cammie said, shaking her head in dread.

Michelle nodded in slow acknowledgment. "She walked into headquarters bright and early one morning, bringing a bowl of fruit. Reid discovered the trick when he reached to give her a quick hug of thanks. He knew what it meant, knew he had seconds to act. The choice was never between her life and his, there was not a shred of hope of saving her; you have to understand that. All he could do was get her away from his men, to save them. That was his duty, his responsibility. He caught her, slung her away from them out into the street. And he told Charles it was the terror in her eyes, and the knowledge of what had been done to her, that haunts him. That and her terrible understanding."

It was long moments before Cammie could speak past the thickness in her throat. "Her uncle killed her, not Reid."

"Yes. But to Reid, it seems he should have known what would happen, should have seen it coming and pre-vented it. Or, failing that, should have held the child as she died."

Reid's pain became Cammie's. It burrowed inward, a consummate horror complete with bloodred images seared into her imagination as they must be burned into his mind. She understood the darkness she'd seen in his eyes on that night at the Fort when she had accused him of abusing children. She could see how a young girl bearing food at the reunion, looking up at him with a sweet and grateful smile, had caused him to instantly recoil. She recognized the wellspring of the aching tenderness of his touch. And acid tears pooled in her eyes, shimmering with the hard thud of her heart.

"Don't do that, or you'll have me blubbering," Michelle said. She turned sharply and ripped off a paper towel, handing it to Cammie before taking one for herself.

Cammie couldn't let Reid know that she knew, not here, not now. She blew her nose and drew a ragged breath. She tried to close off thought as Reid had shown her, and wondered if this was how he'd learned that difficult lesson. She wondered, too, if it always worked for him.

"Anyway," Michelle said unsteadily, "it looks like Reid is beginning to get over it, finally, since he actually held little Reina just now." The other woman slanted a glance both watery and teasing at Cammie. "Could be finding a big girl to hold first helped."

Cammie tried a smile, not very successfully. "I doubt that was ever a problem."

"Reid was not very susceptible that way, at least according to Charles. There was some woman a long time ago who hurt him. I don't think she turned him into a basket case or a monk, but she gave him a certain immunity."

She was discovering a great deal more about Reid, Cammie thought, than she wanted to know. Turning from Michelle, she gave her concentration to serving cheese cake.

The two men were watching the computer screen and talking in barely audible voices when Cammie and Michelle returned to the living room. The baby was asleep, lying as boneless as a rag doll against Reid's shoulder, supported by one large hand. The softness in his face as he turned toward them was nearly enough to cause the return of tears.

"Come look at this," Charles called. "I think we won the lottery."

He had, through methods best ignored, tapped into the FBI's Organized Crime Squad records for the southeastern part of the country, including New Orleans. He had worked with the FBI on O.C. before, and so had a good idea where to find what Reid wanted. It was not as simple as looking through the activities of the local Mafia family, however.

"What you have to understand," Charles explained, "is that, as with most things in New Orleans, organized crime is different there."

Cammie gave a nod of understanding. Her smile rueful, she said, "I once heard someone quip that if crime was organized in the state of Louisiana, it's the only thing that is."

"That about sums it up," Charles agreed with a smile in his voice. "The Marcello family is the oldest Mafia family in the United States. Carlos Marcello, the don famous for his quasiconnection to the Kennedy assassination, is dead now, but things muddle along pretty much as usual. The Marcello version of La Cosa Nostra, as they prefer to call themselves, is relaxed compared to the families of the Northeast. They have their blood rituals and oaths and loyalties, but they don't pretend to control all the crime in New Orleans; there's plenty for everybody so long as newcomers don't step on obvious toes. Also, there's no rigid hierarchy of captains and soldiers. Feuds and fighting for territory aren't the Marcello style, nor is creating mayhem in restaurants or littering the streets with dead bodies. If someone absolutely has to be disposed of, it's done quietly, with a decent funeral, or else the corpse gets recycled in the alligator swamps."

The fluid nature of the crime family alliance, he went on, made it more difficult to keep track of, much less to crack. The FBI had been keeping a close eye on the situation, however, as Reid had indicated, since gambling became legal within the state.

Keith Hutton's name appeared on a list of high rollers whose debts had been turned over to a collection agency operated by a minor Bossier City–Shreveport branch of La Cosa Nostra. He was down for a figure in excess of a quarter of a million.

Reid reached out, being careful not to disturb the sleeping baby on his shoulder, to tap the figure beside the blinking cursor on the computer screen. "I'd say reneging on that kind of money would be enough to earn him a quiet ride out of town, enough for a professional hit by way of example."

"You were right, then," Cammie said, and placed her fingers on his free shoulder, because she wanted so badly to touch him at that moment.

"Only there's no proof," he answered, "nothing to place the strong-arm boys in the neighborhood, nothing to show that anybody expected them to be there."

"You didn't really think it would be that easy?" she said.

He smiled, though his gaze did not quite meet hers. "Maybe not. But it would have been nice."

"So what do we do now?"

"That is, of course, the question," he said quietly.

There was nothing else to be discovered in New York, and no point in staying any longer. At the airport as they waited to leave, there rose inside Cammie a wild impulse to hop the first flight to Paris, or to Venice—anywhere else in the wide world except home. It had to be suppressed. Running away, no matter how seductive it might appear, would not help. They caught their plane.

The things Michelle had told her lingered in her mind. She wanted to speak to Reid about them, but there seemed no good time, no natural way to introduce them. She didn't want him to think she pitied him, and was loath to have him know she and Michelle had discussed him behind his back. In any case, she wasn't sure she could talk about the incident with the little girl without crying.

As she sat listening to the drone of the plane, feeling its vibration, she thought of the woman who might have hurt Reid. Was it possible she was the one? It pained her to think so. She could not imagine failing to return his love if he ever decided to give it. He had so much to offer a woman.

I am nothing if not constant.

He had said those words to her not so long ago. She wondered just what he'd meant by them, how far into the past they extended. She would give a lot to know.

He was so protective, so concerned for her. No woman could ask for a more careful or considerate lover. How much did that stand for, if it stood for anything?

She loved him. She had suspected it for days, but had known beyond a doubt as she watched him hold Michelle's baby so carefully in his strong hands.

It was strange to admit it, perhaps, when she had thought him capable of murder. The heart wasn't logical, of course, or particularly bright. It could be swayed by a glance, a smile, a single word. It had few principles, less sense.

Chimes sounded. The stewardess came over the intercom, announcing the approach into their home airport at Monroe. Cammie checked her seat belt. It was a small airport with a short runway and an approach through the turbulent air currents over the Ouachita River. Landing was always steep, bumpy, and a bit hairy. She reached to slip her hand into Reid's. He turned his head, his eyes warm, steady, reassuring.

She wished she had taken a plane to Paris.

Chapter Seventeen

As Cammie and Reid passed through town on the way to Evergreen, they saw Bud Deerfield sitting in his patrol car parked close to the pizza place. Cammie lifted a hand to wave. Seconds later her cousin pulled out behind them. He followed them into the drive and rolled to a stop a few feet from their rear bumper. Cammie got out and walked toward the sheriff while Reid took her overnight bag from the back of the Jeep.

"I don't mean to tell you your business, Cammie," Bud said as he hauled himself out of the car and came to meet her. "But I have to say I've seen you do smarter things than this."

Cammie lifted a brow as she followed the tilt of his head toward where Reid was setting her suitcase on the steps. Her voice sharp, she said, "I don't see what intelligence has to do with it."

"Well, I'll tell you. I've had people yapping at me about this little jaunt of yours and Sayers's ever since you left. Seems they think there's something funny about you going off so soon after Keith's funeral. It bothers them, makes them wonder about things."

"For crying out loud, Bud! My divorce was almost final!"

"Almost is not enough, not around here. They know Keith had a mind to patch it up with you, because he said so to everybody who would listen. They think maybe he was balking at giving you the divorce and you got mad.

Folks watch all these TV shows about husbands killing wives, wives hiring men to kill husbands, and so on. They're asking themselves if maybe this big brouhaha between you and Sayers over the mill sale wasn't just a smoke screen. They're wondering if the two of you didn't get rid of old Keith between you."

It was so farfetched that Cammie stood for long seconds with her mouth open. Finally, she said in despairing tones, "Where do these things come from?"

"God knows; I sure don't," he said, but set his hands on his hips.

She met his straight gaze. "You don't believe it, do you?"

He wagged his head slowly from side to side. "Don't make any difference what I think; I still have to pay attention. And I say you should have known how it would be, should have known better than to go gallivanting off with Sayers in the middle of all this as if you didn't have a brain in your head."

Reid spoke then as he moved to stand beside Cammie. "It was my fault, my idea."

"Anyway, it wasn't like that at all," Cammie added in anger. "We had a perfectly good reason."

The sky was reflected in the surface of his badge as Budrocked back on his heels. "I sure hope it's one you can trot out for people, because I'm taking heat about this business. People are wondering why I haven't brought somebody in to answer a few questions."

"People like Gordon Hutton?" Cammie did not bother to hide her cynicism.

"Among others. I'd like to keep this all nice and friendly, but it would help if you'd do your part, Cammie. Otherwise, it may have to get unfriendly."

His message delivered, Bud did not linger. As he climbed back in his patrol car and drove off, Cammie stood staring after him with a crease between her eyes.

Reid lifted a hand, running it over his hair and clasping

the back of his neck. "It looks to me like it might be better if I make myself scarce."

"Why?" Cammie demanded. "We've done nothing wrong."

"And nothing right. We both know how things are in Greenley."

The corner of Cammie's mouth tightened briefly before she sighed in acquiescence. "You know, I think I just might be able to get used to someplace like New York, where nobody knows who you are, or gives a damn."

"In the meantime, we have to deal with here and now." Reid stepped close to brush a quick kiss across her mouth. "I'll call you," he said, his gaze direct. "Don't forget to lock your doors."

Cammie watched him pull away down the drive before she went into the house. She had never felt so alone in her life.

She busied herself unpacking her suitcase, putting the dirty clothes into the wash, hanging away what was left. Persephone, not knowing exactly when she would return, had left nothing cooked for dinner in the refrigerator. Cammie took a pound of ground chuck from the freezer and set it out to thaw with some vague idea of making spaghetti.

At loose ends, then, she wandered around the house, watering and grooming houseplants, picking up a piece of half-finished needlework and putting it down again, leafing through a gardening magazine. She was so unsettled in her mind, however, that she couldn't concentrate on anything. It was a relief when the phone rang.

The voice of her great-aunt Beck came through clear and irascible over the line. "Where in the name of Heaven have you been? I've been calling and calling, and you're never home."

"The answering machine was on; you should have left a message," Cammie said.

"I hate those tomfool machines, make a person feel

like an idiot, talking to somebody who's not there. I like answers when I ask questions."

"Yes, ma'am," Cammie said with a private grin. "What can I do for you?"

"You can get yourself over here. There's something I've been wanting to tell you for ages. You don't hear it soon, I'm liable to turn senile and forget. Or pass on."

"That'll be the day," Cammie said.

"Smarty-pants," Aunt Beck said, and hung up with a sharp click.

The elderly woman was in a better mood by the time Cammie had driven the eight miles of country roads out to her house. The only thing that set her up more than making her relatives step around was having a visitor.

Aunt Beck had her little rituals. She enjoyed hot tea, a rare habit in Greenley, where iced tea reigned supreme. More, she liked it made just so and served from her ancient Georgian silver service into eggshell-thin china cups. Something dainty to eat was a necessity, and so were damask napkins with a tatted edging done by her own hand.

Cammie usually enjoyed the small ceremony, and copied it on occasion when she felt the lure of family tradition. Now it strained her patience, since Aunt Beck refused to impart whatever was on her mind until after the choice of exotic tea blend had been made, the water boiled and poured, and the tea in the cups.

Finally the elderly woman settled back in her chair. They ran through the usual civilities. Aunt Beck then asked about Cammie's version of Keith's death, and listened carefully to the answers. With these things out of the way, the old lady sat for a moment, watching Cammie with a shrewd light in her eyes. When she spoke at last, it was in an entirely different tone.

"I told you, didn't I, that I knew Reid's grandfather Aaron? That was Justin Sayers's son?"

Cammie felt stillness close over her like a cloud. "I think you mentioned it."

"A handsome boy he was, too. I let him kiss me once out behind the barn when I was a giddy girl. But there was your great-uncle, and nothing ever came of it."

Cammie allowed herself to show only mild curiosity as she reached for a finger sandwich. She was half afraid her unpredictable great-aunt would change the subject if she guessed her intense interest.

"Yes, well. My sister Maybelle was older, and she married first, married your grandfather Greenley. What you might not know is that the reason that came about was because our mother was Lavinia Greenley's best friend, and one of the few people who stood by her in her troubles after her husband was killed. It was natural that their children should get together, so to speak."

"I had never heard that," Cammie said, pausing with her sandwich halfway to her mouth. "Is it possible—do you remember Lavinia?"

Her great-aunt's smile was sardonic. "As if it were yesterday. My mother was widowed early, and never remarried. She and Lavinia had a lot in common. In their later years the two of them traveled here and there all over the South and Southwest, even Mexico, in a beat-up old Ford coupe. They used to visit the old plantations that were going to rack and ruin back then, before preservation became a big deal; they were great pals with Cammie Garret down at Melrose close to Natchitoches, the woman who took in all the writers and artists. You were named for that Cammie, you know, in a roundabout way."

"I didn't, no."

The old woman gave a decisive nod. "Everything has a purpose, I always say."

"So Lavinia built a life for herself when all the scandal was over," Cammie suggested in order to get the subject back on track.

"Oh, she was something else. There weren't many of the politicians she didn't know back then, nor much that went on at the state house down in Baton Rouge that she didn't have her say about. She supported Huey Long when he was first getting started—and kept up a connection with other members of the Long political machine for years. That was how she came to donate the land for the game reserve."

Cammie sat forward. "You know about her land transactions?"

Aunt Beck gave her a crooked smile. "Why else do you think I called you?"

"The mill land?"

"Especially that. I never heard such ridiculous stuff in my life as this business Wen Marston has been telling me about you owning the mill land. The very idea, thinking Lavinia had no right to give that acreage away if she took the notion. Lavinia was as sharp as they come, and Justin Sayers was no dummy. Why would they arrange their business in any such haphazard manner? It makes no sense whatever!"

"I have to agree, but there does appear to be some kind of legal problem because of the secret divorce."

"Secret divorce, my eye; it was no secret in the family. You, of all people, Cammie, ought to know better. As for the land, I have no patience with all these people who take it for granted that whatever property Lavinia had must have come to her from Horace. Did it never occur to any of you that she might have had control of the property herself, in her own right?"

Cammie put down her teacup with a sharp click, afraid she would drop it. She felt stunned, not so much by the revelation her great-aunt had just made as by the fact that she herself had fallen into the same stereotypical way of thinking as everyone else. She said slowly, "If you mean that Lavinia had a legal right to sell the land, then she must have owned it before the marriage, or else bought it after the divorce. But if she had bought it, there should have been some record. . . ."

Aunt Beck's head was high and her dark old eyes were bright with scorn. "She inherited it when her mother died—her mother's people had been in this parish every bit as long as the Greenleys, maybe longer. So it made not a particle of difference whether Horace divorced her in that sneaky fashion. She had a perfect right to give away her property, and anything else she might have fancied, to Justin Sayers!"

Cammie picked up her cup again, holding it in one hand while she ran a finger around the rim. Her tone pensive, she said, "I've thought a lot about their affair in the last few days, for obvious reasons. I suppose nobody can say what really happened after all this time. But since you knew her, why do you think she came back here again after running away with Justin to the Northeast like that?"

"It's my belief Lavinia came back because of her son. He was so young, not quite three. It's hard for a mother to leave a child, even for a lover. Of course Horace held on to the boy, wouldn't let her see him. He wasn't a forgiving sort of man."

"He had his revenge."

"You could say so, though I don't think it gave him much pleasure. Divorce was a sin in his day, and he was a godly man."

"Do you think Lavinia killed him because of it?"

Aunt Beck was silent so long Cammie thought she might not have heard. She was about to repeat the question when the elderly woman finally spoke.

"Things were different back then, some seventy odd years ago. There was no such thing as a crisis center, and nobody noticed much if a man knocked his wife around, especially if she had shamed him by running off with another man. I heard my mother say one time that Lavinia was entitled to whatever peace she had found, because her married life had been hell on earth. I think if she killed Horace Greenley, she had good reason."

Cammie absorbed that idea for a moment before she said, "What about afterward? Why did she and Justin never get together? I mean, I know he was married by then, but he could have divorced his wife if he cared at all for Lavinia. They could have gone back East and started over if theirs was such a great love affair."

"I gather there were a lot of reasons. Lavinia was never arrested for murder, but the suspicion was there. A decent woman could get away with a lot back then, but there might have been some serious questions if she had upped and married her lover before her husband was cold in his grave. Then, the woman Justin had married on the rebound was a nice, sweet lady who was going to have a child; she didn't deserve to have her home broken up because of Lavinia's mistakes. More than anything else, though, I think Lavinia was ashamed: ashamed of leaving husband and child and breaking her marriage vows, ashamed of the wreckage of her marriage, ashamed of destroying a human life, ashamed that she had so misread her own heart that she betrayed her love to return to her husband. She had ruined everything, you see, and so deserved to lose everything."

"You think it was her, something inside herself, that kept them apart?"

"Well, I know my mother thought so. She always said that Justin Sayers would have walked through fire for Lavinia. It's likely he would have given up his marriage if she had asked it. But she didn't. Then he had a son, and she couldn't ask him to leave his child behind, since she hadn't been able to do the same for him."

"I suppose I can see that," Cammie said. "But what about the mill land? How does it come into it?"

"Who knows? It was something between the two of them, apparently. Though I've wondered once or twice if it didn't have something to do with compensation of a sort, you might call it a dream to replace a dream."

Cammie exchanged a long, considering glance with her older relative. Finally, she said, "You think Reid is legal owner of the mill, then?"

"There's not a shred of doubt in my mind."

Cammie finished her tea and set down the cup. Sitting

forward with hands clasped loosely together on her knees, she said, "I suppose I never really expected anything else."

"Have you considered—" Aunt Beck began, then stopped as if to collect her thoughts. When she began again, she said, "If you stop to think about it, Cammie, there are such parallels between what happened with Lavinia and with your troubles. Have you noticed?"

"Because Keith and Justin were both shot? I hardly think—"

"You were both near the same age and with independent means, both married, both having husband trouble, both involved with other men. Your husbands were both shot, and you are both suspects in the killings. Doesn't it strike you as odd?"

"What are you suggesting?"

"I may be a cynical and suspicious old woman, but I wonder if someone didn't plan it that way."

"Oh, no, surely not," Cammie said. She believed Reid's theory, that Keith's gambling debts were the cause of his death.

"Stranger things have happened. You will be careful, won't you, not take any foolish chances?"

Cammie looked down at her hands. "This whole thing—the problems with the mill, Janet Baylor's disappearance, the missing records, Keith's death—it's all so unbelievable. But you know, I think the thing that bothers me most is the way people are talking, the things they have said to me and about me."

The older woman's white hair caught the light with a silver glint as she nodded. "Talking is what people do best. But I've noticed myself the sheer meanness in what's going around. It's not natural, I can tell you—like this tale I heard just yesterday about you and Reid being caught naked and fornicating in the woods, and Reid shooting at the hunter who walked upon you."

"Dear God." Sickness curled inside Cammie for the

way the simple episode had been blown up into something ugly.

"I told the woman who dared say such stuff that she had a mind like a septic tank," Aunt Beck went on in sardonic tones. "Couldn't be true, I said, not my Cammie. But it seemed to me, after I thought about it, that maybe there's somebody spreading nastiness for the fun of it. Or for a reason we can't see."

"You mean as a part of all the rest?"

"Call me a paranoid old biddy, but I'm only telling you what I think."

"Sometimes," Cammie said wearily, "I feel like resigning from the human race."

"And leave things to the perverts? They would like that too much. I prefer to give them Hades."

Cammie, watching her frail great-aunt calmly sipping lukewarm tea from her fine china cup, had to laugh. It was better than crying.

She drove home with her thoughts jostling each other for position in her mind. There were a few things she had not mentioned to her great-aunt. It wasn't because she thought the elderly woman would not be interested, but rather that Cammie could guess too easily what her reaction would be. And she didn't want to hear it.

There was the gossip, for one thing. Aunt Beck's suggestion that it was being spread deliberately made excellent sense. Information might make the rounds at warp speed under normal circumstances, but the details of what she had done and was doing had spread so fast, it was nothing short of amazing. More than that, though the stories were grossly distorted, they had a bedrock of truth. It stood to reason, then, that whoever was behind them was no stranger. She hated the idea, but it had to be faced.

There had to be one person who, at any given time, was perfectly situated to know exactly what she was doing, when, and how.

Then there were the similarities between her troubles

and those that her great-grandmother had endured. It gave her cold chills to think of someone manipulating her life, arranging events and circumstances so that they made the same deadly pattern. What earthly reason could there be for it?

She could think of two, offhand. The first was a species of arrogance, a need to play God either to satisfy a twisted impulse, or else to inspire fear when the design was recognized. The second was to make it look as if she was herself following in Lavinia's footsteps, trying to emulate a proven plan for murder.

There was one person who would have had a better opportunity than anyone else to orchestrate events, creating the parallels pointed out by Aunt Beck.

There was a single man who had the best possible reason for influencing public opinion, making her appear both immoral and guilty of murder.

The reason was money.

The man was Reid.

Cammie didn't go home, but turned her car toward the Fort. She would have no rest until the maddening suspicions were answered. And if the answers soothed her heart, there were things Reid should know about Lavinia and Justin.

No one answered the bell. She left the front door and rounded the big log house, to see if Reid's Jeep was in the garage. It was then that she noticed the drift of smoke in the air, hanging in a gray-blue veil touched with lavender from the evening twilight.

She stood still, gazing around her. The house seemed all right, as did the garage with its shop addition. The thickest smoke haze seemed to be coming from down a slope toward the back of the property, near the woods. With a frown between her brows, Cammie moved in that direction.

The air was cool, yet with currents of balmy warmth that was the last remnants of the sun's heat wafting from the earth. In the quiet, insects and tree frogs sang their spring songs. The woods were shadowed with the approach of darkness. She breathed in the scents of honey-suckle and damp earth and green growing things, and also the acrid tang of smoke. It was almost enough to bring peace. Almost.

She saw the red heart of fire first. It was a fairly large blaze, burning with resolute brightness. The ground around it had been raked clean to prevent sparks and embers from escaping. A man moved toward it from the shadows at the wood's edge, tossing an armful of dried limbs and green brush onto the flames. As it leaped and crackled, snapping sparks toward the sky, Reid's face and bare arms and chest reflected the yellow-orange light with a bronze sheen.

He was clearing the tangle of undergrowth at the edge of the tree line that crowded the Fort. An axe and a small chain saw lay nearby. She should have known he would be in control of whatever was in progress there.

Her steps easier, she moved forward until she stood within the golden-red nimbus of the firelight. She halted, waiting.

"I thought," he said in tones laced with half-exasperated amusement as he reached for another load of brush without looking at her, "that we were supposed to act sensible and not be seen together. If I had known you were coming, I'd have cleaned up."

She had almost forgotten, or rather, it had been driven from her mind by other things. "I won't stay long. I just needed to talk to you."

"I'm not complaining." He made a gesture with one arm toward the cleared space behind him. As she moved in that direction, he dumped the brush he held on the fire, then stepped to where his shirt hung on a tree limb. Shaking it out, he spread it on the ground under a great pine a few feet inside the tree line. When she moved in nearer, he said, "We could walk back up to the house, but I should stick close to the fire until it burns down a bit."

"Won't you be cool?" She allowed her gaze to rest an

instant on the width of his chest, with the musculature burnished with the faint sheen of perspiration and the fine mat of curling gold hair tipped red with firelight.

His smile was rueful as he met her gaze. "I've been working," he said. "Besides . . ."

"What?"

"Nothing." He avoided looking at her as he touched her arm briefly, indicating she should take the seat he had made for her. As he dropped down on his heels beside her, he kept a little space between them, not enough to be obvious, but enough that there was no chance of an accidental touch.

He had meant that she warmed him. It was nice to know, since she felt the physical attraction between them like the low vibration of an electrical charge. Dragging her mind away, she explained the things Aunt Beck had told her, then waited for what he would say.

"She's a smart old lady." His tone was without inflection.

"Yes, but is she right?"

He picked up a dead twig, breaking off tiny pieces and dropping them. He glanced up at the fire then back at what he was doing with a wide, unseeing gaze. "How do you expect me to answer that, Cammie? I don't know."

Nor did she. Why had she come, then?

Because she couldn't stay away. Because she refused to allow others to dictate to her. Because she had an unsuppressible urge to live dangerously since she had always been so safe.

All these, and more.

What she wanted, she saw, was reassurance rather than answers. And she was not sure that could come from words, after all.

There was a piece of trash in his hair, a curling dead leaf. She reached up to flick it away, then trailed her fingertips through the fine blond strands above his ear, which were damp and darkened by perspiration. The ache of longing she felt was intense, almost painful, though it was not possible to tell whether it was physical or only emotional.

That he had some understanding of what drove her was plain in his face. He caught her hand, pressing a quick kiss to the fingers before touching them to his chest. Beneath the heated skin, she felt the heavy throb of his heart. "I'd like to hold you," he said on a husky note, "but I'm too dirty."

There was a fine dust of ash across the width of his shoulders, and he smelled of wood smoke and healthy, warm male. But the freshness of the outdoors and fresh-cut oak and new grass also clung to him like natural aphrodisiacs.

"I don't mind," she said, and spread her fingers wide over his chest, absorbing his heat and the feel of him as she leaned to offer her mouth for his kiss.

The contact was brief, yet tingling. He drew away with a smile. "You taste like tea and cake. I could eat you in a single bite."

"Do," she murmured, and smoothed her hand across his collarbone to his shoulder, clasping, drawing him to her.

He came willingly, settling to the ground beside her. There was more than humor in his voice as he warned, "Careful. We have some unfinished business in a spot like this."

"Several spots like this," she agreed, thinking of the wild attraction that had sprung between them that first evening when she ran away from Keith, and later, when she had found him in the woods behind her house and they sat talking in the dark. They were fully as memorable as the afternoon they had been discovered.

"You, too?" he said on a low laugh as he reached to span her waist with his large hand. "What a waste."

"Don't waste this time," she whispered, and turned against him, fitting her body into his, wanting, needing, the touch of him along its entire length, needing to feel his strength against her.

He came to her, rolling her to her back, giving her what she needed. As she felt his hard maleness, his weight, desire spiraled up within her in hot coils. Refusing to think, avoiding all doubt, she buried her face in his shoulder, holding him with tight, desperate hands, wrapping her legs around his with taut muscles. The yearning for him to be everything she thought him, everything she needed, was a hollow emptiness at the center of her being that only he could fill.

Concern threaded his voice as he whispered, "Cammie, what is it?"

"Nothing, everything. Oh, Reid—just kiss me please, and don't stop. Don't ever stop."

She felt his hesitation, knew he realized the suspicion she was trying to escape. Felt, too, the instant that his angry despair turned to passion. Then he lifted his weight from her to lie with his broad shoulders blocking the fading light, and also the view from the Fort.

His hands upon her were hard and sure. He knew her now, knew the caresses that drove her mad, the touch that turned her bones to jelly and left her mindless and pliant under him.

She was the same. She knew how to tease and torment him, how to drive him to the last, gasping edge of control.

He pushed his hand under the denim skirt she wore with a periwinkle cotton sweater, resting his hand on the soft mound he found there. Following its crease with firm strokes of his long fingers, he inserted a knee between her legs, opening them wider, extending his access. She gave way with consummate grace, gasping with the shock of pleasure as he slid a finger under the elastic of her panties to seek more perfect contact.

She dipped her head, finding the buried coin of his pap, nipping it, laving it with her tongue, suckling. At the same time, she wrenched the copper button of his jeans from its hole and slid the zipper down. Pushing under his briefs without ceremony, she grasped the heated firmness of him, tugging, rubbing, inciting.

He pressed a finger into her hot, moist softness. Convulsions of fierce pleasure fluttered her abdomen muscles, and she clenched around the finger, which probed and aroused. He ground the heel of his hand against her with slow, steady intent.

She lifted her head. He took her parted lips, tasting them with laps of his tongue, thrusting between them with tender friction that made them tingle with sensitivity. He pressed deeper, invading, retreating in a firm, sure double rhythm that stimulated and promised.

A soft moan sounded in her throat as heated wetness seeped from her, and she lifted her hips, fitting herself more firmly into his hand. He made a rumbling sound of rich satisfaction in his throat. Leaving her mouth, he bent his head to take the nipple of her breast between his teeth, searing it with his hot breath through layers of cotton and silk.

Suddenly, it was too much and not enough. They stripped impeding clothing away, leaving what did not matter. Hot and hard, heated and giving, they came together in fluid, interlocking connection. He twisted his hips, reaching deeper, driving into the beating core of her. She opened to her greatest depth, taking him to the exquisitely tender center of her innermost self.

It was a passionate trial by combat, a fury of competitive ecstasy, of supplicating lust, an anguished craving to make right by might. Flesh against flesh, they drove each other in an unrelenting quest for answers that remained elusive. Yet it was a splendid clash, a fine meshing of mind and spirit with the melding of bodies.

It was glory. It was sensuality incarnate. It was an entanglement from which there was no surcease, no surrender.

And no defeat.

Chapter Eighteen

▨ ▨ ▨ *Cammie was comforted yet depressed as* she drove away from the Fort. She had made love to Reid, and accepted the love he made to her, as if there were no tomorrow. But there was always a tomorrow.

Maybe that's what she was afraid of: she didn't want tomorrow to come.

She hadn't wanted to leave. Reid had insisted. He thought it best, for her protection. As if it mattered.

He had done his job of protecting her too well. She no longer felt safe unless he was near.

What did that say for her common sense?

She still hadn't got a straight answer from him about Janet Baylor. Fear, that was what kept her from pressing the issue. What would she do if he confessed to getting the paralegal out of town, either through threat or bribery?

Then there was Keith. She was haunted by images of how terrified he must have been when he knew he was going to die. Courage had never been his long suit; he would have begged to live. Or maybe not; it was impossible to judge, and more than a little presumptuous.

The headlights appeared in her rearview mirror almost immediately after she left the private road leading to Reid's house. Whoever was in the car came on at speed, moving in close behind her. They hung on her back bumper.

Tailgating of that kind was unsafe anywhere, but out

here on the dark and winding game reserve road, with its many blind curves and deer crossings, it was downright homicidal. There was no excuse for it; the chances of being able to pass were nil. It had to be a joyriding idiot, or else some teenager showing off for his friends or some girl he had brought out into the woods.

Cammie tried increasing her speed. It didn't help; the other car clung like a burr. She tapped her brake pedal a couple of times. The car behind her fell back for an instant, then came on again.

It was a relief when the main highway to Greenley appeared ahead of her and she turned on it. She expected her tailgater to pull out to pass at the first empty stretch of road. She slowed and pulled over closer to the shoulder to make it easier.

It didn't happen. The other car barreled along behind her, almost touching her back bumper. She speeded up again.

For the first time, fear brushed her. There seemed to be something personal in the high-speed hazing. Who would do such a thing? The possibilities were wide, if she thought about it. It could be the same person who had killed Keith. Or it might be any one of the dozens of people who resented her opposition to mill expansion. She held her speed steady while she tried to decide what to do.

She realized after an instant that there was no need to panic. The outskirts of Greenley, with its streetlights and business signs, would be showing up any second. She would be able to see whoever was back there then. If they did not drop farther behind her, there would be too much chance of being recognized.

Unless the driver decided to fall back from easy view, then follow her home after she passed through Greenley.

The big convenience store and truck stop at the edge of town was lit up like an airport at Christmas. Cammie flipped up her signal blinker, hit the brake, and wheeled into the entranceway. Rocketing between the gas pumps and the front door, she came to a halt.

Behind her there was the shriek of brakes, then the other car shot around the gas pumps on the far side, swung in a tight curve and slammed to a stop. The driver wrenched himself from behind the wheel and swung in her direction.

Cammie was half out of her car on her way toward the store door when she saw who had been driving the other car.

Gordon Hutton.

Anger swept through her with the force of a wildfire in dry woods. She didn't wait for her brother-in-law to reach her, but stalked toward him. "What in the world do you think you're doing? You could have killed us both!"

"I was trying to chase you down," Gordon said with a sneer on his round face. "I've been needing to talk to you for days, while you've been flying high, all over the country. I saw you leaving Sayers's place just now and decided to stick to your tail till you stopped."

"You could have called to set up a meeting," Cammie said in cold distaste.

"I've left a half-dozen messages with your house-keeper, for what good it did me. It's my belief she only passes on what she wants you to know."

Cammie had not checked with Persephone, though she saw no reason to tell him so. "So what did you want?"

He moved closer, curling his big, too-white hands into fists. The fumes of bourbon wafted toward her along with stale body odor and the sickly, bitter sweetness of some cheap men's cologne. It was all Cammie could do not to take a step back, if only for the fresher air.

"It's about time," he said, "that we come to an under-standing, now that you've got your hands on a piece of the mill. Your meddling with the sale got my goat before, but I was willing to overlook it because I knew it was a silly female way of getting back at Keith over the divorce business. Now I want it stopped."

The contempt in his voice was enraging; his calm assumption that he could tell her what to do destroyed any hope he might have had of persuading her to listen to him. With chill disdain in her eyes, she said, "This may come as a shock to you, Gordon, but I've never been particularly interested in what you want."

"Bitch," he said, and clamped his teeth together so hard his jowls shook. "You always were selfish, never gave a damn about anybody or anything. It's no wonder Keith had to leave home to find the kind of woman he needed."

Cammie wondered, for a bare instant, if he was right, if her lack of caring had driven Keith away. Then memory and sanity returned. Her smile was grim. "You can turn that around, you know. Maybe I learned to care about myself because no one else ever did."

"That's a crock. Half the men in this town have been drooling over you for ages. And you know it."

There was something in his fleshy face that made her skin crawl. It wasn't the first time she'd noticed it, though it was the first that she had acknowledged its source. Gordon Hutton coveted his brother's wife; he always had. She lifted her chin as she answered, "It isn't the same thing."

He snorted. "You've solved your little problem, though, haven't you? You've got Sayers where you want him—in your favorite position, on his knees."

Keith had been a sullen drunk. Gordon, it seemed, turned crude when he had too much. Alcohol didn't change character, it only brought out traits usually kept hidden. The results could be instructive.

"I don't have to listen to this," she said, distaste congealing on her features in the blue-white fluorescent light from inside the convenience store. "If you want to discuss the mill, call Fred Mawley when you're sober. I'll meet with you in his office."

Gordon's eyes widened in shock. "Why, you—"

Cammie didn't stay to listen. Ducking into her car, she

slammed the door and put the Cadillac in gear. She reversed in a wide, fast swing, then pulled away.

The squeal of tires behind her told her Gordon was coming after her again. That he actually thought he could get away with harassing her like this turned her anger into a clear-headed rage she had felt only a few times in her life. She wasn't going to stop again for him. But neither was she going to run away. And if he had the gall to follow her all the way to Evergreen, Keith's brother just might hear a few home truths he would prefer not to know.

Gordon's headlights still glared in her car mirrors when she turned into the drive. Though she parked in the garage, she thought he was going to ram into the Cadillac before she could get out of it.

He piled out of his own vehicle and stood blocking her way as she stalked from the dark garage interior. Gordon's stumplike legs were spread and he had his hands on his hips.

"Nobody talks to me like that, sister," he began, grating ugliness in his tone.

"Nor would I, if you hadn't pushed it," she replied, countering him with a sharp refusal to be intimidated. "Since you have, there are a few other things on my mind. To start with, I don't appreciate you sneaking around spying on me, or following me."

"That's ridiculous. I was just driving by the Fort—"

"Sure you were," she said in scathing disbelief. He had made a tactical error by defending himself, but she didn't intend to allow him to recover from it. "For another thing, you may have thought it was smart to encourage Keith to force himself on me to stop our divorce, but you came close to getting your brother killed then. Not that you cared. All you wanted was to be sure you got your precious money for the mill. Money, that's what you love, and Keith knew it. That's why he was afraid to tell you he was up to his ears in gambling debts. That's why he was so desperate that he embezzled from the mill instead of coming to you for help!"

All expression vanished from Gordon Hutton's face, leaving it dull and stupid with shock, there in the stabbing brilliance of his car's headlights. His voice was hoarse as he said, "He what?"

"Embezzlement. A half million, at least. And you never missed it, never even guessed it was gone. Reid had to discover the loss."

He opened his mouth for a gasping breath. "I don't believe it. Keith wouldn't do that. Why, taking money from the mill would be like taking it out of his own brother's pocket."

"Reid's too, you might remember," she reminded him.

His eyes blinked as he absorbed the implications of what he had heard. "That's why Sayers went after him—"

"If you mean the day Keith got beat up, that wasn't Reid. The best bet is that it was a reminder from the people he owed."

"God." Gordon's face turned pasty and his shoulders sagged. "I'd have helped him find the money if he'd come to me. Why would he—the Huttons don't do things like that. Ah, God, it'll kill Mama when she hears."

Cammie felt a stir of compunction. He had cared after all, it seemed. He also had his pride: in his family, in the mill, in a long tradition of fair dealing. There had never been any indication that he or his father, or his grandfather before him, had been anything except honest men. To know that his brother had held none of it of value must be a blow.

Abruptly, he straightened. "If Keith took the money, it was because of you, because he hated you having more than he did."

"I'm not to blame for his ego problems."

"You made him feel half a man. But I don't believe any of it, not of my brother. You're a lying bitch. It's not enough for you to force him from his home and destroy him—you have to ruin his name, too."

Cammie gave him back stare for stare. "Keith did a fine job of ruining himself without my help."

Gordon lifted a fist, shaking it in front of her face. "Shut up! Shut your lying mouth. If I hear you're spreading this story, I'll make you the sorriest woman who ever drew breath. You're just trying to queer the mill deal by making out there's financial problems. I won't stand for it. You hear me? I'll see you dead first!"

"Be very careful," she said, her voice lethal in its softness. "The last man to threaten me didn't live long."

His head came up. "You mean—Keith?"

She made no reply, only watched him with an unwavering gaze.

He took a step backward. Swearing under his breath, he whirled and threw himself into his car. He backed down the drive so fast the smell of burning rubber was left hanging in the air. Within seconds his taillights had disappeared and the sound of his engine was dying away.

Cammie let out the shuddering breath she had not known she was holding. She turned away, fumbling with the keys in her hand, though she was shaking so badly that she couldn't seem to untangle the back door key from the rest.

A shadow moved near the steps. She halted with a small scream catching in her throat.

"It's only me," Reid said.

There was something in his voice, a wariness she had never heard before. There was no smile on his strained features. His chest was rising and falling as if he'd been running. She had left him so short a time ago. He must have started through the woods for Evergreen almost the instant she was out of sight.

When she made no answer, he went on, "I saw the car, heard voices, when I made my usual patrol. I thought you might need help. You didn't."

His usual patrol. She had known, of course, even if she hadn't admitted it to herself. That consideration was wiped from her mind, however, as she realized what he had heard.

The words she had spoken to Gordon could have sounded more like a threat than the warning she had intended. And he already thought it was possible that she had killed Keith. Or so he had pretended.

"You're wrong," she said. "I did need you."

"Why," he asked, tipping his head to one side. "Would you like me to kill him for you instead. Is that why you're keeping me around, after all?"

It wasn't an offer. Nor was it a joke. He meant to ask if she would like him to murder Gordon instead of doing it herself. He had suggested something similar before in order to provoke a rise from her, and in retaliation for making him admit he was capable of it. This time he was deadly serious; he really thought she wanted Gordon dead.

Cammie flashed him a look of stark and painful disbelief before she whirled from him. She stumbled as she pounded up the steps and across the porch. It took her the third try to put her key into the lock. She pushed inside, slamming the heavy door behind her.

She need not have hurried. Reid did not come after her. When she looked out the window, there was no one there. He was gone.

It was a long time before she slept that night. Images came and went in her mind, changing like a kaleidoscope equipped with sound. Keith and Reid in the dark at the lake. Reid with the little girl at the family reunion. The shadowy figure of a man who was not Reid watching Evergreen. Wen in her boat crossing the lake. The Reverend Taggart speaking of marriage. Reid and Charles with their heads together in front of the computer. Gordon and his mother at Keith's funeral. Bud accusing her of stupidity. Aunt Beck talking of old scandal, and new. Gordon stomping from his car. It seemed there was a pattern there somewhere, some answers that she needed, if she could only see them.

She wondered, as she replayed the words Reid had said to her, if her doubts of his innocence had the power to hurt him as his did her. It was a strange idea, perhaps, since it would only be possible if he was, in fact, innocent. But didn't it show that if he thought she might be guilty, then he could not be? He could not suspect her of a crime he had committed himself. That was elementary. But only if it was possible to trust him.

Shall I kill him for you?

She had been so certain of his meaning as she faced him there at the steps. Yet, in the dark hours of the night, her doubt returned. It was possible she had misunderstood, and the words had been an offer of service after all. Wasn't that the position he had taken with her from the beginning: unrelenting, altruistic, all too competent service?

There were dark circles under her eyes and the tightness of a tension headache behind her forehead when she got up early the next morning. The idea of staying at home with nothing to do except think, staying where people could find her to complain or accuse, was intolerable.

She decided it was time to reestablish some semblance of a routine to her days. She had been neglecting the antique store. It was unfair to leave Wen to carry on alone for so long. Pulling a full skirt of grass-green twill and a matching cotton sweater from her closet, she began to get dressed.

Cammie spent the morning at the shop, helping unpack the most recent acquisitions from an estate sale. There was a great deal of junk in it: rusting silverplate, furniture store prints in flaking gilt frames, boxes of old books from which silverfish ran at the slightest touch, a collection of salt and pepper shakers shaped like farm animals. But there were also several pieces of Rockingham and Majolica earthenware, a Limoges porcelain chocolate service, plus a rosewood parlor set from the 1860s that still had the original silk brocatelle upholstery.

The grimy work and change of interest, not to mention Wen's caustic and irreverent comments on the things people thought worthy of saving, gave a lift to Cammie's spirits. She was beginning to feel halfway normal by the time noon rolled around.

Wen had gone to the kitchen in the back to heat home-made vegetable soup for their lunch. Cammie stayed in the front with a customer. She was wrapping the Britannia-ware candlestick that the woman had bought when the brass shop bell rang.

The lanky shape and fine blond hair of the woman who stepped inside were instantly recognizable. Keith's girl-friend, Evie Prentice, flashed a quick, tense smile, but made no move to approach, wandering instead toward a grouping of old teddy bears. She bent to pick one up, caressing it softly, then held it an instant against the swell of her body under the oversized T-shirt she wore. When she put it back down, there was a wet sheen of tears in her eyes.

Cammie finished what she was doing and rang up the sale. When the door bell had clanged with the customer's departure, she moved slowly toward Evie. Her gaze rested on the dark circles under the girl's eyes as she said quietly, "How have you been, Evie?"

"Fine, just fine." Evie's smile was overly bright as she swung to face her.

"I looked for you at the funeral, but you weren't there."

The smile faltered. "That kind of thing is for families. I know Ed down at the funeral home; he let me in after everybody else left. I got to say good-bye, and that was—the main thing."

"And the baby? You're feeling all right?"

"Yes, but—I saw your car out front, and you were so nice before. I thought—"

Cammie touched the other girl's hand briefly. "There is something wrong, then; I thought so. I expect you would like to sit down. Come over here and tell me about it."

There was a back corner where a motley group of old chairs were pulled up around a potbellied stove with ornate chrome trim. There was no fire in the stove today, but the corner was quiet and out of the way. Cammie gestured toward a rocking chair, while she took a side chair with swan-neck arms.

"I guess just about everything is wrong," Evie said as she settled into the rocker. She looked at Cammie, then glanced away again with color rising under her pale skin. "I don't mean to say anything bad about Keith, really I don't. I loved him and I—I think I would have been good for him. But he left me in sort of a mess."

"How is that?" Cammie made the words as encouraging as possible.

"Well, he was paying the note on my trailer and the utilities, buying the groceries. He made me quit my job, so the only thing coming in was what he gave me. I didn't like it—with the other men I let come around, I kept working so as to be independent, see? Not that there was that many, only one or two. But there was the divorce coming up, and it seemed important to Keith to be supporting me. At least, until lately. Anyway, he got behind on the trailer note, and I always had to remind him when there was nothing left to eat. I had a little saved, but it—didn't last long. With him gone now, I've got no money. And nobody will hire me, not with the shape I'm in, not in this town."

"I can imagine." From the bitterness of the last words, Cammie thought the other girl had not had an easy time of it with her job-hunting.

"I purely hate the idea of going on welfare, though I guess I've got as much right as anybody. I've already seen about having the baby over at the medical center in Shreveport, where it won't cost anything, so that's all right. But what I'd really like is to get away from Greenley and everything that's happened. Only there's not much chance of that, what with everything being the way it is."

Beyond where they sat, the door from the back opened and Wen stuck her head out. As she saw who Cammie was talking to, her face went blank with surprise. Cammie gave a slight shake of her head. Wen rolled her eyes but withdrew, though she left the door open a crack.

Evie Prentice, oblivious to the byplay as she stared down at her hands resting on her swollen abdomen, went on. "I hate to come bothering you again, but I don't know where else to turn. My last hope was Reverend Taggart. I thought maybe there was some church fund—" She stopped, as if to regain control, then went on again in broken tones. "You'd think a preacher would know all there was about forgiveness for sin and Christian charity, wouldn't you? But he had nothing for me except a sermon. Told me I had made my bed, and I could lie in it with whoever paid the price. Only thing I despise more than welfare is a hypocrite."

There was pain and desperation in the girl's voice. In an effort to help her regain her composure and save her the necessity of asking, Cammie said, "Tell me how much you need."

Evie looked at her with doubt and hope shining through the tears in her light blue eyes. "I couldn't take your money. Honestly, I couldn't. But Keith said—he promised he would take care of me and the baby, no matter what. I know it's weird to ask you, but I thought maybe you knew of a bank account or something he might have set up for us."

There was nothing, Cammie knew that with absolute certainty. The only thing Keith had left at the bank was an overdraft. "I'm not sure what he may have done," she said, "but I can look into it for you."

"Would you? Really?" The tears in Evie's eyes over-flowed, running in wet tracks down her face. "I was so embarrassed, so ashamed to face you with my problems and how it was with me and Keith. I just—"

"Never mind," Cammie said soothingly. "I'll look into

the money situation and call you in a day or two. All right?"

"I can't thank you enough. I—I loved Keith, and I was furious when he told me he was going back to you. But I never blamed him for wanting to, not really. I see what he was after."

"I don't think you do," Cammie said. "If it's any comfort, I think his sudden change of heart had more to do with money."

Evie Prentice scanned Cammie's face, her drowned gaze considering. Slowly, it turned desolate. "No—" she said with a catch in her voice. "I don't think it is—any comfort, I mean."

Cammie walked to the door with Keith's girlfriend. As Evie drove away, Wen came from the back to stand beside her.

"So you're going to find the money to help Keith's main squeeze."

"She was more than that," Cammie answered absently.

"Yeah, she was the other woman, the one he was shacked up with, the one he was going to use to make you a laughingstock just as soon as he had what he wanted."

"Maybe."

"So is it because you're sorry for her, or because you want her out of your hair?"

"Maybe I'm grateful to her for freeing me of Keith."

"Oh, sure."

"It's possible," Cammie protested.

"Yes, and maybe you're a softhearted idiot."

"Softheaded, you mean."

"That, too." Wen muttered an expletive. "Cammie, honey, you can't fix the world."

"Yes, I can," she answered with a determined lift of her chin. "Or at least my part of it."

Chapter Nineteen

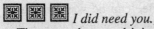 *I did need you.*

Those words were driving Reid insane.

Nearly as disturbing was the answer he had made to them.

The two phrases had rung in his mind all night and half the morning, along with the confrontation he had witnessed between Cammie and Gordon Hutton. He hadn't slept; the thought of eating made him feel sick to his stomach. Long ago he'd learned the difficult lesson that sleep and food were needs you didn't ignore if you wanted to stay alive. Nothing, not even the explosion at Golan, as he referred to it in his mind, had gotten past his defenses enough to disturb these basic habits. Until now.

He was losing his carefully built numbness. It was being stripped away bit by bit, leaving nerves and feelings as exposed as worms discovered under thick mulch. Try as he might, he could find no protection for them, no surcease from the raw pain.

It had begun at Golan, of course; he wouldn't deny that. But it was being close to Cammie that had made him so exquisitely vulnerable.

The Fort seemed like a prison, and Lizbeth's eyes, as they followed him, were all too knowing. She had always understood him better than most. She had a husband and family of her own and a farm north of town, but in his memories of growing up, she was always in the house.

He could remember one hot summer when he was

maybe four or five years old, standing beside her in the kitchen where they were now, watching while she drank a glass of water. The inside of her mouth, he noticed, was as pink as his own. After that, he'd always known she was the same, under her soft brown skin, as he.

She turned her head now, sparing him a glance from the green onions she was chopping for a casserole. "What's the matter, Mr. Reid, the mulligrubs got you?"

"You might say that," he answered, propping his elbow on the table and resting his head on one fist. Keeping his gaze on the coffee cup he was turning in slow circles, he said, "Tell me something, Lizbeth, just what does it take to please a woman?"

She tilted her head forward to give him a look under her brows. "Now, you know that as well as I do."

"I'm serious," he protested, "and I don't mean sex or money or muscles or things like that."

"Are we, by any off chance, talking about a certain woman in town, or just women in general?"

He gave her a straight look without answering.

"I thought so," she said with a judicious nod. "In that case, I'd say there's not much you can do except to love her. She'll either come around or she won't."

"I had a feeling you were going to say that."

"Then why did you go and ask me? Seems like what you need is to get your mind off things for a while, maybe go fishing."

"And get out from under your feet?"

She shook her head before she turned her broad back on him. "You know better than that."

"Maybe," he answered with dry humor. He paused a moment, considering her suggestion. Finally, he asked, "Ty still home on leave?"

"Got another week before he belongs to the Air Force again," she said, scooping up green onions and dumping them into a sauce pan where butter sizzled. Glancing over her shoulder, she added, "Want me to call him?"

"Tell him to meet me out at the lake," he answered, and let his smile convey his gratitude for her understanding.

He and Ty had a lot in common. They were the same age, and had played together from time to time when Lizbeth brought him to work with her during the summer. Together, they had roamed the game reserve, two boys pretending to be mighty hunters, cavemen, or soldiers. They had gone to the same school during the first flush of local integration, and both had tried out for one of Greenley's first integrated football teams. Ty had played halfback, making it his special project to protect Reid as the quarterback in tight play situations. Reid not only appreciated the coverage, but gave his halfback full credit for most of the important plays.

Ty had joined the Air Force out of school, becoming a helicopter pilot. He had worked his way up to a colonel's rank and was still climbing. Over the years, he and Reid had met in various out of the way places around the world to share a drink and catch up on the home news. The last time had been in California nearly two years ago. Reid had been intending to get together with Ty while they were both in town, but his time had been taken up with other things.

The day was perfect for fishing, the temperature hovering around seventy, wind calm, sun coming and going behind ragged and dingy white sheets of clouds. Reid and Ty launched the fiberglass bass boat, then took off down the lake channel. After a few minutes they eased into a long, tree-crowded arm of the lake well out of the traffic.

Using top-water bait, they cast with the easy competence of long habit, reeling in without wasted motion, but also without hurry. Neither of them really cared if they caught anything. It was enough to drift lazily over the tree-sap brown water with its surface tinted blue with sky reflection, using the trolling motor now and then to reach where rod and line could not take them.

They found the bass, great Florida-type monsters

weighing from four to eight pounds, caught their limit and put them on ice. They were careful how they hooked what they caught afterward, since they needed to release them back into the lake.

Reid felt the tension leaving him by slow degrees. It had been with him so long that its departure left behind tingling discomfort.

He and Ty popped a beer or two as the day grew hotter. While they drank, they talked in a desultory way, damning politics and politicians, taking the past seasons of the Saints and the Cowboys apart, raking over the latest dust-up at the Pentagon. It was the kind of wide-ranging and impersonal talk resorted to by most men when they got together. When the two of them had nothing to say, they were silent.

Out of a long period of floating with the sun on his face and watching a blue and green dragonfly perched on his rod tip, Reid asked, "You ever think of getting married, Ty?"

The other man flashed a grin as he tipped his dark head. "Now and then. Right time, wrong woman. Right woman, wrong time. You thinking about it again?"

"Crossed my mind," he allowed.

"Hear you seeing a lot of Cammie Greenley." It was a statement that could be answered or left alone.

"Hutton," Reid said without expression. "Cammie Hutton."

"Right. You always did have a thing for her, didn't you? I remember after a football game, bunch of guys started asking some joker who dated her about how he scored. One idiot got down and dirty with his questions, and you took him apart."

Reid shrugged without looking at Ty. "Seemed the thing to do at the time."

"Ahuh. And as I recall, we used to circle back through the game reserve past the Greenley place so often we wore a trail like a super highway."

Reid gave him a quick look. "You remember too much."

"Like that time the field mouse got in the building, had all the girls screaming and jumping on the desks. You caught the thing, all macho with your bare hands, and it bit the hell out of you? But when Cammie Greenley said don't kill it, you took it out and let it loose behind the baseball field. Then you walked around for days with the stupidest look on your face, all because she said you were kind. Yeah, man, I remember that, too."

Ty was kidding him, but Reid didn't care. He let the memory the other man had raised, bright-burnished and sweet, seep into his mind. And suddenly he felt an icy chill begin around his heart.

Cammie could not possibly have killed anyone. In spite of her courage, regardless of her bravado, she didn't have the hard inner core that would permit it.

Her threat against Keith's brother last night had been empty, if it had been a threat at all. He, of all people, should understand Cammie's ability to drive away those who could hurt her with a salvo of knife-edged words.

The only possible way she could have caused the death of a human being was if she'd been allowed no other choice.

He had known that simple truth before. How had he forgotten?

The answer was, he hadn't forgotten at all. What he'd done was ignore it.

He had ignored it because he'd been an idiot. He'd heard and seen her rout Gordon Hutton, and had been miffed because it seemed she didn't require his protection any longer.

He wanted her to need him because that was all he could use to hold her. And he'd wanted that hold on her desperately.

I did need you.

The words she'd spoken had remained with him because hidden in them was a tiny hint that she might require something more than a strong arm and a warm body. He'd almost missed it in his concentration on his own needs.

Almost.

What if he was wrong? What if there was nothing in what she'd said except what he was reading into it, nothing except his own hope?

He loved her; he had for years. It seemed there had never been a time when he did not love her.

There had also never been a time to tell her so.

Maybe that time was now.

He'd tried once, and failed. And failing made it impossible for him to see her for years.

What if he made it impossible to go back to the physical relationship they had established? There was such near-intolerable pleasure in being able to touch her bare skin, to watch her face as she took the release he offered. There was such mind-stunning glory in finding his own surcease in the depths of her body. Could he endure being denied it?

What if he made it impossible to ever see her again?

It was a chance he would have to take. He had risked more before, and won.

He had also lost. At least one of those times, it was love he'd lost, though of a different, more gentle kind. And it was not he who had paid the price. Could he chance that? Could he bear it, and live?

What else was there? After all this time?

It was late afternoon by the time Reid took his leave of Ty, cleaned his share of the fish, cleaned himself up, then gathered together everything he would need. Hoping Lizbeth wouldn't fuss too much about the way he'd torn up her kitchen with his rummaging, he left for Evergreen.

Cammie wasn't at home, but that was no great problem. He let himself into the house with his handy lock-picking kit and headed straight for the kitchen.

He couldn't wait to see her face when she found him there, he thought as he set the deep fat fryer he had brought on the cabinet. He plugged it in, then reached for the gallon of peanut oil to fill it. If it came to that, he couldn't wait to hear what she might have to say. It was entirely possible she would do her best to annihilate him. It wouldn't make any difference; he could take anything she dished out.

That hadn't been true at one time. He hadn't known her as well then, or himself.

It would be a relief to finally come out of hiding, to—what was that phrase used by writers of spy novels? Come in out of the cold? He'd never heard anybody use it himself, not in all his years in the Company. It was descriptive, though. Being alone in your own mind was a cold and lonely thing.

There had always been warmth in thinking of Cammie, even when he'd known she was married to someone else. He had to admit that.

Holding her in the quiet aftermath of sex, or just for the sake of feeling her against him—with passion of a mental kind, yes, but without lust—had warmed someplace hidden inside that had been iced over for years. He loved being quiet with her, too, reading, watching television.

He loved watching her enjoy things, the way she had in New York. Maybe they could travel other places together. It would be a great way to spend a winter evening, choosing and planning trips, arguing over which sights they should see for the pleasure of coming to terms. He knew exactly how much it would take—or how little—to make him agree to go anywhere she wanted.

The peanut oil was heating just fine. He unwrapped the bass fillets, rinsing them under cold, running water before he lay them out on paper towels to drain. Dumping several cups of white cornmeal into a bowl, he began to rummage through the cabinet shelves for salt and pepper. He hoped his taste in seasoning suited Cammie, because he only knew one way to do it.

He saw that Persephone had been there during the day. She'd left supper for Cammie, pork chops and fresh mustard greens. Maybe he could heat the greens to go with the fish; that would be good. There was also a coconut pie for later. Persephone was one of a dying breed, like Lizbeth. They would both be retiring soon, and it would be impossible to replace them.

He and Cammie could take care of things together when that time came, he thought. He didn't mind cleaning, and he liked cooking. Well, he liked cooking some things; he was no expert.

Where would the two of them live? He didn't care. Either house would make a great museum, if the town wanted the donation. Or they could save the spare place for their kids.

A grin tugged a corner of his mouth. He might be getting just a little ahead of himself, but it was fun, anyway.

The oil was hot as blue blazes, just right. There might have been a bit too much water left in the fish under their coating of meal. The oil crackled and spat with the sound of an miniature artillery barrage as he dropped the fillets into the fryer.

What next? Peel the potatoes. Persephone was a smart cook; she knew a sharp knife was safer than a dull one. She didn't mess with dinky little paring knives, either, or poor quality blades.

Was he expecting too much of Cammie, he wondered, coming here like this? It wasn't fair to make a single person responsible for your whole happiness. Of course, she couldn't know how much it meant to him, had no idea the power she held over him.

She might begin to understand it the minute he told her how he felt. Hell, knowing Cammie, there was no doubt about that part.

Could he stand it if she took what he said and used it against him? Maybe. What he couldn't stand would be if she heard him out, then gave him what he wanted of her out of nothing more than unselfish compassion. He suspected that was a real possibility.

He didn't hear the door.

The first thing he knew was a wafting of cool air on the back of his neck and the brush of a touch on his back. So little, and yet it was enough.

Instincts, laid aside for the first time in long, careful years while he concentrated on his task and his plans, sprang to life in the space of a single heartbeat. They had only one hard-drilled purpose.

The knife turned in his hand as he came around. Sharp edge uppermost, point forward, he drove it with every ounce of his strength toward the soft vitals of whoever posed this incipient threat. Perfectly timed, lightning in execution, there was no possible defense.

A drift of gardenia scent combined with fish and hot peanut oil. A familiar, incomparably necessary presence, felt rather than seen.

The warning screamed through his brain in a red-hot vapor trail of pain. Mind and instinct clashed. Muscles cramped, tendons creaked. Bones wrenched, bending under opposing pressures. The cry that tore from his own throat mingled with a soft, feminine sound of terror and regret.

Too late. Cringing, soul-sick, he felt the instant that steel slashed cloth, sank into tender, giving flesh, ripped free again.

Cammie.

She spun away from him, falling with an impetus half his doing, half her own reaction to danger. Her eyes were wide and dark with pain. The blood, spreading, was bright red against the soft green of her sweater.

He moved like a whiplash, unfurling to catch her before she struck the floor. Slinging the knife across the room to clatter against the wall, he gathered her against him. There was a rough voice babbling. His, he thought, though he had little sense of the words.

"Not—your fault," she whispered against his chest. He

felt the heat of her breath through his shirt, and he shivered. Then her lashes fluttered down, and he stopped living.

He was there, but also not there, for what followed. Ripping the plug of the deep-fat fryer from the socket. Putting Cammie into the Jeep. Cursing the nurse in the emergency room for being so slow, for hurting Cammie while she undressed her, for waiting until the wound was exposed before she sent for the physician on call. Refusing to release Cammie while the doctor explored the wound and stitched up the slashed opening. Barely listening while he was told that nothing vital had been touched, that the wound was clean—hearing only that the knife blade had passed within minute fractions of an inch of the main blood supply of the body.

He had known it could be no other way. It had been, God help him, his target.

By then Cammie was awake and trying to excuse him while he explained. She hadn't wanted anything for pain, had tried to refuse to take it. He had snatched the syringe from the nurse and, shivering, pressed the needle into her soft flesh himself.

He drove her home. On the way, he kept his mouth shut tight on all the things he longed to say. And he watched her, imprinting the memory of her white face and clear, absolving gaze somewhere in the recesses of mind and heart where it could never be erased. Against future need.

She hadn't wanted anyone to stay with her. He was all the help she needed, she said. He called her aunt Sara anyway.

She scowled and told him he was a bully. He didn't answer. It was true.

The sedative took effect at last, though she winced in her sleep as she tried to move. He allowed himself to come close then, kneeling beside the bed, holding her hand to his lips, watching the rise and fall of her chest under the bandaging. Counting the pulse that throbbed under his fingers. Touching the soft, gold-brown silk of her hair. Brushing her cheek with his knuckles. Watching the shadows of her lashes merge with the shadows spreading under her eyes.

Until her aunt came. He let the fussy, frightened old biddy hustle him out of the room then. He was even grateful to her for preventing him from doing anything stupid, such as kissing Cammie good-bye.

His Jeep was in the driveway, but he forgot it. Walking out the back door of Evergreen, he turned automatically for the woods.

The darkness of them closing around him was welcome. He didn't stop, however, but kept walking, winding through the trees, crossing creeks, scaring up deer that were bedded down in thickets, driving deeper and deeper into the cool, covering blackness.

The effort caught up with him at last. His breathing had sunk deep into his lungs; he could hear it rasping, labored, in his ears. His heart pounded with sickening crashes in his chest. Sweat poured from him. His steps took on a jerky, locked-knee cadence.

He tripped. Reaching out to catch himself, he grasped a saw brier vine. The stinging pain ripped through his hand, piercing into the blackness in his mind.

He sat down as if he was the one who had been knifed. There was no point in going on; he couldn't outrun this new horror any more than he could leave behind the last one.

His chest hurt as if his heart was dissolving in the corrosive acid of unshed tears. He would not let them fall. It was too late for that. He would lock them away, just as he must lock away every plan, every endearing dream.

It had been his fault, and he knew it all too well.

He should never have tried to come so close, never thought of reaching for more than he had been given.

Killing, maiming, was all he knew. Maybe it was all he was good for.

The thing he had wanted most was to love and protect

Cammie. The best way to do that, it seemed, was to stay
away from her. Far away.

He would manage it this time, if it killed him.

And it might.

Chapter Twenty

⧉ ⧉ ⧉ *The bedroom was dim when Cammie* opened her eyes. She lay for long moments, letting her mind catch up with her body. It seemed she'd drifted for some time. She remembered waking off and on, and being handed medication to swallow with water. Her aunt Sara had been there. Strange.

Memory returned abruptly. She turned her head, expecting to find Reid beside her. No one was in the room. He'd been there, she knew; it seemed she still felt the imprint of his hand on hers.

But it couldn't be. She had slept through a night and most of another day. The last time she'd seen Reid, it had been completely dark.

She slowly lifted her hand and settled it over the bandages that swathed her midsection. She was touchy and sore under them, but it was nothing to make such a fuss about. Her back was just as sore from lying so long in bed.

She rolled to her side and levered herself up to a sitting position. Her stitches protested a little, but nothing dramatic happened. Pushing to her feet, she moved carefully toward the window. Her balance wasn't the best in the world, but that seemed to her the effect of the painkillers. She wasn't used to anything much stronger than an aspirin.

Beyond the window curtains the evening was sultry and still. A gray-blue bank of clouds spread across the sky above the trees. There was a greenish tint to the fading light, as if the rich spring color of the grass and leaves was being refracted through the humidity-laden air as through a prism. It was going to rain; there might even be a storm building to the north.

As she stared out toward the woods of the game reserve, uneasiness invaded her. Where was Reid? Why hadn't she seen him today? He'd been so upset in his quiet, desperate fashion, so withdrawn.

She was to blame for the whole thing. He had laid out the rules, and she'd failed to follow them. She had just been so surprised to see him, so fascinated by what he was doing in her kitchen. And she had somehow taken it for granted that he was always aware of every little noise and movement around him. She had thought, in her conceit, that he would always know when she was near. So stupid.

She'd tried to tell him, or maybe she dreamed it. She didn't know, really; her brain felt as if it had been wrapped in quilting batting and put away on a back closet shelf.

"Good gracious, Cammie! What are you doing up?"

Cammie turned as her aunt bustled into the room, bringing with her the smells of onions and baking chicken. She forced a smile. "I'm all right. I was tired of being in bed."

"You'll hurt yourself. You've been cut wide open."

"I don't think it was that bad," Cammie said in dry tones.

"No thanks to Reid Sayers," her aunt returned in indignation. "When I think of him turning on you like that, my heart fails me. Your uncle tried to warn you. Now I hope you'll listen."

"It was an accident, that's all."

"He could have killed you as easy as not! You don't know that he didn't intend it, too, not after the way Keith was shot in cold blood."

"Reid wouldn't dream of hurting me." Cammie tried to keep her tone firm.

"How you can defend him is more than I can see or understand. I was never more glad of anything in my life than when he took himself off last night. It made my skin crawl to be in the same room with him."

"Don't be ridiculous," Cammie said sharply.

"You'll think ridiculous when he comes after you again. Things like that happen, Cammie. You see it all the time on television and in the papers. There are people in this world who would just as soon kill you as look at you!"

"Reid isn't one of them." She turned her back on her aunt, moving to her closet, where she jerked down the first thing her hand touched, a pair of jeans.

Her aunt followed her. "What do you think you're doing? Get back in bed right now!"

Cammie pulled a blue oxford cloth shirt from its hanger and turned to face the other woman. The look in her eyes was both firm and sad as she said, "You're my mother's sister and my only real kin, Aunt Sara, and I love you. But I'm long past the age of being told what to do, even for my own good. I'll be fine. Why don't you go on home?"

Her aunt's face crumpled. She turned away, then sank down on the bed to sit staring at her hands.

Cammie closed her eyes, then opened them again. She tossed the clothes she held across the bed and dropped down next to her aunt. Putting her arm around the older woman, she said, "I didn't mean to hurt your feelings. You can stay, if you like."

Sara Taggart gave herself a shake, then lifted her head, trying to smile though her eyes were red-rimmed. "It's not that. It's . . . nothing important. I'm just being silly."

Cammie hesitated, uncertain her aunt was telling the truth. Still, prying had never been her way, and she wasn't sure she could deal with another problem just now, no matter how small.

"I'm a witch for turning on you when you've taken

such good care of me. Please say that wonderful smell coming up the stairs is your famous chicken and dressing, because I'm starving."

She meant it as a diversion, but when Cammie had dressed in her jeans and a loose shirt over her bandaging, and made her way downstairs, she felt the first stirring of actual hunger. The chicken and dressing, shrimp mold, asparagus, and coleslaw her aunt served at the kitchen table smelled delicious. She picked up her fork to attack it.

It was then that her glance was caught and held by a kitchen appliance shoved to one end of the cabinet near the door, with a cluster of paper bags and boxes around it. She stared at them for several seconds before she realized what she was seeing.

A deep-fat fryer.

Her appetite vanished as there bloomed in her memory once more the smell of peanut oil and frying fish and fresh-peeled potatoes. Her stomach muscles contracted, and her stitches burned as they pulled.

What little conversation there was between her aunt and herself died away. They went through the motions of eating, but little more. Cammie insisted on helping her aunt put away the remains of the meal and tuck the dishes in the dishwater. Afterward, when her aunt mentioned, in a tentative way, that she might go home after all, Cammie's protests were no more than halfhearted. Possibly Aunt Sara sensed it, for she began to gather her things together.

Wind lifted the ends of Cammie's hair and flipped her shirt collar against her cheek as she walked with her aunt out onto the back porch. She could see it shifting the branches of the trees with a restless motion. The cloud bank she had noticed earlier had moved almost directly overhead. A storm was gathering, the light fading. The mercury security light at the end of the driveway had already come on.

It was that light reflecting in the polished finish of

Reid's Jeep that made her turn in that direction. The
vehicle was still sitting in the drive, pulled well up in
front of her aunt's battered Oldsmobile.

Cammie turned a questioning gaze on her aunt. "I
thought you said Reid left?"

"He walked." Her aunt's lips tightened, then she
seemed to relent. "Beat all I ever saw. He just disappeared into the woods like some injured animal. I
reminded Lizbeth, when she called to check on you, that
the Jeep was still here. Nobody came for it."

"Lizbeth called?"

"Four times. At least, she did the talking. I could hear
Reid there somewhere in the background, though, telling
her what to ask."

The fear that had clenched inside Cammie eased a
little. "He did make it home, then."

"So it seems. The key's in the Jeep; I looked. I can see
if Jack will come drive it over to Reid's house to get it
out of your way."

Cammie shook her head, the hair trailing down her
back swinging between her shoulder blades. "Never
mind. I suppose Reid will come after it when he wants it."

Aunt Sara gave her a long look, as if she knew what
Cammie had in mind. She made no comment, however.
A swift hug and a few more reminders of things Cammie
shouldn't do, then her aunt was gone, pulling away down
the drive.

Cammie went back into the house. She walked to the
kitchen, where she stood for long moments staring at the
deep-fat fryer on the cabinet. Reaching out, she lifted
the glass lid. It was full of cold oil with cornmeal floating
on top of it like scum, and pieces of soggy, half-done fish
at the bottom.

In the other paper bags were potatoes, half peeled; plus
cabbage and carrots for coleslaw; onions, pickles, and a
covered plastic bowl of what appeared to be hush-puppy
mix. It was all the ingredients for a feast, southern-
country style.

Reid had gone to so much trouble, and now it was ruined, most of it. It made her heart ache to see it.

What had he been thinking as he fried and mixed and sliced? She wished she knew.

Keith had never in his life dreamed of doing such a thing. He had never once put her pleasure before his own comfort and convenience. She had always been the one expected to do that.

However, Keith had made a serious tactical error. He had shown her, inadvertently, that she could live alone without fear, without a man—without him specifically— with no trouble whatever. After that, the rest had been easy. When he'd come back, wanting to start over, she discovered that all trust was gone, that she didn't and couldn't believe anything he had to say. And she'd known beyond doubting that she didn't love him, had never loved him.

What was between her and Reid was so much more complicated. They had brought such excess baggage into their relationship: the old family problem, the brief teenage attraction between them, the difficulties with her divorce, Reid's background, the problems with the mill ownership and the decision to sell, and later, Keith's death. The weight of all these things had spelled disaster. It was amazing to her that they had managed to wrest a few shining moments from the tangled mess.

And yet, was it really so complicated? Wasn't it barely possible that she could unravel the whole thing using a simple formula?

Three questions, three touchstones for future happiness. A set of criteria by which to judge a relationship. All she had to do was ask what she felt, instead of what she did not feel.

Did she trust Reid? Did she love him? Could she live without him?

All she had to do was find the answers.

She moved through the house in fits and starts, her thoughts and feelings as unsettled as the threatening weather. She stared out the front windows, thinking of Keith and Reid and the differences between them. She gazed out the back windows at the woods of the game reserve, thinking of Reid at the Fort on the other side of them, wondering what he was doing, and if he was thinking of her.

She stretched out on the couch in the living room, pressing her hand to her stitches, remembering the look on his face as he knelt beside her on the floor. She knew then that she had plunged him back into the unremitting pain of that other time, and she hated it, regretted it, with virulent passion.

She got up again, walking to the sun room, standing for long moments looking up at her own portrait with its too careful smile and the eyes wild with longing. Climbing the stairs, she walked into the guest room where she and Reid had made love that first night. In the dark, she touched the bed, and was startled by the visions that sprang, vivid and erotic, into her mind.

Finally, she walked out into the windblown darkness and opened the door of his Jeep. She climbed inside among the smells of oil and leather and Reid. Slamming the door, she settled into the seat where he'd sat. She closed her hands on the steering wheel he'd held. Through her mind ran the times she had pressed against him, the times he'd held her. And she stared ahead through the windshield at nothing, and at everything.

There was no conscious decision. She simply reached for the key and turned it. The engine sprang to life. She swung the Jeep in the direction of the Fort.

Lightning flashed blue fire overhead, a dim glow beyond the headlights. The vehicle jolted along, swaying with the surging of the wind. Her stitches pulled with every movement, every bump, but the pain was nothing to the ache of doubt in her heart.

She had her answers. Now all she had to do was convince Reid to listen to them.

There was a single light burning at the old log house. It

shone through the narrow windows of Reid's study. To Cammie it meant that he was home, and most likely alone.

The wind nearly jerked the door of the Jeep from her hand as she swung it open. Limp green leaves were flying through the air, along with dead twigs and bits of bark. There was a crackling sound to the spiderweb of lightning that spread overhead. She put down her head and ran for the front door.

She heard the bell chime somewhere inside as she leaned on the button. Regardless, it was endless ages before it was suddenly dragged open.

Reid stood there with the light behind him, haloing the wild gold tangle of his hair, leaving his face in shadow. There was anger in his voice, however, when he spoke. "What in the name of all Hell are you doing here? You should be home in bed."

"I have to talk to you. It's important."

His gaze was riveted to her face for long moments. Wrenching it away, he stared at the long strands of her hair that swirled around her. Then, as if he could not help himself, his gaze dropped to her hand, which was pressed lightly against her bandaging. He stiffened. His tone scraping like steel on steel, he said, "Go home, Cammie. Forget it. Forget everything."

He was going to close the door. She saw it begin to move and shot out a hand to hold it. "How can I forget?" she demanded. "Tell me that, and I might go."

He drew breath, though whether to answer or to take some action to dislodge her, she could not tell. In that instant the light went out behind him.

It was a power failure, perhaps, from a falling tree limb hitting the lines; it happened all the time in bad weather. The blackout might last two minutes or two days, depending on the damage and how much outage there might have been in more populated areas. In a way, Cammie was glad of the dark. It made her feel less exposed in what she was trying to say.

She removed her outstretched hand from the door panel, shifting to touch the solid, warm wall of Reid's chest, feeling him flinch from the touch. "Please," she said. "There's so much I have to tell you. I know this may not be a good time or place, but if I don't do it now, I may never find the courage again."

"Don't." The ragged command cut across her plea. He clamped his hand around her wrist, dragging it away from his body as if he could not bear the touch of it.

She swayed toward him, pulled a little off balance by his hold. It was then, in the sudden glare of lightning, that she saw the suitcase and duffel bags stacked beside the door.

"Oh, Reid, you can't!" she cried. "You can't go away again. I don't intend to push you into anything, or even to say what you might not want to hear. But I can't stand it if you go." She reached out to grasp his shirt in her free hand as she moved closer. "What happened last night was an accident, nothing more. I won't let you—"

The shot exploded with a flat, hard report. Above Cammie's head there was a rushing, soundless whistle. The door frame shattered into stinging splinters.

She was yanked forward with hard strength, caught in a rough embrace. Immediately she was spun free. She tripped over a duffel bag and came up against the side wall with a jar that made her draw a gasping breath of pain and protest. At the same time, the door of the Fort slammed shut.

"Get down," Reid rasped.

The solid thud of a bar sliding into place at the door was echoed by the blasting of a rifle in quick succession. The shots thumped into the thick, heavy door. Reid ducked away in haste, a moving shadow among the dark shadows of the room.

Cammie slid to the floor, glad to relax her trembling knees. Her voice a strained whisper, she said, "Why? For God's sake, why?"

"He wants us dead."

She ignored the irritation in his voice for being forced to state what he considered the obvious. "Yes, but for what reason? And who can it be?"

Reid was moving in and out of rooms, slamming what appeared to be shutters of some kind over the glass in the windows. "For now, he's just a sniper. One who made a bad mistake."

Reid's voice seemed disembodied as he advanced and retreated in the dark. At the same time, it was so quietly lethal that it sent a chill along her spine. She moistened her lips. "What are you saying?"

"He's in my territory, he's going one on one, and he's shown his hand. More than that, he picked the wrong first target: you instead of me."

"Me?"

"You moved, or he would have had you." Reid's voice came to a sudden, compressed halt, as if his words were cut off by lack of air. When he spoke again, the sound was closer, almost at her side.

"That won't happen again, not ever," he said with grim and implacable promise. "Whoever is out there may not know it yet, but he's mine."

Chapter Twenty-one

⬚ ⬚ ⬚ *Reid swung and glided from the room again.* Cammie listened to his swift, almost silent retreat. If moving around was safe for him now that the windows were shuttered, it had to be safe for her. She got to her feet to follow, leaving the entrance area and trailing his moving shadow along the hall. Her tone urgent yet soft, she called after him, "We need to phone Bud; he can have a patrol car out here in ten minutes."

"I don't think so."

She had been afraid that would be his answer. "You can't go alone after whatever lunatic is out there."

He came to a halt outside his study. It was a moment before he spoke. "Whoever is out there has killed one person, maybe more. Now he's after you, and I expect I'm next on his list. If the police take him, he'll plea bargain attempted murder or maybe cop an insanity plea. He'll get seven years and be out in four or less. I don't like the idea of looking over my shoulder for him again that soon."

"The police frown on taking the law into your own hands these days. You're the one who'll wind up in prison."

"Maybe."

He was moving away from her again, into the study. There was a sudden gleam of light, as if from a pocket flashlight. In it she could see him crouching over an array of electronic equipment on the desk in front of him.

311

She stepped toward him with her hands clenched at her sides. "That isn't all of it. You want to be rid of whoever is out there because that's the only way you can feel right about leaving. Do you think I don't know why you've been watching me? I'm not blind."

"Especially now that whoever is after you has shown his hand." The words had a bitter edge.

"I've known since you took care of Keith at the camp house," she corrected him. "I guessed even before that, when I found you in the woods behind the house. What I don't quite understand is why."

She waited with tightly held breath for his answer. There was none. His concentration seemed to be on whatever piece of equipment he was taking from a heavy zippered bag. Her lips tightened before she tried again.

"So now you've decided that you don't want to be my bodyguard anymore, and you think a permanent solution to the problem will give you the most peace. There's only one thing wrong with that. I can't let you take the chance."

He paused in what he was doing to flash the intense beam of light in her direction. He held it steady a blinding instant, then flicked it away again. His voice hard, he said, "If there's anyone who could stop me, Cammie, it would be you. But since I'm doing my best to keep you alive, I have to follow my own judgment."

Her teeth snapped together in exasperation. Turning from him without another word, she made her way in the darkness back down the main hall toward the rustic staircase. Under the stair steps was a telephone alcove of the kind that had been built in old houses back when a single, centrally located phone was considered adequate for a household. There were other phones in the house now, she knew, but this one was in the most protected place.

She was surprised that Reid didn't follow her. She realized why when she lifted the heavy black receiver of the old fashioned telephone.

The line was dead. Phone service was out along with the electricity. Or, more likely, both had been cut off.

Cammie dropped the receiver back into its cradle. As she stood there, she heard a quiet drumming overhead. The rain had begun. Heavy and insistent, it hit the house in windblown waves.

Somewhere out there the sniper was waiting. Or he might be moving, maybe disabling the Jeep and the Lincoln in the garage so they couldn't leave, circling the house, looking for entrance. Or he could be setting a trap outside the exit he thought they might use for an escape.

One thing he would not be doing was sitting still where it was safe and dry. He might think he had chosen his time and arranged matters so they had few chances to get away, but he had to take them soon, in at least the next few hours. The storm would end, people would start moving again, daylight would come. The Fort was isolated, but there would be traffic on the road by good daylight as people who lived farther back in the reserve went to work. He couldn't risk a commotion then.

What was Reid going to do? There was no percentage for him, so far as she could see, in remaining inside the Fort. He had to be planning on slipping out of the house and going after the sniper. That meant that he had put the safeguards, the bolted door, the shuttered windows, in place for her sake. He was going to leave her shut up inside the house.

It came to her abruptly, as she stood there, what he was doing in the study. That zipped case he had been handling; it was the kind that held a cellular phone. Among the equipment in the room was the computer on his desk. No doubt it had a battery power supply used to save work during the frequent power outages. The cellular phone could be hooked up by modem to Charles Meyer's computer in New York, completing the circuit for the distress signal Michelle Meyer had described with such fond humor.

Reid was setting up a final safeguard before he left her.

As soon as that was done, he would be gone out into the night. That was why he had let her leave him just now: he knew she couldn't use the phone, and he hadn't wanted her to see what he was doing.

She whirled, running back toward the study. She heard the hum of the computer even before she came through the door. It sat on the desk with its message blinking in neon blue and white on the screen, while the indicator lights on the cellular phone indicated transmission. Reid was standing before the gun cabinet on the far wall, methodically loading a high-powered rifle with a light-gathering scope.

"Why?" she demanded. "What's the difference between you sending your signal code and me calling Bud?"

"Two things," he answered tersely. "Number one, letting Charles make the calls gives me the extra ten minutes or so I need to get rid of our sniper. And two, he'll reach a wider circle of police protection, just in case."

"In case you don't make it? Or—just in case it could be Bud out there?"

His face was grim as he gazed at her in the dim light of the computer screen. "In case of need, period. I prefer to cover all the bases."

He had finished loading. Zipping up the dark, close-fitting jacket he had put on, he began slipping extra cartridges into the pockets. His preparations were almost complete.

There was about him a sense of distance. In some peculiar way, he was not just getting ready to leave her, but, rather, had already gone.

As she watched, he reached inside the gun case and took a small, compact pistol from the top shelf. He walked to the desk and placed it on the polished surface.

Without inflection he said, "This is for you. It's not very big, and you'll have to pull the hammer back to fire it, but it's loaded with .22 long hollow points that are guaranteed to stop a man in his tracks. If you decide to use it, don't do anything foolish like shooting over the target or into the ground. Aim for the body and shoot to kill."

"Surely, you don't think—"

"I don't know," he interrupted her in hard, overriding tones. "Don't ask questions, just listen carefully. This is what's called a safe room: inside lock, solid walls, one exit, no windows allowing entrance, and a phone for calling help, if necessary. I want you to stay here with the door bolted until I get back."

He was a stranger, a commander issuing orders, expecting obedience. It was as if he had put away all feeling, donning the impenetrable efficiency of a machine at the first sound of gunfire. If there was any trace of the man she had laughed with and loved, he was gone. It was almost as if Reid, with calm and deliberate intention, had killed him.

Cammie felt bereft, and more alone than ever in her life. Still, she couldn't give up. If he was in the midst of a fight, then so was she.

"It's because you hurt me, isn't it?" she said slowly. "That's why you're like this. It happened in spite of everything you did to prevent it, and you can't stand that. Somewhere in your mind you've put me together with the little girl who died in Israel. You have to save me because you couldn't save her. I know—at least, I think I know how much her death hurt you. But you didn't choose to see her die any more than you chose to injure me. These things happened because of other people, other agendas. You aren't to blame."

He made a small gesture of protest, but she went on without pause. "More than that, Reid, I'm not a child. I'm nobody's victim, and I'm not dead. You didn't kill me because you couldn't. You drew back; I felt it. You saved me, not only from Keith and from whoever is out there, but from yourself. You are not now and have never been an animal who kills with no mercy."

But he was gone, retreating from the words she spoke as he might before advancing danger. One moment he was framed in the doorway, his face pale and strained and his eyes dark hollows of pain. The next, there was only empty space, and silence.

Cammie bit her bottom lip and squeezed her eyes shut. Nothing. She had accomplished nothing.

Except possibly the wrong thing. If ever Reid needed to be a killer, it was now. If he was not, or if she had disarmed him with what she had said, he might well die out there in the dark.

The pistol really was very small. As she moved slowly to pick it up, it fit easily into her palm, with the barrel not quite as long as her middle finger.

She stood with her fingers gripped around it, listening while her chest ached with the press of unrefined terror. One of the greatest moments of danger for Reid would be when he stepped outside. The sniper could be waiting, expecting him to leave the cover of the house.

The minutes slid past. Everything remained quiet except for the steady pounding of the rain and an occasional rumble of thunder. Surely Reid was outside by now.

Cammie slipped the little pistol into the top of her jeans pocket, though more because Reid had left it for her than because she felt the need of it near her. Moving to the door, she put her hand on the dead bolt.

Lock it behind him, Reid had said.

The urge to go after him was so strong. She didn't want to be locked away where she couldn't see or hear; every instinct rebelled against it. It was even possible that she could be of help to him.

She might also get in his way, especially if he didn't know she was anywhere near him. Even if he did know it, keeping track of her could be a distraction he didn't need. He was capable of handling the situation alone, if anyone could.

She was held back, she thought, by the same old considerations that always kept women out of a fight. That they had validity didn't make them any easier to bear.

She flipped the lock, then turned back toward the

center of the room. Her gaze fell on the cellular phone and computer. The message was completed, the line of type on the screen told her so. The telephone was free.

Reid had trusted her not to use it. The exact words had not been spoken aloud, but had been implicit in the explanation he had given her. She moved forward and put her hand on the receiver anyway.

She took it away again. She couldn't interfere with what he had done. If he was right, and something happened to him because of her, she couldn't stand it.

There was a folder lying on the desk next to the computer. Slightly longer than legal size, it was yellowed by age to a dark golden color verging on brown. The edges were curled and worn, and there rose from it the mustiness of age and a faint hint of cigar smoke.

Cammie had seen enough turn-of-the-century office files in the antique business to recognize one when she saw it. It was curiosity that made her reach out and lift the edge of the folder.

There was a single handwritten document inside. The penmanship was looping and graceful, done in black ink with a sharp-nibbed pen. The language was formal, with a scattering of legal phrases, though the intent of the writer could not have been more plain. The subject was a transfer of property. There was not one tract of land involved, but two, and both were described in exacting detail. The signatures had been witnessed and notarized. The names inscribed at the bottom were perfectly clear.

Lavinia A. Wiley Greenley.

Justin M. Sayers.

Cammie let the folder fall closed. How long had Reid had it? Where had it come from? Why in Heaven's name hadn't he produced it? Or at least mentioned it?

What did it matter now? She knotted her hands into fists as she swung away.

The room was too small and cluttered for pacing. It seemed to be closing in on her. What if the sniper decided to burn the house down? She might never know it until it was too late. If she came running out at the last minute, killing her would be too easy.

Was Charles Meyer making the calls that would bring help, or was the message blinking in New York in an empty room? If he got it, who, exactly, would he contact if not Bud? Would the state police come charging in with sirens blaring or descend in a helicopter on the front lawn? Would CIA friends of his and Reid's, or maybe regional FBI operatives, arrive in a motorcade with horns blasting? And how long would any of it take? How long did Reid actually have to complete his self-imposed mission?

Where was Reid now? She could see him in her mind's eye, gliding through the wet, dripping night, ducking under tree limbs, pausing to listen. Did he have some idea based on logic and past experience about where to find the man with the rifle? Was he closing in on him? Would he confront the sniper head-on, or would he try to circle and come in behind him? Would he fix the man in his sights with the light-gathering scope, or would he close in for a quiet coup de grace?

When the knock came, she jumped and spun to face the door. It was not that close, however; it sounded lighter and farther away, as if it might be coming from the Fort's front entrance.

Should she ignore it or check it out? Should she stay where she was, or venture far enough out of the room to discover what was going on?

The knocking could be Reid, trying to get back inside. For her to be safe, he had to have locked whatever exit he had taken behind him. What if he was injured, in no shape to get back in the same way he went out?

She flipped the dead bolt, opened the door a narrow crack.

The sound was definitely at the front door. She moved along the hall and through the living room toward it with some trepidation. Then she heard a familiar voice speaking in low concern.

"Camilla? You all right in there? I thought I heard shots."

"Uncle Jack," she said, bending her head toward the door. "Is that you?"

"Somebody told me they saw you heading this way in Sayers's Jeep. It was so late, I thought I'd see if everything's all right. Let me in, Camilla."

There were times when a meddling busybody could come in handy. He had been in Vietnam; he must know something about snipers. Besides, she couldn't leave him out there where he might be shot by mistake. She pushed up the metal bar, then turned the locks.

He had been in Vietnam; he must know something about snipers—

Recognition exploded inside her. The sniper was her uncle. She leaned against the door to hold it as she snatched at the lock to turn it again.

The heavy door panel slammed into her. She careened backward, hitting the wall and bouncing off it. Agony ripped through her, radiating in burning waves from her abdomen. She cried out, a sound quickly strangled. Staggering, she tried to catch her balance, then her feet went out from under her and she crashed to the floor.

In a stunned haze she saw the hefty figure of her uncle bearing down on her. It was so black inside the house with the windows closed off that he was silhouetted against the lesser darkness outside. He carried a long weapon in one hand, a rifle.

Following the sound she had made, he lashed out with a kick. She rolled with desperate speed. He missed her, though there was a grinding pain at the point of her hipbone from her weight on the little pistol high in her pocket. She reached for it, dragging her loose shirt aside, feeling for the grip even as she scuttled away over the polished floor.

The door into the living room was just behind her, she thought; she could feel the slight draft from the open space. She plunged through it on hands and knees, rolling behind the protection of the wall before she surged to her feet. Skimming through the room, she tried to remember exactly how the house was laid out. Her best advantage at this moment was that she had made her way through this area in the dark twice already tonight and her uncle did not know the house at all.

She rounded the sofa, skirted a rocker. She was almost sure there was a door leading into the dining room somewhere just in front of her.

"Come back here," Jack Taggart grunted in frustrated rage.

A shot blasted, whining. It struck the wall where Cammie had been seconds before. He was firing at shadows and sounds; he couldn't actually see her.

The small pistol came free of her pocket. He made no better target than she did, however, and if she fired, he would be warned that she was armed. If she could make it back to the safe room before he closed in on her, she might be all right. She had only to pass through the dining room and back out into the hall, then down two doors to the study.

She stood still, trying to control her breathing. She could feel the seep of wetness against her shirt and into the waistband of her jeans; she must have torn her stitches.

There was no time to think about it. She had to recall where the table was sitting and how the chairs were arranged. Moving with great care, she picked up one foot, took a step, then another and another.

She was almost to the hall door when she brushed a china closet. Dishes toppled with dull thuds, crystal ringing musically as glasses bumped together. Orange fire spat from across the room.

Cammie whirled away from shattering glass and china and lunged for the door. Hurtling herself through it, she flew down the hall. She felt the stream of wind in her face, heard the splatter of rain. Then she saw a shade of movement, and blind terror gripped her.

She was racing toward the rear of the house, away from the open front door. If she felt the wind, it was because the back door was open, allowing it to sweep down the hall. Ahead of her, she saw the gray rectangle of the opening, saw also the shifting shadow of a man carrying a gun.

The man brought the rifle to his shoulder. His voice quiet, yet savage with authority, he said, "Hold it right there."

Cammie skidded to a halt. Behind her, she heard her uncle's heavy footsteps pound once, twice more, before they ceased. He cursed, a sound suddenly shocking in the same voice he had so often used to pray.

The man with the rifle to his shoulder was Reid. His order had not been for her.

"My bead's on Camilla," Taggart snarled. "Fire, and I take her out with me."

There was a moment of electric silence. Lightning pulsed, sending its pale glow through the open door to illuminate the frozen tableau in the hall. Cammie saw both men standing poised and ready. Reid had moved nearer, almost directly opposite the study door. In the steady beam of the computer screen's light, his face gave no hint of yielding. Her uncle held his firearm close against his body, but it was pointing straight at her.

The small pistol was heavy in her hand.

"Now then," the Reverend Taggart said, gloating rising rich in his voice. "Put your weapon down, Sayers, or I'll kill her anyway."

The only sign that Reid had heard was the tightening of the skin around his eyes. He said evenly, "You'll kill her no matter what I do. You can't let her live because she's in your way."

"So are you," Cammie's uncle said in implicit agreement, "but I thought, you being such a gentleman, that you would want to go first."

Silence returned, stretched. Reid did not look at Cammie directly, but she thought he missed no detail of her appearance, from the red sheen of wetness at her waist to the gun half hidden in her fingers where her hand hung at her side. He made an infinitesimal movement, as if he meant to take the rifle down from his shoulder.

"No!" Cammie cried.

Reid turned his gaze in her direction. His tone weary, he said, "There's nothing else I can do."

It wasn't like him to give up, that much she knew. An instant later she saw what he was doing.

It was not a surrender, but a sacrifice.

"No," she said again, but it was too late. He lowered the weapon in his hands.

"All the way to the floor," Taggart said, his own rifle unwavering as it covered Cammie.

Reid let the rifle fall. Before the thudding clatter died away, Cammie's uncle turned the muzzle of his rifle in the other man's direction.

"Stop!" Cammie said, bringing up the pistol in her hand.

The heavyset man's eyes widened and his mouth tightened, but he held still. A moment later his face cracked in a sardonic smile. "You won't fire. You're too soft."

Was he right? She didn't know. If the pistol had been in her hand when he first came at her in the dark, it might have been automatic. This was so calculated.

She had pointed a gun at Keith and pulled the trigger. The difference was that she had shot at the headlights on his Rover, at the ground in front of his feet, anywhere except at him. His injuries, small as they were, had been an accident.

All she had inside her now was a deathly fear for Reid, plus a strong need to slow what was happening until she decided what she would do next.

"Why?" she said, bringing her other hand up to steady the pistol that was trembling in her grasp. "Why are you trying to kill me?"

"Don't be stupid."

"It's simple," Reid answered for him. "His wife is your closest relative. She is also your legal heir, according to the forced heirship laws of the state, since you canceled your portion of the mutual will you had with Keith. It makes no difference whether you hold title to the mill land plus a portion of the operation, or only Keith's share of Sayers-Hutton alone; either way, he stands to gain control of a sizable chunk since his wife is under his thumb. Though it wouldn't surprise me to learn your aunt Sara is scheduled for a nice little accident as soon as you're out of the way."

"But what about you?" she said. "Why try to kill me here, where you are, when it would have been so much easier somewhere else?"

"Shall I tell her," Reid said to Taggart in jibing tones.

"Why not? You haven't done half bad so far."

Reid dipped his head in grim acknowledgment. "I think," he said, not taking his eyes from the other man, "that I'm cast as the scapegoat. I imagine our bodies are supposed to be found in the classic murder-suicide position—everyone knowing how I killed Keith and was trapped in a sordid and hopeless affair with you. That the sale of the mill will proceed more smoothly with me out of the way is a plus."

"You killed—" she began, then stopped. "No. You couldn't have."

"No," Reid agreed in soft satisfaction for her conclusion. "I think Keith's mistake was maybe trying to borrow money from your uncle here—as well as from a mob-controlled finance company. That and muscling in on the preacher's fun with the choir girl."

Cammie saw what Reid was doing. He was killing time, talking long enough—enough for what? To let her nerves settle? To give himself an opening? Or was he waiting for whoever would come in answer to his message? The least she could do was help him.

"Choir girl?" she asked.

"Evie, as if you didn't know," her uncle answered in scathing tones. "My God, even Sayers heard the rumors. And don't forget I saw her at your house, the two of you with your heads together, whispering about me. Why you would listen to such a little tramp instead of your own uncle—"

"You," she whispered. "You're the one who hounded her when she walked out on you, the man who kept trying to get her back."

"She was the only exciting thing that ever happened to me. I did everything I could think of to have her, even trying to get you to give Keith another chance so he would drop her and I could step in. That smartass husband of yours figured it out at the reunion, had me meet him in the game reserve. He wanted a loan, and as collateral he could deliver Evie on a platter. Bastard. But he fixed himself by mouthing off about the wills, his and yours. It all came clear while he sat there sneering at me."

"Money and jealous rage," Reid said softly, "a lethal combination."

"It was so simple. Kill Keith, Cammie inherits. Kill Cammie, and Sara gets the money."

"Kill Aunt Sara," Cammie said in appalled comprehension, "and you have it all. In the meantime, Evie is alone and broke, and when everything is over—"

"I'll be there to comfort her and take care of her, and there will be all that money from the mill sale to make her come around."

"How can you be sure she will? When you won't lift a finger to help her right now?"

"It's too soon," the reverend said with rough anger in his voice. "I can't afford to set the old cats squalling about me and her again like they did last year. I've got them going my way, smacking their gums over you and Sayers and all that old rot I fed them about Justin and Lavinia. They do love a sex scandal, the juicier the better."

"But wait," she said in frowning thought. "It was you sneaking around the house at night; I know it was, because I saw you. And that was before Keith was killed."

"Me and Sayers. I could have laughed myself silly, watching him moon around. He thought he was the only one with any skill at stalking. He didn't know I was infiltrating enemy lines before he was dry behind the ears. Why, he never knew I was there."

"Wrong," Reid said. "My mistake was in thinking you were a dirty old man. About the time I decided you needed a lesson in manners, you stopped."

The other man scowled. "I had to know whether that husband of hers was coming around at first, to see if they were getting it together. Later, it seemed a good idea to keep tabs on when she went to bed. And maybe who with."

"Which was about the time you picked me out as the fall guy," Reid said in soft suggestion.

"You had it coming. It was your fault the Baylor girl disappeared. She came to me all in a quiver, asking me as her pastor what was the right thing to do about what she found. I told her to sit tight, but you helped her run out on me, and that cut the amount Camilla might have inherited. You didn't want my niece having the whole show any more than Keith or Gordon Hutton, did you Sayers? You're just as dirty as the rest of us."

"That's true," Reid said, his voice even.

Cammie wanted to turn and force Reid to meet her gaze so she could judge for herself what he meant. She couldn't; she had to watch her uncle. The strain in her arms, and in her mind, was becoming unbearable. The fine trembling that shook her was almost a rigor. She had to do something. Soon.

Her uncle laughed, his gaze on Reid. "I'm sure the Lord will forgive me for killing a sinner like you, then. Your soul is black, Hell is waiting for you, and I am only an instrument of His will. If He wants to save you, He can. Would you like to pray for a miracle before you go?"

"Don't," Cammie said, her voice taut with warning.

"Camilla—Cammie, honey," her uncle said, smiling at her. "I'm the man who used to hold you on my lap and feed you pecan pie off my plate. I'm the man who used to hide you behind me so your mother wouldn't spank you. I'm the one who stood by you when your mother and father died, and who let you cry on my shoulder. You know you're not going to shoot me."

"I will." She cocked the pistol with her thumb to show him.

"Put that toy away now, that's a good girl."

"It's Reid's life or yours, mine or yours. It isn't much of a choice," she said with what had the sound of a plea even to her ears.

"Cammie," Reid said in words barely above a whisper. "If you back slowly this way, I'll take the gun."

Did he mean to push the issue? Or was it only an effort to relieve the strain she was under, to take responsibility himself? In fractions of a second the questions and options went through her mind. She could do as he suggested, but if he shot her uncle, who would believe it could not have been avoided? It was different for her. If she killed him, Bud would believe she had no choice. Was this the way it had been for Lavinia and her Justin?

"I wouldn't try that," the Reverend Taggart said. There was sudden finality in his voice. He brought the rifle up a fraction, centering it on Reid's chest. The muscles of his face and mouth tightened. They set.

It was all the warning she had. There was no more time to talk, no more time to decide.

Cammie felt a great calm settle over her. It stilled fear, soothed anger, dissolved doubt. She aimed for the full body and squeezed the trigger with care. She didn't close her eyes.

The report was hard, loud. The pistol recoiled in her palm with a stinging blow, jerking her arm upward. Her uncle was thrown, sprawling in an ungainly huddle.

But the rifle he held went off with a thunderous discharge. The flame reached out in the darkness toward

Reid. He was flung backward, turning with the pale glow of lightning gleaming in his hair. His face was blank, his eyes wide with shock and acceptance. He fell full-length and lay still.

And in the distance, beyond the sound of spattering rain, there came the steady beat of a helicopter's rotor blades cutting a path toward the Fort.

Chapter Twenty-two

░░░ ░░░ ░░░ *"No. Please, no—"*

The words were no more than a whisper. Cammie dropped the pistol she held as suffocating horror welled inside her. She stumbled toward Reid, falling to her knees beside him. With shaking hands she searched his chest, his abdomen, for the wetness of a wound. She could find none, though his jacket was torn and charred.

Leaning closer, she placed her fingers on either side of his face, molding the angles and planes with trembling, caressing fingers. She turned his features gently toward the faint light shining over her shoulder from the computer screen in the study. They were pale, lax. There was no sign of injury.

His chest lifted in a harsh, difficult breath. His face contorted, lips parting as he gulped more air. His eyes opened with an almost audible snap. For long seconds he gazed into her face, which hovered so close, searching her tear-glazed eyes and the loving compassion and lingering terror mirrored there.

With a sudden wrench of iron muscles, he pulled away from her, dragging himself to a seated position against the wall behind him. "Save your pity," he said in striated tones. "I only had the—breath knocked—out of me. The jacket—"

"Bullet-proof?" Cammie guessed as he stopped to breathe. She had felt the stiffness, the heaviness of it.

He gave a nod. "Lucky thing I turned—as he got me.
Might not have taken—direct hit."

There was not much luck in it, Cammie knew. She had
seen the moment when Reid moved, knew he had tried to
judge the shot. She knew, too, from the look on his face,
that it had been a last ditch effort, the most he could or
would do to preserve his own life while hers was hanging
in the balance.

That knowledge gave her a sense of power. She prayed
it was not misplaced.

There was no time for further discussion. The sound
of a siren, coming fast, was nearly drowned by the air-
whipping chop of the helicopter. The screeching died
away out on the drive. Immediately, there came deep-
throated shouts. Through the open door she could see
men in uniforms and raincoats approaching the house.
They ran through silver arrows of rain and into the bright
white spotlight of the hovering helicopter, waving it in.

She got to her feet, pushing at her hair, which blew
around her face. The glaring light outside sent a shaft of
illumination down the hallway. In it she could see her
uncle's limp form with the red stain spreading from a
dark hole in his chest, see the opaque stare of his open
eyes. She thought, in a dazed way, that she should see to
him, be certain he no longer lived, but she dreaded going
near him; she felt an unreasonable fear that he would
suddenly revive and threaten them again.

Reid, following her glance, pushed to his feet with
slow care. He stepped to the fallen man and leaned over
him. He pressed long fingers against the pulse point in
his neck, then looked at Cammie with a shake of his
head. Reaching down, he picked up the rifle that had
fallen across the Reverend Jack Taggart's throat.

"Hold it right there! Don't move a muscle!"

The shout came from the doorway. An instant later the
hall was filled with men. Reid was caught in the beam of
a powerful flashlight, held under the cover of a half-
dozen guns.

He went still, holding his crouch. Not even an eyelash flickered.

"Drop the rifle!"

"No," Cammie cried, moving toward the men.

"It's all right, ma'am. Just stay back out of the way." The man wore the uniform of the state police. He barely glanced at her as he spoke.

"Never mind, Cammie," Reid said. "I can handle it."

He meant to take what she had done on his own shoulders, to shield her from the consequences of having killed a man. It was barely possible, since he had sent the message that had brought the authorities, that he would get away with it. It would be, for him, only one more among many.

But it wasn't fair, and it wasn't right.

Pushing through the men in the hall came a burly form that Cammie recognized. She stepped toward him, catching his arm with urgent hands. "Bud," she said, her voice steady and perfectly clear, "make them stop. I shot him. I killed my uncle."

Bud gave her a keen look. He stared at the man on the floor, and at Reid standing over him. Releasing himself from Cammie's hold, he strode toward Reid, taking a handkerchief from his pocket. Relieving Reid of the rifle with the protective cloth, he turned toward the others.

"Relax, boys," he said in bluff assurance, "there's more here than meets the eye. Let's get some light in here, then these two can tell us all about it."

The statements took some time; there was so much to tell, so many details to explain.

A few things were left out, some by Cammie, some by Reid, and a few by both in silent and mutual agreement. If Bud noticed, and it was highly likely that he did, he said nothing. The questions he asked were shrewd, showing a good grasp of the situation and the preceding events. He was even able to add a little here and there due to his own official and semi-official inquiries.

It had begun with the prospective sale of the mill. Reid's father, in going over the books to be sure everything was in order, had discovered the discrepancy in Keith's department. The stress had helped trigger the heart attack that killed him. Before his death he had placed the call to his son that had brought Reid home. However, he died before he could provide a full explanation of the problems at the mill.

Keith had either been confronted with his theft by Reid's father or else realized an audit of the books made necessary by the sale agreement would disclose it. He had borrowed right and left to make up the shortfall, but it had not been enough. With the usual gambler's confidence, he tried to multiply the borrowed cash on the gaming tables. He'd wound up in deeper trouble.

The results of the title search, which made it likely Cammie would prove to be a wealthy woman from the sale of the mill, had encouraged Keith to return to her. He was certain he could sweet-talk her into taking him back, then handing over the money to fix all his troubles.

Cammie gave Keith more trouble than he'd expected. Gordon, misunderstanding his brother's motives, had encouraged Keith to rough measures to stop the divorce. Cammie's husband had been willing enough to use them. It took Reid's intervention to convince Keith to look for another way out.

However, it had been a major error in judgment to tap Reverend Jack Taggart for a loan.

As they reached that point in the inquiry, a small silence fell. Sheriff Bud Deerfield frowned in Reid's direction. "This deal with the Baylor girl—it was you seen hustling her out of town?"

"Not one of my more successful operations," Reid said with a grim indentation at the corner of his mouth. "It slipped my mind how many eyes and ears small towns can sprout. But it seemed too many people might be dangerously interested in what Janet had discovered. I had her meet me in Monroe, then drove her across the state line to Little Rock. From there, I gave her a plane ticket along with instructions for enough hub changes to wipe out the trail. She's been enjoying a beach condo in Florida, one managed by an army buddy, ever since."

Bud grunted. "You might have told me what you were up to and saved a lot of trouble."

"I had in mind to do that, until Keith died," Reid answered, returning the other man's gaze with a steady look. "His killing—the clean shot, the stolen weapon—had all the earmarks of a professional job. There were three possibilities that I could see: organized crime, the military, or—"

"Or the police? I see what you're getting at," the other man said. "But what was my reason supposed to be?"

"Keith was making noises about your family history that could be embarrassing in the next election. Plus, he was giving Cammie a hard time, and it seemed a warning about it might have gotten out of hand. If you add that it wouldn't be the first time somebody involved with gambling and embezzlement had a hammerlock on the police—"

"One that needed breaking? Makes sense, in a screwy kind of way. Not that there's anything to it, mind."

Reid gave a slow nod of agreement. The two men seemed to understand each other very well.

"Right," Bud said, gathering up the papers spread out over the kitchen table. "Looks like a cut-and-dried case of justifiable homicide to me, and I expect the D.A. will see it the same way. I think the boys are about ready to wind things up out in the hall. Must be about time we got out of here, let you two get on with your rat killing."

It was not the best euphemism for that moment, as natural as it had been. Bud seemed to realize it. He ducked his head, wincing, before he opened his mouth as if to mend matters. He was saved by the shrill ring of the cellular phone from Reid's office.

"That'll be Charles," Reid said. "I'll go let him know the cavalry came in time, if that's all right with you."

The sheriff lifted a hand in a dismissive wave. Reid strode from the kitchen. After a moment they heard the low murmur of his voice followed by the pauses of phone conversation.

"Well, Cammie," Bud said, tucking his notebook under his arm, "all I can say is that I'm mighty sorry about all this."

She tried for a smile that didn't quite come off. "There isn't anything you could have done, or anyone else for that matter."

"I suppose I'd better go break the news to your aunt. It's not a job I'm looking forward to, I can tell you."

"Aunt Sara is stronger than you might imagine," Cammie said. "I'll come with you, though, in case she needs somebody to stay with her."

Bud pursed his mouth, looking at her from under his brows. "I don't think that would be such a good idea, now. I mean, do you? Considering the circumstances?"

It was a moment before Cammie, in her concern for her mother's sister, realized what he meant. For all Aunt Sara's affection for her niece, she might not want to be comforted in her grief by the person who had killed her husband.

"Oh. Yes. I suppose you're right."

Bud reached out and took her hand. "You sure I can't call out the doc, get him to give you a pill or something?"

She shook her head. "I'll be fine."

"I can buzz Wen. She'd be glad to come take you back home, stay with you." He smiled as he added, "She'd love hearing all about it firsthand."

"Call her for Aunt Sara. She may need her more."

He squeezed her hand, then released it. "Whatever you say. But don't do anything foolish, like going back to that big house by yourself. You're a damn brave girl, and my hat's off to you, but there's limits to everything."

"Don't worry about Cammie," Reid said as he appeared in the doorway again. "I'll look after her."

The sheriff gave him a close look, then nodded. "That's

all right, then. Either one of you think of anything else important, anything you want to add, let me know."

It took another half hour before the ambulance crew had removed the body and everything had been cleared away. Finally the helicopter cranked up and lifted away above the trees. The taillights of the squad cars disappeared down the drive. Reid closed the front door and locked it.

He turned to face Cammie, who stood in the hall where she had said her last thanks and good-byes to the departing officers. Walking past her into the kitchen, he took down the brandy from the cabinet and poured healthy shots into two coffee cups, then added coffee from the pot that had been kept in constant operation for the past hour and more.

Cammie, following him, watched him set the two cups on the kitchen table. There was about him still the air of armored invulnerability. It did nothing to give her hope.

His sudden hard gaze as he turned on her caught her unprepared. "All right," he said. "I can tell there's something on your mind you didn't mention to Bud."

"Several things," she agreed warily.

"So out with it." He waved toward the cup in front of the chair that he held for her.

"I don't think now is a good time," she said in low tones.

"Now or never. Come on, give me hell and get it over with."

She heard the pain under the harshness of his tone. Turning from him, she walked down the hall to the study, where she picked up the old, yellowed file folder. Returning to the kitchen, she sat down and placed it on the table in front of her.

He made a sound that was half laugh, half groan. "I might have known."

"That I would find it, or that I would find out eventually?"

"Both, and at the most inconvenient time." The look on his face was tired, but resigned.

"When was the time going to be convenient?" she asked as politely as she was able.

"When I was on the other side of the world."

She had known, but her breath still left her in a rush. Her voice constricted, she said, "Where did you find it? Or did you have it all along?"

"I've been going through the account books at the mill. The safe where they're kept is a relic, a monster that's been there since the mill was founded. I found a bunch of Justin's old ledgers in the back of it; I suppose they were kept there for their historical or sentimental value, or else got shoved to the back and forgotten. Anyway, I started looking through them, and that folder fell out."

She held his gaze for a long moment. There seemed no reason to doubt what he had just told her. "I understand what it says," she said, reaching out to touch the musty-smelling paper. "My great-grandmother agreed to sell three hundred acres of land to Justin M. Sayers in exchange for the sum of one dollar plus goods received, to wit, a plot of three thousand acres of land. And services rendered, I mustn't forget that. What I want to know is what it means."

Reid raked a hand through his hair and clenched the back of his neck. Keeping his gaze on the table, he said, "The document is what's known as a Counter Letter. It's a binding agreement between two parties for the private transfer of property; Louisiana is one of the few states where it's legal. By this agreement, Lavinia agreed to transfer to Justin three hundred acres of land in exchange for three thousand that he owned elsewhere. The dollar is just a legality. Don't ask me about the services rendered, because I don't know.

"According to the description of the three hundred acres, the land was a part of Lavinia's mother's estate, which she inherited on her death, a parcel of land fronting on what was then the only highway leading into Greenley. There is no question that it was hers to dispose of as she pleased.

"The land she got in return was virgin timberland with a river boundary and several creeks running through it, though with no major access roads at the time," Reid pointed out. "All in all, I don't think it was such a bad deal."

She gave him a look of irritation. "It was an excellent deal from a business point of view. Do you realize that those three thousand acres eventually became the game reserve? Do you have any idea what it would be worth today?"

"I know, and it occurred to me, yes," he said dryly.

"So my great-grandmother and your great-grandfather, who had once been lovers, lived on opposite sides of the game reserve with nothing between them except a lot of trees."

Reid propped an elbow on the table and rested his chin on it. "With a well-worn trail between them, one still visible when I was a boy."

"You're joking," she said.

"Cross my heart."

Cammie met his open gaze for a long moment before she looked down at her coffee cup. She took a swallow of the coffee-laced brandy and felt its warmth and strength flowing through her. Putting down her cup, she reached out again to touch the musty document. "There's nothing in this we couldn't have guessed, if we'd tried," she said. "So why didn't you show it to me?"

He shrugged without meeting her gaze. "You seemed so sure of what you wanted to do with the mill. Maybe I thought you ought to have the opportunity."

"What about all your concern for people instead of woodpeckers?"

"So I'm not a man of strong principles. Does it matter?"

"I think you are," she said soberly, "and I think it does.

I think, in fact, that you decided Lavinia got the short end of the stick years ago, and you intended to make it up to the present generation, which is to say, to me. Never mind that it was your great-grandfather, and his son after him, and his after him, who built the mill and worked to make it a success. Never mind that it was your heritage."

"You're wrong," he said tightly.

"Am I? Tell me, then, that you weren't going away and leaving it? Tell me that you didn't intend to present your heritage to me for the sake of—of past love and even services rendered. Tell me, what makes you think that I would take it, knowing it wasn't rightfully mine!"

"Now, Cammie—" he said, his head coming up in alarm.

But she hurried on without stopping. "I'm not like Lavinia, Reid. I need more than generosity and memories. I don't intend to retreat from the trouble and the gossip and devote my life to charity and good works. I'm not ashamed of a thing we've done. And I won't settle for less than love."

He stared at her, his eyes wide and unseeing. Abruptly, he sprang to his feet, turning away from her to stand with his hands braced on the cabinet. Over his shoulder he said with strained vibrancy, "You don't know me, Cammie."

"What is there to know? You were trained to do a job for many and good reasons, and you did it to the best of your ability. Men have done it before, and not been branded killers or animals for it."

"Kindness," he said quietly, almost to himself. "Do you know that's the first thing I remember noticing about you? You were maybe five or six, and we were at vacation Bible school. A little boy, just a toddler, fell down and scraped his knee. You dried his tears and wiped away the dirt and blood with the hem of your dress. Then you picked him up, though he was nearly as big as you were, and carried him to his mother. I remember . . ."

He trailed off, then began again, his voice softer. "And

I used to watch you walk around wildflowers instead of stepping on them, and pick up spiders and throw them out the window instead of killing them. I watched you for years, for the pleasure of it, and because you made me feel—glad inside. And I used to pretend that you were my sister. I showed you all my favorite places, and sometimes, when I was out camping or fishing, I'd talk to you, tell you all sorts of things. Because I watched you so closely, I knew you understood people, knew their strengths and weaknesses and the things they most disliked about themselves. I knew that you kept them at a distance, kept them from trespassing on the too-tender places inside you by using words, turning their weaknesses against them."

"That wasn't so kind," Cammie said.

"It was self-protection. If you hadn't used words and anger for defense, there would have been nothing left of you; they would have taken it all. Somehow, I never thought you would do it to me."

"But I did."

He bent his head, even though she couldn't see his face. "I decided, in my teenage arrogance, that I didn't want you for a sister, that I needed more than that from you. So I caught you where you couldn't get away from me easily, and I tried to show you. And you took the gladness and used it to keep me away. Only I had no defense against you, had never needed any. And so—I was torn apart inside."

"No," she said, "you couldn't be."

A short sound between a laugh and a groan shook him. "Well, I thought so, at any rate, though I suppose I did it to myself. I left, went into service, refused to feel much of anything for anybody, even the woman unlucky enough to be there when I decided I could get married if you could. And it worked, for a long time."

He was silent for so long, lost in memories of which she had no part, that Cammie was afraid he couldn't, or didn't intend, to go on. Forcing the words from her tight throat, she said, "Until Israel."

"Yes," he said on a whispering sigh, "until Israel. Shall I tell you about it? Do you really want to hear?"

"Please," she answered, the single word no more than a ghost of sound.

He tilted his head back. "There was this little girl. We called her A. J. because that was as close as we could come to her name. She was five or six, and her hair was soft brown with red-gold lights in the sun. Sometimes when her baby brother fell down, she would pick him up and dry his tears and clean his scratches with the hem of her skirt. Then she would carry him home to their mother, though he was nearly as big as she was. She had a smile like the sunrise and she loved to laugh. She was so gentle, and reminded me in so many ways of you. And she trusted me."

"Reid," she said, her voice aching.

"No, wait." His voice was ragged and there was a faint shiver along the tops of his shoulders. "I felt the explosives taped to her with miles of duct tape that day, too much to tear away, too tight to cut. I saw the terror in her eyes. She knew what her uncle had done to her, Cammie. She knew. And so did I, because I had read the reports just in on him the night before. Too late to stop her coming. Too late to stop the gladness she gave me. And I had to choose. I had too—"

"You did the right thing," Cammie said in desperation for the pain she heard in every strained syllable he spoke. "There was nothing else."

"Did I Cammie? Did I? I felt the explosives and I saw the timer, and I knew there were only seconds left. Seconds can be a lifetime, Cammie. God—do you remember how I held you at Evergreen, how easily I could have broken your neck?" He stopped. When he went on, the words were no more than a vibration of sound. "Her neck was smaller, more fragile. She was dead before the explosive went off. I killed her, Cammie, as I held her."

The soft intake of her breath was the only sound. He didn't need it.

"There might—just might—have been a tiny chance that I could have ripped the explosive off her, one infinitesimal chance for life. But I had to choose, and I chose life for me and my men, death for her. I killed her. I did it, no one else. And I don't know, will never know, if I did the right thing."

She was on her feet, plunging toward him before the last word left his lips. She caught his elbow, turning him to her. She saw his eyes, feverishly blue and brilliant with tears, before she wrapped her arms around him, holding him tight with her face pressed against his collarbone. The deep breath he drew told her she was hurting his chest, bruised by the bullet that hit him, though he would not let her know. Immediately, she eased her grasp, though she would not release him.

"Listen to me," she said with a fierce sob catching in her throat. "You are only a man, not a god with the power of life and death. People do terrible things to each other for mindless reasons, but you are not responsible. You did what you were trained to do and what compassion and love required of you. You kept that child from pain, but you did not cause it. Mourn the death of a precious, living being if you must, but you are not allowed to destroy yourself over it. You can't, because I won't let you."

She drew back to look at him, her eyes wide with the fullness of giving she felt inside. Taking the hem of her shirt, she wiped the salt moisture that was caught in the hollows under his eyes. In sure and steady tones, she went on. "I love you, Reid, for all the things you are inside, all your tenderness and caring, and yes, for the strength of purpose that can make you kill—or permit you to stand and face death for some stupid reason that has nothing to do with bravery. Love can heal, I promise, if you will let it."

"Cammie—" he whispered.

"No, it's my turn. I knew you watched me, and I wanted you to, all those years ago. Only I was too afraid, too shocked to my soul at how you made me feel, to let you come close to me. I married Keith because you went away and I thought you were never coming back. If you go away from me again, I will follow you, whining, every single step you take, every mile, every league, across every body of water. You will not bury yourself in some sadistic contest for a cause that should stay lost. No, and nor will you go looking for an easy death. Before I let you do that, I'll kill you myself. I'll do it with love and compassion, because it may be a better choice, if not the only one."

The old house creaked in the abrupt, breathless quiet that fell as she stopped speaking. Outside, the wind blew and the rain made a soft drumming.

"I suppose you might at that," he said with bemusement in his face. He touched her hair, stroking it, watching the red-gold lights that shivered along the strands. A line appeared between his eyes. "God, but I was so afraid you wouldn't be able to pull the trigger back there. I thought only two things could make you do it, self-defense or—"

"Or what?" She couldn't prevent herself from pushing for an answer.

"Fear for someone you loved." The words were fretted with doubt.

Her hold tightened. "You were right."

"Do you have any idea how I feel about you? Can you even begin to understand what it meant to me to have you come to me that first night at Evergreen? You are my naked angel who banishes nightmares. You are everything that is bright and good and perfect that ever happened to me. But I won't let you spend the only life you have standing between me and my demons, and I won't let Greenley turn what we had into something ugly."

She stiffened a little. "My life is my own, and how I spend it is my business. As for what people say, I'm sorry that they have no other interest, but they can't make the rules for what I do. Nor can you."

"I wouldn't try," he said. "But I have to live for myself, with myself."

She pushed against his chest a little, carefully avoiding the place where the bullet had bruised him. "What of the mill?"

"Keep it, sell it, do whatever you think best."

"It isn't mine." The words were tight.

"Let Gordon sell it, then. Only hold on to all the environmental safeguards you can."

"Fine, that's settled."

"What, no plea for the trees and the birds?" he asked, his voice soft.

"Woodpeckers. And yes, I still care, and would like to save every sapling, every single feather of every bird of all kinds, every rabbit and squirrel and raccoon and armadillo. But as a wise man once told me, people are more important."

"There will be a fair-sized amount of money coming from the sale. You can take it and buy all the old stands of mixed timber you can find, then dare a single soul to cut a tree or harm a creature."

"I could, but I won't be here."

He stared down at her with the blue of his eyes turning slowly dark. "No?" He paused, then tilted his head, a crooked smile curving his mouth. "You'll be behind me? Every step? Whining?"

"Screaming, more likely."

"You're certain?"

That he was not was plain in his voice. She said firmly, "When do we leave?"

He stared at her for a long moment with an odd look of reverent dread and yearning on his face. He took a sharp breath. "I left you for only a moment, a few hours back, and you almost died. Suppose I told you I came near to changing my mind then, when I saw your uncle with a rifle pointing at your heart? Suppose I said that I half decided in that single moment that you need a permanent bodyguard. Would you understand that I'm afraid to risk anything happening to you while I'm not around, because that would be my fault, too? Would you understand that if I'm to take on that duty anyway, it may as well be here."

A slow smile curved her mouth, though she looked at the top button of his shirt. Her voice husky, she said, "It makes perfect sense to me."

He caught her close against him, holding her fast while he whispered soft and incoherent words of love against her hair.

"Reid, your chest," she protested, "I'll hurt you."

"Never," he said on a gasping laugh. Abruptly, he let her go, to hold her at arm's length. "But you, your stitches? Did I hurt you?"

She lifted her head to look at him with love shining warm in her eyes. "Never. We can never hurt each other."

His features tightened a fraction. "We may, but it won't be physically, or on purpose, or for long."

It was enough. Cammie said quietly, "Shall I take you home with me, then?"

"Or can I take you home, since you came in my Jeep."

"Yes." She paused. "You know we'll have to get married. Greenley will expect no less, and I can't— quite—see myself thumbing my nose at them that much, especially if we begin a Greenley-Sayers dynasty."

"Or Sayers-Greenley. Either way, I like the sound of it. When? Tomorrow?"

She laughed, a strangled sound. "Next week is soon enough. Or next month."

"Next week. I can't wait to begin my guard duties."

She sent him a glance under her lashes that turned into a frown. "I can't believe you let me go on and on, asking you to stay, proposing like the most shameless female."

"My favorite kind."

"I should do something wicked to you for revenge."

"Should you?" he said, his voice not quite steady. "Maybe I'm the one who needs a bodyguard."

"You just may," she said, slanting him a look of promise.

He met it, his smile rich with anticipation. "Now I really can't wait," he said. "Let's go home."

*Lorrie Morgan was born to be
a country-western music star.*

In FOREVER YOURS FAITHFULLY,
she tells us her tempestuous story of sweet
triumph and bitter tragedy.
From her childhood as a Nashville blueblood
performing at the Grand Ole Opry at the tender
age of eleven to her turbulent,
star-crossed love affair with Keith Whitley,
a bluegrass legend she loved passionately
but could not save from his personal demons,
to her rise to superstardom,
she lays bare all the secrets and great passions
of a life lived to the fullest.

And her story would not be complete without
the music that has been her lifeline.

**A special six-song CD featuring
never-before-released material,
featuring a duet with Keith Whitley,
is included with this hardcover.**

FOREVER YOURS FAITHFULLY
by Lorrie Morgan

Published by Ballantine Books.
Coming to bookstores everywhere
in October 1997.

LOVE LETTERS

Ballantine romances are on the Web!

Read about your favorite Ballantine authors and upcoming books in our monthly electronic newsletter LOVE LETTERS at www.randomhouse.com/BB/loveletters, including:

·What's new in the stores
·Previews of upcoming books
·In-depth interviews with romance authors and publishers
·Excerpts from new romances
·And more . . .

To subscribe to LOVE LETTERS, send an E-mail to
loveletters@randomhouse.com,
asking to be added to the subscription list. You will receive monthly announcements about the latest news and features.

So follow your heart and visit us at
www.randomhouse.com/BB/loveletters
for sample chapters from current and upcoming Ballantine romances.